Two Paths Diverge

Two Paths Diverge

To Matt, Kim, Anna, Becca

John Roberts

John Roberts

Matador
9 Priory Business Park,
Wistow Road, Kibworth Beauchamp,
Leicestershire. LE8 0RX
Tel: 0116 279 2299
Email: books@troubador.co.uk
Web: www.troubador.co.uk/matador
Twitter: @matadorbooks

ISBN 978 1838594 220

British Library Cataloguing in Publication Data.
A catalogue record for this book is available from the British Library.

Printed on FSC accredited paper
Printed and bound in Great Britain by 4edge Limited
Typeset in 11pt Aldine401 BT by Troubador Publishing Ltd, Leicester, UK

Matador is an imprint of Troubador Publishing Ltd

For my youngest grandchildren, Jack and Molly
and my great friends
Ian Plimmer (1937-2019)
and
Martin and Diana Roberts

PART ONE

1.

AT THE MEETING HOUSE
1613

He must not laugh.
    Must. Not. Laugh.

Will Nailor, just eighteen years old, stood at the left-hand end of the wooden bench. Head bent, eyes closed, mouth clamped shut, controlling his breathing, hands clasped tightly together behind his back – he held his whole body rigid. Behind his eyelids, it felt as if there were a fuse burning towards an explosion. The corners of his mouth twitched.

Not daring to join in the chanted psalm, he forced his mind to concentrate on the words and shut out everything else. Especially Alice. "Amen" at last sounded along the small gathering, fifteen of them, on the two wooden benches. There was a shuffling and Will sat down with the rest.

Alice, nearly eighteen years old, sat at the right-hand end of the other bench, at the far side of the room, with her father, mother and younger brother Henry. He knew she would be surreptitiously watching him from the corner of her eye, knowing exactly what he was feeling, what he was struggling with. Watching for signs of a loss of control: a splutter into a handkerchief, a deep breath and shoulders back. Wishing for it! Hoping for it! Such cruel mischief in those beautiful green eyes.

The pre-sermon ritual would now begin, the ritual they had analysed together, whispering and giggling among the bales and bolsters of cloth in snatched moments at her father's warehouse, where Will was partway through his apprenticeship. And where Alice had found more and more excuses to visit.

It was just after nine in the morning on Sunday 8th September 1613 in the township of Worsley, near Wigan. They – the Brethren of the Separatists, as they liked to call themselves -- were in the parlour of Will's home, which served as their Meeting House. He had helped carry in the benches from the kitchen last night.

In the silence after the psalm, Will's father Richard, their pastor, stood with eyes closed. From opposite sides of the room, awaiting the expected movements, Will and Alice stared at him, their gaze arrowing in on his face. The pastor turned, took a step forward and knelt, none too easily, on the stone-flagged floor. He reverently steepled his hands and looked up past the pewter plates on the dresser towards heaven, through the stain of damp on the ceiling with its thin edging of black mould. A stain shaped like a sheep's head, Alice had said; more like an old boot, Will had answered.

Mysterious, the portals to heaven, they both knew they thought at this moment. Will swallowed hard three times, remembered the servant girl polishing the pewter yesterday, dusting the dark furniture, sweeping and washing the floor, not lighting the fire though – that wasn't allowed until November.

Mind tricks. He was in control again.

Without warmth, the weak autumn sunshine shone through the small windows behind the gathered brethren. Will knew that the divine inspiration his father sought for his sermon would come in exactly forty seconds. It always did. Will counted in his head: that forty-second silence, as His humble shepherd waited for God's help, was part of the show.

Will knew that Alice was counting, too. She'd laughed when he'd told her of the timing. Now it was a secret link between them across the room, along the row of prim, earnest faces and upright bodies of the brethren: the women in their

4

buttoned-up waistcoats and white bonnets, best aprons over their skirts and petticoats; the men in doublets and breeches, polished shoes. Respect, not vanity, they would say. The seconds simultaneously ticked in their heads louder and louder until Will wanted again to explode into laughter. 38… 39… 40. Exactly on time, his father gripped the corner of the dresser and levered himself up, knees cracking, inspiration received.

In the gloomy room he stood and faced his flock again, head perfectly positioned to catch the sunlight, another part of the performance, the stagecraft. His white ruff and cuffs accentuated the black of his doublet. Black because it was sombre but also because it was the most expensive colour. Vanity. Self-importance. Will wanted so much to glance across at Alice, to share this moment of recognition. He dared not.

His father's eyes slowly ranged across the gathered souls, holding contact with each one's eyes until they bent their heads: his look was an accusation, as if it were more an affront to him than to Christ that they had sinned. For they all had surely sinned.

When his father's eyes met his own, Will stared back unblinkingly. Will tried with all his heart to convey in his look hatred, anger, contempt. Alice, he knew, would do the same.

It was his father who turned away and Will felt a surge of triumph. Now his father reached for his sermon notes, next to his black felt hat on the dresser. Heavenly inspiration still required supporting notes. Next, he would tidy them in his hands. Yes. Glance at them, riffling through the sheets. Yes. Replace them on the dresser. Yes. Draw a deep breath and expand his chest. Yes. Clear his throat. Yes. Stretch out his arms to encompass them all. Yes. A pause. Yes.

And begin.

"Their foot shall slide in due time. Deuteronomy, chapter 32, verse 35."

Will wondered by what route this time his father would lead them all to the usual guilt and inadequacy – guilt that most of the brethren seemed to feast on, to need as succour in the daily struggle. Alice, he was sure, would follow her usual practice – she had vouchsafed it to him – of creating an irreverent picture: maybe today of a shoe skidding on a pile of cow muck, or an embroidered slipper deliberately slipped from beneath her skirt. The forbidden fruit of the hint of an ankle.

Will and Alice had agreed they had no fear of the Lord: how could the good Lord be concerned with such flippancies and humour? But each sometimes was afraid they were wrong, aware of their own hypocrisy in relying on the mercy of the Lord to forgive their youthful defiance. It wasn't – yet – that they no longer believed in God, just not the dour, punitive one Will's father presented to them. They preferred to imagine a jovial God.

"Their foot shall slide in due time," repeated Pastor Richard Nailor.

Now began the sermon, the delight his father took in rebuking his followers. Will did as he always did these days: let his father's deep ominous voice drift over him as he, Will, replayed two scenes from last February. They were scenes he never wanted to forget because they had given him the knowledge of his father that he had always suspected.

February, dirty frozen mud-snow on the ground, a bitter wind, dusk; Will walking back from a secret gambling rendezvous in a woodman's shed deep in the forest, cards, jokes, the banned arousing poems of John Donne on well-fingered pages passed round, innuendoes and laughter with his disapproved-of friends, winnings in his pockets. Passing the dirty hovel in the lane, hearing a woman's weeping and peering in. In the smoky gloom, in the far corner, a heap of rags and the pale face of Andrew, a boy he knew: gaunt, spectral, huge hollow eyes, coughing. His mother wiping the lad's forehead and looking round at Will, framed in the doorway.

"He's starving, Master Will. Near to death."

Her own face thin and pale, voice and eyes weary.

He had given her most of his winnings, tipping the money into her dirty hands, nauseated by the smell of damp and cold and dirt in the hovel. Hurrying on, the gamblers' laughter suddenly obscene. Guilt and anger, wanting an explanation for this poverty and suffering permitted by a loving God.

At home he had knocked on his father's study door and gone in without waiting for an answer. His father was bent over his desk, quill in hand, and had turned his head at Will's entrance, candlelight showing his look of disapproval, of dignity offended.

But Will had stood there, demanding: "Why is your God allowing Andrew Boon to die of starvation?"

His father had turned back to his desk.

"Tell me, why?" Will, amazed at his own blunt challenge. "An innocent young boy who can have done no wrong."

This time his father turned round in his chair. "Andrew's father is a drunkard, a slothful blasphemer." The words slow, resonant, even relished.

"But Andrew…?"

Will's father reached round and laid his hand on the Bible on the desk. "The Lord will visit the iniquity of the fathers on the children, to the third and fourth generation. Exodus 34, verse 7."

And that was all. His father gestured him out of the room.

Will had stumbled out in a helpless rage.

Now he heard his father's sermon voice rising, dramatic pauses, finger pointing. Will knew that Alice was using the same ploy as he had to confirm her disgust. She had her own scene and her own perspective. She had eventually told Will about it, voice low and quivering, tears in her eyes.

7

She'd been very ill in bed and her mother had called Will's father round to pray and appeal for God's help. The curtains had been half-closed, the room stuffy from a blazing fire, the smell of sickness, Alice shivering in the heat. Will's father, sitting close to the bed, had asked Alice's mother to leave them alone, closing the door behind her. He had taken Alice's hand in his and, bowing his head, had recited prayers softly, almost chanting. Silence, only wood spitting in the fire. The pastor with his hands on her bared arms, stroking them, drawing out the humours. Then Alice had felt her hand drawn off the coverlet, Will's father placing it first on his thigh. Alice, startled out of her fever, looked up. The pastor's eyes were closed, his head slightly bent, his breathing louder and more intense, sweat on his brow. He moved her hand to his groin, pressed it into him. She felt a hardness in his breeches, her hand forced to rub against him, rubbing, rubbing. He gave a gasp and groaned. She wrenched her hand away, lay trembling in bed. Will's father raised his head and stared at her, his mouth fierce, eyes threatening.

He stood. "May the Lord bless you," he said, and left the room.

She had told no one but Will. "Who would believe me?" she asked him. "Me a girl in a fever, and him a man of the Church."

Will believed her.

He looked up. Now the sermon was rising to its climax, a sweat shining on his father's face.

"And if your foot slides…" he said, his blazing eyes travelling over each of them. "If your foot slides away from Christ, that world of misery, that lake of burning brimstone is extended abroad under you. There is the dreadful pit of the glowing flames of the wrath of God; there is hell's wide gaping mouth open; and you have nothing to stand upon, nor anything to take hold of; there is nothing between you and

8

hell but the air. It is only the power and mere pleasure of God that holds you up."

The end – and now, past the subdued, rebuked bent faces, Will looked across at Alice. To his surprise she was looking directly at him. She smiled at him, then stood up. The brethren's faces turned to her in shock; Will's father stood open-mouthed. Calmly Alice moved away and along the back of the bench – her dress rustling on the floor – towards the closed door of the room. She opened it and, without glancing back, closed it behind her.

There was a general gasp and all heads turned towards their pastor. They saw his face fashion itself into sadness, a small shake of the head in disbelief. And then:

"Mark my words. Return to your homes and keep the Sabbath pure."

They filed out and Will saw his father touch the arm of Alice's father, as if he needed to support a man in mourning, and followed them out.

And Will was left sitting there alone, a huge surge of laughter rising in him. He let it out, reverberating around the empty room, scattering the sullen gloom of his father's words.

Alice! How strong she was! What wrath she would bring on herself from her father.

Alice, confronting his father's hypocrisy.

Hosanna!

2.

INTERVENTIONS

1613

Not a word was said in Will's home that evening. His father went into his study, his mother to her prayers in her bedroom. Will heard her mutterings. The maid brought him a supper of bread and cheese and beer but had obviously been ordered to remain silent. So Will sat at the table and chewed, stared up at the sampler which had been on the kitchen wall for as long as he could remember. The colours of the embroidery were now faded but the words were as un-nerving as ever: *The Lord see-eth all.*

Yet again he conjured the moment of his conception: in what convulsion of lust and guilt, gritted teeth and apologies had his life begun? Marriage was ordained by God for the procreation of children and as a remedy against sin and fornication. Certainly not for pleasure. Alice and he had kissed – and more – enough to promise far greater pleasures. If their God created such pleasure, why did the men of the Church disapprove of it?

But God had been merciful. Will smiled. Given a helping hand, so to speak, the dry-mouthed widow to ease men's trials.

While his parents were probably praying for Alice's soul, his father doubtless also seeking divine vengeance for the humiliation she had inflicted on him, surely a wise and good God – all-knowing, as the sampler stated – should be applauding her. Those were Will's thoughts as he finished off the cheese. Only four knew of the episode at Alice's bedside: Alice, Will, his father – and God. And all of them knew the truth of it. Was his father agonised by the memory? Was it a single moment of weakness? How many other times had he fallen from grace? And if this God existed, did he follow the old rule: *Do as you would be done by*; therefore forgiving the forgiving man but punishing the punitive man?

But it was the glorious, beautiful daring of Alice that filled Will's mind as he lay awake in his room that night, already the damp of autumn in the stone walls, rain on the window pane. She was able to bake bread, brew beer, embroider, help her mother manage the household; she dressed modestly as a good Puritan woman. But there was a lightness in her step, the arch of an eyebrow or curl of a smile, a brief unexplained laugh that somehow mocked or questioned all that virtue and respectability. A spontaneity that demanded to escape, a mind of her own. A glance, just caught, across her father's warehouse, could make his heart beat fast. For Will it was utterly provocative – all that and the wisps of soft black hair that she allowed to escape from her bonnet, her startling so-direct green eyes, her slender fingers. Had she always been conscious of her effect on him? She was now, and she enjoyed the game as much as he did: the secret game played in snatched, illicit moments. He remembered the softness of her lips: the danger, the excitement, part of the restless questioning and disobedience they both shared.

He was in love, uncontrollably. She was in love, too, he was convinced, but still in control of herself. And needing to be, to hold him back.

He slept little but woke late. Why had he not been woken to get to the merchant's to start the working week on time? Downstairs the maid gave him a plate of cold meat, told him – with a knowing look – that his mother was ill in bed, his father was in his study and Will was to wait in the kitchen until summoned. He was not to go to the Ainsworth's.

11

So there was to be an aftermath, a one-to-one sermon about Alice's disgraceful behaviour yesterday. A necessary evil, a tedious ritual and then he could go.

"Will." The stern voice came from the closed study.

Will raised his eyes to the maid, who pursed her lips. He stood up, crossed the hall and knocked on the study door. A silence. Then: "Come in."

He entered.

"Close the door behind you."

His father stood at the window, back towards Will, looking out at the rain, his head silhouetted in the light. The stiff, straight back, the certainty of one of the elect, selected by the grace of God not by strength of faith or good works. Wasn't that their curious, self-centred belief? The pose amused Will. What terrifying Bible quotation would his pastor father begin with?

His father cleared his throat, still looking through the window.

"I forbid you ever to see that girl, that young woman, again."

Now he turned, stiff-necked, his face in profile, set in that obdurate, strait-laced way, thin-lipped and mean.

"Understand? Never."

Will almost reeled. A body blow.

"But—"

"No buts."

Will's hatred was pure. He clenched his fists.

"And your apprenticeship at Ainsworth's is over. As of now."

"But—"

"I said no buts."

A second blow. Will wanted to smash that smug face.

"You are confined to this house until you leave."

"What?! Leave?"

"This morning I go to Mr Ainsworth. He will agree. He has already spoken to me about the goings-on between you and Alice. He is not blind, he is not a fool, and his workers are loyal. He sees you as a bad influence on his daughter. He wants you away. My son, a bad influence! The disgrace of it."

So that's what drove him: his own humiliation.

"You will be going to London, to a merchant. I have my own contacts. There is paperwork to be done, agreements to be signed to continue your apprenticeship. It will take a week or so for it all to get to London, I reckon. You will follow it down. You will be leaving my house for good. If you wish to sin in London, it will be beyond our sight. It will be you responsible for damning your own soul."

Will's father turned back to the window. Will stared at his back. His father prized respectability more than his own flesh and blood.

"I wash my hands of you."

"Like Pontius Pilate," snarled Will.

His father turned and lunged towards Will. Will set himself, shoulders crouched, fists bunched, teeth bared. At last, nothing to lose.

But his father stopped, backed away

"You blasphemer," he growled. "To your room, to your Bible."

Will glared at his father then stood straight.

"You hypocrite," he said softly. "You to your Bible, Father. Remember: *God sees everything.*"

Will turned and left the study, leaving the door open. At the foot of the stairs he looked back. His father still stood there, but his head was bent.

Up in his room Will thought only of Alice. There would be the same restrictions, confined to the house: making bread, doing embroidery; reading limited to the Bible and *Foxe's Book of Martyrs*. But inside she would still be smiling and

13

defiant. Self-possessed and somehow above it all. But did she yet know he was being banished to London? Would she be self-possessed about that? Would she go with him or join him later? And suddenly Will saw that his world had crashed. How much of him was invested in Alice! Something of that had to be rescued. He had to have some hope.

And he would show his father. In London he would succeed – on his own terms, not his father's. Money granted freedom in this world, so he would make money. But he would make it fairly and do some good with it. Not his father's kind of good but the kind of good that would not allow Andrew Boon to starve to death.

The sins of the fathers should stay with the fathers.

He heard the outer door slam shut, ran to the window and saw his father mounting his horse. Somehow he had to get a message to Alice, see her, make decisions.

He wrote the note: *Meet me on Wednesday, 11 in the morning, at the hut by the river.* Sealed it. He didn't sign his name.

Two days to wait, for things to calm down, for them both to sort their minds out. If she wanted to, she would find a way to meet. Just as he would, no matter what the restrictions. Neither of them would be in irons.

He would now wait for Andrew's younger brother John Boon to pass along the lane. He could trust him to use his initiative to deliver the message in person.

★

That same afternoon Alice sat on the straight-backed chair by the window in her bedroom. She had wrapped her shawl around her and was gazing out at the grey September sky. Allowed downstairs only for meals, she had been exiled to this chilly room since returning from the meeting house. Her father had not raised his voice, just given his orders in the

14

kitchen in front of the entire household. His trust had been betrayed by his daughter. This time his authority would not be gainsaid.

Will would be sent away to London by his father for being disobedient and disrespectful, Mr Ainsworth told them. Alice, too, must learn the hard way to obey her father and act with propriety. The incident at the end of the pastor's sermon had been disgraceful, wrong and embarrassing. But now she could not stop herself from smiling at it.

She turned to the book her father had instructed her to read: *The English Housewife: Containing the Inward and Outward Vertues Which Ought to be in a Compleet Woman.*

Written, of course, by a man: Gervase Markham.

She flicked through the pages. How could her father know so little about her! The book had the opposite effect to the one he wanted. It made her blood boil, it made her scoff, it made her despair, it made her determined.

She found the place that summed it all up. Her fingers traced the words:

Next to her sanctity and holiness of life, it is meet that our English housewife be a woman of great modesty and temperance, as well inwardly as outwardly. Inwardly, as in her behaviours and carriage towards her husband, wherein she shall shun all violence of rage, passion and humour, coveting less to direct than be directed, appearing ever unto him pleasant, amiable and delightful.

Outwardly, the housewife's garments should be comely and strong, made as well to preserve the health as to adorn the person, altogether without toyish garnishes or the gloss of light colours, and as far from the vanity of new and fantastic fashions as near to the comely imitation of modest matrons.

To conclude, our English housewife must be of chaste thoughts, stout courage, patient, untired, watchful, diligent,

witty, pleasant, constant in friendship, full of good neighbour-
hood, wise in discourse but not frequent therein, sharp and
quick of speech, but not bitter or talkative, comfortable in her
counsels, and generally skilful in the worthy knowledge which
do belong to her vocation.

Alice closed the book. Was there such a recipe for an English husband?

Her dear mother downstairs. This bedroom exile had punished her mother as much as her. But her father would not have seen it. Her mother: ailing, pale, weary beyond words, exhausted and downcast by two miscarriages and two stillbirths. It was a miracle that Alice had survived, another wonder that she had even been conceived. It was hard to believe her mother had felt the same surges she had with Will. Had she just been *amiable* and *dutiful*? And men's urges – her father's, Will's, Will's disgusting father! Were they just allowed to be? Were they blessed by God?

And women punished because of Eve. That original sin. But Eve was fashioned from Adam's rib, his side: near his heart, to be his equal.

Alice could sit no more, and strode across the room. Her exile must end sometime and she was impatient for the summons to the kitchen that her father had promised.

"Alice!" His voice sounded up the staircase. Odd, she had expected the servant girl to have been sent.

Alice composed her face. Deference without submission, she was aiming for. Stately down the stairs, not hurrying. Into the kitchen. Her father sat in his chair at the head of the scrubbed and polished table. On one side bench sat her brother, who looked up at her and winked as she entered. Opposite him, sat her mother, wrapped up, bonneted and gloved. Face pale and lined, grey hair. Such resignation in her eyes.

"Sit down, Alice."

She sat next to her mother, smiled at her, but there was no response.

"I have sent the servants to Wigan for supplies," said her father. "I wanted no eavesdropping."

Alice frowned, looked across questioningly at her brother. This was not just about her. Her brother shook his head slightly. So he didn't know either.

"I will come to the point," said her father, leaning forward and putting his arms on the table. "As soon as my business arrangements will allow, we are moving to live in Holland."

Her mother's head slumped, but her brother's eyes lit up.

"I think I should explain my reasons because it will be an upheaval for us all. But one I believe will be worth it."

He paused.

"First," and he looked directly at Alice, "I disapprove most strongly of Alice's behaviour at the service. But I have fallen out of that pastor's way of thinking. He is too grim."

If only you knew what that pastor has done to me, Father. 'Grim' might not be strong enough.

"He sees no beauty in the world. God sent us beauty to enjoy."

He pointed at the arrangement of flowers in a vase at the centre of the table.

"Look at them. Are they not blessings?"

Alice looked at the white and yellow of the ox-eye daisies, the blue and pink of late delphiniums, the skeletons of cow parsley. She loved flowers. It was her father who wanted flowers every day.

"And the pastor disapproves of bowling and archery. Men need fun and enjoyment."

Alice's brother nodded vigorously, but Alice was sure it was not archery he was thinking of.

"Second, and more seriously, we Puritans are more and more frayed out of our wits. Meetings like those at the pastor's house are now illegal. He is a brave man to continue with them, I'll give him that. I will remind you of the law. If we do not attend a Church of England service for a month, we are deemed Nonconformists and we can be sent to jail. If we do not agree to conform to the Church of England and the Book of Common Prayer, we are given the choice of death or exile. But, at the same time, Nonconformists are forbidden to emigrate. So we are forced to flee in secret."

Alice saw tears roll down her mother's face. She sank lower in her chair. Her mother would not survive this.

"Nor can anything be written which is against the Archbishop Whitgift. There is no freedom left in England. Separatists, as we are also known, have been hanged."

He let the image sink in.

"Thirdly, many Englishmen have already fled to Holland, where they are able to set up their congregational government and worship without the hierarchy of bishops. We will be joining our fellow countrymen."

Now he sat up straight.

"Fourthly, our Scottish King, James, has promised to *harry us out of the land*. He has purged the Church of Puritan ministers. They have become the silenced brethren, over 300 of them, I'm told. The King calls us brain-sick and rash-headed. Things can only get worse for us here in England."

He stood up.

"Finally, I am confident that after a short time I will be a successful merchant in Holland and you will be all well-cared-for. I expect that we will set sail in about a month's time, as we need to leave before the winter storms."

As he passed her, he kissed his wife on the head fleetingly. Then he was gone. And now Alice's mother could release her sobs. Alice put her arm round her. Her brother fled. Alice helped her mother to the rocking chair by the fire.

"It will be fine, Mother, I will tend to you."

Her mother drank a little of the warmed spicy posset Alice gave her and in two minutes was sound asleep, snoring gently. Her mother had survived her children's deaths by becoming entirely centred on her home, a home for the four of them: a husband who was gentle but who was away working longer and longer hours; a daughter who was a dutiful companion; and herself protecting herself from her demons by continually tidying and rearranging. How could her father not see it would break his wife to move her from here?

Her mother would be exiled from her centre, but for her brother it would be an adventure. She herself, Alice, would be leaving the home where she had lived her whole life. How fortunate it was that Will would already be gone. It was easier than her leaving him.

She loved this kitchen: it was the heart of the home. Hearth heart. She added two logs to the fire that always burned there, winter and summer. The wood sparked; firelight and sunlight from the casement window glinted on the pewter plates on the dresser. Warmth, food, smells. Cosiness in the midst of the austere beliefs her parents held so deeply. In the side of the brick-built inglenook was the bread oven. She would help knead the dough tonight as always. Over the fire hung the cauldron loaded with vegetables and meat, the smell of promise and comfort. Next to it the iron kettle, the chimney black with soot and smoke. The wooden salt box hung on the wall next to the fire to keep it dry. From the ceiling beams hung gleaming brass and copper pans. There were spoons and ladles and tongs. With them hung bunches of parsley and sage picked from the herb garden, and also tied up was a small sheaf of corn from the recent harvest, signifying good fortune.

She liked the old superstitions; there was a wholesome homeliness to them. Like the old horseshoe over the door which her mother had persuaded her father not to take down. To Alice they were more real than arguments over whether

19

or not she should bow to the altar or kneel at communion. And what kind of a God felt insulted and offended by priests wearing surplices when there were so many other problems to be solved?

She would miss this place but Holland was already becoming an adventure to her, an opportunity, and also a move that would help her deal with missing Will.

She looked at her mother. Would the journey kill her? And would that be a kindness – to end the cycle of pregnancy and tragedy that seemed all her mother's life was about? Her death to end all the previous deaths.

Her own life, Alice's life, would not be like that. Of that she was determined.

3.

SIXPENCES

1613

The river was full after the rains. Leaning on the door frame of the old hut, Will watched the water race past. How he'd loved hearing his father's angry shouts as he had just simply walked out of the garden and turned down the lane, hearing them fade as he crossed the wet meadows in a circuitous route to the woods and then to here. Until this moment he'd been absolutely confident that Alice, too, would find a way out from her home; confident that she wanted to, as much as him.

But it was well gone eleven o'clock. And if she did come, would she be of the same mind as him? He imagined her brushing her way past wet bushes and trees, but with what expression on her face? Eager and loving and defiant, with plans? Sad? Resigned to farewells? Suddenly, he was scared. Her strength could lead her either way.

A dipper was working the river, standing on a stone, mid-stream, tail flicking, then diving into the water. Catching food, surviving, getting on with its business. No heartache.

He heard a rustle in the trees, stepped back into the hut, into the corner shadows. Just in case. Then her skirt appeared, her hand on the frame, her head peering in, the white bonnet.

"Will?" she whispered.

"Alice! You came."

And Will stepped forward, arms outstretched to hold her. But she stayed still, did not reciprocate. He let his arms fall to his sides. Crestfallen.

21

"Of course I came. Did you think they could stop me?"

His eyes brightened. Hope, after all.

"If they take everything away from me, what else have I to lose?"

"The same for me."

Her face was more beautiful than ever, the spirit that shone out of it. Bright in the shadows of the hut.

"I want…" he began, voice trembling in spite of himself.

But she raised her finger to her lips. "And I want, too, Will," she said softly. "But it cannot be."

He had arranged a couple of small boxes into a seat, next to an old bench. He sat down on the box seat. Beaten already? She sat on the bench.

"You know I have to go on Friday, to London?" he asked, not looking up.

"I know. My father told me. You will complete your apprenticeship there."

Her voice was so calm.

"And after that? After three more years?"

He had practised the words of a spousal, of a troth-plight. Foolishly, in his room, oblivious of all else. Needing a commitment. All of that seemed suddenly ridiculous, a fairy tale.

Shoulders bent, he looked up at her sitting so straight on the bench. Composed.

"Alice?" Trying to keep the plaintiveness out of his voice. Was it that easy for her?

"What we want cannot be," she said. "We cannot fight for it."

He wanted to hold her hand, to be held by it, to feel the warmth of it.

"We are being sent our separate ways," she continued.

"I would fight it," he said fiercely, angry at her submission to it all.

22

"How? You are an apprentice and I am a woman. Women are powerless. Do you think I have not thought about it, all through the nights since Sunday?"

Brief comfort there.

"And there is something you don't know, Will. I didn't till yesterday afternoon. Even before Sunday, my father had decided that we will be leaving England and going to Amsterdam."

"What?"

"As soon as my father can arrange things about his business."

"Why?"

Will was dumbstruck.

"There is a strong group of Puritans already in Holland, my father says, free to worship as they wish, not harassed by King James and his bishops, able to ignore some popish practices – as my father calls them – in the Book of Common Prayer."

"And you are going with them?"

"Will, I have no choice. I have no other family here to stay with and, more importantly, my mother is often ill, as you know, and I am the only daughter."

Will nodded. So they were all ashes, his dreams, his stupid romantic dreams. The strong spirit he loved in her had faced up to reality. Her decision was the only possible one, the mature one.

He stood up and went to stand in the doorway. The river rushed noisily past.

"I came to explain to you," said Alice. "It is not what I want. Do you believe me?"

Will turned to look at her.

"Yes, I believe you." But what did it matter?

The dipper had gone, the water greyer now. A breeze getting up, reeds swaying.

"But I must have something," he said. "A token. To know it was real."

"Oh, Will, it was real, it is real. Just impossible."

He came to sit next to her again. He took a red ribbon from his pocket.

"Hand-fasting," he said. "Just the two of us, here. Let me bind our hands together in this ribbon. Just for these few minutes. As a confirmation, an acceptance."

But she pulled her hands away.

"It makes it more difficult for me, Will."

Were there tears in her eyes?

"I need you to help me, Will. I dare not. I would lose my resolve." Her voice was so soft.

How could he see her break? Weaken? That would be obscene, unloving. Slowly he wound the ribbon neatly, tied it and threw it into the back of the hut.

"Of course, I could not know you were leaving here, like me. But we would be separating, anyway. Can we not have something to remember it all by? Something we keep?"

She looked down, her hands in her lap.

"Please," he said, not beseechingly but firmly.

She looked up at him, her face sadder than he had ever seen it.

In his flushed face that childhood scar on his forehead she loved to touch was seared white. She nodded.

From his pocket Will took two coins. They were silver sixpences. He had filed off the face of the King, as was the custom, so that the coins were smooth, then bent them crooked and drilled a small hole in each. He held them out to her in the palm of his hand.

"One for each of us, to keep."

"Love tokens," she said, a hint of a curl in her smile.

His palm still open, he looked her in the eye, bold now.

24

Then she stretched out her palm. He placed a sixpence on it, pressing it lightly into her skin, touching so briefly the warmth of it. She closed her fist on it. He did the same on his sixpence, so tightly it bit into his flesh. Wanting to hurt himself, scar himself, leave a mark.

"I will wear mine always round my neck," he said.

She nodded, stayed silent. Will studied her face for some sign of distress or misery. Perhaps a tremble on her lips. She had this fearsome self-control.

She took a deep breath and stood up, walked to the doorway: her turn to stare at the river. Will watched her: her back, her waist, one hand on the door frame, the other still closed and clutching the sixpence, the nape of her neck, her shoulder leaning on the jamb. A small piece of rotten wood was stuck to her sleeve, like a splinter.

He had never felt so hollow, emptied out.

She shifted, stood straight, turned her head towards him. With the daylight behind her, he could not see the features of her face.

From the shadow she spoke. "I will never forget you, Will."

The brief flash of a smile then she turned and left, the doorway empty, the sudden noise of the river in his ears.

He was still gripping his crooked sixpence. Slowly he opened his palm, looked for a spot of blood, hoped for a spot of blood. There was none; just the bent sixpence lying on white flesh. He watched the pinkness of the flesh return.

The words came back to him:
There was a crooked man who walked a crooked mile;
He found a crooked sixpence beside a crooked stile.
He couldn't remember the rest.

His eye caught a glimpse of the red ribbon in the corner.

He would never come to this place again – unless Alice was with him.

And that could never happen. He in London, she in Amsterdam. Separate lives now. He closed his fingers on the sixpence, stood up and strode out of the hut, out through the woods and across the meadows. London tomorrow. A new world.

★

As she walked slowly back home through the wood, Alice was in a turmoil of emotions: regret, misery, fear. Should she turn back? It would be so easy and Will would be so happy.

Gradually she calmed. She smiled again at the memory of the meeting house. She had been right to make her secret protest. And she had been right at the hut by the river. Both of them had been difficult and painful. She was proud of both her decisions. She felt for the bent sixpence which she would wear on a cord round her neck hidden by the high collar of her dress. Why had she not told she would? That was cruel. But she had had to be hard.

But how she would miss Will. He made her laugh; she loved their shared mockery of hypocrisy; she admired his hatred of unfair poverty; she liked his ambition. There was a strong sense of goodness in him but he could also be restless and contrary. His apprenticeship, she knew, would lead to some kind of quest. She believed in him.

His smile, his tousled dark hair, his soft eyes, his kisses – and the way her body reacted to them: such surges and meltings. She bent her head, breathed deeply. She had to shut these things away.

PART TWO

4.

VOYAGE

1614

Wind howled in the rigging, sails clattered, waves slapped the boat, timbers creaked, the sick moaned and prayed.

Retching and vomiting, Alice leaned over the side of the boat. The wind and tide whipped away her vomit across the surface of the black water. She could not stop; another convulsion would come even when her stomach was empty. Others lined the side, too. The wind was blowing strongly but the smell of vomit remained: on faces, clothes and bulwarks. And still the boat rolled and pitched. "Lord, we beg thee, keep us safe. Deliver us." Steepled hands raised to heaven before they clung to the gunwales again.

And they were still only in the estuary of the River Humber.

But there was also Mary Cheever. Unaffected by seasickness she bustled up and down the boat, arms round a shoulder, words of comfort, cleaning a face, offering a drink, cuddling a child. Mary was a blacksmith of a woman, with bellows bosoms, broad hips, massive forearms, a round face and a loud laugh. She was the only source of cheer in this desolate circumstance.

Alice's mother was down below, out of the cold and gale, tended by her father. God knows what it was like down there, the air fetid and vomit running everywhere, the dark hold impregnated with coal dust.

Alice was terrified: she had never even seen the sea before they'd boarded this filthy boat in Grimsby. Out on the wide estuary, the power of it had taken her breath away. And the expanse of it stretching out into the night. Sick and scared, her excitement had long since gone. She raged now against her father: all this, and the grave danger to her ailing mother, just so he need not bow to the altar or kneel at communion. It wasn't just foolish, it was wrong and selfish. What sort of a God would demand this?

She looked for land but the low-lying riverbank she knew was somewhere to her left was barely visible, just a darker stain that appeared and disappeared as the boat pitched and tossed. The moon appeared spasmodically between banks of blown clouds. She saw her brother Henry, leaning over the stern. So he was suffering, too, in spite of his early manly bluster.

The coal barque *Francis* was taking them to their rendezvous at dawn, upstream and away from settlements and villages to an empty marsh area – Salt End, her father had said – where they would transfer to the ship which would take them to Holland. But she had seen he was worried. Last night eighty of them had boarded the *Francis,* filing up the gangway. People on the dock had stood and watched: it must have been an unusual sight. They might have been reported to officials: their voyage was illegal even though they supposedly had the right to emigrate.

The cold wind lashed her face and the boat lurched again. Her stomach heaved. The boat swung suddenly to the left and the sail boom swung with it over their heads with a great clatter. Seamen yelled and hauled in ropes. Waves crashed over the side and they were drenched in cold water. Then the boat steadied. In a few minutes Alice saw that there were fewer white tops on the waves and the water was calmer. Low land appeared on her left and then also on her right, closing in. They must be in some kind of waterway or creek. Was this Salt End?

Sailors yelled and then there was a great scraping noise from beneath; the boat slowed suddenly and crunched to a halt. More shouts from sailors. "We're aground!" bawled someone.

But Alice felt only relief. The motion of the boat had stopped; there was not even a slight bobble and the wind was less strong. The mad screeching of birds overhead, a dank smell of river mud.

She tried to clean herself up. As the others also felt better a babble of voices rose: "What will happen now? Where are we?" She heard more prayers being said. Gradually people came up from below deck. They looked even worse, pale and stained, ravenously breathing in the fresh air. She was looking for her father and mother. Soon the deck was crowded. Then at last her father appeared, somehow awkwardly manoeuvring her mother up the ladder. Alice pushed her way through the crowd and took her mother's arm. Her mother looked up at her so piteously, as if all she wanted was to meet her Maker now. She was so frail-looking. Her father looked exhausted, too. Alice wanted to ask him, cruelly, if he was still convinced God was on his side. But he had insisted it was he who should stay with her, leaving Alice on deck in the healthier air. Together they helped her to a seat on a hatchway cover.

Mary Cheever had gathered a group of children and was telling them a story: great booming voices, flung gestures, laughter.

"Sunrise!" said someone. Alice looked around and there, presumably to the east, there was a long line of murky orange light.

"See, Mother?" she said.

"Praise the Lord!" echoed round the boat. Alice saw her mother's lips move.

Her father had been to speak to the captain. "We're waiting for the Dutch ship's longboat," he reported.

31

Thin beer was passed around. No one wanted food.

It was Alice's father, Mr Ainsworth, who had arranged this voyage through his merchant contacts. A Dutch captain, sailing back to Holland from Hull, had agreed to offer them passage for a hefty sum. His ship should now be anchored in deeper water, mid-stream in the Humber. Alice had not been totally convinced. Only a year ago a party of Puritans had bought passage on a ship from the port of Boston. But the English captain had taken their money and belongings and handed the emigrants over to the local authorities. They, too, like the present group, had sold their homes and land. Would a Dutchman be more reliable? When he sold up his house and business, her father had kept a considerable acreage of land which he had leased to a local farmer. Alice wondered if her father, a cautious man in business affairs, had held on to this land in case things turned out badly.

Light was increasing and Alice could see that the boat was lodged on a kind of sandbank in the narrow river. Was this deliberate or not? The land on either side was low, mud leading to reeds and marsh. Inland she could just see a hut, so maybe there was access over the land as well as by waterways. What a truly depressing, flat place it was: not a tree or even a bush in sight; the melancholy bird cries in the wan light, trickling water and the sigh of reeds.

"The boat!"

She turned and saw through the thin dawn light a boat being rowed towards them, oars dipping, flashes of white water, a creaking of wood on wood. It surged onto the sandbank.

"Men first!" was shouted in a foreign accent by a man standing in the prow.

Alice's mother seized her father. "Don't leave me, please."

All round were voices of distress from the women, pleadings and imprecations, tears.

"We must be quick; the tide will turn."

And then, hearing the cries of the women and complaints of the men: "Men only; captain's order. We return for the women. No time to waste."

"It's alright, Mother, I will look after you." Alice turned to her father. "You must go, now, on the first boat. It will be worse if you wait."

An agonised look, guilt, and a desperate clasping of hands.

"You will join me soon," her father said and then he stepped over the side onto the brown mud and walked awkwardly across to the longboat. Her mother sobbed, burying her head into Alice's shoulder.

Farewells were shouted and the full longboat pulled way, slowly disappearing into the murk.

The women were concentrating on comforting their children, distracting them from departing fathers and brothers.

A grey light now permeated the scene. Alice saw the longboat returning for the last group of men, which would include her brother.

"Look!"

A woman was pointing in the direction of the hut. A line of horsemen was emerging along the low skyline, and then marching men.

"Soldiers!"

Alice turned. The empty longboat was already turning away to return to the anchored Dutch ship.

"You better give 'em the slip fast," said the *Francis'* skipper to the remaining men. "You'll be arrested. They'll be militia sent from Grimsby, checking you've got an official licence to travel abroad. Which we and they know you haven't."

The men looked confused and indecisive.

"The other way, you fools. The other bank. You'll find a track in about a hundred yards. Run for it!"

The men looked at each other. Alice's brother was the first to move.

"Come on, we've a chance. Better than rotting in jail."

A quick pat on Alice's and his mother's shoulders and Henry was over the side, through the mud and wading across the water to the marshland. Others followed, bending low. And now there was more keening and sobbing on the boat: the women and children left alone to whatever fate had in store. Desperate prayers were said as they watched their men disappear.

"Never fear," said Mary, hands on hips, "we are women now; no men to mollycoddle and look after." She gave a great laugh but Alice could see few women heartened.

As the militia approached they became more frightening; some had muskets, some had fearsome billhooks: long poles with an axe-like blades and spikes at the top. As they splashed into the water Alice turned back to the river and saw in the distance the Dutch ship hoisting its sails and already moving downriver on the tide. Her father was gone; her brother was escaping through the marshes. She was left alone with her ailing despondent mother, marooned on this grounded boat. Was it always to be like this – the men active, the women left to cope, children crying and shivering with cold? Was this God's plan? Was Mary a saint, or possessed?

★

For weeks after being apprehended at Salt End marsh, the would-be emigrant women and children were transferred from one constable to another in Lincolnshire. They were an awkward embarrassment. They could not be sent home because they had sold their homes. To imprison so many innocent women and children because they wished to go with their husbands was unreasonable and would cause an outcry.

Mary Cheever was the only woman travelling on her own. As the party trailed along, she kept their spirits up with her jokes and her ridicule of the authorities, demanding and cajoling for food and drink. Alice had never known a woman like her and was drawn to her. One evening in a jailhouse as they drank thin potato soup and hard bread, Mary told them tales of her rioting. She was from a village in the Fen Country.

"They sent men to drain the fens: the courtiers and gentry wanted more land, wrecking our livelihoods because we lived by fishing. Our men were afraid of being imprisoned for fighting back which would have made things worse for all of us. Hundreds of us women stoned the surveyors and destroyed a dyke, all of us rushing into the fens with scythes and pitchforks to frighten off the men. The authorities didn't know how to deal with us. We were women; had no rights therefore had none to lose. We wives belonged to our menfolk. They called us coverts – we didn't exist in law, like children and imbeciles. We were covered by the men and so it was their fault. But they had done nothing so couldn't be charged. We delayed them but didn't win. But we had a great time. It was wonderful, all us women acting together."

Alice was stirred by the stories. Uplifted.

"And it wasn't the first time," said Mary, laughing. "There were the bread riots, and commons and grazing riots. We were defending our homes, our families and our livelihoods, our rights for fish and game and reeds and fuel."

The rest of the women were shocked by Mary's exploits.

"What yer gawping at? We're pushed around too much. Yer've got to stand up for yerself."

Then, she said, her husband had fallen ill and died.

"I'm a widow now. What bit my husband had is mine. Nobody owns me now. You young ones" – she held Alice's arm – "should aim to be a widow."

She cackled again.

"That's yer aim in life if yer've any sense."

She had had enough of England, she said. She'd heard good things about Holland, wanted a change, a bit of adventure. She was a Puritan, too, had no time for the Church of England, its bishops and robes and hierarchy. But Alice believed this was a less important motive for her than the adventure.

Mary was a fen woman and had sold eels and suchlike at various big houses. A week later it was Mary who arranged for Alice and her mother to be taken in by the Huncote family who lived near Boston in one of those houses. Several Puritan families agreed to take the would-be migrants in, in the expectation that their menfolk would somehow find the wherewithal to get them to Holland. The authorities were glad to be rid of them.

Alice was happy to be a kind of guest/servant because the family looked after her mother so well. The Huncotes were devout Puritans and Alice kept her doubts silent, joining in all their prayer services.

Then in mid-November her brother suddenly appeared on the doorstep. Money had been sent from Holland by their father, through his trading contacts, and arrangements made for them to sail there from Boston Haven. Henry had heard that the authorities would turn a blind eye, just wanting rid of this troublesome and expensive tribe of women.

★

Huddled in her cloak, hood tight around her face, Alice watched and listened to the white breakers bursting on the bare rocky islands they were passing. At last they were sailing south, on course for Amsterdam. Round her, the other emigrants were also recovering. There was still a cold stiff breeze but it was behind them.

They had been at sea for fourteen days and for seven of them had seen neither sun nor moon nor stars. The storm had been terrifying, seeming to punch and taunt them. Never had Alice experienced anything like it: icy water breaking over the ship and pouring down into the hold in which they took shelter; winds howling in the rigging like shrieking demons; the ship labouring up huge waves and then surging down into the trough before rising again; the emigrants clinging to each other but still thrown about.

All around in the dark, hard-timbered hold – waves crashing into the ship's sides inches from their heads – people prayed and sobbed, the children numb and petrified, helplessly clinging to their mothers. Mary Cheever had in the end also succumbed, as sick and weary and resigned as the rest of them, her cheery blustering spirit subdued. Alice was sure her mother had been on the point of death. And Alice herself had prayed – out of mortal terror and desperation.

"Yet, Lord, Thou canst save us! Thou canst save us!"

Now, with the storm past, Alice berated herself for her weakness. At the moment of greatest need she had reverted to the general supplication. What would Will have said? But Will hadn't experienced it.

And the Lord had saved them, it appeared.

"A merciful deliverance He has given us."

"Our faith and patience have been seen."

"A miracle!"

Hungry, aching but unharmed, Alice didn't understand. If it was God who had saved them, it was also God who had imperilled them. It seemed a brutal, calculated test of faith. If her own father had thrown her into the river back home, watched her struggle and go under the teeming water and, at the last moment, rescued her – would that have been a miracle? No. What sort of father would do that: let his loved one suffer in terror, knowing he would get all the plaudits for the rescue?

"The Lord works in mysterious ways" seemed an inadequate answer that could be equally applied to any action of man as well as nature: to Will's father's abuse of her. The explanation was not an explanation, just an evasion of responsibility.

Spray hit her face but it was now refreshing and cleansing. What was Will doing back there in London? She touched the bent sixpence that hung round her neck. She had been right to reject him, to reject the hand-fasting. It was the only sensible thing to do. She could not go with him as a mere apprentice, could not leave her mother, could not disappoint her father who doted on her in his way. But did Will understand she had no choice, that it was the opposite of what she really wanted? She would have gloried in the romance of it, the defiance. She had broken his heart, had been as brutal as this God her fellows were praising and thanking.

So what would he be doing – handsome, broken-hearted, alone – with those London city girls? He would become a successful merchant, she was sure of it: he was a hard worker, was ambitious, was independent-minded.

Oh, Will, what have I thrown away?

These souls she was with were good. They were travelling to do God's work and live righteously. They believed. She would look after her mother and be loyal to her father, but after that, what? To be a wife and bear children and watch them die? Comply humbly with men? Would Holland and Amsterdam give her different opportunities? They welcomed separatists but did they welcome free-thinking women? She was not like Mary – who was so big-hearted she would be welcomed anywhere, so experienced and weathered by life. Besides, Mary was a believer.

No, she was eighteen now, innocent and naive.

For a moment she felt scared again. Then she smiled and hardened her eyes. Henry would be freer, being a lad, but she would make her own way, make her own mistakes. As Will would, too.

38

5.

APPRENTICE

1614/15

Will lay on his narrow bed. The late afternoon October light was fading, rain gusted against the window, the city streets caterwauled and clattered. His muscles ached, his brain ached; it had been a hard week, as usual. His stale, damp, dingy room penned him in like a prison cell.

He was here, alone, because of his father. Sentenced by him. That hypocrite, that bully, that abuser.

Was Alice somewhere like this?

He buried his face in the bedclothes. His father and his cursed Bible.

He could never forget his father's fierceness, how terrified of him he'd been as a young lad. An image of him: even now he could hear his deep voice intoning the verses of St John's Revelations:

And I stood upon the sand of the sea, and saw a beast rise up out of the sea, having seven heads and ten horns, and upon his horns ten crowns, and upon his heads the name of blasphemy. Here is wisdom, let him that hath understanding count the number of the beast, for it is the number of a man, and his number is six hundred three score and six.

Will shivered.

"The Pope," his father would say as he raised a piece of mutton to his mouth, "is the Beast, the Son of Perdition, the Man of Sin. And his Roman Church the Whore of Babylon."

His jaws would work on the mutton. "The Pope is the Antichrist." He would spit out a piece of gristle.

Each Sunday afternoon, his father led his family through *The Plaine Man's Path-way to Heaven, wherein every man may clearly see whether hee shall bee saved or damned.*

His father would glare at him in silent challenge and Will would flinch.

How he had loathed his father's closed mind, scorned his father's complacency about being one of the elect, his father's self-satisfaction which compelled others to damnation. To Will, that did not tally with a forgiving Christ.

As the parlour candles had flickered in the draught of a late winter's afternoon, his father would pause in his reading of his prized Geneva Bible to look up and stare into the fire burning in the grate.

"William Laud," he would declare, his voice rising, "Archbishop William Laud. A pestilential prelate, a great-bellied bishop, an anti-Christian mushrump, the waged servant of the Antichrist. One of the ten horns of the Devil."

He would thump the table and wipe spittle away from his mouth with the back of his hand. Will's mother would cower away and Will would take her hand and stroke it for a moment.

What torment his quiet mother must have suffered. And he had not protected her as much as he should have done.

Will groaned and beat the bed with his fists. What he needed was the tavern and ale, crude laughter and the thrill of dice. At the end of work, he had arranged to meet Ralph there. And the good John Boon had agreed to go with him. Walking home, he had decided to avoid the temptations, but now his resolution broke. To hell with it! He would go.

★

The tavern room was dark. Hides stained with dried grease half-covered the two windows, and pale light seeped in round the ragged edges. In the murk, shapes of men hunched over tables; guttering tallow candles on the walls showed huge bony hands holding tankards of ale, unshaven chins and bad teeth. Two serving wenches shoved between tables, refilling mugs and tankards from stoneware jugs.

There were mutterings and grunts, stools scraped across the stone floor, boots scuffing dirty straw, spit gobbed at spittoons. No laughter. These were tired men, dockers after a shift.

Below one of the windows, around a table that flickered with pale candlelight when not shadowed by bent heads, sat five men. A rough coat sleeve wiped away a spillage of ale and callused fingers put down a box of three dice.

With the back of his hand, Will wiped the foam of ale from his lips and took another swig. Sitting next to him was John Boon, two years older. He was the brother of the starving Andrew Boon Will had seen in the hovel and argued about with his father. He had followed Will to London and, on Will's recommendation, been taken on by Will's master. Will knew John was here because he suspected the man Ralph of bad intentions and wanted to protect Will.

"Start with a farthing," John said.

But the other three laughed in derision. John flushed, angry and humiliated. Will ignored him, chucking his penny into the cap as if it were a sovereign.

"Right to start cautious," said Ralph, standing behind Will's shoulder. Will glanced up at him, eyes narrowed, trying to look shrewd. He could smell the stink of Ralph's rough breeches as they grazed his shoulder.

Ralph had spotted Will earlier at the warehouse; seen him as a country lad, innocent but wanting to impress and join the man's world. Ralph had known there could be money

41

for himself in it but he'd learned to play the long game. He was an experienced warehouseman and he'd helped Will sort foreign merchandise, taken him under his wing to protect him from the mischief of rough dock labourers, bought him the occasional ale at the end of the day. Will had not been the first greenhorn Ralph had targeted. When Will had earned a small bonus from the master for ensuring the prompt delivery of urgent goods to Sir Thomas Verney, Ralph had seen his opportunity. It had been his idea to come to this tavern in the warren of Cheapside alleys so that Will could try his hand at dicing. Dicing had been illegal for a hundred years, Ralph had told him, except for the gentry and aristocrats.

Dick now placed his stake in the cap – another penny. In the wavering light of the candle on the table, teeth gleamed as they grinned at Will, making him feel welcome, part of this new, illicit gambling brotherhood. But their rancid breaths hit his nose like jabs, making him flinch and splutter.

His father! How Will wanted his father here to witness this fruit of his parental and religious zeal: that stern tight-arsed hypocrite seeing his son half-drunk, betting, fumbling with the willing wenches. Will imagined grabbing his father's hair, yanking his head back to force ale down his throat and then have that serving wench push her soft, ample tits into his father's face. Oh, what redemption would he need then! What pitiful prayer-wailing and gnashing of teeth!

His father and Alice: the preacher and the ill young girl.

Alice gone.

He shook his head, took another great mouthful of ale and thumped the tankard down on the table. He took hold of the dice box and jiggled the bone dice in it.

"No slurring," said Ralph from behind, and winked at the man facing Will. "Cast true!"

Will threw the dice and they clicked across the table. Faces leaned into the candlelight.

3, 5, 1.

"Nine," said Dick, his opponent. "Useful throw."

Dick threw next.

2, 4, 2.

"Eight," said Ralph. "That's good, too."

The game was to get a score closest to 31. Over 31 and you were out and lost the kitty.

Will threw a second time.

"2 plus 5 plus 6 equals 13. Add 9 from the first throw equals 22. Tricky," said Dick, smirking.

Dick threw again.

"1 plus 3 plus 5 equals 9. Add 8 from before equals 17. Tidy," said Ralph. "Are you stopping at 22, Will? Or risking it?"

"I'll take the risk," said Will.

He threw the dice, peered at them.

"3 plus 2 plus 3 equals 8. Add 22. That's 30," crowed Will.

"That's nailed it, Nailor," said Ralph. "Your throw, Dick." Another big wink that Will could not see.

Dick clicked the dice in the box, grinned, threw.

"6 plus 5 plus 5 equals 16. Add the previous 17 equals 33," said Ralph. "You're out."

Dick's head slumped.

"You've won, Will," said Ralph and pushed the cap of pennies to Will.

"Another game?" asked Tom, the fifth man, who had been watching silently and cleaning wax out of his ears. "You've coins to play with."

"No," said Ralph. "Quit while you're winning."

"Good advice," said John. "And now I must leave. Are you coming?"

"I'm staying," said Will.

John thought of saying more but simply shook his head and left.

"No more dicing but more ale, Will," said Ralph, calling for a wench who filled Will's tankard, leaning forward, Will's nose in her cleavage.

An hour later, Will left for his lodgings, staggering along the street but his pocket still full of coins. Back in the tavern Ralph and Dick grinned at each other and punched shoulders.

"Twice more to reel him in," said Ralph. "Then he'll be cocky enough to bet all his money."

"And my little beauties will win the lot," said Tom, opening his palm to show his dice – weighted, holes drilled and loaded with quicksilver, the holes stopped up with the black pitch to make the spots.

Will tottered, lurched on and half-collapsed onto the steps of a church doorway. It was starting to rain. He pulled himself up the steps, stood and fumbled for the big iron door ring.

He twisted it and the heavy wooden door opened a bit, the hinge creaking. He pushed it and stepped inside. Cold, dark and empty. A sense of space high above him. He leaned against a stone pillar. The windows above were a paler darkness.

"God's vengeance, Father, you poxy bastard! The same goddamned God!" His half-shout ended in a coughing fit. He slithered down the pillar to sit on the stone floor.

"And where is Alice? My Alice?"

He muttered and groaned to himself, crouched like a foetus.

He felt the bile rising in his stomach, and in his swirling head an idea. He laughed, echoing round the emptiness.

He levered himself up and stood for a few moments to get his balance, his eyes getting accustomed to the darkness, looking round.

He saw the shape he was looking for and stumbled towards it, arms outstretched to keep his balance. His stomach was beginning to heave, felt it rising, sourness in his throat. Nearly there. He lunged forward to grasp the stone edge of the font.

His stomach spasming now, coming up his throat. A wooden lid, heavy. He grasped it and shoved it off. It crashed onto the floor, resounding like the crash of doom. Then it came, irresistibly, his foul vomit, puking into the font, retching, dribbling down his chin, his nose running. Again and again, the stink making it worse. Finally he was empty, his face lathered in sweat, shivering, spent, his ribs sore, leaning on the font.

But his mind had cleared to another idea. A row of wooden stools like pig buckets in the dark. He grabbed one, pulled it over the stone floor next to the font and stood unsteadily on it. Almost right. Should do it. He dropped his breeches and peed. He could just see the line of it, pale and glittering in the dimness, arcing upwards and falling to splash on the vomit and water in the font.

"Father!" he yelled into the vast space. "Are you watching, Father dear? You whoreson preacher!"

Then he saw Alice's face, high up in the vaulted ceiling. She was watching him, sadness and disgust on her face. He howled, his throat raw. Howled at his own misery. He shuddered and trembled, groaned.

With exaggerated carefulness he stepped down, made his way to the still-open door and reeled outside into the rain. He held his face up to it: the cold rain cleansing his face and mind. He felt a vicious peace.

Two men pulling a handcart came round the corner. They didn't see him as they lumbered past, guffawing, cart wheels clattering. The stench of the cart made Will retch again. Night soil men. A sudden pity for them.

He passed doorways with beggars sleeping in them; snoring heaps of rags. The smell of alleys – narrow, dark, threatening places. The trickle of the sewage ditch down the middle of the street: all the piss and filth of half a million people. Faint screams from behind the walls of Bedlam.

A feeling of total loneliness, of loss: loss of his old life, of Alice. His hand went to his jerkin; he clutched it tight, felt the shape of the bent sixpence he always wore hanging on a cord round his neck.

Alice, Alice.

She would be busy with her life, not thinking of him.

★

Will woke in the morning with a sore head and a foul-tasting mouth. But he somehow felt purged. He smiled at his defilement of the church and his father. Today was Sunday, and the one good thing about the Sabbath was that it was a day of rest. And the sun was shining. He would stroll the streets.

After a few months in the city, what had once amazed Will he now never noticed: the endless series of narrow lanes packed with people and carts and animals; streets covered in muck and rubbish, sewage and horse and cow shit; grand churches and smart townhouses next to ramshackle shacks and crumbling taverns, tenements and cottages.

Smells of tanners and chandlers, smithies, smoke; of spices and fruit and flowers; of sour ale and roasting meat. The calls of vendors, curses; black men in flowing robes, big bearded men from the frozen north, the gabble of foreign tongues. The White Tower and St Paul's towering high, clusters of church spires. London Bridge with its shops and houses; above the South Bank gateway a group of skulls and withered heads on spikes. On the Thames a forest of masts from all over the world; two-and three-masted ocean-going vessels anchored in mid-stream or moored at wharves; and amongst them wherries and ferries, rowing boats, fishing skiffs, eel ships and barges. Here were shops and workshops for ropes and sails, masts, victuals and munitions.

Here in St Katherine's, just outside the jurisdiction of the City of London and so unhindered by the authorities and their restrictions, was the warehouse where he worked. Here were the labourers, dockers unloading bales and barrels and crates, the customs clerks and comptrollers.

Will's master, Charles Spencer, had a reputation for integrity in his dealings. He took his responsibilities seriously for training apprentices, seeing future business opportunities in the making. So Will learned to keep accounts, to write bonds and bills, to strip and weigh great parcels of silk from Aleppo, to recognise spices from the East and test the quality of furs from the north.

Will loved to imagine the far-flung places to which he despatched goods: linen, fowling pieces, spirits to the Americas; bales of West Country cloth dyed red or violet, burgundy or green, which were sought all over the Ottoman Empire. And the stuff that came in: indigo, pepper, cochineal, sugar, tin, Persian silks, Turkish mohair. Many things he never even knew existed.

Here he learned of Ralph's sideline – odd for a godless ruffian: smuggling in from Holland illegal religious tracts attacking the King and the bishops; even, once, a printing press, dismantled and packed in crates marked 'Pottery'. Doing it for the money only.

More importantly, he learned how his master had shares in several of the ships that transported his goods – spreading the risk of storm and piracy losses. If Will was really to prosper this was an example he must follow.

Though he worked hard, he played hard, too – in the taverns and brothels round Newgate. He preferred dark and gloomy taverns, mucky flagstones, low ceilings with smoke-blackened beams, the smell of stew in a pot, rough tables and a couple of hounds sprawled underneath.

But for brothels he went upmarket: polished wooden panelling in the hallway, bronze candelabras, ornate tables inlaid with pearl and onyx depicting scenes of seduction; whores in diaphanous gowns who sprawled on sofas and chairs; a card game in a corner.

From those places he would return to his cheap lodging house – the third floor of a tenement off Cheese Lane. Just a small fireplace, a chair, a table, an adjoining bedchamber, no carpets and draughty curtainless windows. There he would feel shame; the thought of his fingers touching the bent sixpence was abhorrent. Alice!

It was soon after he arrived in London that he embarked on this phase of wild living, as if resolved to be as far as possible from romance, love, family and normal life.

And sure enough he was punished. He contracted a sore throat then a high fever and blinding headaches. One of his balls swelled to the size of a fist.

"The clap!" groaned Will.

"Gonorrhoea," said the surgeon and prescribed salivation, a treatment with mercury. Will was bled, purged and poulticed, given a quantity of mercury-based pills and potions and enemas. He sweated and puked, terrified, abhorring himself and repenting but still not resorting to prayer.

Spent, wasted, humbled, he slowly recovered.

Cockfighting, he concluded, would be a safer kind of sport than cock-brandishing.

6.

HOLLAND

1615

A lice sat her mother in the chair in front of the fire and tucked her up as best she could with shawls. She poked the coals, took one last look at her mother's pale face – eyes closed, chin slumped forward on her chest – closed the door and scuttled down the dark narrow stairway.

There were closed doors on landings, stale smells of food, damp that caught her throat and made her cough. Three floors down she opened the front door of the lodging house, stepped onto the littered cobbles and hurried down the alley between its high walls of damp stone and old brick. A cat squirmed away from her feet, baleful yellow eyes contemptuous. Ahead was a tall rectangle of grey light: open street, canal, sky. She paused and drew breath – a different damp, fresh and salty on the breeze; barges on the murky canal; shouts of men. She joined the bustling people: men pulling carts full of sacks and wood, rattling over the cobbles; a woman with buckets of fresh herring; shouts of street-sellers; the smells of fish and horse manure; clanking of buckets, the sound of hooves on stone, the peal of church bells.

She had been awestruck at first by the city: so utterly different from Worsley's quiet lanes and fields and easy pace. But, as she got used to it, her nervousness had changed to excitement: so many different kinds of clothes worn, from different countries; strange languages and unfamiliar gestures; a range of skin colours, even black, which she had heard of but never seen; and the goods on show: silks and fish, cheeses, spices and barrels, pottery. The whole world was here in Amsterdam, buying and selling, money changing hands; words spoken behind hands, hands shaken. But it was the women she was most shocked by. They walked publicly in pairs holding hands, or on their own without chaperones. They sat in public smoking long white pipes, drinking ale and wines and gin; shouting at men, arguing with them, laughing out loud and joking. That was what struck her most. They seemed free and not submissive.

Alice reached the baker's: the heat inside, the smell of sweet cakes and waffles, spiced biscuits and piles of marzipan pieces. She bought a loaf and some sugary pancakes for her mother. Then back home.

Her father was out all day with the merchants, trying to find a niche, her brother was porter to a bookseller. She had ribbons to weave in the light of the small window, food to prepare, rooms to be kept. They had to live on ninepence a week, boiled roots and cheap fish. Mary Cheever she never saw, gutting and salting fish somewhere down at the docks. Alice missed her irresistible boisterousness.

It was a hard grind but she wasn't often homesick. At night before she slept she thought of Will, wondered what he was doing in his own city. Just as excited as she was, she believed, making his way.

Her mother, she knew, was fading fast: walked from prison to prison in England, buffeted by the sea; now in this unfamiliar dingy place, hearing foreign words shouted on the stairway. They had had to carry her up to these top-floor rooms, so breathless was she when she climbed a few stairs. Now her mother was marooned here.

"Why does God not just let me die?" she had asked. It would indeed be a mercy – to her mother and all of them. Though it felt sinful to say so.

Alice had never before travelled further than Wigan, ten miles away from home. She had never imagined a life away from Worsley, even though she had fumed at the hypocrisies she observed. Nor had she had paid work, just helping her mother or commenting to her father on textiles he was selling. Now, on a loom borrowed from other English Puritans and placed on a table underneath the window, she worked many hours a day.

Ribbons were all the fashion: worn to braid hair, trim clothes, to brighten linen and even to ornament furniture. Men attached them to sword handles, to hats, tied them round the knee. So Alice wove gold and silver thread and silk into satin and velvet, the ribbons dyed shades of blue and yellow and red. At first she was slow, earning virtually nothing when she took them to the merchants. But gradually her speed increased, her fingers hardened and she began to contribute to the family budget. Alice understood for the first time what it was to have to work, to be poor, to count the pennies and look for the cheapest food. She had a new respect for the poor: their strength and resilience. And a little more disrespect for the God who had ordained that each had his place and for most it was a low place. If it was God, and not the church of men. There seemed such a difference between Jesus' words and the ways of the Church – not just the papists but Anglicans and even among some of the Puritans.

All this and her mother fading fast just so her father could pray in the way he wished. It seemed to her utter selfishness rather than saving their souls.

She heard her father's footsteps on the stair. The door opened and he stepped into the room. She looked up from the loom and watched him bend to kiss his wife on the forehead. He muttered something but her mother did not stir. Then he peered into the pot hung over the fire and sniffed. She saw little of him these days, long hours working among the merchants and workhouses.

"Herring again?"

Alice stood.

"No, I must ask your pardon," he said, "I did not mean to be critical. These are not easy times. And it was I who brought you here."

He sat at the table and she ladled him some of the soup: potatoes, herring and scraps of cabbage. There was a hunk of bread, too.

He finished his soup and pushed the bowl away, wiped his mouth and sighed.

"Alice, I will be taking us somewhere else shortly."

To a better house? A lighter and warmer one?

"Away from Amsterdam."

Leaving!

"But why, Father? We are just settled here."

"It is good news, really. It is extremely hard for me here. Amsterdam is the capital of the world. There is plenty to sell and buy but the competition between merchants is intense. There are guilds that have heavy controls, and only members have rights. But I have found a Dutchman who wishes to enter into a partnership with me. He wants me to set up in the city of Leiden, which is about thirty miles south of here. A fair city, he says."

Alice immediately thought of her mother. She doubted she could survive the upheaval of another change.

"Your poor mother will find it difficult but we cannot be happy living like this. And we will not be going alone. Other English Puritans are going, too."

"And why is that?"

"Some of us are not happy with what is being preached in our congregations."

What?! With a decent living so hard to make, were they still arguing about words? What about caring for people?

"What do you mean?" she asked.

"Pastor Smythe, from Gainsborough if you remember," – she didn't – "is now declaring that infant baptism is unbiblical. All of us have to be baptised again as adult believers."

They deliberately picked and plucked to find disagreements, never at peace with themselves. More intent on establishing their own cleverness than caring for their flock. And what was wrong with adult baptism? A baby was not capable of choosing to become a Christian. She wanted to yell at him, pummel his stupid chest. But she said nothing: discussions with her father about theology rapidly became arguments, heated on his part while she retreated into silence, appearing to accept his ideas.

"Pastor Smythe also says that during worship services the Bible should be read out only in its original languages of Hebrew and Greek."

"That is ridiculous; it's like the papists and their Latin."

"Yes, I agree, but to be fair, he says it must also be translated on the spot into English. But that is just a nonsense, a waste of time. It is making the preacher with his translation too powerful. Worse still, another pastor is saying that he and the elders can dictate policies to their congregations. That is not our way. As you know, it is our belief that all of us can speak about religious doctrine and debate it. Some of us do not wish to be embroiled in these disputes, which will only get worse. And that is why a group of us are moving to Leiden."

Why can you not have your disagreements without shifting house and home? It was stupid.

He finished his pot of ale.

"It is a fortunate coincidence that it is the city my partner wishes me to work in."

At least he had not said it was the will of God, as if God ordained such mercantile details.

★

It was no surprise to Alice that her brother Henry refused to leave Amsterdam. He had made friends, and even talked about joining a ship to trade and travel the world.

So it was that three weeks later Alice sat in the back of a cart, cuddling her mother among the small number of their possessions, while her father sat with the driver on the buckboard. Another English couple were travelling with them, who had lived in Amsterdam for nine years – Nehemiah and Judith.

A small town they came to seemed strangely empty, the outlying streets silent except for wandering dogs. But when they came to the market place, there was a huge crowd. They could not get through, and from the cart they could see over the heads of the people that a stake had been set up.

"It is a burning; I can see the brushwood," said her father, standing up. "We must leave. I don't want to see this." But more folk had crowded in behind them and their cart was now hemmed in.

"Ask someone what has happened," Alice said to Nehemiah, who understood quite a lot of Dutch. He got down from the cart. People answered his questions eagerly, with gestures and shocked expressions. He climbed back in.

"It is a local woman called Kael. They say she caused a child to fall ill, that she paralysed a pig, that she prevented the milk of a cow from being churned into butter."

"Peasants, seeking revenge for some slight, can make such accusations. It has happened in England," said her father. "I do wonder that the justices believe such stories."

"But there is worse," said Nehemiah. "They say she turned into a tomcat and had sexual congress with the Devil."

Alice found herself instinctively crossing herself.

"And this is a Protestant town?" asked her father.

"Yes," answered Nehemiah.

And this is the tolerant Low Countries, thought Alice. Such superstition!

Then there was a great shout among the crowd and a surge forward. Alice felt herself drawn to watch with the rest. She saw an old woman being led to the stake, head bowed, bare-footed, wearing a rough woollen dress. A man on each side pinioned her arms. The woman was made fast to the stake, her feet on the ground, a chain locked round her waist. Alice was appalled but could not look away. One man raised the woman's chin – her eyes were closed – while the other fastened a halter round her neck. One end of the rope of the halter was passed through a hole in the stake.

Alice wondered if the justices had been merciful and plied her with alcohol, but she had seemed steady enough as she was led out.

Except for a few uncouth male shouts, the crowd had gone silent. How can good people watch this? Now brushwood was piled up in a circle round the stake, covering the woman's feet and the lower part of her legs. Another man appeared with a lighted torch, smoke curling up from it.

Suddenly the woman's voice split the air, high-pitched and desperate.

"Please, strangle me, please." Then she was sobbing and praying, it seemed.

And some of the crowd shouted, "*Ja, ja. Wees barmhartig!*"

"Be merciful," whispered Nehemiah.

But others shouted louder, "*Nee, nee.*"

Alice had never seen such a baying mob. It was crude and cruel.

Judith was weeping, head bowed and looking at the cart floor.

Now the torch lit the brushwood. Immediately flames and smoke rose. There was a great intake of breath from the crowd. Alice remembered being told that sometimes the wood would be chosen because it was damp so that the smoke would kill the witch before the flames burned her. Not here.

The woman was screaming now. Then Alice saw the executioner pull on the rope behind the stake and tighten the halter. He was trying to strangle her. Thank God for his mercy. But then he staggered back; the flames had burned through the rope. The woman shrieked again – such sounds of pain and despair Alice had never even imagined. And a different smell in the air, of flesh burning. Alice gagged, wanted to vomit.

Now the executioner lifted a heavy lump of timber and hurled it at the woman's head. It struck and cracked open her skull. She slumped. Death at last. Many in the crowd now bent their heads and prayed silently.

A tomcat able to fuck with the Devil, but not able to escape the stake.

But the crowd did not disperse. There was a different feeling now. Maybe the same feelings Alice herself had: shame that she had watched, guilt, the knowledge that this was not right.

Now the flames engulfed the woman's body and flew high above the stake, up to the blue heaven. Was this what their God really wanted? Did he approve and even praise such things – whether it was in Hebrew or Greek or Latin or English?

In silence they watched the flames die down, smelled the burned flesh.

As the crowd broke up and wandered away, Alice wondered if the experience would make them harder or softer next time. Would the shame – if they felt it – harden their hearts because what had to be done had to be done?

At last their cart could move on. Her mother had slept through it all, only starting up momentarily when the witch shrieked. Witch! Already her mind had assimilated it. How strong was superstition, how ready the human mind was to be scared, how easy to become a mob!

7.

MARRIAGE

1617

Alice and her parents settled in the fair city of Leiden. Within two months Alice and her father were scattering foreign soil on the coffin of Alice's mother in the churchyard of St Peter's Church, the Pieterskerk. Forty or so fellow English Puritans stood with them among the gravestones and under the trees that were just beginning to bud. They had not been able to contact her brother: away at sea, people said. Pastor Robinson spoke the words: "Ashes to ashes, dust to dust." English words among the Dutch and Spanish grave epitaphs. Her father had his head bowed and eyes closed, but Alice suspected he was not grieving. Alice, too, was not grieving for the woman her mother had become: her death had been welcomed, the end of her earthly travails and, if the pastor was to be believed, the beginning of her heavenly happiness. No, Alice grieved for the mother she had had as a child, back in England: the mother who had bathed her cuts, taught her to read, kissed her goodnight, who was always there. She remembered the touch and smell of her skin that seemed to bring safety and comfort.

But as the gravediggers began to fill in the grave and Alice turned away, not taking her father's arm, she knew she did not want the life her mother had lived. She would not be *The English Wife* of Gervase Markham's book: always obedient to her husband, in thought as well as deed, assuming he knew best about everything beyond the management of the home. Her mother's meek obedience had brought about her death:

not questioning her father's decision to leave England. She realised she had never heard them discuss religious issues. Her mother had let her father take the lead.

Her father had brought her mother to a land in which she was not well enough to thrive. But he had also brought her, Alice, and – quite beyond his calculations – Alice had had her mind opened, had seen things she never would have seen in England. What her father so obviously disapproved of here, Alice liked and was amused by. Perhaps Mary Cheever had started it, back on the estuary boat, not just comforting the sick but berating the sailors, standing up for herself just as she had done later in the Amsterdam fish markets – making her own way, a woman alone.

Her father returned from work one evening to their small house on the Green and sat down at the table. Alice served him his meal: not herring stew anymore, but capon and fresh vegetables. He ate in silence: there were just the two of them now and Alice was weary after a day at the ribbon-weaving loom. She sensed an announcement, something in the way he wiped his mouth after his last forkful of food, something in the way he carefully positioned his cutlery on the pewter dish. He was controlling a nervousness she had not seen before.

She collected the dirty dishes to take to the kitchen.

"I have something to tell you, Alice. Please sit down."

So, she had been correct. She looked at him. He was staring at the fire, not looking at her. She put down the dishes on the table and sat on the bench, her back straight. Was his business venture failing? Might they even be returning to England?

"I will be direct with you: I am going to marry again."

And still he did not look at her, his hands resting on the table, lace cuffs among the breadcrumbs. He took a deep breath.

"Have you nothing to say?"

What did she have to say? She was surprised but not shocked. There had been no indication. She had assumed he was late home some evenings because he was working longer hours. Men did re-marry but perhaps not usually so soon after their wife's death.

Like all men, she thought, her father needed a stable home base from which to sally forth and do manly things and then return to warmth and comfort and food. Until leaving England, her mother had provided that. But not since they arrived here. Her father had struggled to re-establish himself here; it had been difficult – and lonely – for him. Now he could begin to relax a little, be more confident; he wanted that same comfortable home and support. And there was something questionable about an unmarried, prosperous middle-aged man. Unpleasant rumours flew. So it was all natural to him. She could not blame him.

"I would like you to be pleased for me."

And now she had so much to say, as a confusion of feeling flooded into her. But she must be guarded. She must not create hostility between them. His eyes flickered towards her; he was uncertain. And she felt a sudden warmth for him. She smiled.

"Father, I know you have not been happy for some time."

He nodded, moved his hand towards hers on the table. He was going to take her hand. She could not remember when he had last shown her some affection. But he stopped it before he touched her.

"Mother was ill for so long. You have had so much worry over business here; we have not had much money. It has been difficult settling in a foreign country."

Did she see moisture wet his eyes? He bent his head.

"So, if you are happy again, I am pleased for you."

She clasped her hand over his. It was instinctive not deliberate. She was startled. She had not touched him since being a little girl. He must have been shocked, too, but he did not remove his hand. How warm were his fingers.

"It may not be easy for you, I know," he said. "You will have memories of your mother, and maybe you are thinking I have not been loyal to her."

He was right. She felt a sudden pang of resentment, even of anger on her mother's behalf.

"With another woman as mistress of the house, you will have to adapt."

And now at last he looked directly at her. He squeezed her hand.

"But I hope you will be friends."

For five years her mother had been ill, weakened not just by fatigue but by a deep sadness, a lethargy that saw her sink deep into herself with no desire or ability to emerge into the world. Her mother had always been obedient to her father in the big decisions – like leaving England – and in return was mistress of the house. This was how things were, the natural way. But now this new wife would be mistress of her home, and she, Alice, was no longer a child. She was an adult and it would not be easy for two adult women to share the same home. Over the last six months, even though it had been hard, she had come to run their small household as well as bring in a small income. Things would change.

She asked the obvious question: "Who is she?"

"You do not know her. Sarah Clarke. She is a widow, widowed while in Amsterdam, a Puritan like us, from the village of Scrooby in Nottinghamshire. She has money from her husband's estate and some income from property there – like we do from the rented farmland we still own in Worsley. She is a goodly woman and we share the same beliefs."

Alice was not excited by this description. It seemed like an attempt to re-create the past, to ignore the fact they were in a foreign country with its different life. They would stay within their tight Puritan English community. Disappointment filled her. She would be restricted, shut in, with no sympathy for reaching out to new ideas. But it was a sensible match: sensible and logical, calculated even.

"When will you marry?"

He paused. "In about three weeks' time."

That was a shock; it was very soon.

"There is no reason to delay. My partnership at last is beginning to bear fruit. Money is coming in, and with Sarah's income we will be able to think about moving to a larger house."

Alice saw herself in an attic room with her ribbon-weaving loom beneath the window.

"And soon, if all goes well, you will not need to work at your ribbons, unless you wish to be a ribbon-weaver for life?"

He laughed.

So, she would not need to contribute to the household. She would be more a grace-and-favour lodger than a daughter.

"And you, Alice," her father continued, "you need to be thinking of marriage. You are twenty-two years old. You have been brought up to better things than ribbon-weaving."

He stood up.

"I may be of some help to you in choosing a husband." He smiled at her. "And now I must go out to a meeting."

Alice remained seated at the table, the dirty dishes still there.

From the date of her mother's burial it had taken her father only nine months to arrange a new marriage.

And marriage for her? That would be a way out, to be mistress of her own home. But at what price? Her father would doubtless choose an English Puritan for her, but she had seen, with delight, how many Dutch women were not subservient to their husbands. She had seen them arguing loudly in public and felt her spirits lift. This busy city, with its university and inhabitants from all over Europe and even further, was awash with different ideas and beliefs. She had no desire to be shut within the limits of her mother's life.

★

It had started snowing in the early evening and continued overnight. Alice lay awake in bed, picturing it: in the dark, silently, without permission, the snow was slowly transforming the city and the land, single flakes accumulating, obscuring, accentuating.

In the cold and windy morning, she walked through the snow to her mother's grave. There was a simple headstone: *Patience Ainsworth, born in Worsley, England, 1572, died Leiden 1618.* Such a brief summary of a life turned upside down. There in the black and white of the wintry, snowy churchyard, her cloak wrapped around her, she remembered the candlelight flickering on her mother's open mouth on her deathbed: the black hole in the white face, skin drawn tight, her faint snoring, the lack of dignity. Then the weak rattle in the throat and the release of death. A sudden absence in the stale-smelling room. The thought of sponging her mother's body with lavender water and preparing it for burial had revolted her. Her father had to get someone in to do that.

Another life ended – just like all those others buried here. Life was a strange phenomenon: all that getting and labouring, the brief joys and longer disappointments. And they had been a very fortunate family; blessed, as her father would say. Her childhood had been happy – always warm, fed and clothed, with shoes. Her mother had brushed her long hair, taught her to read as well as cook. It was only as Alice became fourteen or fifteen that they had begun to grow apart. She had not been a mother she could talk to, raise questions with, confide in. Alice understood now that her mother had preferred being

62

settled and had not liked disturbances of any kind. Routines, repetition, the security of fixed ideas – with all these she had been happy.

And for a moment, as the cold wind blew her hair loose from her bonnet, Alice envied her mother the contentment she had enjoyed back in Worsley. But only for a moment. What had her mother lived for? To tend her husband – and in return he had brought about her death. To nurture her children – but four had died before they were one year old.

Men protected and provided for their wives; they too loved their children, if only from a distance and sometimes severely. But men had something else, too. They achieved things: built businesses, wrote books, discovered countries, dispensed justice, governed, thought big ideas. Why were women excluded from such things?

She was cold now, shivering.

Why was she, Alice, so different from other women? Was it all down to Will's father in her bedroom when she was ill? Surely what had happened to her had happened to other girls. But it was then that the whole edifice of respectability and the appearance of things came tumbling down. From then on, mockery seemed a natural reaction, mockery and scepticism. Only Will had been an ally. Poor Will! With his ribbon to bind their hands together, a ribbon she now wished she had kept. And his bent sixpence. She felt it now, beneath the collar of her dress. Why did she still secretly wear it? Will was a romantic and she had rejected that. Perhaps it was a kind of guilt, even though she knew she had been right. The time had been wrong. She would never forget the tenderness and fierceness of their stolen kisses and secret embraces. He had burned and she had melted. And the secrecy had been part of it. She shivered. Did he still wear his sixpence? She thought he would, even as he tupped some city girl in London. Out of revenge or pain or a need to forget. He had thought he loved her but it was circumstances. Neither had been old enough to know what love was. Or so she'd thought. Now perhaps she was less sure, but it was too late.

Alice stood up. Did her father visit this grave? There were no flowers on it. What had happened to his love for her mother? Was it just displaced by the new woman? Placed on a shelf like a well-read book? Alice was sure there was an equation, a balancing of books.

She pulled her cloak and hood around her. The winter sun had gone and only the cold wind was left. There were no other footprints in the thin snow. It was a comfortless blanket over her mother's grave. Rooks called angrily from the bare trees.

She walked back into the bustle of the town. And again she marvelled at the pipe-smoking women, the breeches – even wide galligaskins – and wide-brimmed hats some of them wore in a brazen imitation of men. Pinned on their bodices were what she swore were imitation codpieces. Alice laughed aloud. How did they dare?! It would not happen in Worsley. The streets were busy and loud with many languages. It was indeed a new world.

★

Alice and her father had an argument at breakfast. Peter Warren, her father's choice as Alice's husband, was to join them for dinner the following evening – a meal prepared by Alice.

"Your food will impress him. First impressions," said her father affectionately.

But, without raising her voice, polite, determined, she had refused.

"But why?" Her father was angered and surprised, a flare of red on his face. A sudden image of her, around two years old, repeatedly saying No, testing the rules. "How dare you?!"

"I am, I hope, more than a preparer of food."

"Of course you are, Alice," he said, solicitously now.

"It is more important I hear him talk, and he hears me. I don't want to be worrying about whether he likes my pie pastry."

"Hear you talk?" He took a drink of ale.

"Yes, Father. You know I have my own ideas. And I know you disapprove. He has to know that and accept that I may be different from other wives."

"What I do know, Alice, is that you need to marry. And Peter Warren is a good man."

"Maybe he is. I have never met him."

She would make her own choice of husband, she was sure of that. But she would not say that in so many words – yet. And perhaps, by good fortune, Peter would be the one.

"You will serve wine, then."

"Yes, I will serve wine, gladly, and we will have some sweet cakes."

"I will select the best wine we have." He looked at her, his face set in suppressed irritation. "Do not embarrass me."

He cut a thick chunk of cheese and chewed some bread. His look did not invite a response.

So the following evening the table had been scrubbed, there was a vase of fresh flowers and a bowl of fruit. The fire was cheerful and there were smells of herbs and spices. The best goblets had been polished. Their young servant girl had been sent home early having polished the copper pans and pewter dishes, which gleamed in the firelight.

To please her father, to conciliate and, yes, to impress – why not? Mr Warren might, by coincidence, be the man – Alice wore her best dress and had put her hair up under her cap. As she sat waiting – and her father was always punctual – she stroked Will's sixpence, held its metal in her fingers. It would give her strength.

At the sound of the key in the door opening, she hastily tucked the sixpence away beneath her collar. She heard the door scrape across the flagstone. She sat upright in the chair by the window, hands in her lap. Demure, she thought, composed: a way of controlling her nervousness, a nervousness she hated.

The door was pushed open, her father filling the doorway. "Alice, here is Mr Warren."

She stood up and Mr Warren stepped out from behind her father. A minimal curtsey to him. She was surprised: she had imagined an older man, shorter, with a paunch and a round face. She had a vague memory of noticing Mr Warren – as he walked to church or on the steps of City Hall?

He took off his hat and gave a slight bow. "I'm so pleased to meet you."

He was tall, well made, a thin face with a dark beard and longish hair, no grey in it. His black jacket was of velvet, a white collar, laced cuffs spilling from the arms, polished calfskin boots.

"Sit down, Mr Warren," her father said and, turning with a smile: "Some wine, Alice?"

She knew she had been silent so far. Mr Warren must have known she'd be wary. She poured the wine, pleased her hands were not trembling, and sat down opposite Mr Warren.

He began to talk: of his home village in England, his parents who still lived there, of hunting and farming. Alice liked his voice; he spoke well and with expression, eyes bright. There were occasional jokes which she smiled at. He never mentioned his business.

But something about him made her skin crawl. After brief eye contact she saw his eyes ranging over her body, assessing her with brazen arrogance as if she were merchandise. Eating one of the sweet cakes, he would lick his lips with his tongue, just a little longer than was necessary, looking directly at her. And there were his fingers on the goblet or as he stroked his beard: stubby, short. They revolted her. On his right hand two garish gold rings, and over-ornamental lace at his cuffs made the fingers even uglier.

Beneath his charm there was something lewd and base, calculating and lecherous.

She made sure she sipped only a little wine but watched Mr Warren drink copiously.

When he rose to leave, pushing his chair back, he was red-faced. She remained seated, determined not to touch his hands in some farewell.

"I may see you again," he said.

She could not tell whether it was a question or a statement. She looked down at the table.

She listened to the farewells on the doorstep and her father returned. He looked at her accusingly. "You were quiet."

"I answered his questions."

"Not the last one."

"The last one?"

"About seeing you again."

Had her father not seen the man's eyes stripping her naked? How could she ever describe to him the revulsion she felt physically for him?

"He will not be my husband," she said.

Her father blustered and shouted, slammed his fist on the table. "You are throwing away an opportunity. He will give you a good home."

"I do not want to see him again."

Her father stamped out of the room and the house, slamming the door behind him.

His anger would dissipate, she knew, but could they ever be reconciled?

Mr Warren never came again. And somehow she found it impossible to thank her father for that. In the days that followed, there was a silence between them that chilled the house. She did her domestic duties and wove her ribbons. Her father went his ways. They were separating.

8.

BOOKS

1619

Had it become an obsession, making money?

A glass of fine Spanish wine in his right hand, Will's left hand held the latest fashionable clock-watch, which hung from a chain round his neck.

He stood by the window, looking down at the bustling wharves below, where his future income was being unloaded by a gang of strong, rough men.

Well, had it?

His answer was no.

He loved what money could buy; he loved how it had refined his taste. No doubt of that. He stretched his toes in his fine Spanish leather boots – those damned papists could make stuff.

His fingers traced his intertwined initials *WN* engraved on the brass lid of the egg-shaped clock-watch. He glanced up at the Flemish tapestry on the wall. Both objects were expensive, both produced by skilled craftsmen. He, too, was a skilled man – with an eye for quality and a mind for a shrewd deal. Self-taught. He, also, was creating – but a business rather than an artefact or a mansion house or a church.

And to do that he had to take risks. Was risk an obsession with him? More a compulsion – if there was a difference. A weakness for gambling, he had to admit that. Though he had learned a lot since dicing with Ralph – which Ralph, laughably, the cunning whoreson, had later deemed lessons for which Will should have been grateful.

But he'd grafted, put in the hours. He'd only been here six years, two of those as an apprentice. He'd found he had a natural gift for making deals; he'd been shrewd but straight with people, never cut corners for the quick return. His master, Charles Spencer, had trusted him and given him responsibility. He knew his had been a meteoric rise, and he was grateful. His established competitors had not liked it, this upstart off-comed-un, as they would say at home. And he was envied.

He sipped some wine, then turned to his desk, took a heavy purse out of the pocket of his canvas doublet – the height of fashion – and placed it in a drawer. That new breed of goldsmith-bankers, "keepers of running cash", as they called themselves, were gamblers, now dealing in gold coins. Henry Pinckney, whom he had just met at The Three Squirrels in Fleet Street, had gambled in setting himself up to vie with the merchants from northern Italy who had established themselves on Lombard Street. Gambling with their new-fangled banknotes or drawn notes.

He had this very morning deposited a large amount of gold with Henry Pinckney, whom he had known for several years. He had received a receipt for it and given instructions for regular monthly pay-outs. And that was another virtue of money: to do good and maybe assuage a guilty conscience. He had his friend and lawyer Francis Ingilby to thank for the introduction to Pinckney. Now, Francis was a man for whom money and the pleasures it brings, some of them the source of scandal, were the only objectives. They'd become friends playing bowls and skittles, backgammon and shovelboard. Both loved to wager, against each other and against others. But they enjoyed their differences, too. Francis was from a Catholic family in Lincolnshire, a younger son who'd trained at the Inns of Court, his glib tongue honed to a laconic wit. Most of life amused him and he hinted at dubious pastimes.

Will rolled the wine around his mouth. Such a fine taste.

There was a firm knock on the half-open door. Will looked up: the tall shape of John Boon stood there, shoulders hunched slightly, as usual when he approached a doorway.

"Ah, John, come in."

Will pulled open the drawer of his desk and took out the purse.

"I want you to take this to Lizzie. You know where she lives."

John nodded, but Will noticed the slight tightening of his mouth which appeared whenever the subject of Lizzie Brentwood arose. John had become his conscience, the good angel on his shoulder.

"I am making reparations, John. There are two pounds in this purse. Tell Lizzie you will bring this to her every month, to help with Edmund's upbringing."

But John's eyes granted him no blessing. In John's world, if a man got a woman with child, he married her: simple, honest, responsible. Because of Lizzie, Will would always be morally in the red for John.

"Thank you, John."

John pocketed the purse and left.

Will relied on John, would trust his integrity to the end, respected him. But sometimes, like now, Will resented John's virtue, the uprightness of his monastic life with no women and no immoderate drinking. The sheer lack of stain on his character.

And he did feel guilty about Lizzie, leaving her with a child. But from now on she would at least be financially secure, with a better chance of marriage and more able to choose. He had been genuinely fond of her, a seamstress who worked for a friend's business, but he had taken advantage.

He respected her, for not coming after him or asking him for money when he had abandoned her. At the time he had given her what he could. Now prosperous, he had John Boon find Lizzie Brentwood and where she lived and the name of the child: Edmund, his son.

A marriage between them would never have worked. Lizzie was too docile for him, a good young woman but without questions to ask of the world. Alice had set the bar high. Even now, six years after they had been forcibly separated, Will thought about her softly. Did she still have the bent sixpence he'd given her? It still mattered to him. His own was on a cord around his neck, resting on his bare chest – a simple thing from the past, from Worsley, hanging next to a luxury from Nuremberg. And much more valuable.

No, what he had done for Lizzie was best for them both. And John Boon could purse his mouth all he wanted.

John was his right-hand man; no apprenticeship but he had learned fast. He had miraculously taught himself to read and write while still in Worsley. Honest but shrewd in business, John spoke little but always to the point. Two years older than Will but six inches taller, with a thick beard and broad shoulders, he had a physical presence that made other men instinctively respectful – and drew admiring glances from women, which he ignored. John was older than his years, serious to the point of grave, stern and sober as a judge.

Will looked at his polished oak desk, mostly hidden under papers, maps and contracts. He shared this world now with his master. He was on his way up, an unofficial junior partner in the firm. And the world was his to trade with. He walked over to his cabinet, which was the measure of his success, tangible evidence of his connections across the globe. He still marvelled at the infinite variety: furs from Russia; timber and pitch, tar and hemp from the Hanseatic ports of the Baltic; nutmeg and cloves from India; silk from Persia; tea from Bengal; sugar and tobacco from the West Indies; wine, olive oil and merino wool from papist Spain; spices from the East

Indies. And always competing with the Dutch. His cabinet contained small specimens of them all. His trade had enlarged the geography of his mind.

He moved over to the map of the world on the wall. His eyes now always went first to the city of Aleppo in the Levant. This was the place that excited him more than any other. It linked East and West. Already he sent there bales of dyed West-Country cloth and tin. In a complex operation he imported indigo, pepper, cochineal and sugar to England and then exported them to Aleppo. These were sold there and the money used to buy goods for the English and European markets: Persian silks, Turkish mohair. It was a place where serious money could be amassed, more even than in London.

He liked to imagine the caravanserai of camels arriving after desert crossings, bringing gems from India and spices from Arabia. He imagined the people who lived there: Muslims, Christians, Ottomans, Jews, Armenians, Greeks. One day he would go there, be part of it. From austere, damp Worsley to rich, hot Aleppo. That would be a journey.

Worsley. He had left it behind forever. Alice had gone; his father no doubt still prating; his mother getting on with her lot.

John Boon had wanted to bring him to this stationer's for some time: tentatively inviting him as if sounding him out. A test of trust?

It seemed more of a shack than a shop: a wooden structure that leaned against the walls of St Paul's; a door that strained its hinges as it scraped the floor.

Inside, the gloom was silent except for the turning of pages. By each of the dirty windows stood a man with a book, his fingers moving down the pages. Another was unfolding a map on a table lit by a candle that guttered in the draught. They seemed to hide their faces when Will and John entered.

"John," said a quiet voice from the dim back of the shop.

Will saw a plump, white-haired man step out from behind a counter.

"Good to see you," he continued.

"And you," replied John. "I have brought a friend."

He introduced the stationer, Arthur Babthorpe.

Will shook hands and looked around. He was not a reader – except for what related to business. He had never seen so many books. All these thoughts which were ranged around him: men's minds, arguments, principles. Just lying here, stacked, finished, completed, the covers like coffins for dead ideas. Their authors had moved on to other works, or were dead themselves.

But if he opened one and turned the pages? Would they come to life again, dance in his own head? Emerging like butterflies from a chrysalis? In his imagination he travelled with his ships and bales of goods to the ends of the earth, to places he'd never seen. Perhaps it was time to begin another kind of voyage, blown along by ideas.

His fingers brushed the dust off a book. His father must once have found new ideas and made his own way. But that way had led to restriction, dogma and arrogance and then to cruelty. His own journey would be different.

"Can we see your latest pamphlets?" asked John of the stationer, his voice lowered.

"In the back," the plump man said, leading the way.

They passed bookshelves stacked with paper and turned into a small, even darker room. The windows were dusty and cobwebbed as if deliberately obscuring and keeping secret.

The stationer lit a candle. Will saw pamphlets laid on a desk, a pile of books, scrolls, chapbooks and a pot of quills.

"These are from Holland," said John. "Most of them. There are English and Scottish printers over there who print them and then they are smuggled over here in kegs of wine and brandy."

"Why smuggled?" asked Will.

"Because the authorities say they are heretical."

"Heretical?" Will was suddenly interested.

"Yes. They say bishops are evil – and remember, our King James believes *No bishop, no King.*"

"So they are against the monarchy?"

"Indeed. They also say that Archbishop Laud has re-introduced idolatrous abuses into worship, that he is a secret papist."

Will was warming to these writers.

"They call for a new reformation," continued John.

"I can see why the authorities oppose them. Do you agree with the writers?"

"I do," said John, his face firm and strong in the dim light.

"These books and pamphlets," said the bookseller proudly, "are too hot for their time." His eyes twinkled.

"It must be dangerous to stock them."

"Indeed. We have twice been raided by the Stationers' Office."

"He has been in Newgate Prison," said John, "and more than once."

Will looked again at the little plump man with his round face. A brave man, a rebel.

"You said many came from Holland," said Will. Holland meant Alice.

"Yes. There's a Pilgrim's Press, they call it, in the city of Leiden on Vico Chorali, Choir Alley. An Englishman called Brewster runs it, a Puritan. But the English authorities are chasing him, even over there. They tell me he has to be on the move all the time to keep one step ahead, never sleeping in the same place twice."

Alice's father would certainly not be involved. He was devout but too cautious and canny.

"Look at this pamphlet," said John, handing it to Will.

Will read the title: *Against conformity to kneeling in the very act of receiving the Lord's Supper.*

"People risk their lives to write this?"

"As you can see."

Will remembered his father telling him of William Tyndale, burned at the stake for translating the New Testament into English; of the bishops burned at the stake in Oxford, on the orders of papist Queen Mary, with bags of gunpowder hung round their necks. Only forty years before he was born.

Brave men but crazy, mad.

"And these," said John, handing Will two more.

Perth Assembly, Will read. Haltingly he read the next title, in Latin, *De Regimine Ecclesiae Scoticanae.*

"What are these about?" They didn't exactly get his blood racing.

"They mock the bishops in Scotland and the Anglican rituals King James is trying to introduce there. There are many other papers defending the right for anyone to preach, not just prelates. These writers do not believe you need Church tradition or ceremony or priests to know God. It is only scripture that counts."

John's voice grew more intense.

"Dissent is what counts," said John. "The right to dissent."

He stopped, as if suddenly embarrassed.

This quiet, sober, hard-working man? He was a rebel? John had mentioned that occasionally he went to hear sermons preached by a cobbler or a stone mason, or a leather worker with the wonderful name of PraiseGod Barebones who held forth at The Lock and Key on Fleet Street.

There was another world out there, a world of questions and debate, sedition, where ordinary men were unafraid to voice their opinions and challenge. And what opinions! Attacking the Church and the King – what bigger targets could you shoot your arrows at? Will had no liking of hierarchies, be they kings or bishops or the great guilds and liveried companies with their grandmasters and privileges. And he despised the concept of the Elect – his father, that foul hypocrite, had considered himself one of the Elect. Will hated people who were so arrogant they thought they were always right – from the Pope down, the Pope with his so-called Papal Infallibility. The Pope and the rest of them were only men like himself. They shat and stank and fornicated.

Will suddenly felt boring and conventional. He was totally outside this subversive surge of ideas, of ordinary men putting their lives and livelihoods at risk. He was only good at making money. In fact, it was all he was interested in, apart from gambling. But now he felt a new excitement. He could spread ideas along with his goods. This would be a bigger risk, another gamble. His blood was up. He loved it. Subversion thrilled him. And Francis Ingilby would not approve.

And good man John Boon had introduced him to it.

He bought copies of *The Defense of Separatism* by a Francis Thompson and *A Little Treatise* by a Robert Harrison.

"They should keep you occupied of an evening," said John. "Mind you, I don't agree with everything they write."

Will clapped him on the shoulder. "That's what it's about, isn't it?"

"In a way. But it's not just the love of argument for argument's sake. It's about changing things, making things better for people."

"Now, don't get all pious with me, John."

They both laughed.

9.

Decisions

1620

A lice leaned in between the shoulders of two men to place another platter of bread and cheese on the table. Then from a jug she refilled goblets of ale.

Hugger-mugger round the table, men's heads bent towards each other, conversation intense; men's voices not bitter, just weary; not defeated but struggling. Disappointment shrouded the room. She saw, in their lined faces and tired eyes, hopes curtailed.

She knew what they were to discuss: possible emigration to America, her father had told her.

Would she go with them? The question had lost her sleep. She liked the Dutch way of life, she fitted in. But emigrating would be a new start, an adventure. There were parts of the past she wanted to leave behind: her father's control, her mother's grave, the memory of Will still present somewhere in her head.

Emigration could also be a restoration of the past. Would she really want to travel with dedicated Christians intent on setting up what might become a sect of saints, with all its restrictions?

Pastor John Robinson's living room was crowded: men sat crushed tightly together along the benches at the table and others stood around. There were twenty-seven, counted Alice, and all seemed to be talking, chewing or smoking pipes – and smelling in the heat of the fire: twenty-seven damp black uniforms of piety and twenty-seven varieties of male sweat drying, combining into a fug that made her want to stopper up her nose.

Alice was ostensibly here to help, to do the women's work, but also to listen.

Pastor John Robinson now called for silence. Chewing and chatting ceased. Prayers were said, bowed heads and closed eyes, humbly asking the Lord for direction and assistance.

John Robinson waited a moment for reflection and then began: "We are meeting because, as you know, there are many among us feeling unease about continuing to live here in Leiden. I thought it would be wise to hear those views – and others – together."

The disappointments were described: independent farmers were now combing wool for low wages; advancing years made it harder to put up with things; religious disputes were becoming nastier and violent; the truce with Spain was coming to an end, the papists would return – catastrophe.

"At least we are free to worship here as we wish." It was her father. Alice had not expected him to speak. He was not a man for public debate.

"We have come here to this foreign place," he continued, "and, yes, we have had to work hard, but we have prospered. We have made our homes here in Green Alley, together like a village. We are settled, we are respected here. Do we really want to break that up?"

A shuffling of arms on tables, shoulders warily touching, eyes flickering at each other.

"I for one am staying," her father concluded and took an authoritative swig of ale.

Alice felt a surge of unaccustomed pride in him. He had not been afraid of speaking out against the general opinion. But then few had prospered like him, or married again.

There was a light tap on the door and it opened. A man stepped in quickly, cloaked and hatted; a brief blast of cold air and then he closed the door behind him.

"William," said John Robinson, rising to shake his hand, "I knew you would come."

Elder William Brewster had come out of hiding for this meeting. He was a brave man, thought Alice. He had run a printing press here in Leiden, published tracts that were smuggled to England by some daring merchant. One of the tracts had attacked King James and his bishops. The King had ordered his arrest and royal agents had been sent to Holland. Since then he had never stayed in one place for more than one night. He was a fugitive.

"Please, continue," said the Elder with a gesture of his hands; his beard and long hair were grey.

"Our children," said George Seoule, still wearing his steeple hat and sounding like he did in the pulpit, "have been led into manifold temptations. Eager to rid the reins from their necks, they have fallen into the licentiousness of the youth of this country."

How he loved that word 'licentious', its four syllables drooling out of his mouth.

Alice had to purse her lips to hide her smile as grunts of agreement ran round the table. What had they seen – young people being happy, natural, acknowledging each other, finding each other attractive? How immoral! So sinful! A brief memory of Will and their soft kisses. So long ago now. A reminder, too, of Will's father. What went on behind these respectable facades? Behind the fierce pieties?

"They will soon no longer be English. They speak more and more Dutch as they spend time with these Dutch buttermouths."

William Brewster responded: "As we have all seen, the Dutch buttermouths do not keep the Sabbath holy – their children are encouraged to feast and make merry on the holy day. And I have heard the women bawl at their men, in public, call them lubbers and other disrespectful names. It is too secular a place."

Grunts of general assent as the men downed their ale. Alice smiled wryly.

William Brewster again: "This city and all of Holland is a melting pot of people and ideas. There are French Huguenots, Anabaptists, Mennonites. Our young people listen to them and hear beliefs different from our own."

More shaking of heads in bewilderment.

Did they really believe they could pen in their children and close their ears? Did they think that was right?

John Robinson again: "We have heard the main reasons why many do not wish to stay. And it is sad to hear."

"Pardon, John," said Brewster. He leaned forward to place his goblet of wine on the table then stood tall. The others waited on his words. "But the greater reason is our wish to go," – he threw out both his arms to emphasise the word – "and to advance the gospel of the kingdom of God in the remote parts of the world."

The challenge in his words took them aback. Then Alice felt a sense of relief around the table, as if they had needed a reminder of a greater purpose; to feel connected with something noble and goodly. Glasses were raised to lips and requests made for more cheese. Spirits had been raised.

"You are right, William. So the next question is: where is this preferred promised land?"

Several voices: "To America. America."

But previous settlements had suffered problems. The savages were cruel.

Alice saw fists tightening on the tabletop, knuckles whitening.

Large sums of money were needed. Other voyages had ended in tragedy.

William Brewster cleared his throat. "I have heard enough of this doubting." In his deep sermonising voice: "Where is our faith and our strength? All great and honourable actions are beset with great difficulties. Leaving our homes in England to come here is an example. But we did it, emboldened by our faith. We have proved that difficulties are not insuperable."

And now a changed tone in the voices.

"We will have our courage to overcome them, and fortitude and patience."

"And the help and blessing of God."

"Our ends are good and honourable, our calling lawful."

"Even if some should lose their lives, we can be comforted that our endeavours will have been honourable."

And now there was a pause, as if the argument had exhausted them but they had been returned to virtue – no one could deny the goodly words of goodman Brewster.

How easily people could be put down and then uplifted.

The pilgrims – as some were already calling themselves – were godly, and this godliness made them brave. For them it would be a voyage to the promised land but it would also be an adventure. Among the prayers and sermons there would be much to do. To start from nothing and to build something against the odds – now, that appealed to her.

Her father was intent on arranging marriage for her, if not with the man he had brought then with another similar. She would not be arranged. And her stepmother was increasingly difficult to live with. She had to bite her tongue too many times. It was as if she were trapped by living here.

They had eaten their fill, though wine and ale were still asked for. But not by the Pastor or the Elder or her father.

"So, where in America would you go?" asked the Pastor, looking round the room.

Now there was a new energy.

Guiana? Too full of tropical disease, and Spaniards already there.

Virginia? But English are already there and we would be persecuted for our beliefs as much as we were in England.

"The Virginia Company," said Elder Brewster, "has extended its charter much further north to an area they are calling New England. There they are willing to grant large tracts of land, up to 80,000 acres, to groups of individuals who undertake to people and cultivate them. The King, we are told, refuses to grant us liberty of religion under his seal but he promises not to molest us provided we carry ourselves peaceably."

"Then we must be satisfied with that," said Solomon.

There was a silence.

Then William Brewster: "That is the place for us. I propose that those who wish to journey to New England decide on messages to the Virginia Company, so we can make contact with merchants who would be interested in supporting the voyage. It is time to act."

"Ayes" circled the room. The spirit of rekindled hope.

"I declare the meeting closed."

Some left, including her father, but many remained deep in conversation.

Alice's mind was racing but by the time the dishes and glasses had been cleared, washed and put away, she had resolved that she would be among those who left for New England and a new life. She was guiltily relieved her mother was dead because she surely could not have left her. She wished Mary Cheever was around and not in Amsterdam somewhere. Mary would be a great companion in the adventure, with her practical abilities, her no-nonsense, don't take it too seriously, cheery approach to life. But no, she would be on her own – and that in itself, though daunting, was exhilarating. It wasn't as if she were leaving safety behind. She was leaving what seemed to be repeated pursuit and increasing danger. To leave would be to break free.

Her father would be sceptical of her new-found piety as a pilgrim. She would argue she was doing only what he had done: deciding to move to another country. He would see the advantages to himself as well and, she hoped, help with the costs of the venture. He was angry with and nervous about her independent spirit; he would be glad to be rid of the responsibility for her, and so would his new wife.

As she helped to sweep and tidy up, Alice thought of that last gathering at Will's father's house, the meeting house. All this had begun there with her small act of protest. She could not imagine that God had ordained and organised this sequence of events; they were the unforeseen consequences of chance happenings. And she liked that.

She walked back, past the apothecaries, dye shops and print shops: the ceaseless busyness of the city. Back at home, alone, her father with Sarah, Alice mixed some spiced ale. She heated a poker in the fire and plunged it into the pewter mug. It hissed and steamed and the kitchen filled with the smell of nutmeg. The ale warmed her stomach; her hands were warm around the mug. The challenge of New England filled her with hope.

Her younger days could never come back: picking the windfall apples in the garden, the smell of summer rain on grass, church bells. Will in the hut by the river with his red ribbon; Will who had helped to free her mind. She would keep the memories but that was old England. She was bound for New England – for uncertainties and maybe danger. But they were what she needed.

10.

AT HAZARD

1620

Will moved further back from his office window, to see but not be seen. He swirled the mug of spiced wine, nosed it, breathed in.

This wine encapsulated what he had achieved – not making money but creating a refinement. His ships had brought the ingredients: Spanish red wine, Flemish honey, spices from the East – cinnamon, ginger, cloves, nutmeg, galingale.

He took a sip, loving the warmth and foreignness of it.

Today was different: one of his ships in from Amsterdam. It wasn't just wine and cloth his men were unloading. The bales on their shoulders, the barrels they trundled over the cobbles, the loaded carts – they were all freighted with ideas in pamphlets and broadsheets that he, Will Nailor, had smuggled in. From here they would be carried by washerwomen, pedlars and coachmen to the city, bought from booksellers like his plump friend Arthur Babthorpe, read and passed on to distant hamlets and towns on carts and milk wagons. Men would discuss them in low voices in inns, maybe share them with their wives at home.

He was seeding men's brains. A good, very good, feeling. Another sip of wine.

"Bringing Adam out of bondage," was how John Boon put it. "For the commons."

Will envied the men below him. He wanted to manhandle the secrets, feel the edges of the barrels' rough iron rims scarify his hands, his fingers chafe under the tight cords of the bales.

The men, of course, didn't know what they were conveying. And if they did, would they care? He heard their curses as they stumbled and laboured under the weight of their burdens, heard their coarse laughter, knew they would piss away most of their wages. These were John Boon's commons. For them he was risking prison, and they wouldn't give a rat's arse. In a way he couldn't understand, this made him more determined.

He poured himself more wine. Trade now had an additional purpose: to fund his distribution of radical ideas. He needed to expand further. Only two weeks ago John had brought news of two ships planning to sail from Plymouth full of Puritans to set up a new colony in North America. Well, if the colony was successful, there would be more trading opportunities. Already he dealt in salted cod from Newfoundland.

Some of the Puritans were coming from Holland, John had said. Immediately Will had thought of Alice. Would Alice's family be among them? Unlikely – he didn't see Alice's father as a pioneer.

If he was honest, it was Alice who had set him on this road to nonconformity, to stirring up men. He owed his new-found satisfaction to her.

★

The press stood in a small room behind Will's new house. It had once been a cold store and dairy, only one small window opening into a narrow walled alley, and a strong, barred door. Having been smuggled in from Holland, dismantled and hidden among pottery and household furniture, the press took up almost half the space in the room, reaching seven feet high to the rafters, three feet wide and seven feet long. It was placed in the middle, leaving just enough space to walk round it. Arthur Babthorpe, his white-haired bookseller friend, had supervised its setting up.

Will watched with pride as his team worked efficiently. All his printing staff were committed and experienced. Courageous, too: they were constantly on the move, as illicit presses like this one were discovered and destroyed by the King's Stationers' Office.

The press only worked at night, as now, candles lit, sacking over the window. It was always busy – news of it had been discreetly spread, and there was a steady stream of dissenters who brought their writings to be printed as tracts, pamphlets and broadsheets. There was no conversation, just occasional instructions or requests, short pauses for drinks of ale. It was thirsty work. There was always an alertness in the air: an ear cocked for a shouted warning from outside or a knock on the door.

"Good work, John," said Will.

John Boon nodded and smiled.

"The Lord's work," he said.

"Maybe." He preferred to think of it as men's work, the fruit of their brains, no need for some vague spiritual overseer.

In the restricted space, the team moved well: composing sticks were locked onto the flat stone bed. Ink was rolled onto the typeset. Dampened sheets of linen paper were lifted from a stone trough and laid onto the frames, lined up and pinned into place. A wooden handle was turned that pressed the plate over the paper to make the inked impression. Then each page was lifted off and hung on wooden racks overhead to dry. Will loved the logic and mechanics of the machine, its craftsmanship: human genius.

This was a different kind of paperwork from the business and bureaucracy of the Custom House. This was more like planting and pollinating. These printed sheets were like seeds – spinning, whirling, gliding in the wind, taking root in men's heads, creating new growth, disturbing the ground.

Will moved to the shelf of completed pamphlets. *Of Kingly Power and its Putting Down, All Men Brothers.*

He picked one up, *Liberty no Sin,* opened it and read:

Whereas we know that in the beginning He created them man and woman, that is to say that Adam was the grandsire and Eve the grandma of all mankind, none excepted, and that man and woman, is to say, all men and all women, how comes it that since then are sprung up so many Kings, Lords and Squires that tread their fellows under foot and are loath to call them Brother?

So the Lord, perhaps, was having second thoughts. Or, more like, men were thinking for themselves, asking questions.

The real value of his money was that it furthered this questioning.

Today he didn't need wine to make himself feel warm inside.

★

Next afternoon Will stepped into the enclosure. Bedlam, hullabaloo, pandemonium – disputes, bawling, yelling, wagers laid. Blood was up after eleven cock matches, and now there was only the big one left: Will's gamecock versus Francis Ingilby's gamecock. The top two cocks in London, they were both victors of twelve previous fights, champions. And this was the top place – The Old Red Lion Cockpit behind Gray's Inn Walk – and Midsummer Day, a holiday.

The arena was packed, rich men and poor men alike. Drawn by the gamble, the passion, the bloodlust, the violence and bravery instinctive in the cocks, the certainty of the loser's death. Bare-knuckle boxing didn't go half as far. The men were seduced, like Will himself. An English tradition for hundreds of years. Tiers of spectators looked down on the ring: twelve feet in diameter, surfaced with turf and surrounded by a four foot high wooden palisade. The turf was patched with sawdust thrown over the blood of previous fights.

Will pushed his way through the crush, through the stink of whisky and wine and ale, pipe tobacco smoke, stale sweat, blood and chicken dung. Mouths gaping, blackened teeth, eyes ablaze, men yelled for him or against him, arms waving, thumping him on the shoulder, supporting or opposing depending on where their money lay.

As he reached the palisade, Will saw Francis Ingilby pushing his way through on the opposite side. Francis was not just his lawyer but had become his closest friend. Today he was the rival. This was what the crowd was excited by: the battle of the champions. They cheered and booed.

This was the last chance to bet – most had already done so after inspecting the cocks in their pens or at the weigh-in when both birds weighed 4lb 11oz. Odds were yelled, answered across the ring, fists thrust out and waved.

Will glanced up at the big wicker basket that hung overhead. One man crouched in it, covering his head with his arms. The pit master had had him put there: a drunk or a danger or, more likely, someone who had welched on a debt. There he hung, to be pelted at times with gristle and burnt crust from pies, with apple cores, with the dregs of ale, ridiculed and pilloried.

Will and Francis faced each other across the pit, dressed in their finery as if for a grand council meeting of the liveried company of Merchant Adventurers. They stared at each other, doffed their felt hats and grinned. The crowd roared their approval.

The pit master stood and waved his arms for silence. The noise abated.

"What are your wagers, gentlemen?" he asked.

Francis took the initiative. "I'll lay 1,000 crowns for my Joslan to win."

The crowd gasped and cheered.

"You seem not so confident," smiled Will. A pause, the crowd waiting. "I'll raise you to 2,000 crowns."

Another roar that quickly subsided. A rooster crowed from somewhere behind.

"That's one of your ship's whole cargo, Will," said Francis quietly. "You have faith."

"Indeed I do, in my Hotspur. What say you?"

"We are friends and I do not wish to ruin you, Will. But, if you insist, I'll raise you… to 3,000 crowns."

The crowd sucked in its collective breath. Mouths gaped. This was unheard-of money.

Will stared at Francis, a wry look on his face. This wasn't about the cocks anymore. This was about pride and prosperity. Vanity. Losing face. One of them would surely rue this. He knew that afterwards, over expensive spiced wine, they would admit they were both fools, borne along by the tide of the crowd. But one of them would be seriously hurt in his pocket.

Francis was smiling at him, the challenge laid down, the gauntlet thrown.

To hell with it! He had two ships due to arrive in two weeks, stuffed with money-spinning spices from Aleppo. Where was his spirit? Take the risk.

"4,000 crowns, then," Will said.

The crowd's faces turned to look at Francis. There was a strange silence: a silence that expected, that pressured, that wanted the duel to continue.

Francis's face was impassive. "Done!" he said.

It was the price of a city house.

And now the crowd roared the release of its tension.

"Your wagers, gentlemen," said the pit master, unmoved.

Will and Francis each wrote out and signed a slip of paper. It was passed round the ring to the pit master by eager hands.

89

"I held it," they would say later at the inn. "The wager that ruined – or made – him."

The pit master stuffed them deep into his pocket.

Two ships' worth of cargo, both Will and Francis thought. Storms or pirates or the Dutch could do for both of them.

But the deed was done. Each gave the other a smile and a nod across the pit. Will cast a glance at the hanging wicker basket. For fools.

"Bring in the cocks!" shouted the pit master.

The crowd made room for the two setters-on. They pushed through, each carrying a sack, and stepped over the fencing into the pit. They stood and faced each other, eyes glaring, the sacks at their feet bulging and stretching as the cocks inside lashed out against their restricted space.

"Untie the birds," said the pit master.

The twine that held the sacks was loosened and each setter-on held his bird close and threw away the sack.

Magnificent creatures – the crowd stamped their feet, drummed against the wooden fencing, yelled and cheered – ten feet apart across the pit.

Will looked at his setter-on: Harry, stern-faced, responsible. He was a good man who was master of his trade and looked after all of Will's gamecocks. He knew the best diet for them, how to train them: to run them for endurance, flirt them to strengthen their wing muscles so they learned to flap their wings for balance, to spar them with sparring muffs, to fly them so they could rise eight feet into the air from a standing position. Will had watched it all, this last week. He had held Hotspur in his own hands, felt the bird's pulsating warmth, its straining legs and head, its firm muscles and fine feathers. Hotspur was in top condition. But then Francis's man had done his work, too.

Both birds were winners, fighters to the death, their natural aggression honed and intensified by training and fighting experience. They knew what to do.

"Arm the cocks," instructed the pit master.

Both setters-on first fitted to each yellow, horny leg a cockspur – a leather bracelet with a silver spike, two and a half inches long, sharpened to a point.

Then, where the cock's natural spurs had been sawn off, tight hide coverings were fitted over both stumps and the sockets in the silver gaffes slipped over the covered stumps and tied with waxed string. The points of the gaffes were sharp as needles.

Harry took a pipe from a spectator, filled his mouth with smoke and blew it over Hotspur's head. It was to irritate it even more to fighting pitch.

"Bill your cocks," said the pit master.

Both setters-on brought the birds across the pit, cradled in their left arms, holding their feet to avoid the cuts of gaffes and spurs, and stood sideways at the centre, just two feet apart. These cocks had never met before, never fought each other before, but they were deadly enemies already. Virtually face-to-face, there was murder in their eyes and their feet strained to slash, striving to leap to get in the first pecks. Plumes of glossy black tail feathers, auburn feathers on the back, blood-red wattles and combs, yellow legs: they were arrayed to be braggarts, but elegant, too.

"Pass them," said the pit master.

Holding the gamecocks at arms' length, the setters-on passed them in the air with a circling movement and then backed away and squatted on their heels, opposite each other, setting their straining birds on the turf.

The pit master rang the bell.

"Pit!" he shouted.

The setters-on let go of the birds and jumped out of the pit. The crowd roared.

Hotspur was the slower bird. He missed with both spurs as Joslan sidestepped. Hotspur was on his back with a spur in his chest.

"Handle," shouted the pit master.

The setters-on leapt into the cockpit. Harry disengaged the spur from Hotspur's breast. No shake of the head from Harry: it wasn't fatal. He wiped away the flowing blood and pressed his thumb into the wound to stop the bleeding.

"Pit!"

Joslan was over-confident now and Hotspur extra-vigilant. Joslan tried two aerial attacks but failed to get above Hotspur. Now with mutual respect, they circled in tight patterns, heads low above the floor, hackles raised, eyes angry. Hotspur tried a rushing feint that worked. Joslan dodged, and Hotspur strutted up his spine and struck a gaffe home beneath Joslan's right wing.

"Handle!"

The gaffe was removed. Hotspur's wound no longer bled but Harry held his thumb over it nevertheless and made him stand quietly, facing him towards the fence so he couldn't see his opponent.

"Pit!"

The birds were released and immediately Joslan outflew Hotspur and fanned him down. On his back, Hotspur struck with his feet. Both birds fell over, joined together by all four gaffes like knitting needles in a ball of twine.

"Handle!"

It took a full minute for the setters-on to disengage the heels. Both cocks were now severely injured. They were sponged down with water. Harry sucked Hotspur's comb to warm his head, held his beak wide open and spat into his open throat to refresh him, gently massaged his legs.

"Pit!"

Stiff-winged, the two cocks advanced towards each other and clashed wearily in the centre. Too sick for aerial combat, they buckled. Joslan fell over limply, breathing hard, and stayed there. Hotspur stood quietly with his head down, bill touching the turf. The pit master waited but there was no action.

"Handle!"

The bout had to continue to its inevitable end.

"Pit!"

Hotspur crossed the turf towards his enemy on shaky legs. Joslan remained squatting at his place. Hotspur pecked savagely at Joslan's weaving head. Maddened, Joslan shot into the air and came down on Hotspur's back with blurring, hard-hitting spurs which pierced his spine. Hotspur fell, paralysed and unable to move from his head down. Joslan went in for the kill and his long silver gaffe sliced cleanly through Hotspur's kidney. Then Joslan slumped exhausted to the turf.

The crowd was suddenly almost completely silent as they watched the tableau of the fallen birds. Both were dying and the crowd knew it. If Hotspur died first, Joslan would be declared the winner because he had inflicted the last blow, even if he then also died.

Will looked over at Francis. For both of them the intoxication and the fervour were over. There was only horror as they looked at the damage inflicted on their brave and noble birds, compelled now by wounds to cower but still unyielding.

There was no cry of "Handle!" No one was allowed to touch the birds. All eyes watched the rise and fall of the birds' breasts as they breathed their last. Hotspur was the first to lie motionless. There was a sigh from the crowd. Moments later Joslan died. There was a minute's silent respect for the warriors and then bedlam broke loose again as bets were settled and money paid out.

Will still stared at Hotspur: saw the same irrational blank, glittering black eyes as when he was fierce and fighting. Then the setters-on bundled the corpses into sacks and took them away. Slowly the crowd dispersed and the pit master called Will and Francis over.

"Francis Ingilby's cock is the winner," he said. "I have the wager slips. You, Mr Nailor, must pay your debt within a week. You know how it is. If you do not, you will be banned from all cockfighting in London and the surrounding areas."

Will nodded. The two friends shook hands in front of the pit master.

"I will pay," said Will.

But there was no sense of victory on Francis's face. For both of them it was defeat.

The pit master turned away and left.

The two of them were left in the empty cockpit – silent, stinking, hot.

"We can settle this between ourselves over time," said Francis.

"No, a wager is a wager, especially between friends. I know the rules. I will write you a slip, with a copy to my banker Henry Pinckney, that the cargoes of my two ships due to arrive shortly will be paid over to you to the value of 4,000 crowns. I will do that today."

"They fought well," said Francis.

"Warriors," said Will. "But cruel none the less."

Francis nodded.

They shook hands again and went their separate ways, Will to his office and then to The Three Squirrels in Fleet Street.

11.

1620

20 JULY 1620

So it was that we left the goodly city of Leiden, left my father and his wife Sarah, and travelled to a town sundry miles off called Delfshaven. There we had a small ship fitted out, called the Speedwell. All things were ready for us. My father had provided me with ten pounds' worth of provisions for the voyage – salted beef, hardtack, beer and other victuals – and this earned me one share in the New England Plantation. He had also bought me a second share for another ten pounds. My father was generous to me in spite of our differences, and I am grateful for that.

He did not accompany me to Delfshaven. He and Sarah bade me farewell on the steps of our house. My father hugged me and this startled me: he had not done so since I was a small child. I could not help but think that if I were his son, he would have been proud of me leaving to make my own way in the world. But as I am his daughter, my leaving is something of a humiliation for him: I am not doing as he would wish.

All single people – and I am the only single woman on the ship although there are other adult daughters with their parents – will have to stay with one of our families when we arrive. I will stay with Robert and Susanna White and their son Resolved, with their two servants. *They gave me a warm welcome and I think I will enjoy their company. They are devout but not without humour. Susanna is with child and I hope I can be of good service to her.*

21 JULY

At Delfshaven we were granted a great feast by the congregation of Leiden. There were tears and singing of psalms. It seemed the sweetest melody that ever mine ears had heard, even if I believed few of the words. I thought of my dear mother. And Will, of course. I will never see him again. I will be on the far side of the ocean. So the night was spent with little sleep and many tears. I was foolish and sentimental enough to kiss Will's bent sixpence.

22 JULY

On the quayside we had a sermon from Pastor Robinson. When the time came to form a Body Politic, he said, he urged us, "to let our wisdom and godliness appear". He beseeched us always to choose "the glorious ordinance of the Lord and a virtuous mind" over the ways of the world.

It is a good company but I fear the ways of the world are strong.

We knelt on the ground and the Pastor led us in prayer. One man I took exception to: Samuel Wilton. He seemed intent that the sound of his amens and prayers be heard above everyone else's, his fat florid face and blubbery lips veritably straining with piety. I feared his veins would burst.

But the tide was turning and we needed to leave. We boarded and watched the sails hoisted and the lines loosed. We waved to those left behind and they

waved to us. It was not easy to be brave. I had to think
of the future and adventure, not the past and loss.

17 AUGUST

We are still in England. We sailed from Delfshaven
to Southampton in our Speedwell and there joined
another ship, the Mayflower, which contained more
pilgrims. But our vessel was as open and leaky as a
sieve, and if we had stayed at sea but three or four
hours more she would have sunk right down. That is the
view of some of the men. So here we are at Dartmouth
with shipwrights aboard trimming her while waiting for
a fair wind. Some see this as a bad omen and want to
leave the ship, losing all they have put in. But the others
see all this as crosses to bear, like their Lord.

Wilton is most loudmouthed in his complaining.
He has paid for several shares in the settlement, as he
boasts. It is clear he aims to be a very prominent citizen.
He is fleshy before his time. He boasts he is of the gentry
back in Shropshire (of the lowest rank, I would think) and
that he gambled away his inheritance, as if this were a
clever achievement. He is an arrogant man with all the
superficial airs but none of the graces of his class.

One of the servants with our family, Edward
Thompson, a frail man who had been with the family
many years, died of the bloody flux.

25 AUGUST

Another false start. The Speedwell again sprang a leak,
this time out in the Atlantic, and both ships limped back
to England, to Plymouth this time. It has now been
decided – by the men, of course – that we shall cram all
passengers onto the Mayflower and go to America with
the single ship. More have abandoned the enterprise.

97

Yet those who remain on board are wonderfully steadfast. And perhaps we will succeed better if we have only those who are strong in their faith or in their bodies or, like me, in resolution.

And here at Plymouth my mistress Susanna gives birth to a boy. I tried to amuse little Resolved while more experienced women assisted at the birth. They call the new baby Peregrine, which I think is a fine name. The peregrine is the fastest hunting falcon: maybe the name is a prayer that, after our slow and interrupted start, we will make God-speed across the ocean.

It is strange and sad to think this is the last time I will be on the same piece of land as Will. I must be busy.

6 SEPTEMBER

We leave Plymouth but it is now very late in the season. We are two months behind schedule and there will be storms ahead. Plymouth Sound was blustery and the wind filled our sails.

Soon there was seasickness again, and only a few of us – I was fortunate to be among them – were able to come up on deck to watch Land's End disappearing and only the open ocean all around. There is so much left behind and we are so few in number; our ship is tiny in this vast grey expanse of long rolling waves.

It was marvellous to see the cargo we are taking with us: victuals of biscuits, beer, butter, cheese, peas, oatmeal, vinegar and aqua vitae. Tools including thwart-saws, hammers, nails, mattocks, grindstones and augers, pickaxes. Kettles, frying pans, pots and platters, bread baskets and flaskets, candles. Fishing hooks and lines and nets, canvas.

All this planning strengthens me. I begin to think we are either very brave or very foolish. I do not have the faith in the Lord that the others have. It is a great comfort to them: if they perish it will be the Lord's will. If I perish it will just be by chance, and that is far less comfort but, strangely, makes me stronger. I am on my own.

And I trust in Captain Christopher Jones: he seems a wise experienced seaman and, more importantly, can keep a clear head. His master's mate, John Clarke, and his other pilot, Robert Coppin, have been to these lands before. We might be sailing into the unknown but they are not.

28 SEPTEMBER

A sad day. One of our number, an apprentice named William Button, dies and his body is consigned to the sea. Spoken prayers were whipped away by the wind, and we few on deck, drenched by icy spray, lurched and clung to each other as the ship tossed and swayed. Yet the few minutes of sea air were a relief from the dark airless stench 'tween decks where we live and can barely stand upright. Susanna is preoccupied with her baby so it falls to me to be with Resolved. I am teaching him to read. That is not easy as it is dark down here.

7 OCTOBER

Mistress Elizabeth Hopkins gives birth today to a boy and they call him Oceanus. It is a fitting name. I wondered if her husband Stephen had sought her agreement to the voyage or whether he himself had decided what they should do and she had no say. Life is hard enough on this ship without the travails of being with child. She had work enough to do with one child already of their own and two more by Stephen's previous wife. I am in awe of the strength of these women – how they stay so hopeful and caring while doing all a woman's tasks. How I wished Mary Cheever were with us. The men I see, though godly men, seem at a loss for what to do most of the time. It is the women who bear the load of their families here: feeding, keeping their children clean and warm.

There are twenty-four families, fifteen from Holland and nine from England. There are, so well as I can account, fifty men and twenty-three women, with fourteen youths and nineteen children younger than twelve. There is also a spaniel and a great slobbering mastiff, with their noise and mess. Among us, I slowly learn, are a merchant, tailors, a printer, a carpenter, a physician, a blacksmith, a tanner, a cobbler, a hat-maker, a cooper, a sawyer and a soldier (but only one). So, if we survive, we are well provided to make a settlement, if not to protect ourselves against the savages.

I have not before mentioned that half the passengers are what we called Strangers. These were men from London who the investors, the Adventurers, had added at the last moment to the ship. They too are here to make a new life – not better in terms of religion, but better in terms of money and success. Our Puritan leaders regard them with suspicion.

17 OCTOBER

Sometimes, in spite of myself, I hate these goodly people.

For weeks now, a young seaman has taunted us daily for our faith with great profanities, mocking and cursing us, even as prayers were said. He wished us dead and cast overboard. The women stopped their ears and scolded their children for laughing. The men were silent, not wanting to be hostile with the crew on whose work our lives depended.

But it was his body that today was cast into the sea. He was struck for two days with a most grievous disease and died in a most desperate manner. Nor did I grieve for him.

Elder William Brewster declared it was the just hand of God that had fallen upon the young seaman. He made a short sermon to us, down in our dark quarters.

"The Book of Nahum, chapter 1, verse 2," he intoned. "God is jealous and the Lord revengeth; the Lord revengeth and is furious; the Lord will take vengeance on his adversaries and he reserveth wrath for his enemies."

There was a great chorus of amens.

I remained silent. Are these Christians? I thought.

It was their amens, their sanctimony, their lack of compassion. Perhaps that young sailor had suffered, as I had in childhood, from some pastor or priest or even from his parents.

Do they pick and choose which word of God they wish to believe?

How can anyone be so certain they are right?

And yet it is their rightness that gives them the strength to be here and endure.

3 November

We have been at sea now for fifty-seven days.

Faith is being sorely tested.

There is some scurvy among us and it is horrible to see. I am free of it but I see legs swollen, bodies sore so they cannot stir hand or foot, gums swelling, loosening teeth and foul-smelling breath.

Others have the flux, including Mr Robert, my master – painful gripes and bloody diarrhoea. He shakes and shivers, yet has a fever. He has a great thirst and his tongue is covered with a kind of white mucilage. It is the adults who suffer more than the children. Susanna looks after him with great care and strength. Baby Peregrine and Resolved are so far free of these terrible ailments.

And then Samuel Wilton became ill with the flux. What a change. Now we saw him for a whimpering, complaining milksop. In his extremity he was calling for his mother as well as the Lord – like an infant. So unlike Robert, my mentor, who suffered his flux in silence, bravely. I and other women tended Samuel Wilton, wiped his brow, cooled him, gave him to drink, cleaned off his liquid stool. All with no thanks.

If we had left England on time, we would be in America by now and had fewer storms to endure.

9 November

It has been a momentous day.

At daybreak today, as the sun rose behind us in a clear dawn sky with a thin slice of moon overhead, we looked to the west and saw America!

At last!

Waves rolled in on high sandbanks, and further off were forested hills wooded to the brink of the sea, which had changed from deep blue to pale green. Seagulls flew over us and their squawking was strangely familiar in this unknown place.

Thanks were given, prayers offered, pilgrims – for that is how most see themselves – embraced each other. Even I instinctively lifted up my eyes unto the Lord. But of course there were no cottages or a lighthouse or any fortification or warm inn. It was bare, and no one to welcome us. No one talked of it but all, like me, must have seen the challenge of it.

Robert has thrown off the flux, and our family, though ill-fed now and often cold, is as healthy as anyone aboard.

10 NOVEMBER

All day there has been discussion and argument among the men. Some of the Strangers we had realised from shouting matches had no desire to live in a religious community, one or two even holding the pilgrims in great contempt. Some said they were at liberty to live and do as they wished with none to command them.

We heard the men's voices all day: sometimes quiet, sometimes raised, sometimes fists thumped on boards, sometimes laughter. We women could only imagine they were deciding what would happen when we landed, how we would be organised. But at last the discussion ended.

As night fell we hove to off the north of Cape Cod. The ship was stiller than it had been since we left Plymouth. Even the wind in the rigging was almost silent.

Then Pastor Brewster came down to us. He said agreement had been reached by all and a Compact written, to be known as the Mayflower Compact.

Children were shushed and he read it to us.

When he finished there was a silence.

I will never forget that brief silence in the dark, stinking 'tween decks living quarters which had been our home. I admit there were tears in my eyes. We were exhausted, many sick, many apprehensive. Yet this was a pure statement of goodwill and determination. And hope. Where the others were in their minds I do not know. I wanted Will to have been a part of this. I was for a moment back in that hut by the river at Worsley, saying goodbye before, out of sight of Will, I wept. My fingers searched for the bent sixpence and squeezed it tight. But we were in separate worlds now and would remain that way.

During the evening I persuaded Robert to let me see the Compact. I copied it because I was so moved by it.

Having undertaken, for the glory of God and advancement of the Christian faith and honour of our King and country, a voyage to plant the first colony in the northern parts of Virginia, do these present solemnly and mutually in the presence of God and one of another, covenant and combine ourselves together into a civil body politic, for our better ordering and preservation, and furtherance of the ends aforesaid; and by virtue hereof to enact, constitute and frame such just and equal laws, from time to time, as shall be thought most meet and convenient for the general good of the colony, unto which we promise all due submission and obedience.

I write this on deck with a candle in the dark. A cold mist surrounds us but the Compact is a heart-warming statement.

11 NOVEMBER

Today at daylight, with all passengers crowding the rails, we entered into Cape Cod bay and anchored in the sheltered waters.

Here, at last, arrived in a good harbour and brought safe to land, the pilgrims allowed themselves to fall upon their knees and bless the God of Heaven who had brought them over the vast and furious ocean. We had crossed a sea of troubles.

Elder Brewster led the prayers of thanks. I gave my thanks, too, in my own way. Fortune had favoured me. Our family embraced each other.

But in front of us the land we looked at was bleak and had a weather-beaten face. The woods and thickets were wild and savage. There would be unknown wild beasts and maybe wild men, savages. Behind us were thousands of miles of ocean. The nearest English communities in America were five hundred miles away. We were alone.

Now the real work would begin.

The men were called into the great cabin and each signed the compact, forty-one of them. Some were too sick to sign and some were seamen only hired for a year. I watched Wilton, now fully recovered, go in to sign. But I fear he means none of it. Naturally, none of us women were invited to sign. It would not have entered the men's minds. They then elected a leader, John Carver, whom I had seen was a godly man.

Captain Jones could sleep at last.

I watched from the rail as sixteen well-armed men loaded into the ship's small boat and rowed to shore. We saw them fall upon their knees and wander over the dunes. With darkness coming, they returned to the small boat and rowed back to the ship. They had brought cut lengths of red cedar which smelled sweet and strong – of land at last. In the evening a fire was lit. There was gentle chatter and the laughter of children.

But so many of us had still not touched dry land.

I felt lonely and wrote this.

12 NOVEMBER

It is Sunday today so no work is allowed, nor play. Elder Brewster led us in prayer morning and afternoon. This was a great test for Resolved and the other children. There is something unnatural, I feel, about how obedient they are. There was an icy breeze.

And now I must confide what I have hitherto hidden; it is the right time. I have an enemy even before I step foot on this new land. Samuel Wilton, I fear, is a dangerous man if he is thwarted. He stands there now, with his hands on the ship's rail, as if he is already parcelling up the best land for himself. A bully. I took a dislike to him the first week of our voyage. He is a single man.

He is a pious, praying Puritan, humble in his beseeching of the Lord. And there is nothing ill in that. But he has been officious, interfering in the discipline of other people's children, wagging a finger, shaking his head in disapproval, telling even the youngest The Lord see-eth all. But though he came with us as a Puritan he is more like one of the Strangers imposed upon us by our sponsors. He is here to make his money, as he is not shy of telling us.

Two weeks ago he sought the permission of my mentor Robert to seek my hand in marriage. He said he would buy out my shares so that Robert would lose nothing. When Robert approached me I was horrified, only just managing to control my anger. Robert did not try to persuade me and said it was completely my choice. Of course, I said no.

Robert reported this back to Samuel. At which he shoved Robert aside and came storming up to me. He gave me such curses and foul language I was afraid he would strike me. He sprayed me with his spit as he berated me.

"I will not forget!" he shouted. "I swear to God you will be mine."

He cared not who heard – confident he would be superior to them all in the new settlement.

Susanna comforted me.

There, I have written it.

And now in spite of him – he has just turned and given me a baleful look – I am desperate to set foot on land.

13 NOVEMBER

And today we did. We women were allowed ashore – for the great washing of clothes and children and ourselves at a small freshwater pond we found.

We found abundant mussels and untold numbers of ducks and geese. Whales played hard by us.

But we have seen no people.

12.

FORTUNE

1621

Next morning, head down, worsted cloak round him, Will walked into a blustery cold east wind blowing along Fleet Street. Everything oppressed and hemmed him in: horses barging through the crush of people, dogs cringing or barking, the yells of tradesmen, filth in the street, stench, rubbish blown in the wind.

He stopped short of The Three Squirrels and leaned against a stone wall at the corner of an alleyway. In his pocket he had the promissory notes for Francis Ingilby, signed and sealed. He knew their import and, for once, was full of foreboding. Overnight, restless in his bed and with too much wine, the defeat of Hotspur had become more than a cockfight. The gallant, flamboyant cock lying with its spine severed had swelled into an omen. Had he taken too many risks at the same time, ridden his confidence too hard?

But he must keep his word. On his word was everything built.

He scraped the muck off his boots on a doorstep. A gust of wind whipped out of the alley; there was rain in it now. He stepped into The Three Squirrels and crossed the taproom which smelled of last night's ale and food. A young woman sweeping the floor paused and looked up at him. He nodded to her and made for the back room and Henry Pinckney's office.

He knocked at the strong wooden door.

"Come in."

Will entered and closed the door behind him.

"Ah, Master Nailor, the very man in my thoughts. Take a seat. Allow me a moment."

Pinckney had a document in front of him on his desk, and a quill in his hand. His head was bent as he read, his grey beard sunk into his lace-trimmed ruff, hair to his shoulders, ears with pearls in the lobes, his long thin nose pointing down, lips compressed. A man in control, thought Will, in this quiet, orderly room, with large candles burning on the desk so it was spooled with light in the surrounding dimness. A successful man.

His quill scraped a signature, the sleeves of his fashionable maroon doublet split with yellow sliding across the paper, expensive leather gloves neatly folded at the corner of the desk.

Somewhere a door banged; rain spattered the single window.

Pinckney laid down his quill and leaned back in his chair, his face out of the candlelight, just the glitter of his eyes.

"What can I do for you, Master Nailor? I heard your champion fought gamely last night."

Will got a sudden scent of apples, startlingly fresh against the ale of the taproom and the reek of the streets. Pinckney must have combed a pomade through his grey hair.

"Yes, sadly."

He placed the promissory notes on the desk and explained.

Pinckney leaned his head forward into the light and read the documents.

"Very clear. Let's hope your ships return safely."

Let's hope so indeed!

Pinckney leaned his long body back again in his chair, his hands on the desk, golden signet rings glittering in the candlelight.

"I have bad news for you, sir. No good beating about the bush."

Will's stomach lurched.

"In the light of your success as a merchant I loaned you considerable money. You invested most of it in that fenland project of the Earl of Bedford."

"Yes?" A guarded response.

"I had news two days ago. It has not worked out as expected."

Will remembered clearly: 95,000 acres of fenland being drained, of which he would gain 8,000 – after five years the marsh and mudflat would be excellent arable farmland, ready for selling at huge profit. The great Dutch engineer, Cornelius Vermuyden, in charge.

"What went wrong?" His throat was dry. He felt a tightening in his chest. The dead Hotspur as omen.

"I do not know the workings of it," said Pinckney. He lifted his right hand to stroke his beard, the pearls glistened mockingly.

"But it seems that building sluices over tidal rivers is a very difficult enterprise. Three were built and all collapsed in a great storm. There are suspicions of sabotage, the embankments deliberately undermined."

"Who would do that?"

"The fenland people, those who live in the marshes, a wild people, foresaw their lives and livelihoods wrecked. Maybe they did it."

Will closed his eyes, swallowed, felt himself sink into his chair. So much of his fortune gone; too brash, too big a gamble.

"It was a bad place to work: ague and sickness took many workers, others fled, frightened by superstition. They dug up urns and ashes and were afraid of the spirits they let loose."

Pinckney leaned forward again into the light, shadows and brightness playing on his long bony face.

"The result," he said, "is that Vermuyden has fled. Levels half-built are sliding back into the water. You knew you took a risk, Master Nailor – and it seemed a fair one – but this time your luck is out."

Will gathered himself, kept his voice as steady as he could, did not want to plead.

"Can you extend the repayment of my loan?"

"Sadly not. You know the terms of the loan. To tell the truth, I have lost money, too, in the project. I need to retrench."

Though he didn't look as if he did.

"The debt is due in a month and must be paid."

Will stiffened his face and stared at Pinckney.

"I will see to it."

The two men rose and Pinckney opened the door for Will.

"I am sorry for this, Mr Nailor. I hope you understand."

Indeed he did: contracts were contracts. Otherwise, business was impossible.

Will gave a curt nod and left.

Bankers, whoreson bankers! They always came out on the right side.

The rain was now a thin drizzle, the wind less blustery. He paced slowly down Fleet Street and came to St Paul's churchyard. He looked at the bookshop where the other part of his life had begun. His press printed pamphlets about fairness and justice, about equality. Because he had money, he had tried to prosper more. Was his greed, his hypocrisy, being punished? Was he as bad as his father?

He came to Thames Street, smelled the salt from the sea, saw beyond the alleyways to the ships moored in the river, the forest of masts – all were ventures, all were risks. And he had loved that – the gamble of it. He could only repay Pinckney's loan on time if he sold his house and everything he possessed, and use every penny he had saved. And then what?

111

He kicked out at a cur that nosed around his boots. It slunk away, turned its head and snarled at him, yellow teeth bared.

★

Two days later news came from another vessel arriving at Puddle Dock. Its captain reported that Will's two ships had been attacked and captured by Barbary pirates, their cargoes and crew to be sold in the markets of north Africa.

As the words sank in, he slumped in his chair but his mind reeled: no ships, no cargoes, no income. His last hope ripped away. He slammed his fists on the desk, felt the walls of the room close in on him. Its riches mocked him. He leapt up, compelled to escape, to flee from his failures.

He mounted his horse and rode east out of the city across the East Marsh of Poplar, a wild and empty place of reeds, mud and oozing channels of water with occasional half-collapsed wooden huts. It was a still day and the stink of rotting vegetation was thick. The emptiness oppressed him, made him feel like a crawling thing.

Along Blackwall Causeway he passed a few carts heading to the new docks being built. This was an ancient way but now the ghosts of people past just emphasised his loneliness. Finally he came to the Artichoke Inn on Blackwell Stairs, paid an ostler to brush down and feed his horse, bought a tankard of ale and descended the Stairs to the water's edge. Out on the Thames rode the ships of the East India Company which the new docks were being built for.

The ships were busy with tenders ferrying cargo. That was the promise and the adventure of the last seven years, his rapid ascent to success. But lapping at the bottom of the stairs was the filthy water with its scum of muck, rubbish sidling and twisting in the current. And in the taverns and lodging houses the brutal men who laboured here, and the whores who serviced them. Beneath the finery, his finery, was poverty and unceasing struggle, brutalised men, abused women, starving kids.

Far from winning his way, he had lost his way.

Alice had opened his eyes, given him his moral compass, shown him mischief and laughter, led him to be positive. He had lain with women over the years, fathered a son, but there had been no feeling so tender as when he kissed Alice and they lay chaste side by side in the grass and he felt himself elide into her warmth and softness, his body passing like a spirit into hers. How he needed that escape now, that comfort, to be wrapped with her.

Here on the stone stairs among the mud and disgusting sucking of the water, its ooze and lurking, all his striving had arrived at nothing.

With Alice he knew he could start again. She would encourage him, restore his nerve, renew his confidence. He believed it utterly.

And believed, equally utterly, that this could never happen. She was gone, maybe even dead. He could not believe she would think on him as he thought on her. He was alone.

A gust of cold wind whipped off the water.

He shivered and suddenly felt his vulnerability, here alone in his rich clothes, no one knowing he was here. He could be cudgelled, robbed and his body flung into the Thames, and the world would go on undamaged and unaware.

He strode quickly up the steps, fleeing the unseen threat, collected Flint and rode back to the city.

In his office he called for a goblet of mulled spiced wine, closed the door and sat at his desk.

What would Alice do in his position? If she were with him, what would she say? He imagined her sitting opposite him, her green eyes frank, self-possessed, one hand stretched out to hold his, a half-smile as she talked, her words clear and uncompromising.

"You are a good man," she would say. "You have worked hard and fairly and deserve your success. Your love of risk is both a strength and a weakness."

And here her eyes would momentarily flirt with him, sharing a secret.

Yes, he had been reckless at the cockfight, borne along by the excitement and his desire to best his friend. Reckless, stupid even, but not malicious or bad.

His fens investment?

"Many others," she would say, "respectable and experienced businessmen and aristocracy – even the King himself – had believed it a good investment. What had gone wrong was out of your control. You are not to blame. These things happen. In this world you win some, you lose some."

His captured ships? That was always a risk, inherent in foreign trade. A storm would have had the same effect. Again, out of his control.

"You still have your position, your knowledge and skills as a trader, your networks." And now she would lean across the desk with that mischievous smile, kiss him on his furrowed forehead and on his weary eyes.

"You can do it, Will, start again."

His debts could be paid from his savings and the sale of his house. For a time, at least, be cautious, limit the gambles he took. He would succeed again.

As she turned at the door, she would add: "Just keep the press going, Will. We are helping to spread ideas."

We, she would say. A partnership as well as a marriage. It would surely have been a marriage.

She was right. It was easier to make money than change men's minds. That was now what really excited him, though he needed money to do it.

He took a long deep breath and a warming swig of wine. This was a setback, not the end. He'd made mistakes, not failed. He could succeed again, even without Alice. Learn from experience.

There was one mistake he had not made: his press. Pamphlets printed on his press were talked about at inns. He'd heard the low voices. Even in gatherings of traders, over wine when the deals were completed, he'd heard ideas exchanged, warily and with cautious glances. He was playing his part in a movement that was stirring men's minds, provoking questions, making men restless.

Enough of brooding! He needed to get out of his head, see something positive. His press was the only place. He shoved back his chair, closed the office door and walked briskly past the warehouses deeper into dockland. The chill wind now invigorated him. He turned out of the alley and onto the cart-wide cobbled street that led to his storehouse. And stopped.

A month ago he had shifted his press out of his home to a storehouse. Four men with muskets stood outside this storehouse. Will stepped into a doorway and wrapped his cloak around him. Two other men carried out piles of pamphlets and books and threw them in a heap onto the ground. There was a struggle at the doorway and two more men with pistols drawn dragged out the plump old white-haired bookseller, Arthur Babthorpe. He stood there, bare-headed, his arms pinioned. It had happened to him before, Will remembered. Then another man and a woman were brought out. Will recognised Ruth, one of the typesetters. She seemed to be shivering.

Will waited, terrified that John Boon would be next.

A small group of labourers was now gathering, eager to see some distraction. With his hat pulled low, Will moved forward to the back of the group. Now he could hear the sound of hammers smashing wood inside – his press was being destroyed, chests of papers ripped open.

The musketeers' boots shoved the pile of books into a tighter pile. Wrecked timber was brought out and added.

115

Then a burly man carried out an armful of pamphlets which he dumped into a small handcart. Evidence, thought Will. The man slammed the door behind him. The officer had a sheet of paper. He impressed his signet-ring seal into a blob of green wax on it, took the hammer from the musketeer and nailed the paper to the door.

He turned to the group of spectators.

"Seditious manuscripts and dangerous books. The King forbids them. Burn them."

Two of the musketeers took their flints and sparked them onto oily rags. The rags flared up and were flung onto the pile of books and papers.

As the flames and smoke rose, the watching group was silent. Will had thought there might be cheers. He looked across: Arthur Babthorpe and the printers had their heads bowed.

It was then that Will felt a strong grip on his arm. And his heart jumped. *My turn,* he thought. A voice in his ear.

"Come, Will, you must get away now."

It was John Boon, dragging him away.

Will resisted and looked back. Through the smoke he saw the old bookseller looking straight at him.

"You can do nothing, Will. It is the Stationers' Company. We have been betrayed."

Will heard the words only vaguely. Was the bookseller's look pleading for help or urging him to escape?

"This is folly," said John Boon and wrenched at Will's arm.

They hurried away

Half a mile away, John ushered them both into an inn. They sat in a shadowy corner and John called for ale.

"The Stationers' Company agents will be after you at this minute," said John.

But Will could not get Babthorpe's look out of his mind.

"What will happen to them?" he asked.

"Same as before: taken to Newgate, up before the Committee of Examination, a fine maybe, a short time in prison."

"What can I do?"

"Nothing. If they capture you it will be worse for everyone. You cannot return to your house or your office. Agents will soon discover, if they don't know already, that you are the owner of that store and therefore of the press."

"Does that woman Ruth have a child?"

"I don't know."

Will was sunk into himself, his world turned upside down.

"Where can you go to be safe?" asked John.

Will wrenched himself away from the faces behind the smoke, from despair.

"Where can you go to be safe?"

Suddenly the vast crowded pandemonium of London seemed to slide away and leave him exposed. Who did he really trust? Who might take a risk on his behalf?

The only answer was Francis Ingilby. His only real friend. But should he ask him, put him in a dilemma?

What would he, Will, do if the positions were reversed? If Francis wanted help but did not ask him for it, Will was certain he would be angry and offended. It would be an insult to their friendship.

"Francis Ingilby," said Will quietly.

"I will go to see him," said John. "You must walk the streets, keep on the move, stay in the crowd. In three hours we'll meet at Ludgate Circus and I'll bring you his answer."

Will nodded and John Boon left. Will did not even finish his ale. He had to keep a clear head. Outside the tavern Will found himself looking in every direction for suspicious characters – the very thing he must not do. *Act normally.* So he walked.

He walked fast to escape his guilt. He had left the bookseller and his workers to be taken to prison. They would suffer because of him. He was responsible. No matter how hard and long he walked, he could not avoid that. Would a braver man have thrust himself forward, confessed to the officer who he was and asked for their release? Was he a coward?

He stopped to peer into a baker's shop. He was suddenly hungry, wanted warm bread running with butter in his mouth.

A young woman came out of the shop. He watched her walk away. Alice! What would Alice have counselled? She was his touchstone, but this time she was silent.

How had they been betrayed? Careless talk, a distributor, an agent sent to spy on Arthur Babthorpe and then follow him? Ralph – perhaps it was that bastard Ralph, for a few gold coins, for the price of his next dicing?

By the time he approached Ludgate Circus, Will had made decisions: he must flee abroad, with or without Francis's help; he must give John or Francis the legal power to sell his house, which would pay his debts, and for lawyers to defend Arthur and the printers. He would somehow succeed abroad. Then he would return – to England and London.

Then he saw John Boon coming towards him.

★

The following morning, as a drizzly dawn slunk out of the night and the tide turned to ebb, Will skulked on the deck of the *Leopard*, keeping out of the way. Sailors shouted, the capstan creaked round as the anchor cables were hauled in, a stink rose from the brown river. In the shadows, a damp cloak wrapped round him, hat pulled low, William stood, still stunned by the last twenty-four hours.

His life had been transformed from prosperous merchant to penniless fugitive, but the dank air of the river was better than the dank air of a Newgate cell. Francis's connections had saved him. The *Leopard* was under the command of General Captain

William Rainborowe, on the instructions of Parliament and the Committee for the Captives in Algiers, bound for the port of Sallee in Morocco. Mission: to free Christians captured and enslaved there by the Barbary pirates.

He moved to the stern and gripped the rail. He was grateful Rainborowe had taken him on, no questions asked. A breeze caught the sails. Will shivered and felt the first movements of the ship getting underway. The Tower of London was left behind. He heard the hull beat into the river, felt spray on his face, watched sailors scramble up the rigging and others coil ropes.

He'd never been to sea, never fought with sword or pistol, knew no one on the ship. It wasn't just the cold that made him shiver.

13.

BLACKBERRYING

1623

It was Tuesday afternoon in the last week of August; there had been days of hot sunshine and no wind.

Alice decided to bake an apple and blackberry pie – a favourite of all the White family. Late summer always made her nostalgic – not just for England but for her childhood and, still a little, for Will. It was three years now since she and the other Pilgrims had landed in New England, ten years since Alice had left Worsley. Never in a million years could that young girl in Worsley have imagined how life would change.

Alice, with her basket, wandered through the field of cows, walked round the edge of the field of corn and stopped at the gate into the wood. She looked around at the small settlement: the nine farm cottages, smoke rising straight from their chimneys, the neat fences, cattle lying chewing the cud, the rich yellow of the corn, occasional shouts of men, a dog barking, the rhythmic blows of an axe chopping, a hoe being sharpened on a whetstone. There was a peace here, a peace born of hard effort and community. And that familiar smell, too, of manure and dried fish that still made her nose wrinkle. A cock crowed.

She was happy: a valued member of the White family, busy, part of this great pioneering project, proud of what had been achieved against the odds. Pleased with herself, too. She was her own person here, not a person shaped by custom and parents and the Church to fit in with what was expected. Life in Holland had changed her.

Being single had helped, being young, being a companion and maid-of-all-work, too. She felt a freedom that the older women, with their husbands and children, could not. She had learned so much from them, especially Susanna and especially about bringing up children: the two boys, Resolved and Peregrine, had flourished.

And marriage? She was twenty-six, a good age for marrying. The looks cast by men proved she was attractive; a few had even spoken with her, but none had made her pulse beat faster. Will still cast a shadow, ten years on and an ocean away. She had met no one with his sense of fun, his sharp eye for the ridiculous or the hypocritical; no one whom she sensed combined his gentleness and strength. They were good men, no doubt, but men of narrow vision who would be suspicious of women who chose their own path; men who believed that virtuous women should abstain from laughter, that there was little point in their learning to read and write, that they should live under obedience. And there weren't that many single men, although more arrived in the colony every year. Settlements were growing up all along the coast.

She breathed in the warm air. Time enough for that. It would be chance, not God's will, that would decide what happened next. One of the things she had learned was that nothing was predictable anymore, but that didn't scare her; it enthused her.

She saw, two fields away, Resolved feeding the hogs. She didn't wave. She wanted to wander on her own, without the chatter of the young lad. Alice turned into the woods. There was only a thin trail, barely a path, just signs of bushes pushed aside and a way made. It was used sometimes, she knew, as a shortcut to the main track that led north ultimately to Boston, and south to the trading post at Aptucxet.

There was a dazed warmth in the wood; even the birdsong seemed lazy. Maple, ash, beech and chestnut rose above her, no sign yet of leaves turning but a sense of completion. She pushed her way through the shrubs, the trail dry and hard with horses' hoof marks dried into it, to a small glade where blackberry bushes flourished in the sunlight. She stood and heard scurrying in the undergrowth, then silence.

The bushes were crammed with berries, full and glossy. She crouched and began to pick them, the clustered berries making it easier. She tasted some, so sweet. Soon her fingers were stained purple and scratched from brambles. The basket was filling up quickly, a pile of glistening berries, some half-crushed and leaking juice. She moved on to another bush and it was then she heard a sudden spate of alarm calls from blackbirds. Then a whinnying. A horse emerged from the path into the clearing. It was a creamy-gold buckskin with a black mane. Black gloves held the reins and pulled the horse to a halt. The rider, a man, was bare-headed, black hair down to his shoulders. A plum podgy face. He smiled. And with a shock she realised who it was.

"Who have we here?" said the rider, hands crossed on the pommel, his voice suave and amused.

Alice's heart was pumping. Samuel Wilton from the *Mayflower*.

He dismounted ponderously, wheezing as his feet hit the ground, threw the reins over a branch and walked towards her.

"Sweet Alice Ainsworth."

"Good morning, Mr Wilton," she managed to say, forcing her voice to remain steady.

"This is a pleasing coincidence. I was coming to visit you."

There could only be one reason for that, to continue where he had left off three years ago. Instinctively she looked around: no one else was there; she was out of earshot of the settlement. And doubtless no one was expecting him and didn't know he was there.

She clutched her basket to her belly. He stood in front of her. She could smell tobacco, leather and brandy. He was a broad, heavy man. He took off his gloves and pushed them into his pockets. Those short thick fingers, now with a gold signet ring on the right hand.

"And do you know why?" he asked. His smile was somehow threatening, eyes hard.

She could only shake her head. All that self-confidence she thought she had had suddenly disappeared. Her legs felt weak. She felt a blush in her face and was furious with herself.

"There is no reason you would visit me," she said.

"Oh, but there is."

He laid his hand on her arm.

She shook it off, holding on firmly to the basket.

"You refused me on the ship. I was angry at that. But I have reconsidered."

She took a step backwards.

"I understand your refusal. You knew nothing of me. We were going to an unknown place. You could not predict the future. How could you take such a risk?"

Alice thought it better to keep silent.

"But now it is different: the colony flourishes, there is peace, the future is good. And I am a wealthy man now. I would make you a good husband. I have a fine house and could give you fine clothes. I am a magistrate now as well as an elder. My wife would be a respected citizen."

The smile had gone; his face was stern. He had rehearsed this. And somewhere inside him he maybe meant it. His eyes glanced away from her face, down to her breasts and looked up to her again.

"Do not spill your berries," he said, "you have worked hard for them."

He tried to take the basket from her. She clung on. But his fingers were strong and unwrapped her fingers from the handle.

"That's better," he said, taking the basket from her and laying it carefully on the ground.

She wanted to run but knew that in her wide skirt it would be impossible to escape him. She held her arms in front of her, fists clenched pathetically.

"Do not touch me, sir." Her voice was strong.

"Touch you? I only want to hold you. I want you as my wife, Alice."

He took her hands and separated them and lunged in to kiss her. She wrenched her face away and he kissed only the edge of her bonnet.

"Get off me, sir. This is no way to win a wife."

But he was angry now, humiliated, urgent.

"I will have you, woman."

She cried out but he grasped her head roughly in both hands and turned it so he could kiss her, his tongue forcing her mouth open. She wanted to gag, her fists thumping at his head, pulling his hair. Fear lent her strength.

"God's blood, you are a minx."

With one hand he forced her head back; his other hand grabbed her breast and squeezed. Alice cried out in pain. Then he was forcing her down to the ground. She fought but he was too strong and bulky and she fell. Immediately he was on her, his foul breath enveloping her, his weight crushing her, his hand beneath her skirts, forcing her legs apart. She squirmed and yelled but he forced one hand over her mouth. She writhed but could not escape, felt his hand on her thighs, tried to bite him.

Her eyes were screwed shut when she heard the voice, felt the body on her suddenly grow still.

"You can feel my sword point, sir, on your neck. Doubt not that I will pierce you with it unless you get up."

Samuel Wilton levered his body off her and sat up. Alice opened her eyes and saw a young man standing behind him, his sword now at Wilton's throat. She began to retch, turned sideways and vomited. The young man stretched out his left hand towards her. She grasped it and he helped her up. He gave her a kerchief to wipe her face. She was trembling and sobbing. Could not get the taste of Wilton out of her mouth.

"I may have misunderstood," said the young man. "Do not take me as a prude. But tell me, was this man, as it appeared to me, forcing himself upon you against your wishes?"

"I was not, sir," growled Wilton. "She wanted me." He stood up and brushed down his waistcoat.

The man looked at Alice.

"He was going to… rape me," she said, her voice cracking.

"Do you know who he is?" asked the man.

"Samuel Wilton. We came over on the *Mayflower* and he is now an elder and magistrate in Boston."

"Is he now?"

"On the ship I refused his offer of marriage. He was coming here to ask me again when we met by accident here."

"And would you have refused him again?"

"I would, sir, I told him. And then he set about me."

Her courage was coming back.

"So now we must decide what to do," said the man.

"The woman lies," said Wilton. "She wished to seduce me and trap me into marrying her because I am a prosperous man."

The young man laughed. "I think not. Stand against that tree."

He pointed to a chestnut tree.

"I will do no such thing."

"Or I will send your horse away and leave you here, trussed and gagged, hidden in the bushes. Maybe a man will find you or maybe a forest beast. It will be God's will for you, an elder of the Church." A smile, and a slight tremor in his voice, she thought.

Wilton scowled and moved to the tree.

The young man took Alice aside and whispered to her: "If you were to lay a charge and take him to court for assault and attempted rape, it would be your word as a woman versus his word as elder and magistrate. I fear the outcome for you." He spoke fast, almost nervously.

Alice nodded tearfully, smoothing her dress and tidying her hair.

"Best, I think, to let him return to Boston. But with him knowing that we know. I have friends in Boston and am well thought of there. He will want to pretend this never happened. What do you say?"

His words were clear but his lips quivered for a moment.

"It is a sad thing, but you are right. We are supposed to be a godly community although I am sceptical. But some things don't seem to change. Let us do as you say."

The young man nodded, gritted his teeth and approached Wilton, who seemed to have regained his self-confidence. He knew his power and the way of things.

"Mr Wilton, you are free to return to Boston. But remember, I know what really happened here…"

"Nothing happened here."

"… and your Church might be interested to know about it."

Wilton harrumphed.

"Now, mount your horse and be gone."

The young man whacked him across his back with the flat of his sword. But Wilton refused to scamper. He sauntered defiantly across the clearing, mounted his horse, gave Alice a long hateful look and disappeared along the path.

Alice saw the young man's shoulders rise as he took a deep breath. Then they drooped and his head slumped. Clumsily, he sheathed his sword. She saw his hands trembling.

When he turned round, his face shone with sweat.

He did not look at her, fidgeted, pulled at his cuffs. He swallowed.

"And now for my horse," he said. "When I heard you scream, I left him in the trees and rushed here."

"And I am so grateful," said Alice. "He would have raped me."

"Your berries," he said, picking up her basket and giving it to her. An awkward smile. "If you wish, I will walk with you back to your village."

Alice saw he was more agitated than she was.

"I would like that."

A hesitancy. "Perhaps you should know my name: James Parker, farmer and merchant from Duxbury."

"And I am Alice Ainsworth, maid and companion to Farmer White and his family here in Plymouth."

James retrieved his horse. They walked slowly along the trail through the woods. She could sense him begin to relax. What an effort that confrontation had been for him – yet he was broad-shouldered and strong, had seemed so self-assured.

"How long have you been here in America?" asked James.

"Three years. I came on the *Mayflower*."

"One of the brave pioneers."

"Pioneer but not so brave."

"I think, if I am not mistaken, we speak with the same accent," said James.

"I think that too. Where did you come from in England?"

"A little place called Walkden, in Lancashire. I arrived last year."

"Walkden? I don't believe it. I come from Worsley."

"That is only a few miles away," said James.

But he seemed as worried as surprised. He turned away from Alice and stroked his horse's neck.

"The world is a small place," said Alice.

They walked in silence then, and soon the village appeared through the trees, smoke from the chimneys, cocks crowing, the sound of the axe still chopping. Life had just gone on.

"You are safe now," said James. "I will leave you. I am on my way to Aptucxet." He mounted his horse. "I am glad I could help you."

And with that he waved to her and moved off at a slow trot.

Alice watched him leave. As his horse came to a bend in the track, he turned and waved. Quickly she waved back. And then he was gone. A morning that had started innocently had become terrifying, almost shameful, and had ended in relief.

James had been so decisive but not cruel, had been sensible and kind but also shrewd. Yet there had been a tentativeness about him. His voice was rich, his smile open and honest, his eyes soft. He had a strong weather-beaten face; he was a handsome man.

And from near home. Did that mean anything in the great scheme of things? Of course not. That was fanciful. Just happenchance.

Five days later, as Alice was kneading bread, there was a knock at the door. It was James, standing in the drizzle, holding the reins of his horse, a shy smile on his face, rain glistening on his hair.

"Passing through, on my way home," he said. "Thought I'd stop by to see how you were."

"Come in," said Alice, not caring that tongues might wag.

And so began the first of several conversations they had together as he made his journeys over the next two months – conversations in the house, sometimes with the Whites, walking in the fields, by the small lake. He was primarily a farmer, with cattle, sheep and tobacco, but he had also set up a small store and – a scandal among the good burgers of Duxbury – had appointed a Pequot Indian and his wife to help run it and to trade with Indians beyond the settlements. When James talked of the efficacy of Indian healing herbs and potions, Alice could add her own experience for she had formed a friendship with an old Indian lady who had helped her plant the Whites' medicinal herb garden. It was something they had, again by chance, in common. James told her of his botanical studies. He was gathering together the Indians' knowledge of healing herbs, writing down the varying conditions in which the herbs thrived.

"Perhaps you might help me with that?" he asked.

"Gladly, sir, I would learn a lot, too."

At his house, he told her, his Indian workers and servants sat at the same meal table with him and ate the same food. Alice had observed the same in Holland and how the English Puritans had not taken up the custom. He was interested in what else she had seen in Holland, in why she was so sceptical of the Church. She did not tell him of her encounters with Will's father but spoke in general of hypocrisy and innocents suffering.

They grew closer and Alice was disappointed James did not ask to stay the night on one of his journeys. That would have been no problem – many men and women on journeys would stay overnight, often innocently sharing a bed in the small houses.

14.

TARRYING

1623

He arrived in the middle of the morning on an unusually warm late October Sunday. Alice was siding away dishes in the kitchen, contentedly wondering when she would next see James. Then came his distinctive knock on the door, almost like a code now. Her heart leapt; she had not been expecting him. Smiling involuntarily, she quickly wiped her hands on her apron, flicked wisps of hair behind her ears and hurried to the door.

He stood there, his strong brown hand, with sunlight fairing the dark hairs, leaning on the door frame. The brim of his hat shadowed his face but he was smiling.

"I have bread and cheese and cider in my saddlebag," he said, nodding in the direction of his horse which stood still, neck lowered. "I hoped we might go to the lake for an hour or two."

She smiled up at him. "I can think of not a single objection to that. I'll bring some cherries. I picked them only yesterday."

He loved her uncomplicated good spirits, the bright sparkle in her eyes.

"I must leave a note," she said. "They are all at church – being instructed, no doubt, with more lessons on how to live the godly life."

She laughed lightly and accidentally brushed his hand as she turned back inside.

"That's why I chose Sunday," he said, wanting to touch her shoulder or her hand, to share in her easy cheeriness.

They chose a spot at the far end of the lake where a fallen tree trunk lay on a pebbly beach. Leaves in their russet autumn colours rustled in the slightest of breezes; sunshine flickered and wavered over them; shadows dappled the shore.

Alice sat on the log and James sprawled on the ground beside her, his back leaning against the log. His black hair brushed her skirt; he could have lain his head on her thigh. He sensed the heat of her and closed his eyes. She looked down at him, wanting to ruffle his hair.

Alice watched James lobbing pebbles into the water. They watched the ripples spread and the water reform its smoothness. A pair of ducks paddled across the little bay, dived, surfaced, paddled, dived again. They heard a child's distant laugh.

She heard James take a deep breath. He was staring out at the ducks.

"Do you find me an agreeable companion?" he asked.

She was sure there was that tremor in his voice that she had heard before.

"What a strange question," she replied. "Do you not think I do?"

When she looked down at him, she could see only the side of his sunburned face, his hair glossy in the sun and stirred by the breeze. His jaw was set.

"But do you?" he asked again, this time more tensely.

"You know the answer, James. Haven't we walked and talked, held hands and kissed over these past weeks? I would not have done that if I did not find you – as you put it – an agreeable companion."

He was silent, appearing still to study the ducks. He threw another pebble. The ripples spread. The water settled.

Something needed to be added, she thought, but she could not decide what. James had never been so ill at ease, she never so lost for words.

Without moving his position, his left hand resting on his raised knee, he said:

"Enough for you to consider marrying me?"

His voice was eerily expressionless. She sat, stunned.

Then at last he moved, turned, knelt on the pebbles, looked up at her, took her hands in his and said again: "Am I agreeable enough to you for you to consider being my wife?"

In that strong open face she had never seen such shyness, such uncertainty.

She felt his hand tighten round hers, watched his face relax. He smiled and she saw the bold candour return to his eyes.

"How crazed I am to spring this upon you," he said.

Alice felt tears in her eyes.

"Crazed? You foolish man! Stand up off your knees."

She helped him up and they stood together. With both hands she gently cradled his head and kissed him on the mouth, a long and tender kiss. She felt him press his body to hers, felt his heart beating strongly, even through her skirt felt his arousal.

She stood back, hands on his shoulders. "You are my man," she said, and kissed him lightly on the nose. "And I will gladly be your wife."

With a startling flapping of wings and beating of webbed feet on the water, the pair of ducks flew off. Arm in arm they returned from the lake to the Whites' cottage in Plymouth Settlement.

James's self-confidence had also returned and he immediately approached Robert, sitting on a stone wall with his pipe and in his best Sunday suit, to announce his wish to marry Alice. For a daughter to marry it was necessary in the colony to have her parents' consent. Though this did not apply in Alice's case they had both agreed it would be more politic and kinder if they had the agreement of Robert and Susanna.

Often had they conversed with James on his visits, found him respectful and good-humoured. They knew from friends and neighbours that he was successfully making his way in Duxbury.

"Alice, do you want James as your husband?" asked Robert.

"I do," replied Alice.

They gave their immediate and complete approval.

"Well, now, of course you must bundle," said Susanna with a knowing smile.

On their way back from the lake, Alice and James had discussed whether the Whites would approve of a custom that was common in the colony but not universal. They had paused in the wood, embraced and kissed – in anticipation – the idea itself excited them. It was as if James's proposal and her acceptance had released a pent-up flood of physical need and desire. Both were loving and passionate but Alice was also nervous. James no doubt had had several women – she would never ask him – but she, Alice, was a virgin. How restrained and honourable Will had been, she realised now, though they had been much younger.

"We call it tarrying where I come from," James had said.

"Well, that was Walkden; it certainly did not happen in Worsley."

Alice laughed. Worsley thought it was more sophisticated.

A shadow suddenly in her mind: her memory, that secret. Should she tell James about him? Would it sully his happiness, spoil their bundling? But it had happened twenty years ago; she had been a child, compelled against her wishes to do something wrong. She was neither guilty nor sinful. James would understand that. But something told her not to tell him.

And now Susanna looked up at Robert and quickly kissed him on the cheek.

"We bundled ourselves, back in old England," she said.

Robert nodded shyly.

"I remember it well," he said.

The short October evening seemed to linger forever in the warm family kitchen as Alice and James sat on the pine slat-backed chairs, each with a mug of cider, contemplating the low flames in the fire, each with their own imaginings. Resolved was learning to read with his mother. Peregrine was asleep in his cradle. Robert smoked his pipe and drank his ale.

But gradually the light did dim as the sun sank lower. Providence was sent to bed. Though candles flickered, the corners of the room darkened.

"Time for us to go to bed," said Susanna. "We must be up betimes tomorrow."

Robert was nodding in the chair, chin on chest.

"Robert!"

"Oh!" He started up.

Susan nodded towards Alice and James.

"Oh, aye!" muttered Robert and stood up.

"I have left you blankets on the bed," said Susanna. "That is the traditional way. But it is a warm night and maybe you will choose to lie on top of the covers."

Robert and Susanna said goodnight and went upstairs. Alice and James heard them move about, and then the latch fasten the bedroom door. They waited for five minutes, Alice suddenly prim as James put his arm around her. Then he followed her up the narrow stairway, built around the central chimney, up to the first floor. Their bare feet padded up the rungs of the ladder that led to Alice's bedroom in the attic, the last daylight pale in the dormer window.

There was a braided rug on the floor and the corded bed was simple, the bedposts unadorned. On the bed, neatly folded, were two blankets.

"At least there's no board down the middle, which is sometimes the custom," said James. He stood in his shirt and waistcoat and breeches, his boots and jerkin left in the kitchen.

Now, again, Alice saw this strong decisive man was hesitant – like earlier at the lake. His own man but unsure. She loved him the more for it.

"It is too warm for blankets, the heat always collects up here in this attic," she decided, breaking the awkward hiatus. "We will lie on the coverlet. Come, to bed."

She took his hand and they lay together on the bed.

"I have lost my wits," he said.

"Wits are not needed for bundling, I believe. Kiss me."

He laughed, turned his head and looked into her eyes, which seemed to be sparkling with new mischief.

"You do not know what you unleash," he said, and kissed her on her mouth, her ears, her neck. "Must you lie all night in this unwelcoming voluminous skirt?"

She sat up, her elbows on the pillow.

"Is it safe, if you are to be… unleashed?"

"This night, remember," he said, "is to advance our knowledge of each other, is it not? That is what they say. That is its purpose."

"Then look away," she said.

She felt strong and confident, though no man had seen her in anything but full dress. She unlaced and unbuttoned her dress, let it fall to her feet and stepped out of it. She let down her hair – and then saw the bent sixpence at her neck. She almost staggered at the shock of it; she had completely forgotten about it.

A quick glance at James: he was dutifully turned away. A decision. She took it off and pushed it down under the clothes in the top drawer of her dresser.

So rapid this was, so simple – this putting away of the past. No more than a moment of sadness, then a look in her mirror: the odd experience of seeing her face as James would see it.

She returned to the bed and James turned back towards her. He kissed her, and his hands roamed over her – delicate, tender, urgent – and sensations spread through her she could not have imagined. She loved his hand cupping the fullness of her breasts. She undid the buttons of his shirt and stroked his warm, hairy chest. He groaned and shifted and, as he moved, her hand brushed his hardness. And she was back instantly in her childhood bedroom, the darkness, Will's father forcing her hand on him; the revulsion and terror she felt, the sharp smell of brandy, tobacco and sweat.

James sensed her grow tense.

"Are you not happy with this?" he asked.

And then she slammed close the shutters on that part of her past. She was glad she had not told him of it. She never would.

"I am happy," she said. "It is just… unfamiliar."

"But you usually like the unfamiliar, something new and different."

"Indeed I do."

She closed her hand around his stiffness, felt his heat even through his breeches, and the past was an irrelevance.

But James, too, had a secret – a secret he was afraid to share with her, yet knew he must sometime. But not tonight. Tonight was for other explorations and pleasures. So they touched and chattered, laughed quietly, giggled as they listened to the snores of Robert and Susanna below.

And then one particular touch of his made her gasp, so exquisite a sensation. From her rapidly crumbling reason she managed to whisper, her mouth at his ear, "We must not betray their trust."

"We won't, trust me."

She was ready to believe him; she relaxed and gave herself up to him.

His fingers were on her lips.

"Wet my fingers in your mouth," he said.

And she did.

"So that we do this together," he said.

And his fingers stroked her, soft and rhythmic, then harder. She felt her thighs shudder; her back arched, and she was flooded with pleasure. She cried out and James put his hand over her mouth.

"Sh, sh."

Slowly she came back to herself.

"I think," she said, "we are truly extending our knowledge of each other. And I of myself."

They laughed and cuddled.

"Have you never done that to yourself?" he dared to ask.

"What?!" She was genuinely shocked. "Do women do that?"

"How do I know what women do? But it is rumoured, when the ale flows."

"If I had, I would not have been so astonished. You have a clean slate to write on, James."

He laughed.

"And your opening verse certainly got my attention."

"And now I need your attention," he said softly.

"I am at your service," she said, newly emboldened and uninhibited in her new realm.

"If I stay like this," he said, and put her hand on his hardness, "I will ache all night and not be able to sleep."

"But we cannot…"

"I know. I would dearly love to but it would not be right."

"So?"

"So?"

He unbuttoned his breeches and placed her fingers round him. She felt his naked hot stiffness.

"Move your hand up and down," he said. The momentary image of her dark childhood bedroom, her small hand gripped and forced to rub him, the rough cloth and then the slimy dampness as the minister groaned. Her hand now didn't move, held him but still. She set aside the image and breathed deeply.

137

"I will wet your fingers," he said.

He took her hand into his mouth and sucked her fingers. She began to move her moistened hand, delighting in pleasuring him.

Then he shuddered and groaned and her fingers were sticky. How bizarre and wondrous is evolution, she found herself thinking.

"Like milking a cow, but upside down," she said, and giggled.

"It's not supposed to be funny," he said, his voice drowsy.

"But it is an odd way of going about things. Never in a million years would I have imagined doing that. Those women I see going to church in their bonnets and with their prayer books, do they do it? I can't believe it."

"It is a way of avoiding being with child," he said, the words still only slowly surfacing.

"I enjoyed it, feeling you, hearing you. But now look at it!"

James hastily closed his breeches. Then he sat up, back against the painted wooden wall. He held her hand and looked at her slender body in her shift.

"Bundling, as you said, Alice, is a way of finding out about each other before we finally decide to marry, yes?"

"Yes."

"And now, after this, do you still want to be my companion?"

"Why do you need to ask?"

"I need to hear you say it."

"Well, then – I want to be your wife."

He looked at her; the faintest of moonlight lit up his frown, his eyes shadowed beneath his bushy eyebrows.

"Then there is something I must tell you," he said. "I see now I should have told you before we reached this point, but I was afraid."

Now she was afraid. Would there be a price for not revealing her own secret? Would his confession ruin everything? Like a knife into her heart the thought came: he is already married, a wife left in Walkden. But, whatever it was, she had to know.

"Tell me," she said.

"I did not come to America for religious reasons," he said.

"Neither did I."

She had to ask him.

"And are you already married, to a woman back in England, whom you have fled?"

He looked at her, taken aback. "I would not be here on this bed with you if that were so. How can you ever imagine that?"

And she found herself apologising.

He held out his hand. "Stop. This is madness. It is I who has the apology to make." He took a deep, deep breath and rubbed his hand across his forehead. "Back in England I killed a man."

He was about to say more but stopped.

She stared at him, swallowed, thought before she could stop herself: is that better than a previous marriage?

"That," he continued, "is why I am here in the colony. I fled to escape trial and hanging."

"So you killed a man." He nodded. "But you must tell me the circumstances."

"He was an elder of the Church and I drowned him in the river, our local river, the Worsley Brook."

James looked to see if there was a reaction but Alice's face showed nothing.

"I drowned him, Alice, holding his head under the water while he struggled, until he went limp. I held him under until I was certain he was dead. And then I let go of him, let the river take him. I watched his body twist among the rocks, get snagged on a tree branch. And then I ran."

James's body shuddered.

He did not tell her of the brandy he had had to drink to build up his courage, nor of sitting afterwards on the riverbank, trembling and sobbing like a girl, in terror at what he had done.

"But you haven't told me the important bit. Why?"

"Because he was a filthy old man. Because he abused my little sister, made her do things to him. I hated him. He did not deserve to live."

And her memory shot back again.

"You may know him," continued James. "He was a pastor in your village – Mr Nailor."

Kneeling on the bed next to James, Alice swayed and almost fell. James grabbed her.

"I am sorry. Are you so shocked?"

Now, if ever, was the time to tell him. But she could not. It was her secret. She might have to tell more than she wanted.

"I'm alright. I think it is just everything. So much has happened in these past few hours."

"Now you know, can you still accept me?"

"Of course. How can anyone condemn you for what you did, even though it is against the law and the commandments?"

"One more thing, since we are stepped in so far. I promise you it is the last."

"More?"

"My name, James Parker, is not the name I was christened with. That was James Fenton. And I chose America and New England because distant relatives – the Rainborowes, well connected – already had family members here. But once I was here I realised, with my crime and my new name, I could not make myself known to them."

"And that is the end of your confession? Nothing more?"

"There is one more thing."

Then silence.

"What is it? So terrible you cannot tell me?" She was nervous again now.

He cleared his throat. "I was betrothed back in England, to a woman called Ellen."

She sat up, leaned on one elbow and looked at his face. But she was remembering Will and his ribbons by the river.

"And do you still love her?"

"It was a different life, I am a different man. Three years ago."

"That's not long." Will's sad face, pleading.

"It's you I love now," he said.

She lay back. It had been almost the same for both of them, but she still didn't want to tell him of Will. Men could be strange about such things, jealous, insecure. Let sleeping dogs lie.

They lay on the bed, side by side but not touching. They were exhausted and emptied, not estranged but at a kind of peace. His fingers stretched out towards her hand and she held them.

And Alice had learned she was not the only victim of the pastor, that she had not somehow brought it on herself, as she had often agonised. At least that vile man could not harm more children. She was glad he was dead. How had Will reacted to his father's death? He would not have grieved overmuch. All that was over.

She tightened her fingers on James's, but he was asleep.

In the morning James left early to return to Duxbury. He rode away in happy certainty about the future.

Alice, in a happy daze, helped feed Peregrine at the table. Susanna looked round from washing pots.

"The bundling went well, I see."

"It did. Thank you."

"Well," said Susanna, "you can be as well-behaved there as anywhere or as mischievous."

There were knowing smiles between them, a complicity.

Alice wanted to tell her how she felt James loved her for who she was: sometimes wilful with ideas of her own, liking to challenge, unwilling to be subservient. When it came down to it, she wanted to be someone to be reckoned with – like a man. And James encouraged this.

Like Will had done.

Later that morning Alice went up to her bedroom and retrieved Will's bent sixpence from the drawer where she had hastily hidden it. She slipped the cord over her neck and pushed the sixpence out of sight beneath the collar of her dress.

She walked back to the lake. It was warm and sunny again, though clouds were building far to the west. She sat on the same log as yesterday and unslipped the sixpence. She held it in her fist tightly so that it nipped her flesh. James's touch was still on her, his words still clear in her mind. And Will? Was he finally in the past, as she had resolved last night?

She opened her fist and looked at the battered coin in her palm. She had come here to throw it into the lake, to finally close the past so she could unequivocally set herself to the future. She stood at the water's edge and coiled the cord around the sixpence; imagined it looping through the air, flashing in the sunlight, landing in the water, sinking, tiny ripples forming and disappearing until the blank water was still again.

Lost forever, settling in the mud, rusting, corroding. It was as if she were signing Will's death warrant.

She could not bring herself to throw it, could not relinquish it and abandon him. He was an authentic part of her, not to be denied. She would hide the sixpence well in the home she had not yet seen. James would never find it. Yes, it was a deceit, but what James never knew could never hurt him. Will, however distant he might be, would always be a part of her. Why erase part of herself? It had been a good, awakening time for her, a time she wanted to save and preserve – in a corner of her mind, like a bygone carefully wrapped in an attic.

She wondered if Will ever thought the same. She hoped so but doubted it. But that should make no difference to her.

So she uncoiled the cord and placed it back round her neck. She felt truer to herself; it meant no disloyalty to James.

In four months' time Alice and James were married and living in Duxbury. Their cellar was filled with cranberries in firkins of water; there were baskets of apples and pumpkin and squash. There were sacks of wheat flour and cornmeal, barrels of cider, heads of dry corn mixed with peas, pots of salted pork and salted cod, boxes of candles.

Three healthy boys were born to them over the next six years; the farm and store prospered. Then in 1633 they heard that a group of Plymouth Pilgrims, led by Roger Ludlum, had founded a new settlement at a place called Windsor, further south in Connecticut. James and Alice agreed it was an opportunity for the family to expand their horizons and consolidate their prosperity, and an adventure. So they moved, bought land and the Windsor Trading House. The farm and the store would be perfect for three strong healthy boys to develop.

But within a year Samuel Wilton also arrived in Windsor, among rumours of troubles he had created in Hartford. Alice had thought she was rid of him.

"Purely business," he'd explained when he stopped her outside her store. But his leer said otherwise.

PART THREE

15.

ONE EVENING

1635

Fifteen years later, as a pale sun set and darkness drifted in with the flood tide, Will stood amidships on the deck of the *Phoenix* and watched the Tower of London approach. The catheads were in position, sailors ready to loose the anchor, its cable in, carefully laid out on the deck in great loops. The tide rippled comfortingly along the hull.

Will was warm in his fur-collared coat. But he loved the familiar fresh chill of the air on his face, the Thames smell – had longed for it in the heat and marshes of Aleppo, and in the caravanserai of the deserts.

The fugitive was returning as a rich man – a seaman who had weathered great storms, a soldier who had killed men, a man who had overcome failure and error. He was pleased with himself but knew fortune had smiled on him and this gave him a proper humility. And awareness of this humility made him even more pleased with himself.

The *Phoenix* was now passing moored ships, the river busy with small torch-lit boats ferrying cargo, the splash of oars, the shouts of men in his own language at last. He glanced up at St Paul's. In his mind's eye he mapped the streets he would tread again tomorrow. Tonight he would sleep on board in his cabin, his ship firmly anchored to the Thames mud. He would roll with the tide and the flow of the river, feel the ship swing on its anchor. And sleep the sleep of being home. Tomorrow he would seek out Francis Ingilby and John Boon and tell them his story. He had given no notice of his arrival. He didn't even know if they were still alive.

That same evening, seventy miles north of London, Oliver Cromwell, Member of Parliament, was writing a letter to his cousin. In the six years since King Charles had angrily dissolved Parliament in 1629 – what a day that had been: denunciations of Archbishop Laud, rank refusal to pay Charles' tonnage and poundage taxes, the imprisonment of six MPs – Cromwell had been treated for melancholy in London, lost a battle in local politics and been compelled to move out of Huntingdon down the social ladder to a farmstead in St Ives. Here he now lived as a mere tenant farmer, renting grazing land.

But, for the first time in a long time, he was happy. This evening the shouts and thundering footsteps of his six children as they played around the house did not irritate him; the bleating of his sheep in the fields beyond his bedroom window and the squawking of his hens in the yard were sounds of peaceful domesticity. Elizabeth, his wife, he knew was in the kitchen packing eggs for the market tomorrow.

Dear cousin, he wrote at his small scrubbed table, and his eyes shone with a new zeal. *You know what my manner of life hath been. Oh, I lived in and loved darkness and hated light. I was the chief of sinners. I hated godliness, yet God had mercy on me. Oh, the riches of his mercy.*
And here his eyes brimmed with tears so that he had to wipe them away. Tears of guilt and relief. He dipped his quill in the ink.

Now I trust the Lord will bring me to His tabernacle, to His resting place. Truly no poor creature hath more cause to put himself forth in the cause of his God than I.
Miraculously released from his melancholia and inspired by the sermons of Dr Samuel Wells, he had a new direction and a restored faith.

The Lord be with you, he ended, *Your truly loving cousin,*

Oliver Cromwell.

He got up from the desk and caught a glimpse of himself in the looking glass. He paused: he was not the most beauteous of the Lord's creatures with his caricature of a nose and his warts. But what was important was understanding the Lord and praying for his help. His burly figure turned to the window. He looked at the vast grey sky and the flat fields, the dull light, and the ash tree shaking in the breeze.

He gritted his teeth and punched his right fist into his left palm.

"Praise the Lord!" he muttered to himself. "There is work for me to do."

Seventy miles south, King Charles sat on a gilded, red satin chair at the end of the Banqueting Hall in his Whitehall Palace. Courtiers simpered around him. Charles closed his eyes to shut out the scene and listened solely to the music. He loved it: the soaring notes of viol, lute, guitar and harpsichord took him out of his thoughts. But only for a moment.

He opened his eyes and gazed at this extravagant spectacle: the costumes, the scenery. Inigo Jones knew his value and charged for it. But his wife loved it. There she sat in a bower, Henrietta gorgeously attired, attended by six countesses, the foliage around them heightened with gold and interwoven with flowers. Behind them a painted scene of a green hillside with fountains gliding down the slopes.

His dear heart wife was Chloris, Goddess of Flowers; and Ben Jonson – always a man to the main chance – had concocted various rites in which other characters brought her gifts and praise. She loved flattery. She loved to act in these masques, though many considered it a scandal for women to be on stage.

149

She was indeed the embodiment of love and beauty, smiling as Zephyrus and Cupid bowed to her and danced.

Smoke now rose from the floor and his dwarf entered, prancing from the gates of hell, cloven-hooved, grinning fiendishly and waving a devil's tine. And immediately Charles' mind was filled with the image of John Hampden's face: the man who led the refusal to pay Ship Money. Those damned Parliamentary Puritans who had denied his right to raise taxes without their consent and for which defiance he had dissolved Parliament. He needed money – for war and for his wife's extravagance. He was king by divine right, he would not stomach their impudence.

Tomorrow he would order the ruthless collection of Ship Money, or imprisonment. He would use his authority.

And now the music stopped and the Goddess of Flowers stood and curtsied to the audience. There was obsequious applause.

Charles thrust away his thoughts. After every performance, Henrietta came eagerly to his bed. And he could lose himself in her, released from his responsibilities and worries.

Eight minutes' walk away, John Lilburne, twenty years old and almost out of his apprenticeship to draper Thomas Hewson, arrived at Gatehouse Prison just outside Westminster Abbey. He had come to see Dr John Bastwick, imprisoned for printing publications in Latin which attacked bishops. Lilburne was astonished when the gaoler showed him to Bastwick's place of confinement. He had been expecting dark, dank stone passageways, the clink of chains and clank of doors, groans and cries for help.

Bastwick had two rooms where he lived with his two children and his wife who cooked them meals. Of course, it would have cost him, Lilburne knew.

"John Lilburne, sir."

"Good to meet you. Comfortable, eh?" said Bastwick, shaking Lilburne's hand. "And they allow me visitors like you and give me writing equipment." He pointed to a small desk with a manuscript on it, quills, an inkpot and books. "Some beer, wife, please."

"Is there beer here?"

"This gaoler appreciates gifts." Bastwick laughed. "But you need money."

Bastwick's wife arrived with a jug of beer and two mugs, left the room and closed the door behind her. Lilburne could hear the chatter of the children. Bastwick poured the beer.

"Now, why have you come? I do not know you."

Lilburne took a drink of ale and nodded towards the desk.

"I hear you are writing a book."

"I am indeed. At the behest of John Warton. Do you know him?"

"No."

"He is a hero, eighty-two years old, a bookseller of so-called illegal books, hauled in front of the Star Chamber, fined, stock destroyed. And yet still he fights. He loathes bishops and has asked me to write a book on that subject. But in English, not Latin, so the people can read it."

"That is what I had heard. And have you begun it?"

"Nearly finished it."

He moved to the desk and picked up the top sheet of the manuscript.

"It will be called *Letany.* Perhaps this sentence sums it up: *From plague, pestilence and famine, from bishops, priests and deacons, good Lord deliver us.*"

He replaced the sheet with a flourish. "Do you approve?"

"Of course," said Lilburne. "That is why I am here."

"And?"

"I believe in what you are writing. I am going to seek work in Holland and know men who wish to print books like this.

151

And I want to organise smuggling them in to this benighted country."

Bastwick looked down at Lilburne, still seated.

"You are a godly youth."

Lilburne looked up, and Bastwick saw the zeal in him.

"I will think on it," said Bastwick, "and talk with John Warton. Come back in two days."

They shook hands.

His head whirling with excitement and high hopes, Lilburne strode purposefully back to his lodgings. He was entering the game, part of the protest against the creeping return of popery, against the King.

Barely two miles away, Francis Ingilby stepped out of the Ship Inn in Twyford Place. He did not look cautiously round like others did as they left. That just looked suspicious if agents' eyes were watching. Only occasionally, usually when he woke feeling aroused, did Francis go to the illegal Mass that was held there. It was dangerous, life-threatening, to attend – and this somehow swelled and refined his lust. While the itinerant Jesuit intoned his holy chants and held up the chalice of wine to be blessed, the small congregation all had tankards of ale on their tables – just in case there was a raid, so they could pretend innocence. Somehow for Francis, the smell of stale beer and the smoke of many tobacco pipes was more uplifting than a swinging censer of incense.

Nobody there ever talked. They were strangers to each other, come only to accept the sacraments. Ignorance of each other was safety.

Which didn't apply to his next port of call, where there was equal danger but less virtue. And a different kind of benediction to be sought and given.

He smiled to himself. He loved this walk, about three-quarters of an hour to anticipate and savour the pleasures to come, sins confessed, Hail Marys said, soul purified before the delights of defilement. A walk between two very different sorts of heaven and each a matter of faith for him. Each a part of the truth of him.

Dusk was imminent as he reached Finsbury Square, beyond the City walls. Sodomites Walk as it was known. He felt a certain ludicrous pride in that, a sense of bravado and recklessness. And there, on the opposite side of the square, was Miss Muff's Coffee House. Or Miss Muff's Molly House as its regular customers knew it, customers with similar tastes and drives which vanquished discretion.

He opened the door and entered. This room was the coffee house: the roasting pan and cauldron on the hearth, coals burning, the serving table, the smell of coffee. He glanced around: a few he acknowledged with a nod, some looking spent, others – eyes unnaturally bright and a tautness in the face – deliberately waiting before they made the next move; one or two unfamiliar faces, looking nervous and unsure. Miss Muff would soon put them at their ease and make clear to them, in her incomparable way, what their choices were.

Francis moved to the door at the back of the room, the threshold to the magical world he craved. He opened it, went through and closed it behind him. Immediately the dim, mysterious light of candles, perfumes heavy in the air, vases of flowers, the quiet chatter of girlish voices, giggling. He raised a hand in general greeting and moved to a further room where his clothes and accessories were stored in a chest with no identifying name – just a small painting of his code. He unlocked it and changed into his costume.

He loved sloughing off his workaday, legal identity and donning his secret persona. Today he chose rustling petticoats, a white gown and scarlet cloak, fine-laced shoes and, of course, a red silk garter round his thigh. Looking in the mirror he put on an elaborate feminine wig with curls around his forehead, adjusting it carefully, painted beauty spots on his cheeks and powdered his face. He was now transformed into Garter Mary. He stood for a minute, letting himself relax, closing his eyes, entering again into the body and mind of a woman. It was, at the same time, intensely arousing and totally comforting.

He placed his lawyer's clothes in the chest and locked it, put the key in his purse, took a last look in the mirror, fluttered his fan, curtsied to himself and returned to the room of magic.

For the next hour or so he giggled with milkmaids, sat on the laps of shepherdesses, protested at precocious male hands – "Lord, how can you serve me so!" – kissed, tickled, hugged and danced. He twirled his fingers, stroked the hair of his wig, fluttered his eyelashes. He loved the foppery and frolic, the pretence of passivity while he knew he aroused his partners.

At last he chose his partner, Pippin Millie. Arm in arm they entered another room, known as the chapel, where they would be 'married'. And there, at last, all restraint and pretence abandoned, they would slake their lust in the luscious vice of buggerie.

Tomorrow, restored and at peace with himself, his imps of mischief laid to sleep, he had an appointment with Lord Howe, a military man, very correct but with a land dispute to settle. The rich always wanted even more money. Francis didn't crave only money. What he craved more was bodily pleasure and sensation.

Three miles away, John Pym, MP for Tavistock, called the meeting to order.

The main business for these influential Puritans in attendance, members of both Houses of Parliament, prominent lawyers and merchants, was how to oppose the Ship Money and forced loans being levied by the King.

"These are crucial matters," began Oliver St John, lawyer. "Since Parliament refused to levy taxes for him, the King has been desperate for money. First he sent letters to all Justices of the Peace asking his subjects to, as he put it, "lovingly, freely and voluntarily" gift him money. Unsurprisingly, few did. Next he levied on the nobility and gentry loans, forced loans in truth – which of course will never be repaid. You will recall the five knights imprisoned for not paying them. This was arbitrary use of the King's powers – these were not seditious conspirators against the throne but respectable men making a legitimate objection. The King was acting above himself."

Nods of agreement around the table. "Indeed, indeed!"

"And the second matter is just as vital. As you may well know, I am defending John Hampden MP for his refusal to pay this Ship Money which the King has levied. We have fought long and hard to establish that only Parliament can levy taxes on the people. It is a key principle of our Parliamentary system and of our democracy. If the King can levy taxes himself he is eliminating the need to have a Parliament."

"True," said Lord John Robartes. "If ship money is legal, non-Parliamentary government has come to stay."

Wine was drunk, tobacco smoked and opinions confirmed as voices grew louder. This king, with his Catholic wife and his papist Archbishop Laud, with his contempt for Parliament and his belief in his divine right to rule – this king must have his wings clipped. Two hours later, as the meeting dispersed, John Pym was a happy man. There was much to plan, connections to be made, papers to be written, but the impetus was undoubtedly there among very influential men. Thank the Lord!

An opposition was forming.

Two miles east of Puddle Dock was Edmund Brentwood, aged eighteen, slumped against an old gravestone in the churchyard of the lime-washed St Mary Matfelon on Whitechapel High Street, outside the City walls. The stone was hard and cold on his shoulders and the early evening light was dimmed by the yew trees. No one else was there:

the mourners had shuffled away, giving him brief sympathetic glances. Just five of them, five at the end of his mother's life to give her their respects. Was that all she merited?

Dead at thirty-eight. Her whole body covered in lumps, like beads under the skin, pustules and scabs. On her tongue and in her throat. Her agony. He shuddered as he remembered, and snarled in anger.

Nobody deserved to suffer like that. And where had his father been? A sudden bile of bitterness and rage. He had never known him. His mother had told him the story when he began his apprenticeship in the bell foundry, a kind of coming of age when he was fourteen: a brief fling when she was a maid but she had loved him; her being with child; his father's regular payments delivered to her even from before his birth on the agreement that she would never divulge his paternity; the full payment of the fee for his seven-year apprenticeship. She had never said a word against him.

On her deathbed, Edmund had asked for his name but she would not break her promise. It had maddened him but made him love and admire her more. So strong she was, so true. As she breathed her last and found peace in that small dark room with the fire hot, he had felt completely alone for the first time in his life. He realised too late how he had not valued her enough and he was wracked with guilt. Too late, too late.

He levered himself up from the ground. Five mourners only but she would have a headstone with her name on it. He would not allow her to just disappear. Somehow he would find the money.

He stood by the bank of raised earth that was her grave and stared at its ordinariness. Another death in this place of the dead. But her soul was safe in his heart, her memory kept warm there.

His father?

156

His father he would find. He had to find him, if he was still alive. He must be a prosperous man. Yes, he would thank him, then tell him how his lover had died so painfully and in such meagre surroundings, then hold him to account for abandoning her, no matter how generous he had been.

Now he must go home, face all the evidence of his mother's life in their two small rooms and live alone there.

He would not drink ale. He did not want to diminish the day.

She had no more tears; her eyes were dry and red.

Jane Nowell sat at the window of her bedroom, throat sore, ribs aching with sobbing, exhausted from no sleep. Her black mourning dress felt strict and unforgiving, harsh as a hair shirt.

Into her misery had seeped anger and bitterness. Her beloved Rowland killed in the North Sea protecting the English herring fleet from Dutch fishermen and their guardian men-of-war. It was cruel and ludicrous. Not even a battle, just an exchange of fire, and Rowland had been unlucky.

Unlucky! So her father had told her. A soldier loyal to the King, he had given his life for King and country! She should be proud of him.

"Given!" she had yelled at her father. "He had it taken away. No one gives his life for fish!"

And on one of the ships you built, she had wanted to add, *built for the King's brand new navy.* The *Merhonour,* the Admiral's flagship. She blamed him, her beloved father, who doted on her, his only daughter. Blamed him, the wealthy shipwright, and the King and the Ship Money tax collectors and the merchants who paid it and the fishermen – all men. A man's world.

So now she sat alone – her father, hurt and turning away; her mother, whose sympathy she rejected as irrelevant. She needed to be on her own. To remember Rowland's gentleness behind his strong manliness, his smile, his loving eyes, his nervousness as he courted her. He was handsome in his officer's uniform. She had felt so safe with him. She had been so proud of him, as she walked with him, her arm in his. How proud Rowland had been to be posted to the flagship.

And now a stab of guilt: had she encouraged him? Was some of the blame hers?

She stared out with narrowed eyes at a ship being constructed in her father's shipyard. So many men at work, like pygmies bustling and busy. Another coffin was being carefully built; more women contracted to weep.

The wedding they had planned for six months' time. And now she was like a widow, at twenty-four years old, a widow.

How fortunate she was, she had to remind herself. She must give thanks not aim blame. How different her life was from those she helped at her parish church, St Mary Matfelon. Those poor orphaned and abandoned children, hungry, unloved, unshod. The money she gave helped to feed them and train them in spinning and weaving so they could build themselves new lives.

Her grief was a luxury.

Or so she reasoned.

And then the emptiness came again, bitter and piercing. She too had been abandoned. She was alone. Self-pity enveloped her.

She wrung her hands, pale against the black dress, sobbed but no tears fell.

Not far north of Whitechapel High Street, John Boon sat on the front of a cart, holding the reins loosely as the cart horse clumped along the cobbles and the wheels rattled. Behind him were boxes of vegetables, sacks of oats and a couple of casks of ale – all partly hidden under an old cloth. But underneath, out of sight, were the sections of a dismantled printing press.

He was heading for Goodman's Fields, a place of allotments, gardens and an old farmhouse with outhouses. There he would meet others who would unload and set up the press again. Tomorrow they aimed to have another pamphlet on the streets: a ballad, *A true and plaine genealogy or Pedigree of Antichrist*. That would make Archbishop Laud rant and rave.

John smiled as he bumped along. The thrill of the chase, keeping one step ahead. But this had been a close one. Last night he'd been busy printing at a secret press in Coleman Street. A sudden crashing at the door, hammers thudding into the wood, yells. The Stationers' men! He and the two others had escaped down a rope out of a back window and into the garden. But William Larner, whose house it was, had been arrested and was now in Newgate Prison – and not for the first time.

Safe in a tavern a mile away, a quick discussion and decision: the hue and cry was getting closer, there must be an informer. Dismantle the other press in Bishopsgate in the morning and take it to a safer place. They had a routine, had done it several times before.

So here he was as dusk was falling. Fleeing but winning. The streets were still busy but the cart lumbered on, unsuspected. John sipped on his pipe, a man at peace and at war. The steady clomp of the hooves, the taste of the tobacco on his tongue, his lips on the clay bit, the fragrance of the smoke in his nostrils, and revolution under the cabbages.

16.

OVERSEAS

1635

Will had dressed carefully, quality but not show. From a belt round his waist, concealed under his dark cloak, hung a scimitar in its scabbard. At his neck the bent sixpence. He would return with it as he had left with it. Sentimental, nostalgic, pointless. But something real still clung to it, like verdigris.

Rowed from the *Phoenix* to the docks, Will shivered in the chilly morning breeze. But it refreshed him. He stepped off the boat onto Blackwell Stairs and paused on the wet stone steps, breathed in the dank stench of the foul river, and remembered the last time he had stood here: a ruined man, pursued as a traitor by the King's Stationers' men. He shook his head, watched the scum of water lap the stone. The same tide, the same troubles, no doubt. A new king now, he'd heard. What else had changed? But a new life for him to lead. Alice! How little he'd thought about her while he'd been away. He turned and climbed the steps.

He needed to walk, to find his bearings, to be at home again, to smell the familiar smells and hear the familiar cries of London. A city was a city, packed with noise and people. But Scanderoon, the seaport for Aleppo, had mosques and Greek Orthodox churches, caravans of camels, marshes, fogs, jackals roaming the streets, pelicans and porcupines in the surrounding hill.

Here it was colder, greyer. A tripe-seller yelled her wares; he smelled honey cakes and frying sausages; a beggar boy sat in a doorway; the bell of St Paul's tolled.

The same chicanery, the same struggles and cruelties, the same brave attempts to love, the same brief glimpses of beauty. Will felt his old life re-gather around him: Alice, Lizzie, Edmund, Hotspur, John Boon, Pinckney, Arthur Babthorpe. What had happened to them all? And Francis Ingilby, towards whom he was now walking. He would surely have survived.

Not only survived but prospered. No surprise. Good for him. Over the doorway, in gold letters on black, his name and the title, Attorney; next to the door, a brass plaque engraved with a set of scales; the stone of the building scoured clean of city grime; an office either side of the door. The business, it seemed, had doubled in size.

Will smiled to himself and entered. He was in a reception room, with three clerks at three tables, shelves of files from floor to ceiling. A clerk looked up.

"I need to see Mr Ingilby," said Will.

"He is very busy. Do you have an appointment?"

"No, I don't – but it is urgent."

"I will see, but his diary today is full. Your name, sir?"

With the clerk at the door to the staircase, Will replied: "Tell Mr Ingilby it's about cockfighting."

"Cockfighting?"

"Yes, about Joslan."

"Joslan?" Incomprehension on his face.

But then the clerk hadn't been there fifteen years ago.

Will heard the clerk's feet hurry up the staircase. Two minutes later, they hurried back down.

"Come with me, sir," said the clerk.

Upstairs, Will was ushered into a large room. At the far end, in front of the fireplace, he saw Francis's head bent over a desk, writing. He didn't look up.

Will nodded thanks to the clerk and the door was closed.

"A moment, sir," said the bent head, not looking up. "Please sit." He gestured to an upright chair placed out of the sunlight by a high shelf of dark, thick tomes and ribboned scrolls. Will sat. The scrape of the pen, rustle of paper, settling of coals in the fire, smell of smoke and old documents.

The pen scrawled a signature with a flourish.

"That's that. Sorry to keep you waiting."

He sprinkled a generous portion of pounce on the wet ink.

"Joslan, you said," said Francis, slipping a red ribbon around his paper. "That intrigued me."

Only then did he look up.

Will saw his lawyer face, set for a client: quizzical, curious, agreeable but promising nothing. Will watched it change. It froze. There was recognition, then astonishment. A full smile.

Francis stood up, shoved his chair back and bustled round the desk, arms outstretched.

Will stood up. They hugged each other with much clapping on shoulders, then stood back.

"Whoreson Will Nailor! In God's name! Will Nailor back from the dead! This is resurrection indeed!"

"Goodman Francis. You prosper, of course. Your belly is rounder."

"And why not? A celebration. I will call for my best wine."

He pulled a bell rope.

"Not wine, Francis, if you please. Some good strong English ale. I have tasted none for fifteen years."

"It shall be done, of course."

The summoned clerk arrived.

"The best beer, the best fresh warm bread and the best cheese. And as quick as you can. And cancel all my appointments for this morning."

"But it's Lord—" began the clerk.

"Never mind, invent a reason. Go."

"Ah, England!" said Will with a smile.

Francis poked the fire up and placed two chairs in front of it. "So," he said. "Tell me all."

162

"You helped me escape, Francis. You saved my life. So, first, a token of my gratitude."

Will took off his cloak, unbuckled the belt and handed it and the scabbard to Francis.

"A weapon; you think I need a weapon?"

Carefully he unsheathed the sword.

"A scimitar," said Will. "From the Mohammetans. It will look good over your fireplace instead of that portrait of King Charles and his wife."

Francis's fingers stroked the handle, inlaid with jewels which sparkled in the firelight. He placed his thumb on the blade edge, gave it a sudden flourish.

"Sharp and vicious, that curve looks more savage than a straight sword."

He placed it carefully on the desk.

"I thank you, sir. It will suitably impress my clients. So, you are still a rebel, Will. You must take care. Things are happening here in England: conflict between King and Parliament – and Charles is married to a Spanish Catholic."

Will shook his head. "Well, that will suit you."

"Leave it, Will; plenty of time to argue, now you're back."

"I look forward to it." A smiling challenge.

Francis frowned, voice more serious, "But you should know: the King has dismissed Parliament because it would not grant him money. Parliament has passed a Petition of Right. Rights!" Francis spat into the fire. "And the King's Archbishop Laud has enraged the Protestants."

"You seem in the thick of it. Not just the quiet lawyer, coining it in."

"You're talking to Francis Ingilby, Member of Parliament."

"Member of Parliament!"

"For a place called Grimsby. I have family there. It cost me money."

"Everything can be bought, no change there."

"Indeed. But good for contacts, good for business."

"So no change there either."

"And these radicals must be opposed. They would turn the world upside down."

A knock on the door and two clerks came in with jugs of beer, mugs, bread and cheese and pewter platters.

"Thank you."

"The smell of that bread. You cannot imagine how much I have wanted it."

"Help yourself."

Francis poured the ale; Will ripped off a piece of bread and placed it in his mouth.

"This, Francis, is as close as I will get to heaven."

"No more of politics, Will. Your adventures."

"We start with business." Will took out his purse. "A paper order for the 4,000 crowns I owe you for that cockfight. Take it to my banker next week, after I've deposited some of my funds. Is he still at The Three Squirrels?"

"Pinckney? Indeed not. He now has his own offices. If you think I have prospered, wait till you see him. These English bankers."

"I will be seeing him, to pay my creditors involved in that disastrous fenland venture."

"So, how have you done it?"

They each took a drink. Will drew a deep breath.

"I killed men."

A silence, flames crackling in the grate. Francis took a swig of ale.

"To make money?"

"No, not directly."

"To free the Christian slaves, on that mission with Rainborowe?"

"Yes. It was a just cause – but that doesn't excuse me. The point is: I killed men and enjoyed it."

Francis frowned. "Enjoyed?"

Will stood up in front of the fire. He let himself remember the cannon and pistol shots, his hammering heart and trembling legs; he heard the yells and curses, the screams of the Barbary pirates, the clash of cutlass on cutlass.

"It was kill or be killed," he said.

The sudden truth: a sword coming at him, thrashing at him, and the answering surge of blood in him, his own yell in his throat, his leap forward, the feel of his sword slamming into the pirate's stomach, skewered and falling in blood. And in him a feeling of such rage and power and victory. Killing more, like a man gone mad, in a frenzy. The ecstasy of inflicting pain instead of being inflicted with it.

He shuddered and turned to face Francis

"It was bloodlust. Afterwards, when the battle was over and the pirates captured, I was terrified of myself, of what I had become. In the moment, I loved the killing, I loved it." Will closed his eyes. "It wasn't Christian slaves I was fighting for, it was myself."

Francis stared into the fire.

"It was survival, Will. You had no choice. It was instinct."

Will sat down again.

"Have you ever killed a man, Francis?"

"No, thank God I've never had to. But now, with this bloodthirsty scimitar…"

He turned to look at it on the desk behind him, firelight flickering on its scalloped blade.

Will took a large bite of bread, still warm and crusty. He savoured it.

"So, you freed the slaves?" asked Francis.

"Yes."

"Mission successful, then? Maybe two years after you left, a young man came to see me. Said he was the brother of someone called Alice, and that you had rescued him from slavery."

So Henry had got safely back. Alice was a secret he would still keep from Ingilby: too precious for Francis's unsavoury pastimes to sully. He wrenched his mind back from her.

"Yes, three hundred of them, men and women. They were in a terrible state. Many of them had been captured by European pirates, including English ones, and sold on to the Mohammetans in the slave markets." Will broke off a chunk of cheese. "Are you not shocked by that?"

"No, Will, I am not. One thing I have learned above all as a lawyer – that greed rules many."

"Even you?"

"To a degree, like you. Look at our clothes, our money, the home I have, the house you will shortly buy with the new fortune you have somehow accumulated."

"But we have both worked fairly for it," replied Will. "Neither of us inherited anything, no silver spoons for us, no land and rents."

"True, but both of us have more than we need and much more than most. We want the pleasures money can buy. You cannot deny it."

"I don't deny it," said Will.

"It is the way of the world. Whether Mohammetan or Christian, Catholic or Protestant, Ranter or Fifth Monarchist – it matters not. Original sin is the making of us lawyers." Francis laughed and took a drink of ale.

"You sound like the Devil," said Will.

"Every venial and mortal sin I have witnessed. And the godly Puritans are as bad as the rest – fraud, cheating, challenging wills, conflicts over property and boundaries."

Will looked up at him. "But you have morals?"

"Yes, Will, I do. The same as you, I believe: the morals that are good for business. I don't cheat, I give value for money; I don't overcharge or make fools of people. That's how you ran your business, was it not?"

"Yes, it was. And is."

"People need me, Will. Rich people. How can I turn them away? I solve their problems, make things fairer."

Will laughed. "Yes, yes. And you have come to need them."

"Indeed I have, but no more than you need buyers with money to spend. We both offer a service and that service is valued."

Will nodded.

"You are successful," continued Francis, "because you have never been a vain man, never sought prestige, no swagger."

"Thank you for that. But I am not the same man you helped onto Rainborowe's ship."

"I should hope not. Fifteen years in those exotic places. It would be unnatural if you had not changed."

"I saw such luxury and such poverty, such cruelty – all out in the open and easy to see. As if there was no shame."

"But the same is here, Will, as you know. My life differs from the girl who scrubs my pots. It is more hidden here, perhaps. Cruelties are more privately done. We sit here, warm and comfortable, well fed. But to get here you will have walked past beggars, maimed soldiers and starving children."

Will stood up and went over to the window.

"Yes," he said. "Which is why I intend to use my money to make things better. I don't know how yet but I will search out ways. John Boon will run my business again, I hope. Is it still as dangerous to publish seditious pamphlets?"

"More so."

"I must be more careful this time, then." He turned back to look at Francis. "And I will find a wife." He grinned.

"A wife? Now, there's an honest endeavour. One you don't need my help for. I am not skilled in such things, as you very well know. It is not to my taste."

Will had never enquired into Francis's private life. Even when both were drunk, the subject was bypassed. He knew of Francis's occasional foppery, had heard rumours of molly houses. But each to his own and no harm done.

"You still haven't told me how you amassed this second fortune which you are going to use so charitably," said Francis.

"A long story that will pass an evening or two in a tavern. In a nutshell, I met merchants in Sallee where we freed the slaves. They pointed me to Aleppo as a place to make my way. So I went."

Will took another bite of bread and cheese.

"And?"

"Well, actually, I first went to Scanderoon, a seaport. A terrible place: bogs, fogs and giant frogs. I set up as a factor-marine, meeting the English boats when they arrived and sending homing pigeons to Aleppo, one hundred miles inland, with the news. I worked my way up to become a factor in Aleppo itself. You cannot imagine it. It's a fierce place; life is cheap. I don't know if it's the heat and the light and the colours but there was a barbarity about the place. It was frightening. So many different people and clothes and skins and beliefs."

"Exciting, though, I'll wager."

"Yes, London is pale by comparison, grey and cautious. Watching the camel trains, sometimes 3,000 camels come in from the desert to camp outside the city gates, the white houses and the palaces of the Turks, the citadel. I set up on my own and fortune favoured me. I am richer than before."

"Not just fortune; hard graft, Will, as ever with you. Were you safe?"

"We never felt safe. The Ottomans did not like us. We lived in khans – which combined warehouses with stables, trading areas and living quarters. There was a curfew from dusk to dawn and we never left the khan without armed guards."

"And women, Will, you haven't mentioned women."

168

"Women! With painted bellies and pierced nostrils – extravagant creatures. You have not seen the like. But remember the pox I had?"

"Before my time and my moderating influence!"

Will scoffed. "For fifteen years I have not been inside a woman's thighs. But they have other ways to relieve a man – subtle ways, slow and teasing. But to sleep with a Muslim woman there means death."

"I understand why you seek a wife."

"Enough of this."

"Details later? You know I like the details." Francis grinned.

"Maybe, but now I must visit John Boon. He is not expecting me either. I presume he will still be as radical as ever."

"Ah, John Boon. He will have news for you about your father."

"Is that old hypocrite still prating about hell and damnation?"

"Maybe, but he is dead, drowned a dozen or so years ago one January."

Will felt not a trace of grief. He had long ago removed his father from his mind. Now he realised his loathing and contempt for the man had not abated one jot. But he was dead now and could harm no one else. A good thing. Drowning? That was odd, but not worth a second thought.

"And my mother?"

"John will tell you, she is well. He arranged things for her."

He imagined the eulogy. He would have been hardly able to stop himself from mocking the hypocrisy: the piety paraded by those God-fearing souls under the bare trees, with rooks cawing. The prayers snatched away by the cold wind.

"To my mother," said Will, and they toasted her health.

"John Boon has indeed become even more of a radical, an independent. He and Babthorpe spent some time in prison

169

for your illegal printing press. It's men like him who must be controlled. One of my duties, as I see it, in Parliament."

"Is that so? Then I must become an MP also, and oppose you."

"Let's drink to that – and to the memory of Joslan and Hotspur, our game fighting cocks."

They clinked their tankards together and drank their ale.

"To a wife for you!" said Francis.

17.

PEQUOT WAR

1637

Youngest son Giles shovelled up horse shit, still steaming, from the track and dumped it in a wheelbarrow. The carter trundled away back to Boston; his two horses had left generous donations for James's fields.

"I'll go down to Peter now with this lot," Giles said with a grin. "Then I'll give him a hand."

Eldest son Peter was mending fences round the prized orchard of Roxbury russet apples. James waved an acknowledgement. Both good lads, workers. He and Alice were both proud of them. It had been hard but rewarding work bringing up a family, establishing the farm and store. Their only worry was Nicholas, their middle son: middle sons seemed to be a not uncommon concern among many families.

James and Nicholas carried the newly-delivered goods into the store. Nicholas had a bunch of spades, mattocks and fire shovels. Outside the door stood boxes of kitchenware, pewter spoons and metal pots, sacks of seed potatoes and corn meal, packages of clothing, casks of wine, bales of cloth, barrels of beer and cones of sugar.

Inside, Alice checked the paperwork while the Indian assistant, Nukpana, examined a pile of beaver pelts his Indian hunters had brought in. Two wampum belts they'd also brought lay on the counter.

James was on the threshold, turning into the store, a sack of meal over his shoulder, when he heard the sound of tramping feet. He turned to look: a troop of men in rough marching order, boots raising dust, muskets over their shoulders, bandoliers and shoulder belts, staring straight ahead, some ragged whistling. The newly-gathered militia.

And at their head, of course, a familiar figure in his royal blue coat, striding out in his long cavalry boots, paunch in advance, chin in the air, sweating in his helmet, gauntleted right hand on his sword pommel: Magistrate and Elder Samuel Wilton, farmer, merchant, landowner, braggart – and charlatan, it was rumoured back in his previous hometown, Hartford. Stories of debts that he denied.

Wilton had already built himself the biggest house in the settlement: a grandiose statement that he was here to establish himself as a man of power and influence. Alice detested him.

"Squad, halt!"

Wilton had stopped directly in front of James's store.

"Attention!"

Wilton stamped his boots together and pushed out his chest. Sunshine gleamed on his ridiculous ornamented spurs. Pretentious fool! Now military leader. To think that this was the man, hairy arse half-bared, assaulting Alice, that he had once had at sword point.

"At ease!"

The men lowered muskets, relaxed and shuffled about. James knew them all and they him. Some looked sheepish, others aggressive.

When Wilton strode forward, James went inside to dump his sack before returning to stand in the doorway. James glared at him with disgust but Wilton was oblivious.

"We're going to teach these Indians a lesson, Mr Parker," said Wilton. "We have been far too patient. As you know, they have ignored our demand that they hand over the warriors responsible for Stone's murder, and now there is John Oldham killed. We must find them ourselves. Are you with us?"

It was a deliberately public challenge. James looked at the gauntlet. Wilton, and the others, knew James's views on war with the Indians. This confrontation was just part of Wilton's continuous campaign to discredit him, alienate him from other settlers and destroy his business: revenge for the humiliation of the attempted rape.

The waiting troop had been watching, muttering, laughing, most enjoying James's discomfort. Most of them had heard James at the general meeting, arguing for more negotiation. Any sympathisers were silent now.

"We leave tomorrow from the quay at first light," he said. "Expect you to be there. And bring your medicines."

He gave a knowing, challenging smile. He knew he'd put James on the spot.

"For the King!" he ended, with a salute. "Form up!" Wilton waved the troop back into marching formation.

What a loathsome man! James watched them march away.

The King! Charles! James hated the monarchy. His elder brother Stephen, a keeper in the Royal Forest of Rossendale, had been killed when a royal hunt passed through. One of the hunt had been the Archbishop of Canterbury who, aiming at a deer, had shot a crossbow arrow through Stephen's chest. A royal commission had found in the Archbishop's favour, and Charles' father, King James, had signed the pardon. There had been no compensation. One law for the rich; no one should be above the law. Anyone who tried to topple the monarchy had James's support. Fight for the King? Not a hope.

"Are you going, Father?"

Nicholas's voice, from the shadows, standing just inside the door, out of the sunlight.

His sixteen-year-old son was for the war party.

"Let's go inside."

Alice was sitting on the chair by the counter.

"Thank you, Nukpana, you can go now," said James. "Remember us to your wife."

Nukpana, face impassive, nodded his thanks, collected his cloak and left.

James sat on a cask of wine. He watched the dust dancing in the sunlight of the door, breathed in the smells of earth and sacking. The shelves were filled with goods. The store was doing well, in spite of Samuel Wilton's efforts. He looked up at his son Nicholas. He was a strong broad boy, a good worker, but lately he had been associating with young men who had no respect for Indians, drank too much hard cider and roamed round the village in a loud group trying to impress the girls.

"You are surely not thinking of joining them, James?" said Alice, putting her papers down.

"I am still deciding, Alice."

"But you know they are wrong. We must live alongside the Indians, not fight them. You have always argued so." Her voice was quiet but certain.

"I know what I have said. I still believe it."

Then Nicholas, his arms folded: "You may not want to fight them but they fight with us. Two weeks ago they killed John Oldham. He was a man you respected and traded with, an honest man on a trading visit to Block Island. His crew were slaughtered as well and his ship looted. His murderers are still free, given sanctuary by the Pequots."

"No need to remind me, Nicholas. I know full well what happened. John was a good man. You are right."

"So why are we wrong to want to bring his murderers to justice?"

"We?" How far was he in with these people? His son was drifting away from them.

"He's not the only one murdered by the savages," continued Nicholas. "Two years ago there was John Stone

174

as well. The Indians lie all the time, they cannot be trusted." Sneering, dismissive.

His mother: "That is a terrible thing to say. Do you not trust Nukpana and his wife?"

"I do not know they do not cheat us." Sullen.

James jumped up from his seat. "No more of this!" he shouted. "I will have no more of this sort of talk." His fists were clenched. Nicholas lounged against the door post, not flinching.

Quietly from her chair, Alice said, "I would not be alive if it were not for the Indians."

"I know, you've told me many times." Nicholas yawned and slouched.

James, still standing: "You will not talk to your mother like that."

"Well, I will tell you again," said Alice, "since you seem to forget."

James watched his son's face but there was no expression.

Alice continued: "Half of us pilgrims died that first winter. The Indians, on whose land we had built our seven houses, could easily have attacked and killed us. Instead we made an agreement with them. They gave some of their seed corn to plant, told us how to fertilise the soil with dead herring, planted their own beans and squash for us which thrived while the barley and peas we brought from England suffered in the foreign soil."

Nicholas said nothing but his sulking face was unimpressed.

"Your mother is right. The only future is for us to live together."

Nicholas, in the doorway, turned his back to the sunlight. He spoke from a silhouette.

"They have said they want someone from each family in the militia. Giles is too young; Peter is a farmer not a fighter; you, Father, do not want to go." He paused, a slight deepening of his voice, even an appeal. "And your reasons I respect. So I will go. I will represent the family."

"You most certainly will not," said Alice. It was a tone James knew well – not to be gainsaid.

Still from his face unseen in the shadow: "We will be taunted. Father, they will call you a coward."

There was some truth in that. "I will fight if I have to but only when I think the time and cause are right."

It sounded legitimate but Nicholas's eyes seemed to be seeing into him.

"And you think our store and farm will prosper if we do not support our community?"

"At last you speak some sense," said James. "No doubt that Wilton will use any excuse to convince people not to deal with us. He has his reasons and you, Nicholas, do not know the whole story."

He glanced across at Alice, who looked down.

There was a silence then Nicholas shuffled his boots on the boarded floor.

"So, you are forbidding me to go," he said, the words heavy with challenge.

"Yes," James said, "we are."

Nicholas snorted.

James continued: "Because I will go myself."

Alice jumped up from her chair, leaning forward onto the counter; "You? But—"

James held up his hand. "Nicholas is right. My first duty is to look after my family. And that means we cannot cut ourselves off from our neighbours and customers."

Nicholas's face was a mixture of victory and disappointment.

"But your principles, James, and your brother Stephen," pleaded Alice.

"I know. I must bend them and he will forgive me. The expedition is going to capture the murderers not kill them.

And Wilton said I was to take my medicines. I will go as medical man."

Alice knew James hardly slept that night, tossing, turning, sighing. Was it fear? Wrestling with his principles? Anger over Nicholas? But his decision to go to war meant that Nicholas would not, and for that she was grateful. She wanted to put her arms round her husband but she was certain he would push her away, caught in his own travails.

Next morning just after dawn, James left for the quayside, sword at belt, haversack of medical stuff over his shoulder, musket in his hand. Still locked apart, they had not kissed farewell.

Two weeks later, as dusk fell, he walked wearily into his home; he was greeted with silence. There was no hug from Alice who, at the kitchen sink, merely turned her head towards him and then continued to wash pots. Peter and Giles sat at the table, heads bowed as if in prayer. Nicholas stood by the fireplace, chewing tobacco. He spat into the grate when James took off his pack and threw back his shoulders to ease the stiffness.

News of the trip must have got there before him.

Alice placed five plates of mutton stew on the table and sat down. Stony-faced, she looked around at her four men, nodded curtly, and the three sons began to eat. James, hands on the table, looked at her, a frown on her face. She took a mouthful of stew.

"How many Indians were killed, Father?" asked Nicholas innocently.

James saw the sardonic half-smile. How to start to tell his version?

Alice put down her spoon.

"I do not want to talk about it," she said. "Not today, not ever. It was a shameful business."

"I—" began James.

177

"I know, you saved a man's life. But that does not excuse what else happened."

"I did not—"

"I know, you did not kill a man. And I thank heaven for that. Now, no more. I will have no more about it."

But James glared at her. "Don't tell me what I can and can't say," he snapped.

She saw his sudden resentment, a belligerent set to his face, heard a new harshness in his voice.

"If Nicholas wants to know, I will tell him."

He swallowed a mouthful of stew. "Wilton lied to me." His voice steady now, controlled. "When our orders came, they were to kill all the men in the village and capture the women and children. But I could not back out then. So we sailed to Block Island. The Indian village we found was empty. They must have known we'd landed; fires were still warm in the wigwams."

Alice bent her head, not looking at him, but the boys were listening. James finished another mouthful.

"Oh, you would have been proud of us, Nicholas, brave men with our muskets."

Nicholas curled his lips.

"Yes, we looted everything, all the food and corn. We torched the wigwams, smashed the canoes and cut the throats of seven horses."

"A successful expedition, then," said Nicholas.

James leapt to his feet, his chair crashing onto the stone floor. He brought his fist down onto the table.

"No!" James shouted, flinging the word like a spear, eyes blazing at Nicholas. "No, you young fool."

Alice looked up, shocked, half rose to put out a hand to calm him but James dashed it away.

Quieter now, he said, "We don't even know if these Indians were guilty of anything. We destroyed their homes

178

and livelihoods simply because they were there. They were scapegoats."

He sat down again, shoving his plate away.

"You think you know everything, Nicholas. But this was a defeat."

Nicholas was about to say something.

"No, better to keep your mouth shut."

James paused then continued, "It was a defeat, a defeat for our way of life. The Indian tribes will surely band together; there will be reprisal raids on equally innocent English people. Working in the fields and woods, we will now have to be constantly on our guard against arrows in the gut and hatchets in the skull."

He looked round all of them. "It is the end of co-operation, of community concord. Is this what we fled England for? We will reap what we have sown."

Silence, half-empty plates on the table, tension.

Nicholas stood and went outside. Alice began to side the pots.

It was Giles who spoke first. "They told us you saved a man's life, Father. Nathaniel Endicott from the next village."

James sighed, lifted his head, nodded, closed his eyes and put his hand through his hair.

"Yes, I did."

"How did you do it?" continued Giles. "I really want to know."

A silence from the sink, Alice listening. Giles leaned forward, elbow on the table, head on his hand; Peter leaning backwards, his chair creaking.

"Nathaniel was hot in the chest with an arrow. The arrowhead was made of antler bone, notched and barbed to make it harder to get out. We gave Nathaniel brandy, plenty of it."

James took a drink of ale.

"He's a brave man, never a murmur. I had to probe the wound to make it larger to get the arrowhead out."

Alice had turned and was watching. James shivered.

"Your mother had given me a twig to use as a probe, dried and stitched into purified linen and infused with rose honey as an antiseptic. Then, when it was wide enough and deep enough, I took some small metal tongs so they grasped the arrowhead and with my other hand holding the unbroken arrow shaft I slowly pulled it out. It must have been excruciatingly painful."

Peter and Giles were enthralled.

"Then, with cloth soaked in brandy, I dabbed the wound clean and applied a cold smear of thyme oil and bandaged it up."

A silence and then Alice began to scrub the pots again.

"I'm to my bed," said James.

Alice went up much later. She saw his eyes were closed but sensed he was not asleep. She undressed quietly and eased herself into the bed. They lay side by side. She knew he did not want her to touch him.

She had angered him, and he had never spoken to her with such harshness before. She had been unfair, unthinking.

She listened to his breathing, soft and easy, but she knew she had wounded him. Some kind of trust had been fractured.

18.

RING AND WHIP

1639

Just after two o'clock in the afternoon of Friday 25th November 1639, at the church of St Katharine Cree on Leadenhall Street in Aldgate, Will Nailor gently held the left hand of Jane Nowell and slipped a gold wedding ring onto the fourth finger.

"With this ring I thee wed," he repeated after the minister, "with my body I thee worship, and with all my worldly goods I thee endow. In the name of the Father and of the Son and of the Holy Ghost."

For a moment Jane looked down at her hand, then raised her head, looked up at him and smiled. Will saw her grey eyes were soft with love.

Then they knelt together and the minister continued, "O Eternal God, Creator and Preserver of all mankind..."

But Will wasn't listening. Eyes open, he was looking up at the rose window at the end of the chancel, high above the altar. Dull November sunlight still made the coloured glass blaze in blues and reds. Beautiful. But all part of a fairy tale he had long ceased to believe in. He'd had no choice in the setting of his marriage. Jane and her parents, all virtuous churchgoers, had insisted on it. It was not a battle worth fighting. And he had wanted Jane to be happy. Jane, who was now his wife.

As he had stood at the front of the church, waiting for Jane and her father to enter, he had looked up at this same window, and the face of Alice had materialised among the shining colours: an ironic smile but her green eyes affectionate and understanding. A sudden lurch of loss in his heart, a terrible silent isolation as the organ played, a need to be cradled by her, to rest with her.

Then behind him the church doors had clanged open and the congregation rose with a great swishing of skirts and scuffling of boots. He had closed his eyes tight to hide from the revelation of the window, turned and seen Jane, her silver dress catching the candlelight. And his heart had leapt at her beauty. He had turned to the front again. What sort of man was he, who could hold these contrary, treacherous feelings at the same time?

Will was startled back to the moment when the minister took hold of his and Jane's right hands. The minister joined them and said, "Those whom God hath joined together, let no man put asunder."

And he felt a great, guilty affection for this young woman whose beauty drew men's looks but whose diffidence disconcerted them.

As they turned and walked back down the aisle, arm in arm, he heard the bells peeling. A sudden image of his father, enraged: appalled by the papist ring-giving, by the organ and the bells; his father's supercilious smile, leering at Will's hypocrisy. *So much for you, Father*, thought Will, and strode on. He spied Ingilby, who nodded his head and gave a droll smile. It was Francis who had introduced him to Jane at some guild event. Will had been attracted by her artlessness, intrigued by whether or not it was a subtle ruse. He knew now it was natural but that she was aware of its effect.

Outside the church porch, wheat grains were thrown over them and trumpeters played in celebration.

Then they were caught up in the general good cheer and celebration. Their friends and fellow businessmen assured them it was "a good match". Most of the crowd were from Jane's side but John Boon was there and the old bookseller

Arthur Babthorpe, even Will's banker Henry Pinckney and, of course, Francis.

They moved into the wedding feast where expensive yellow gloves were given out to guests as a sign of friendship. Many of the women wore ribbons to symbolise the tying of the knot. Will could not prevent a memory: the ribbons Alice had rejected at the riverside hut.

The feast was lavish with an abundance of roast peacock, their feathers decorating the tables. Rich wine was liberally poured, the elaborately iced and decorated bridal cake was cut, and the groom cake diced into pieces and presented to guests in little boxes. It was all very fashionable, as was the dancing that followed: too much French baroque for Will's taste. But he enjoyed the swirling gavotte and the gigne.

At a pause in the dancing he noticed John Boon and Arthur Babthorpe standing together and slightly apart from the rest of the company. Will could guess their views on the luxury and extravagance. Suddenly ashamed, he wanted to tell them of Jane's Christian charitable works at the church in Whitechapel. And then an idea: he would endow a school for the children of his workers. Where did that come from? As the musicians played on and laughter grew louder around him, he let the idea develop: there would need to be a nominal charge to encourage commitment; the children would learn to read, write and count; no Latin or Greek and certainly no religion; some practical skills. The more he thought about it, the more enthusiastic he became. John or Arthur would know a suitable schoolmaster. What he needed now was suitable accommodation – not a problem.

He wondered what his father-in-law would make of it. Richard Nowell would approve his charitable purpose but perhaps not the schooling of the poor. They might get ideas above their station, read dangerous pamphlets. Will had kept quiet about that aspect of his past – and his intention to continue. Richard was a man who had done very well out of the status quo and opposed anything that might threaten it; he was comfortable in his views and never loathe to express them. He enjoyed what his money could buy, displayed it, but had no side. Will liked him for his forthrightness. He was a burly man with strong, muscled calves and a well-nourished belly, a severe jaw and thick neck. Remnants of thin grey hair were arranged carefully across his pate, an incongruous touch of vanity. He seemed soft and indulgent only with his daughter, their only child.

Will had charmed Jane's mother, Ann. He liked her, too: quiet but not submissive, she appeared to manage her marriage with great skill. There was great affection between husband and wife – a mature companionship.

During their first nights in bed together, Will had quickly learned that Jane was not completely innocent. That did not trouble him. There was much for them to discover about each other. Jane was eager to comply but less confident to pleasure or be pleasured. Will sometimes felt her making love with him was somewhere between a duty and an act of charity. But it gave him the release he needed. And she wanted a child.

★

Jostled by the crowd as they surged forward for a better view, their angry shouts mingled with chanted invocations to the Lord, Will watched as John Lilburne's shirt was ripped off him. Stripped to the waist, his hands were bound and he was tethered to the cart's arse.

"Welcome to the cross of Christ!" shouted Lilburne, his head thrust up defiantly.

The crowd roared their approval.

As the executioner drew out his whip, Lilburne said to him: "Well, my friend, do thy office."

184

Will heard the reply: "I have whipped many a rogue before, but now I shall whip an honest man."

Under a blazing sun, the horse and cart, prisoner walking behind, proceeded slowly along its two-mile journey from Fleet Prison to Westminster. Every three or four paces, the three-thonged corded whip with knots upon it lashed his bare back as Lilburne cried out: "Hallelujah! Hallelujah! Glory, honour and praise be given to thee, O Lord, forever."

The watching crowds shouted words of comfort to him. Many accompanied the prisoner, and Will walked with them. The lash cracked in the air, blood ran from the man's back, his sweat glistened in the sun. Every time the whip landed, Lilburne's body jerked and Will flinched. He could not comprehend the repeated spasms of pain Lilburne endured, knowing there were far more to come. The cart wheels creaked round with infinite slowness, the horse's hooves stirred up the dust of the streets in a slow plod – but the man uttered no groans.

Will was horrified but spellbound: one man inflicting pain on another, licensed by the law; the other, victimised by the law, glorying in the pain he received. Something primitive compelled Will to watch, something shameful but fascinating roused his blood. He too wanted to yell and fete the man's bravery. But he saw too that it was a collaboration, another martyrdom. The Star Chamber needed a victim and the victim wanted to be a martyr. But Lilburne – 'Freeborn John' Lilburne as he was called – was not here primarily out of some religious ecstasy. The knotted cords raked his back because he was a champion of free speech and because he had refused to accept the authority of the Star Chamber. That seemed to Will a nobler cause – not fired by a religious zeal for his own soul, which can unbalance a man, but by a belief in the possibility of manmade justice.

The power of preachers' words. How easily they could convince people so eager to believe. There was a hunger in people's hearts that needed feeding. Or a terror that needed appeasing. The Day of Judgement, Doomsday, was prophesied by preachers for 1666. Predictions that fuelled fear, like dry sticks thrown onto a fire

As Lilburne was hauled into New Palace Yard in the Palace of Westminster, he stumbled, his knees buckling. The crowd held its breath but he regained his balance and did not fall. His back and breeches streamed with blood, his shoulders swelled almost as big as a penny loaf with the bruises, and the weals were bigger than tobacco pipes. The pillory was ready for him up on the platform. Horse and cart stopped, the crowd halted. Lilburne was untethered from the cart. He stood, swayed, and drew himself upright. Will shivered as he imagined the weals on the man's back stretching and cracking open. Freeborn John's face was drawn in pain. Will reckoned he had received 500 strokes, making 1,500 stripes to his ruined back.

Will looked up to the windows of the six-gabled Star Chamber. There were no faces yet but he knew they would be there, waiting: the members of the Star Chamber who had found Lilburne guilty and set the penalties. Archbishop Laud, member of the Privy Council, would be there, and Bishop Juxon, the Lord Treasurer, and Chief Justice John Finch. Sipping the new modish brisk champagne, tasting fancy French sweetmeats – kickshaws, as they called them – they would be smiling and equivocating.

A door opened in the Star Chamber building and a pot-bellied man with a fleshy face emerged in robes. Will did not recognise him. A lawyer, he presumed. The crowd hissed. The lawyer stood in front of Lilburne. Will could just hear the words, coldly spoken:

"Do you admit your error?"

Lilburne shook his head.

The lawyer signalled and turned away.

Lilburne bowed towards the Star Chamber before he was led up onto the platform and, stooping, his head was clamped in the pillory. Will looked up. Faces were at the windows of the Star Chamber now. Implacable, expressionless. The Law. Laud relishing his Christian revenge.

The crowd gathered close and Lilburne began to speak, at first haltingly, then fluently. He had been found guilty by the Star Chamber of "a very high contempt and offence of dangerous consequence, and was an evil example". He told the story of his arrest for the "unlawful printing and publishing of libellous and seditious books, including *Letany*" which he had smuggled in from Holland. Will remembered that *Letany* was the book which had called bishops "the tail of The Beast". Lilburne explained why he refused to take the ex officio Star Chamber oath "because they have no power to demand it. Oaths can only be sworn before magistrates, and the law of the land allows no man to accuse himself. As a freeborn Englishman I claim these rights. And these rights have been removed by the Bishops who have their authority from the Pope, who is the Beast of the Revelation, who is the Antichrist."

Lilburne shouted these words then gasped for breath. How did he have the energy, how could he collect and organise his thoughts, how could he be so brazenly defiant? Here was a true man.

Will noticed men scribbling as they stood and watched – material for pamphlets which, in spite of the censor's printing laws, would circulate round London and then the country with every detail of the punishment. Once he had been part of that movement. He thought fondly of it but now there were other ways in Parliament. But perhaps he could start again, with John Boon.

The fat lawyer returned and bid him to stop talking.

"I would rather be hanged at Tyburn!" shouted Lilburne.

Again, the lawyer signalled, and this time Freeborn John was gagged, so hard that his mouth bled. But he wasn't finished yet. From his breeches pockets he pulled pamphlets which he threw towards the crowd. They cheered and grabbed for them. For two hours he stood, stooped in the pillory, before he was unclamped. Will watched him leave, accompanied by cheering crowds, as he was escorted back to Fleet Prison, to stay there until he conformed.

Will felt humbled. This man knew with certainty what was right: a freedom to express opinions and let others read them; the rule of law was paramount over secret courts; the rights of freeborn Englishmen. It was simple, really. Inspiringly simple. There was a liberation of spirit, a freedom to speak, which excited Will. England was at the edge of a new age, in spite of what he'd just witnessed at the pillory.

How he wished he could talk about these matters with Jane, but they would only argue.

19.

A DEATH

1641

In the years that followed the Block Island attack, the Pequots raided settlements across the colony. They killed men and women, stole cattle and horses, burned crops. Any English man or woman who ventured outside their settlements was liable to be murdered. No one travelled alone. The whole area was filled with fear and anxiety.

Exactly as James had predicted, mused Alice, as she unpacked new supplies in the store.

She and James had slowly restored their marriage, Alice persuaded that James had done the best he could, given the necessity – as he still believed – for his participation. Nicholas grew further way from both of them, working hard on the farm and giving no cause for complaint, but treating Nakpuna and his wife Fala with studied indifference. In the evenings and on Sundays he spent time with young hotheads. He never spoke about them in the house but listened to conversations between his parents with hints of a supercilious smile which Alice noticed but forbore to react to.

Leaders of the inland settlements met in Hartford and agreed to raise another militia, which would be led by William Mason. As before, Samuel Wilton had taken upon himself to draw up a local group of volunteers. This time James had refused to go, even as a medical man. The topic was not raised in the house. Nicholas had gone about his usual labours with a quiet sense of virtue.

On the morning of 18th May, Alice came downstairs, riddled the fire and placed more logs on it. There was bread to be made. Still half asleep, she picked up the container of flour, took off the lid and was about to scoop some out when she saw a piece of paper weighted down by a tankard on the corner of the table. It was folded over and *Mother* was pencilled across it. Suddenly wide awake, her heart pounding, she took the note and opened it.

For the honour of the family.
Nicholas

She slumped down onto a chair and stared at the note. A sudden realisation, a quick glance at the door: Nicholas's haversack was not there, nor his jacket. He had gone.

For several days she had feared he would: his new friends, the horrible silence between him and his father, the call to patriotism. Above all, the need to prove something. She had also known she could do nothing about it. Her brother had defied her father and gone to sea; Will had defied his father. Now she and James were the parents defied. This was what sons did.

She heard James stamping about in the bedroom above.

James had refused to go on this expedition and she had supported him. So they were both responsible for Nicholas going.

James clumped down the stairs.

"Fried eggs this morning, two, please," he said and kissed his wife on the forehead.

She handed him the note.

He read it. "The stupid young fool." He screwed the note up and flung it towards the fire but missed. "The stupid, stupid idiot!"

Alice laid her hand on his arm.

190

"There was nothing we could do," she said. "He is his own man."

"Man?! A little boy, more like." James ran his hands through his hair. "This bloody disastrous wrong-headed expedition. They are raising wasps around our ears. And it's my fault he's gone."

"James – it's no one's fault or everyone's fault. You cannot blame yourself."

"Well, he'll find out how brave he really is," said James. Alice heard bitterness and anger in his voice, maybe even envy. How was that possible?

James left for the fields with a flagon of cider and a hunk of bread, fried eggs forgotten. All day he laboured and dug and hammered, cursing and losing himself in physical effort. Peter and Giles had dared make no comment; they worked on a different part of the farm. At home, Alice filled the day with scrubbing and cleaning and washing clothes. But in the back of her mind, like a nightmare she could not wake up from, was the picture of Nicholas, covered in blood, his face shattered, crying for her.

Two days later, on 20th May, a travelling pedlar brought news: one hundred Englishmen and fifty Mohegan Indians, who were the traditional enemies of the Pequot, had left by boat for Narragansett Bay. Among them was Nicholas Parker.

Two weeks later, on the afternoon of 3rd June, Alice saw Roger Mather ride into town on the back of a cart, get down and limp home on a pair of crutches. He was one of Nicholas's friends, son of the cooper. She rushed across to him and he told her Nicholas was unharmed. She then raced down to the fields and told James. They embraced with relief.

James joined the men at the inn that night as Roger, plied with ale as a hero, told his story, leg propped up on a stool. Both Nicholas and the other local lad, Philip Hubbard, were safe when he left them.

"They fought like tigers," he said, "and saved my life."

They had carried him to safety through a hail of arrows, his foot shattered by an Indian musket ball.

The soldiers had breached the palisade of the Pequot stronghold at Porter's Rocks and set fire to the buildings. Five hundred Pequot men, women and children were trapped and burned to death. Those few who escaped were cut down by sword and musket. Only seven survived and were taken prisoner. It had been a massacre.

But that had not been the end. As Roger was being treated for his wound, the rest of the force learned that Pequots from all the surrounding areas had decided to abandon their villages and flee westward. Captain Israel Stoughton was being despatched with most of the soldiers to catch and destroy them. Nicholas and Philip had gone with them but Roger had been invalided home.

James drank little during the evening. He listened intently to the tale and watched the faces of the other listeners, rapt with attention, eyes bright with ale and excitement, living the battle vicariously. The Indian slaughter was greeted with cheers and acclamation. More ale was sunk.

He closed his eyes, heard the mugs thumped down on the inn table, boots clattering on the wooden floor in applause, calls for more ale for the lad, more questions shouted. The place was in a fever, forces loosed. And he was apart from it. For him the battle would have been a terror, the fear of a wound, a shattered limb, the pain.

That night Alice and James lay with arms around each other. Their son was still alive and had bravely saved a man. James was ashamed he might not have done the same but was proud of his son's bravery, misplaced though it was.

Seven weeks later, on 20th July, just after Alice, James, Peter and Giles had finished their evening meal, there was a knock on the door. James went to answer it.

He came back into the kitchen with a tall man, hatless and bearded. James's face was white.

"Captain Israel Stoughton," said the man.

Alice suddenly placed the name and gasped aloud, her hand to her mouth.

"No, no!" she sobbed, shaking her head wildly.

"I have sad news for you," said the captain.

"No…" a long groan from Alice. "Please God, no."

"Your son Nicholas died in battle. It was a brave death. He was a fine soldier."

Peter put his arms around his mother, who had slumped forward on the table, hands over her head. Giles looked at his mother in fear and bewilderment. He had never seen her cry before. James just stood, rooted to the spot.

Alice looked up, face haggard, tears streaming, voice choking. "A brave death," she sneered at the captain. "That makes it worthwhile?"

She hammered her fists on the table. She screamed, "Get out of my house, you murderer!"

"I'm truly sorry," the captain said. "Nicholas was a fine man."

Alice started up from her seat but Peter held her. "Mother, no," he said softly.

The captain turned and beckoned James after him. James started as if from a dream. They went out.

Half an hour later James returned. Alice was seated in the rocking chair, rocking it gently, staring into the fire. Peter and Giles sat at the table, watching her warily, not knowing what to do.

Without looking round, Alice said: "Is his body coming home?"

His two sons looked up at him. The horror of such a question.

"No, it is buried out there. He had a Christian burial, the captain said."

Alice half laughed, half cried – a weird sound that cut through them, made their scalps crawl. "Well, that's all right, then."

Her fingers were drumming on the bare wooden arms of the chair.

"Tell me the story, then." Her voice was flat and distant. "I want to know."

Hesitantly, quietly, forcing himself to remember the captain's words, speaking as if through a thick curtain that shielded him from the content of his words, James spoke.

The colonist militia had followed the fleeing Pequots to their refuge in a swamp. They had then encircled the swamp, firing rounds into the thickets. The release of nearly two hundred elderly men, women and children had been agreed.

The remaining warriors, about a hundred, refused to surrender. Fighting continued through the night but the Pequots held their position until the fog rolled in the following morning. The militia continued to fire with small shot. A few Pequots broke through the English perimeter, and in this successful fight to escape with their chief, Sassacus, Nicholas was killed: two arrows, in the throat and heart. The remaining warriors in the swamp were gradually culled.

James finished. No one spoke. The rocking chair creaked, the fire crackled. The room dimmed as the sun set, the last of the light shining through the pane of glass onto ordinary mugs and plates and pots. Dust danced.

Alice gave a great sigh. "I hate this place," she said. "I'm going to bed." At the bottom of the stairs she added: "I'd like to be alone tonight, James. I'm sorry."

James nodded. He, too, wanted to be alone.

"I will sleep in the barn," he said.

There in the barn, as he heard the hunting owls hoot and the mice scurrying in the hay, he knew it was his cowardice that had killed Nicholas. He had thought it was principle, had convinced himself it was principle that had led him not to fight, but it was fear. The old fear he had had all his life from being a boy. This fear, and his big strong frame, had led him to avoid challenges that might have hurt. He had never proved himself in any kind of fight with a man. He had never told Alice any of this and now never could.

That night, Alice lay in bed alone. As clouds shifted across the sky, moonlight shone sporadically on the wooden mockingbird Nicholas had whittled for her as a child. She watched it appear from the darkness and then merge back again.

At some point in the small hours her tired eyes closed and, at that moment, part of her memory snapped shut like the lock on a jewel box, and she turned the key. She slid the box to the back of her mind, stuffed it into the clogged and dusty jumble there – deeper even than the bent sixpence. It was to be hidden, then forgotten.

At last she slept.

In the pre-dawn mist James went down to the furthest edge of his land and onto the trail into the blackberry clearing where he had first met Alice. Though he had no religion, it seemed right to kneel on the earth. And there he gave his thanks to his dead son, tried to make his atonement, and wept.

He pushed up the sleeve of his jacket, grabbed a branch of bramble thick with thorns, and jabbed it hard on his arm, sharp and stabbing. He watched the bubbles of blood well up. Then he ripped the branch down his arm. An excruciating shock of pain made him grit his teeth, lurch and rock sideways.

Steady again after a few moments, he threw away the bramble. He looked down at his arm and watched the blood seep and run, such crimson threads ravelling together towards his wrist. And felt unburdened.

Alice unburdened herself, too. What she could not live with in herself, she projected onto James. It was James alone

195

who had caused Nicholas to depart secretly in the night and go to war. It was James's principles and pragmatism, not their mutual decision, that James, this time, should stay at home because the war was both wrong and unwise.

It was James alone who had brought about the death of her son.

So in the days that followed, Alice became cold towards him. She could not bear the living warmth of his touch. When he brushed her arm or leaned forward to kiss her, even to comfort her in her grief, she flinched, shuddered and withdrew.

So he in turn withdrew.

There were no hugs or kisses of affection. Both saw to it that was never any accidental contact. They never saw each other naked, preparing separately for their celibate bed, then lying side by side in an unspoken alienation that locked them apart.

Alice was content: the same contrivance of her mind that made James solely to blame also constrained her never to acknowledge or see his hurt.

She never explained. It was a manifestation of her grief, James thought. Or perhaps it was that the death of her son made the act of procreation anathema to her, a basic instinctive horror.

He was patient, tried to understand, and waited. But as time passed and there was no change he became resentful, bitter, frustrated. One night his need was so great that he did make love to her. She did not protest. She permitted him but did not respond; lay there motionless with her eyes open and a blank face. Wifely duty – and it was horrible, gruesome, a kind of rape. He did not repeat it. Instead, despising himself, hidden among the hay bales in the barn, remembering how it had been with her before, he would joylessly relieve himself.

196

But around this huge crater in their lives they somehow contrived, in time, to construct a life that, otherwise, was normal – as if they had reached an unspoken agreement. They worked together in the store, made decisions together about farm and house. Other things changed. Towards Peter and Giles, Alice was sometimes distant, hardly speaking; sometimes smotheringly close, questioning them on their farm work, their experiments with grafting apple trees and growing tobacco. They never knew which mother they would meet, so they became wary of her.

Alice would no longer have any Indian healing herbs in her house or garden. James transplanted them to an allotment area out by the barn. Was it because Nicholas had been killed by Indians and in his wife's troubled mind she had to rid herself of their presence? James didn't know. Even more strange, she continued to get on with Nukpana when he brought furs into the store. James saw no animosity between them but noticed Alice was never as warm with Nukpana's wife, Fala.

James immersed himself in his work and was even more intent on his botanical studies of Indian herbs.

Alice took a new interest in local politics and the church. She began to attend services, but the purpose was to deride what she heard. She scoffed at those in authority, mocked the sonorous sermons. Without consciously recalling her years in Holland, she added bright ribbons to her clothes and shocked the goodly citizens with her gaudiness.

Vanity, they said, and soon lost sympathy for her grief which, to all appearances, had disappeared. Alice found new friends – a few other bold and prosperous women who spoke out as she did against the authorities. Soon she was repeating her conversations with them to James. He laughed, agreeing with so much of what they said. This laughter brought them together again – but still not in bed.

It was a malady in her mind, concluded James, which she was not responsible for and could not therefore be blamed for. They developed a different form of happiness, but for how long?

20.

GAUNTLET

1642

After two years of marriage Jane was with child: proud, serene and sometimes anxious. Will had felt the child's kicks, that miraculous quickening, life pulsating in there, while outside in the world there was tumult.

Will and Jane got along well – provided each kept to their own interests and did not interfere with the other's. But it was more than a relationship of convenience; they were happy. He wondered now if she had been too eager, too needy after the death of her soldier fiancé; but that was no worse than him wanting to settle down and have a family. Each needed a complement. She was a churchgoer and not interested in politics, rather conventional in terms of taste.

He had come to realise that in all this she was the opposite of Alice. Maybe his choice of Jane had been a long delayed reaction to Alice's rejection of him. But he had kept his bent sixpence hidden at the back of a drawer; he could not throw it away.

His private life settled, his business prospering, the birth of his first child due in a month and, with the encouragement of Francis Ingilby, Will had got himself selected as one of the four MPs for the City of London. It had cost him money. Jane was not the slightest bit interested but did enjoy attending dinners and balls on the arm of a man who was an MP as well as a successful merchant.

Being an active MP was new not just to Will but to all MPs. Twelve years ago Charles had dissolved Parliament because it had voted through a proclamation against illegal taxation and innovations in religion. Away in Aleppo, Will had known nothing of this and would not have been too interested anyway. Charles' personal rule had lasted until, bankrupt and fighting the Scottish Covenanter rebels, he had been forced to recall Parliament and ask for more money. Those demands were again denied, and after two months Charles dissolved Parliament again. That was when Will became interested.

Six months ago, Charles had retreated from Scotland, his armies beaten and the Scots occupying the north of England. Even more desperate for money, he had recalled Parliament again and that Parliament included Will. He listened fascinated as the Commons refused any grant of money until the grievances of the people were met and papist practices in the Church of England were banned. He had done more than listen; he had spoken out strongly against the King and the King's statement that "princes are not bound to give account of their actions but to God alone".

And now the day had arrived.

Will guided his horse Flint through the London streets jammed with troops of yeomen and gentry hurrying towards Westminster: clattering hooves, thumping boots, a clash of glistening pikes. Men yelled and punched the air, defiant jaws thrust forward, thin mouths determined.

The city was in a fever. Gangs of armed apprentices roamed the streets, ready for riot; propaganda pamphlets were snatched, read and passed on; arguments turned to blows; strangers were seen lurking in alleyways; unfamiliar customers were reported eating and drinking at victualling houses in the suburbs. Bishops had been assaulted: anti-Catholic mobs had tried to attack Archbishop Laud in his Lambeth palace. Wild rumours had been circulating. Now everyone was waiting for the outcome, today in the House of Commons, of the Grand Remonstrance, the statement of public grievances, the indictment against the King.

And Will was one of its authors.

Westminster Palace courtyard was packed, a hubbub of arguments, restless with shifting groups of men, shouted challenges and greetings. Will left his horse with a stable hand.

It was just before ten o'clock in the morning on Monday 22nd November 1641 when he elbowed his way along the rows of MPs to find a place on the green benches of St Stephen's Chapel. He found a seat just behind John Pym, who sat, still and upright, looking down at the floor in front of him. A brave man, a man of vision. Rehearsing his speech, keeping calm. Already Will's heart was thumping. So much was at stake; so much rested on Pym's shoulders.

It was Pym, Will knew, who had noted his voice in Parliament as a City MP – speaking out against the King's unconstitutional forced loans, against the King's promotion of high-church men with their papist rituals; supporting John Hampden's defiance of ship money. He had opposed any granting of funds the King had demanded.

It was Pym who had invited Will to join the committee of twenty-four, appointed to consider the State of the Nation, and instructed to collect grievances against the King's rule.

Will had been proud to be selected, but wary, too. Did he really want to commit himself further? To be identified by the Royalists as a prime mover?

"Don't run too fast, Will," Ingilby had said. "You are a newcomer. Powerful people, who don't want the social order to change, are watching you."

Will had smiled nonchalantly.

"Parliament has a place, but a limited place," continued Ingilby. "A King by Divine Right can muster forces which can crush you. There will be a reckoning."

"I appreciate the advice, Francis."

But as the grievances were assembled by the committee, meeting in secret, Will's reservations faded away. He had

201

not realised the extent of the rot and unfairness; his opinions hardened against what King Charles was initiating or permitting.

And now the hour was at hand. Will straightened up and adjusted his sword so it lay against his high leather boots. Voices rose around him. They were throwing down the gauntlet to the King. It was still hard for Will to comprehend that he was actually here, at this moment when the King was being challenged as never before in the history of England. This was more than the Magna Carta. And he was part of it. The King had no divine right to be king. After the abuses of his eleven-year personal rule, he could not demand money and ignore the people's grievances. The monarch's power had to be curtailed. Parliament was not to be at his beck and call. The Commons, elected by the people, had to be the prime place of power.

Will realised he was clenching his fist. He opened his hand, let it rest on his thigh.

There had been seven previous debates, starting on Tuesday 9th November: angry, vociferous, learned, impassioned. But this was to be the final one. A vote would be taken at last. Will, dressed in dark brown fustian, shuffled in his seat and re-arranged his sword again. Below the tapestried walls, the Commons was packed: a swathe of Puritans in black, many with cropped hair; most of the Court party in boots and red waistcoats, green and blue jackets, a few in grey wigs or ruffs. Ingilby sat near them. Of course he would: he prospered from the status quo.

"What's that jumped-up lawyer Pym from Tavistock going to insult us with today?" Ingilby the lawyer had asked that morning. "Self-righteous, joyless Puritans – a pox on them." Will never knew exactly when Francis was just bating him.

The air was thick with musky sweat, leather, horse and rosewater. Light from the three high windows angled down onto the green and gold high-backed Chair, surmounted with the arms of England. There sat Speaker Lenthall, cloaked and sworded, wearing his flat black hat. In front of him was the Clerks' table where sat Henry Elsyng, short-sighted eyes peering close to the paper, and his assistant.

Will took a deep breath. He was tense and needed to relax. He was beginning to despise, even hate, those who supported and excused this corrupt king. And he knew the feelings were mutual. If this Remonstrance was passed today, there would be no going back.

Prayers were said and other business finalised, members curbing their impatience.

"At last," shouted a few, and then voices quieted to silence. Will felt the tension rise.

"Mr John Pym," said the Speaker.

Loud cheers and a counter-volley of boos. *King John,* as his opponents sneered; *King John,* as his supporters cheered. Will focused all his own energy and commitment to hearten his leader in his heroic, historic stand.

John Pym rose from his seat, a tall man in Puritan black with a white linen collar, a black steeple hat, a grey pointed beard, wide moustache. He straightened up, holding his speech in his right hand, looking around the chamber, waiting for the noise to subside.

"The Commons," he began, "in this present Parliament assembled, having with much earnestness and faithfulness of affection and zeal to the public good of this kingdom and His Majesty's honour and service…"

The first loud snorts of derision.

"… for the space of twelve months have wrestled with great dangers and fears, the pressing miseries and calamities, the various distempers and disorders…"

Hissing and clapping, catcalls and cheers.

"… which have not only assaulted but even overwhelmed and extinguished the liberty, peace and prosperity of this

kingdom and the comforts and hopes of all His Majesty's good
subjects…"

Shouts of "Hypocrite", stamping of feet, clapping, "Praise
be to God!"

Pym pressed on, then paused, lowered his voice so that the
MPs had to strain to hear.

"The root of all this mischief, the actors and promoters
thereof, has been: first, the Jesuited Papists" – cries of
"Antichrist" – "second, the Bishops and the corrupt part of the
clergy who cherish formality and superstition" – more cries of
"Popery" – third, such Councillors and Courtiers as for private
ends have engaged themselves to further the interests of some
foreign princes or states to the prejudice of His Majesty and
the State at home."

Uproar. Bawling and shouting and brandishing of fists.
Ingilby, arms folded, looked amused.

Pym had drawn the battle lines. Pym had suggested, and
the committee had agreed, that the attack should not yet be
directly against the King but against his pernicious advisors.
That would be the tactic, the pretence. Both Pym's supporters
and opponents knew it.

And so Pym began the list of 204 points of grievance that
Will had helped compile. Will knew them almost off by heart.
As he listened, he felt cleansed, exultant, purified. The braying
cat-calling opponents were the corrupt defenders of tyranny.
Ingilby, by acting as if he was above it all, was part of their
number.

Furrows of fine earth were being turned, their freshness
glinting in the light of a new age. And he, Will Nailor, was one
of the ploughmen.

John Pym spoke on as light faded from the windows
in the late afternoon. He passed from the imprisonment of
MPs and the imposition of ship money to the taking away of
men's rights between the low and high water marks, to the

unfair monopolers of soap, salt, wine, leather and sea coal, to abuses by the saltpetre men, to packed juries. As he spoke, his hands circled, pointed, indicating balance and affirmation. Occasionally he emphasised issues by counting on his fingers. His voice flowed, now high, now low. His shoulders hunched then straightened. Will looked at the audience: grim-faced, turned-down mouths, creased brows, some nodding or sitting with folded arms, chewing tobacco, yawning, coughing, stroking their beards. He counted four asleep.

Candles were called for and lit. A few MPs, bored or outraged, left.

Pym ended with demands for remedial measures, much rehearsed by the committee. "First, Catholics must be kept in such condition that they cannot hurt us. Second, that both Sheriff and Justices be sworn to the due execution of the Petition of Right and other laws. Third, that in future there be only Counsellors, Ambassadors and other Ministers as Parliament may have cause to confide in."

In these ways "His Majesty would see his people united in ways of duty to him, and happiness, wealth, peace and safety derived to his own country."

Pym sat down wearily, spent, Will thought. There were loud cheers and equally loud cries of disapproval. Will knew the traditional deferential arguments their opponents would put forth: the Commons did not have the power to put forward a Remonstrance without the concurrence of the Lords; because the Remonstrance touched the honour of the King it ought not to be circulated among the people. But that world was passing, was being replaced.

The Speaker called for more candles as he could not see who stood up and wished to speak. There were cries for adjournment, the House was agitated, but Denzil Holles, one of the committee, ploughed on, defiant. "MPs are elected and this empowers us to make a Remonstrance. We have a duty to tell the King if he is misled. It is against Nature not to have liberty to answer a calumny; our right is unquestionable."

At close to two o'clock in the morning, answering weary MPs' pleas, Speaker Lenthall closed the debate. Ingilby had long gone. The question was put, whether this Remonstrance should pass. He called for a vote by a show of hands. Arms shot up and waved, determined to be seen. There was a great affirmative and just as great a negative. The numbers were so close he could not declare a result.

"You know the protocol."

So then the Yeas filed out into the ante-chamber, tight packed through the narrow doorway. Flickering glances registered who left and who stayed. Will lingered, wanting to estimate how many Noes remained in their seats. There were many more than he had hoped. Will joined the Yeas. Tension was high in the crowded ante-chamber. Have we enough? There were muttered doubts as the tellers counted them. How much convincing did people need? Why could they not see? The tellers left with their totals. It was an agonising wait, everyone subdued, their excitement quenched. It must be close – tallies checked and re-checked. Then at last the Speaker called the Yeas back in.

The Noes glared at them as they returned, but fatigue and tension had silenced them all. Will sat down, his heart thumping. This had been the biggest ever challenge to the King.

The Speaker stood up, his face half lit by candlelight. He cleared his throat.

"For the Remonstrance 159, against 148. The Yeas have it. Resolved, upon the question, that this Remonstrance shall pass. This Remonstrance shall pass."

Will leapt to his feet and cheered, arms thrust out. Shouting and hullabaloo. Defiance, challenge.

Then John Hampden stood up, gestured for silence which didn't come and shouted, "I move an order for immediate printing."

Will knew this was a prearranged move, agreed by Pym and the committee. The public throughout the country must know the outcome, must be able to read the comprehensive enormity of the grievances.

Bedlam.

"It is an appeal to the people!"

Sir Edward Dering from Kent stood. MPs were still on their feet but the tumult quietened a little. Will strained to hear him.

"I am amazed at this descension from Parliament to people. I neither look for a cure for our complaints from the common people nor do I desire to be cured by them."

Cheers from the Noes. Howls of derision from the Yeas. But it was now three o'clock in the morning and tempers were frayed. Threats were bawled, hats waved, swords unsheathed in the ill-lit chamber. The Speaker proposed the issue of printing be deferred to another day, and the members, exhausted and maybe brought to their senses by the nearness of an unseemly and wounding riot, agreed.

As they filed out into a blustery darkness to collect their horses from waiting ostlers, one member said to Will: "I felt for a time it was like sitting in the valley of the shadow of death in there, that we were going to sheath our swords in each other's bowels."

Will nodded. It was true. Then another took hold of his left arm. Will peered at his face. It was Oliver Cromwell, that melancholy, ill-clad MP from the Fen Country. Cromwell said in muffled tones: "That was a close call. If the Remonstrance had been rejected I would have sold everything I owned, including my property, and gone to the Americas and never seen England again. And I was not the only one to think so. The Antichrist is still among us. Now we wait for the King's response. But be of good cheer."

And he walked off.

As Will rode home through the dark, stinking city, he tried to calm his racing mind. What was it all about? Liberty of conscience and worship, yes. But civil government, too: the right not to be taxed without consent, the right to petition, the right to choose representatives, the right of those representatives to freedom of debate, the right to the pure administration of justice, the right to individual freedom under protection of the law. That was what we were fighting for. That was what John Pym stood for.

Will knew he was on the right side, and on the side of right. They had taken a great step forwards. His idealism filled him with pride. He smiled to himself as he realised he cared not a fart for the King, who would now be mightily provoked. The odds were, the hope was, that in his arrogance he would commit a great folly and weaken himself still further.

Which was the opposite of what Jane and her father would want.

21.

Meeting

1642

One soft late August evening, as Alice was tidying the kitchen, James returned from the store later than usual. As she served his food Alice noticed he never looked straight at her. During the meal he spoke only in monosyllables. Afterwards he sat and stared out of the window. Finally, without a word, he went outside, leaving the door ajar behind him. Alice continued her chores, but something had surely happened.

She went to the door and saw him at the bottom of the yard, leaning on the fence, staring out across the fields. It was a warm, muggy night and the light from a low full moon bathed everything in a ghostly shimmer. She could hear cows munching.

She walked to him and stood just behind him.

"Penny for them?" she asked.

He was startled, hadn't heard her come. He turned to her and she saw a frown, then he looked away.

"Busy day," he muttered. She could barely hear him.

"Problems?"

No answer.

"A bad-tempered customer? Stock not arrived? Come on, James, what's the matter?" And she linked her arm in his. But he did not lean into her as he usually did; she felt him flinch. "There's something you're not telling me," she persisted.

He was still looking away, his face in shadow, moonlight on his back.

"A woman came into the store today," he said quietly. "I was in the back, shifting sacks of maize and beans. I heard a cough."

He stopped. He's taking cover in the darkness, thought Alice.

"And?" she said.

"It's a woman I used to know." His voice was strained, a dry rustle, almost a whisper. "Back in England."

A pause. A distant dog barked.

"In Walkden?"

"Yes," he said. "It was a shock. It's knocked me off balance."

There was more to come, and she knew what it was. But she waited; it was for him to tell her without another prompt. And why did it mean so much to him?

He extricated himself from her arm and faced her, one side of his face moonlit.

"It's Ellen," he said.

Of course it was.

"The woman I was engaged to." His voice was strangely formal.

"Yes, I remember you telling me."

"I didn't recognise her at first. Then when I came to the counter she whispered *James Fenton*. And then I suddenly knew her."

He turned back into the protecting darkness.

"That must have been a shock," she said.

"I was back straightaway in that previous life I'd completely forgotten."

"So of course it unsettled you. It's dangerous, too, having someone who knows who you really are."

Somewhere an owl hooted.

"She would never give me away. I am sure of that."

Careful now. "And you were in love with her. It must have brought it all back."

And that was the substance of it. Had the feelings returned? If Will turned up while she was working in the store, how would she feel? Suddenly she saw his face, clear as a painting. And she felt a surge of affection well up, unstoppable. Had that happened to James?

"It's understandable, James, you were going to marry her."

She wanted to stretch out an arm, reach out for him, bring him back. She felt hesitant. There was an uncertainty, a wavering in him she had not seen before.

Then he turned back into the moonlight, the moonlight on a smile. "It was just the shock. I reeled a bit, I must admit. I'm sorry."

He put his arms around her and kissed her on the mouth. She felt herself respond. He lifted his head away and she rested her head on his chest.

"It was twenty years ago," said James.

But she heard a wistfulness.

They strolled back home across the moonlit yard, heard the horses restless in the stable, sheep bleating in the fields.

"I think you'd like her," said James on the threshold.

"Well, we have something in common."

"What's that?" he asked in some surprise.

"We both fell in love with you."

He laughed.

Alice wanted to know more about Ellen. It might not be a simple matter.

Over the next two weeks James seemed to return almost to normal, although occasionally she thought she saw him dreaming.

Ellen came into the store three times while Alice was working there. She bought sugar and herbs and enquired about garments; there were brief words about the weather. But there was an awkwardness: Ellen seemed reticent, almost shy. Presumably she did not know whether James had spoken about her to Alice. Alice did like her: her common sense, a gentleness, laugh lines at her eyes, her knowledge of medicines and plants.

Alice decided this was a ridiculous situation and, without consulting James, asked Ellen round to her house one warm September afternoon. They sat out in the garden and drank cider.

"We are two sensible women," began Alice. And she explained what she knew. Ellen seemed relieved. It made things more straightforward. And Ellen understood she would put James in grave danger if his real name became known.

Ellen told her story: when James left (he had told her about the murder) she looked after her ill parents. When they died she married but her husband was a brute of a man who beat and abused her. Thank goodness they had no children. So she left him but she was destitute. She had no reason to stay in England. A family she had helped to care for were emigrating to Boston and offered to indenture her; after seven years she would be free. There was a rising fear of Civil War; she wanted to make a new start. She had assumed James would be married. But somewhere deep within her there was still a hope: that he might be unattached or widowed. She had landed three years ago but had found no trace of him there. She stopped looking out for him and wanted to get away. In her disappointment, she was glad her family decided to move away from Boston to a new place: which turned out to be land three miles beyond Plymouth Plantation. Seeing James had been as much of a shock to her as it had been to him. She understood now why James had changed his name.

"I am happy in my position with my family, and in four years I will be a free person."

"And James?" asked Alice.

"I can see he is still a good man. And you are both happy, that is clear. But I have had my fill of men. It was all a long time ago and I am not the young woman I was. The past is the past. Life has moved on."

"I would like us to be friends," said Alice, emboldened by Ellen's plain speaking.

It was Ellen who took Alice's hand. "I would like that," she said.

Their friendship grew, helped by a common interest in plants.

Alice watched in admiration as Ellen made a life for herself; she became the subject of many conversations overheard in the store. From her mother and from looking after her parents, she had learned much about treating ailments. She knew much about English medicinal herbs and had soon established a herb garden on her family's land. She had a green thumb, as they said. From these herbs and from others she bought and collected, she made salves, teas, ointments and poultices. Her pestle and mortar were her most valued implements and she would crush plantain, heal-all, yarrow, comfrey and adder's tongue and many more. Ellen told Alice she believed strongly that plants were put on earth to help human health. The sun and moon and stars infused them with healing essences and the soil nurtured them. Plants and humans were part of the same world.

When Indian women came by she bought from them wild strawberries, cranberries and blueberries which they gathered from nearby bogs and woodland. From one old Indian woman she often bought bark, roots and leaves and learned to value their healing effects. But Alice still wanted nothing to do with Indian medicines.

She would not join Ellen when Ellen went out into the woods to dig up the bright yellow roots of yellow puccoon to make a tea out of it for eye washes and mouth washes; or when she dug up the roots of the skunk cabbage with its terrible stench to make a paste which cured skin problems.

Ellen had begun by just treating members of her family but then neighbours sought help and recipes. She was called for more often than the English doctor. Her fame spread to surrounding settlements and farms and soon she and her mistress were selling herbal remedies in the market and at stores like James's. James was deepening his botanic studies of local plants, with Alice now interested, and they and Ellen would often discuss matters when she came by the store. Respect for each other in their new lives grew and each was warmed by it.

Ellen also admired Alice as, with one or two other brave women friends, Alice began openly to challenge sermons and magistrates, refusing to accept that women should remain quiet on these topics except at home in conversation with their husbands.

Alice congratulated Ellen when, after all her successes and growing reputation as a folk healer, she was made assistant to the local midwife. The only dissenting voice was that of Samuel Wilton. Soon after Ellen's arrival, Samuel's wife had bought herbs from Ellen to help treat their son. But his illness had grown worse and he had only just survived. Samuel blamed his wife for buying from a lowly indentured servant and blamed Ellen because her herbs had failed. His was a loud voice that decried Indian healing methods as born of savages and superstition.

Even Alice disagreed with that. Wilton was a dangerous man. What devious scheme lay behind this?

22.

BIRTH, EXPULSION AND RESTITUTION

1642

"*We, your most humble and obedient subjects, do with all faithfulness and humility, beseech your majesty...*"

Those were the opening words of the Petition which would accompany the Remonstrance to the King. Sitting on the committee that had agreed them, and looking round the table, Will had seen the knowing half-smiles. The honeyed words, believed by no one, were an obligatory part of the great game. Humility was scarce on both sides, and their 'disobedience' blatant. The Petition demanded ('beseeched' was the actual word) that the King strip Bishops of their vote in Parliament, banish Papist practices introduced into the church, purge his advisors. Not much to ask!

On Wednesday 1ˢᵗ December 1641, squalls flung hail at Will's windows as he gazed out, imagining cloaked riders, cursing their luck, heads bent, galloping the dozen miles to Hampton Court Palace to deliver the Petition and Remonstrance. Their emissary had been a canny choice: Sir John Hopton, MP for Wells, had gained approval from the Parliamentarians for speaking out against the King's favourite, Strafford, in the debate about his impeachment, but he was also still a confidante of the King. A group of twelve MPs had been sent, carefully selected to contain some who would be less unwelcome to the King. John Pym was not among them, deciding his presence too provocative.

Next day, Will was in the House when Sir John Hopton reported on the meeting.

The King had said that he supposed he was not expected to answer now to such a long Petition. "I will give an answer with as much speed as the weightiness of the business will permit," he said. He gave them his hand to kiss. As they left the palace, a message was given them, for immediate delivery to the House of Commons.

Sir John read the message: "That there might be no publishing of the Remonstrance till the House had received His Majesty's answer."

All through December they waited, but there was no news. Will and Jane were waiting for other news: Jane was swollen with child, her baby due at any time. She wanted him for Christmas: it would be a good omen. Will had a fleeting thought of Edmund, whom he'd never seen, but that was a lifetime ago.

Banished from his home by midwives and Jane's mother, Will was in a committee room at Westminster, celebrating the printing of the Remonstrance on 28th December, when a messenger called him home. Sitting up in their bed was his wife, tired but looking triumphant, and at her breast was his son Robert. Will gently kissed Jane on her lips and took a closer look at his child. He had never before seen a newly-born baby, and he was taken aback: a wizened red face, skin flaky, brow furrowed. An old man's face. And yet Robert was a miracle, one he and Jane had created together. Though he truly rejoiced, he also felt superfluous: women had the wisdom here.

So he was torn less than he thought he would be between his child and the momentous events happening outside his home in the city.

Thousands of copies of the Remonstrance were sold and distributed throughout the kingdom. There was rejoicing now the people knew their grievances were being heard at the highest level, thanks to the Parliamentarians. But with it went an increase in discontent.

For days London was filled with rumours: the King had moved to Windsor, the King had purged the Privy Council of all Parliamentary-friendly politicians, there was a new Royalist-friendly lieutenant in charge of the Tower of London. The city was seething, on the edge of insurrection.

How long would this charade go on?

Here Will was, at eleven o'clock on Monday morning, 3rd of January, in St Katharine Cree church again, cold, impatient and fretting to get to the House of Commons. Something singular was in the wind. He needed to be there.

The Book of Common Prayer was open in the minister's hands, a black three-cornered hat, trimmed with red, on his bent head, the wide sleeves of his vestment threaded with gold.

Will imagined his father staring down from his elect place in Heaven at the baptism of his grandson: the sacrament given to the child of a non-believer, the papist rituals, the painted church, the high altar and florid rose window. And Will rejoiced with the satisfaction of causing his father deep offence: a benefit, after all, in the belief of life after death. A shame he didn't share it.

The drone of the minister's recited prayer: *"We call upon thee for this infant, that he, coming to thy holy Baptism may receive remission of his sins by spiritual redemption…"*

His son, Robert, barely a week old, had already sinned? Did Jane really believe in Original Sin? They had not discussed the issue. The only outcome would be loud argument followed by long silences, and even more disfavour with his father-in-law when Jane reported back to him. Religion and politics were out of bounds in his household. Since they were both topics that fired him up, quenching them left him staring at a cold hearth.

"… and Jesus said unto them, Suffer the little children to come unto me and forbid them not, for of such is the Kingdom of God…"

The group round the font, heads bent in prayer, was small: just Will and Jane, her parents and two godparents. One was Jane's sister Ann, the other was John Boon. Will knew John was suffering the heresy of this high church ceremony only out of loyalty to him. Will was grateful. He had first asked Ingilby, partly to annoy his in-laws, partly out of irreverence for the whole ritual.

Wisely, Francis had demurred. "A happy hedonist like me? Hardly the right man to, what is it? *Mortify all our evil and corrupt affections and bring him up to lead a godly and Christian life.* But thanks for the offer."

The prayers stopped and the minister took Robert, swaddled in the Nowell family's baptismal gown, from Ann's arms.

The baby was sleeping, his face already neater: his delicate eyelids closed, lips twitching a little, pale down on his roughened scalp, nose like a button. Perfectly formed, thought Will.

"Name this child."

John and Ann together said, "Robert Nowell Nailor."

Gently the minister cradled the baby, dipped his finger in the water of the font and made the sign of the cross on the baby's forehead. Three times. Even Will knew that was a papist practice. His father would now be choking with venom. Will remembered the last font he had seen: vomiting and pissing into it, blind drunk, screaming into the dark church, "Are you watching, Father dear?"

And now, still, his father's presence loomed.

The minister: "I baptise thee in the Name of the Father and of the Son and of the Holy Ghost. Amen."

Robert was now crying, Jane receiving him into her arms, rocking him. For her, all was now well in her world, the child received into "the congregation of Christ's flock".

Then came the minister's endless advice and instructions to the godparents, John Boon closing his ears to words that offended him, determined to do his duty for Will.

And then, at last, the service was over. Eager to leave, Will kissed his son's newly sanctified forehead and made his farewells as brief as decorum would allow. He kissed his wife's proffered cheek before she returned her attention to her baby. But his father-in-law was not so easily pacified.

"I presume," he growled, "that you were one of those jumped-up MPs who voted to publish that Remonstrance thing."

"I was."

"You have stirred up the common people. Now they march in the streets, waving it and demanding their entitlements."

The man's neck and jowls were reddening but Will wanted away.

"It is a list of justified grievances."

"It is an ultimatum, a rebellion against the King who is anointed by God. He has had to leave London. Take care, young man, that you do not turn the world upside down and let anarchy loose."

He was wagging his finger now.

"I have no time now," said Will.

"Back to that Parliament of yours for more mischief? Think of your son – my grandson – and the broken world you are in danger of making for him."

He turned back abruptly to the family group. Will's eyes blazed with anger at his father-in-law's back. Then, with an exasperated splutter, Will strode away, his boots clacking on the stone floor.

The Commons was strangely muted that afternoon, when Will hurried in, the windows still patterned with frost. Something dramatic was expected but no one knew what. Nothing had been heard from the King. Both parties, Royalist and Parliamentarian, were waiting. A half-hearted debate was droning on about dissolving the College of the Capuchins at Somerset House when a herald rushed in from the House of Lords. All eyes turned to him.

Standing by the Speaker's Chair and taking a deep breath, he announced: "The Attorney General has formally charged five MPs with impeachment."

Gasps and cries of outrage, a few grunts of approval. This then was the King's response.

"Who are the five?"

"John Pym, John Hampden, Denzil Holles, Sir Arthur Haselrig and William Strode." As he named them he looked at each of them on the half-empty benches. He continued: "These five must surrender themselves to answer the charges against them."

The debate about the Capuchins was over. Now small groups of MPs, casting looks at the five, muttered to each other, anxious or pleased.

That afternoon, articles were published charging them and Viscount Mandeville from the House of Lords with subverting the fundamental laws of the realm: in a plainer word, Treason. Then messages came in from their distraught wives that their homes had been forcibly searched and papers taken away.

Will and others urged the five to flee immediately to a safe house in the Puritan area, but Pym insisted: "I think that is wise, but we must be back here in this House when we know the King is on his way. Our spies will inform us. Then there will be undeniable evidence that he is the violator of Parliament's independence."

They hid overnight in the Puritan stronghold of Coleman Street in the City. Will had offered his house, much to his wife's disapproval, but as a member of the committee of twenty-four he was deemed too likely to be raided.

Some prayed, some didn't, during the long night, but all were back in the Commons by noon on the 4th of January. The House was packed. The five sat on the front row. Will looked across at the Royalist sympathisers, those who had voted No six weeks ago. Some were smiling. A spectacle was in the offing, and they were like a ghoulish crowd waiting for an execution. He saw Ingilby sitting expressionless, not his usual half-smile at the antics of men. Ingilby understood the implications.

At three o'clock a Puritan MP hurried through the doors and whispered in John Pym's ear.

Pym nodded. "It is time, gentlemen. Time to leave. We have word that the King with 300 men-at-arms has left Whitehall."

Lady Carlisle, their spy at court, had done her work, God bless her.

Pym stood and turned to his supporters and doffed his black hat. "We are making history," he declared, "for our children's children."

Will cheered with the rest: he had a child now. The five, without hurrying, left the House through a back door to be taken down the Thames by barge, back to Coleman Street.

The House waited again. George Digby deliberately left the door of the Commons open so that, as King Charles and his nephew, Charles Prince Elector Palatine, entered the Commons, all had a clear view of Charles' soldiers standing there and the crowd already assembling. The MPs stood up and uncovered their heads. The Speaker stood up just in front of his Chair. King Charles doffed his feathered black hat as he walked the length of the House, bowing to members on either side. The MPs bowed back. Charles, his blue cloak wrapped over his arm and carrying a silver-headed cane, came up to the left side of the Speaker's chair, close to where Will was sitting.

"Mr Speaker," said the King, "I must for a time make bold with your Chair."

The Speaker stood aside. Will watched closely. The King sat in the Chair and looked around the assembled Commons. Chestnut hair down to his shoulders and curling on his forehead, a pearl earring in his left ear, a wide lace collar, the blue sash of the Order of the Garter with the medal of St George pinned to it, his dark crimson doublet, cuffs with lace edges, breeches tied above his knee with a bunch of cream ribbons, square-toed high-heeled boots. This was the King, by Divine Right. Rex is *lex*; the King is Law. But for how much longer?

Then, in the silence of the waiting House, the voice of Charles asked the Speaker if the five MPs were present.

The Speaker, William Lenthall, went down on one knee and answered: "May it please Your Majesty, I have neither eyes to see nor tongue to speak in this place but as the House is pleased to direct me, whose servant I am here. I humbly beg Your Majesty's pardon that I cannot give any other answer than this to what Your Majesty is pleased to demand of me."

Charles nodded with calm dignity and looked around.

"Gentlemen, I am sorry for this occasion of coming unto you. Yesterday I sent a Serjeant-at Arms upon a very important occasion, to apprehend some that by my command were accused of high treason. I did expect obedience. And I must declare unto you here, that no King ever was in England that shall be more careful of your privileges, to maintain them to the uttermost of his power, than I shall be. Yet you must know that in cases of treason, no person has a privilege. And therefore I am come to know if any of these persons that were accused are here."

He paused and smiled. A forced smile. The whole House was still silent.

"Well, I see all the birds are flown."

He stood. As he walked out, a few voices cried "Privilege! Privilege!" and this swelled to a roar as he left. As his coach crossed the courtyard it was surrounded by a hostile crowd which repeated the cry: "Privilege! Privilege!"

As their opponents left the House, surly-faced and shoulders defiant, Will and his colleagues cheered and threw their arms round each other's shoulders. Shouts:

"A despot!"

"A blundering despot!"

"That was nothing less than an armed assault on Parliament."

"A damned attack on privilege!"

Jokes, laughter, bravado. A few swords waved in the air. Ingilby just shook his head and left. Their friendship was a more careful one these days: they still skittled and bowled but their conversation skirted circumspectly around the big issues.

Will and a few other MPs hurried to the Bell Inn on nearby King Street. Over pots of ale and thick slices of brawn, among raucous laughter and serving wenches, they retold the event they had just witnessed. They fell to reminiscing over the revolution they were leading.

"Your first year in Parliament, Will. The Petition of Right: no taxation without the consent of Parliament."

"Bonfires were lit, church bells rang."

"And, best of all, my father-in-law was livid," added Will, laughing. *"What do you think you are unleashing? This agitation, this insurrection, is bad for business. We need certainty."*

Roars of laughter and more toasts.

"No imprisonment without cause shown. I remember," added Will. He had been swept along in the tide of insurrection against the King's arrogance and stupidity. Westminster had been a new world to him.

They raised a toast and clinked their mugs of ale.

"Archbishop Laud impeached and in the Tower," said another.

They cheered and drank to that as well.

"Strafford beheaded on Tower Hill?"

Another drink and cheer.

"The Star Chamber abolished."

That was worth a drink, too.

"And the High Commission."

How feared those courts had been, meeting in secret, above the common law, used to punish dissidents like Lilburne.

That deserved two drinks.

And now Will's brain began to blur.

"No more personal rule by the King," his lips and tongue managed to utter.

They all drank to it.

Will woke next morning with a heavy head and a light heart. Jane was polite but cool. They too were wary of certain conversation. As he rode to his warehouse, he sensed a feverish excitement and suspicion in the rowdy streets. Parliament had mobilised trained bands of local militia. It was if the city was already on a war standing.

Five days later the King and his Court retreated to Greenwich; the City was not safe for him. The day after that, the five accused MPs came out of hiding. Eight companies of the Trained Bands with eight cannon and a mounted guard were sent to watch over MPs and peers from the Grocers' Hall to Westminster. On the Thames, sea captains, masters of ships, mariners, with small barges and large boats sufficiently manned and armed with cannon and muskets and half-pikes – 2,000 men – were engaged to guard the Parliament by water. Standing on a festive Thames barge, the five MPs were cheered by a delirious crowd. Escorted by Will and others, they returned in triumph to Westminster and took their seats in the House.

The day after that, 12th January, the King retreated even further, to Windsor. Parliament issued instructions to the Governor of Hull, Sir John Hotham, not to deliver the city or its store of arms and ammunition to the King without Parliament's permission. Portsmouth also was to hold out against any demands of the King. Parliament transferred from the King to itself the right to commandeer men and munitions.

All was to play for.

23.
SCAPEGOAT
1644

The second winter after Ellen and her family arrived was a desperately cold and wet one. A fever spread through the area and children especially were not as well-nourished as they needed to be to fight it off. The fever turned into a pestilence of influenza and Ellen was called for from everywhere. Other illnesses developed as people's constitutions weakened with disease, cold and malnourishment. Family members all around Ellen's home died but none of her own family. Although Alice shared her own herbs, she watched Ellen's supplies of herbs and medicine run out. She saw Ellen grey with exhaustion. Ellen had to rely more and more on Indian cures. In the depth of winter she went out into the wood to cut and gather the roots of young hemlock saplings, cutting them into pieces and boiling them in beer to make a concoction to bring down fevers. She used her last supplies of Indian sage and wild geraniums for other fever cures. But still people died and her own family remained healthy.

Alice could not avoid seeing people begin to look at Ellen suspiciously. Alice was in church when Reverend Wareham chastised the congregation from his pulpit.

"It is the sinfulness and wickedness of those who have not obeyed the Lord at all times that has invited in this menace."

She looked across at Ellen and noticed many others doing so. Ellen bowed her head. They were already accusing her.

Then two of the Reverend's own children caught the fever and died.

Ellen treated several other children but her herbal supplies were now so few that she could make only weak concoctions. She could make the children more peaceful but she could not save them.

On a day when James was collecting supplies from Boston, Alice was in the store. It was a cold, rainy, wind-blown day and few people were about. The door opened and Ellen staggered in. Her cloak and boots were wet. Alice got up from her accounts.

"You're cold; you need some of our brandy."

"For once I won't say no."

"What brings you here on a day like this? You have nothing left to sell, have you?"

Alice poured her some brandy into a mug and Ellen took a sip.

"It burns my throat," she said.

"That's what it's meant to do. It will warm your breast in a moment."

Alice drank some, too.

"I am frightened, Alice. You will have heard even more than I have. They are calling me a witch, aren't they?"

"Some are, yes. I am afraid so."

"And it is not just the simple folk. All I have tried to do is help people. I have cured many but not all."

"There have been many deaths; some you have treated with your herbs but others have been treated only by the doctor," said Alice.

"But people do not see that."

"Superstition is widespread and people revert to old beliefs when they are helpless."

Ellen broke down and wept.

Alice hurried over to close the shutter over the door and locked it.

She put her arms around Ellen, who relaxed into her, leaning into her, crying softly.

"I am scared to death," Ellen sobbed, "that they will come for me. None of my family are ill and they think it proof I am in league with the Devil. One little girl called me a dark angel, and a dying boy said he saw the face of the Devil hovering beside me."

Alice let her cry herself out, stroking her hair, wet with the rain.

"You are a good woman, Ellen."

Five days later Alice sent James to bring Ellen. Giles was sick with an infection from an axe wound, an accident when he was chopping logs.

Alice's face was desperate when Ellen hurried in.

"All I have left is Indian remedies, Alice, which I made some time ago with the old Indian woman, and something her son brought me two days ago."

"Thank goodness you have come, Ellen. You are my last hope. Giles will die unless something else is tried. I did all I could and the doctor has nothing else to suggest."

"I thought you had turned away from Indian remedies."

"I am desperate. It is the last chance."

She held Ellen's hand in both of hers, her grip hot and tight.

"Let me see," said Ellen. Giles made no sound but held his breath and body taut as she carefully unwrapped the bandages on his thigh. The cut was red and swollen and filled with pus. As gently as she could, she cleaned the wound. Then she dressed it with pine turpentine and the crushed inner bark of the white pine. It was what the Indian had brought. Then she gave Giles an infusion that would help him sleep.

"It is all I have, Alice, but I have faith in it."

The three of them watched Giles slowly relax, his eyelids droop and he fell asleep. Alice at last felt some peace.

Quietly, Alice said: "I have heard the rumours, Ellen. But there is no such thing as the Devil. And I know the many you have cured."

227

"Alice, I can promise you nothing. I have done my best for your son. But I may have come too late. It will be two days before we know."

She gathered together her things.

Alice insisted that James take her but Ellen refused.

"I will walk home, James. Stay with your wife and son."

Next day another story was all over the settlement. Samuel Wilton had been heard outside the courthouse, arguing that Ellen was no better than the Devil's spit. He talked about how she had almost killed his own son; that children she had treated had died of this pestilence, even the child of one of her neighbours who had called out that she saw Ellen was a dark angel; another had seen the Devil's face in her. She was in league with Indians as well as the Devil. Two boys had reported they saw her meet the Dark Lord in the woods not four days ago. Though surrounded by illness and death, none of her own family had ailed.

"It was a bewitchment," it was reported he had declaimed. "She must be watched to see if she shows any signs of cavorting with Satan."

He would bring, he said, the witch-finders' manual his family had recently sent out from England and then they would prove it for sure.

All these things James heard – in whispered conversations in his store, in passing comments on the street, in corners of the inn – he reported to Alice as she watched by Giles' bed. She was terrified by how quickly suspicion could flame up, at the one-sidedness of the accounts, at how old superstitions could be revived. People Ellen had cured were afraid to speak up for her. And Alice also knew that Wilton was manipulating this. This was the scheming she had feared. Wilton was ambitious to be Chief Magistrate: he was wealthy but wanted more direct power. If he could prove himself a hero of the settlement by destroying the Devil's messenger, his popularity would soar.

Maybe Wilton did genuinely believe Ellen might be a witch but he was ruthless enough to send an innocent woman to her grisly death if it suited his purposes and calmed the people. His was a more popular message than that preached from the pulpits about the sinfulness of the people. In his version the people had a scapegoat for their losses.

Two days later, in mid-morning, Alice flung open the store door and rushed in, shouting, "He is healing, James! The pain has gone and the fever with it. He is eating and laughing."

She flung her arms round him and held him tight. Her eyes were laughing and he smelt the scent of her hair in his face. She kissed him full on the mouth.

"He is well, he will live."

She had not touched him like this for two years.

"Ellen saved him. There is no doubt."

She was happy with him, unconstrained.

Alice demanded James take her to thank Ellen.

That evening, a few hundred yards away from Ellen's home, James pulled up the horse and cart. Ahead of them, in front of the house, they could hear a hubbub of yells and neighing horses. Wilton on his horse was shouting orders; other gentlemen and three Deacons were also on horseback. And around them a mob of people armed with muskets, swords and scythes. James and Alice heard a chant start: "The witch, the witch, find us the Devil's witch-wife!"

They heard the Constable hammer on the door and then go in with three burly men. Five minutes later they were dragging Ellen out of the house. She was in chains. The crowd cheered. The Constable declaimed so all could hear: "You are under arrest for complaints of consorting with Satan. You are charged with plotting and carrying out the murders of your fellow townspeople."

Tears were streaming down Ellen's face but she did not struggle. James and Alice jumped down from the cart and ran up.

"She is innocent!" James shouted at the Constable. "Innocent. If the Devil is at work it is here and now."

Alice looked at the faces of the people she knew, faces transformed now by fear and hate and revenge. Grimaces, scowls, raised fists.

"Be strong, Ellen!" shouted Alice. "We will help you."

Gripping her by the arm, the Constable marched Ellen down the path through the settlement. Many of the crowd followed, hurling insults at her. But at some of the houses they passed, people shook their heads in disbelief. Their children Ellen had cured.

She was placed in the prison shed of Samuel Wilton, a place where Alice knew he had kept Indian women and children after the Pequot war before he had sold them off as slaves to the southern colonies. It was cold and filthy.

The Constable ordered that no one was allowed to talk to her and placed a man on guard. Tomorrow, proceedings would start. Later, James and Alice brought food for Ellen but it was forbidden. There was nothing they could do.

24.

TENSIONS

1642-45

25 AUGUST 1642

In his warehouse office, Will stood by the open window: a humid day and a strong stink of river. In his hand was the new contract with the Levant Company.

The door was flung open: Francis Ingilby. He strolled in, moved some papers, sat on the corner of Will's desk and announced, "You have your wish. It was inevitable."

"What are you talking about, Francis?"

"So, I'm better informed than you." He dabbed his face with a handkerchief. "How stifling it is in here, and it smells like a sewer."

Will turned from the window.

"What has happened?" Impatient now with Francis's games.

"War has happened. The King has raised his standard in Nottingham."

Will was stunned. Francis covered his nose with his handkerchief.

"I thought you'd cheer."

But Will was not exhilarated. "It had to be," he said. "Because the King is a stubborn fool. But no one in their right mind wants war." A clang of iron on stone from the quayside. "It's a sad day."

"It will divide the country," said Francis.

"But Parliament must win. Will win. We fight for what is right."

"Right seldom has the bullets and the swords. We shall see." He stood up. "I must go, I have a wealthy earl to counsel about his land."

The door closed and Will remained standing in the middle of the room. Civil war, the worst of wars: neighbours, families, friends, all at each other's throats. His own family even more deeply divided.

Jane would say nothing but her looks and coolness would show she held him personally responsible, him and his radical colleagues.

30 SEPTEMBER 1643

Jane's parents came for midday dinner, a rich spread with roast pike, crayfish in jelly, capons, tasty sauces, marchpane and cheeses, Portuguese red wine and coffee.

The fire was crackling, Robert toddling and falling, newly-born Susannah sound asleep in her cradle, conversation about the children and domestic concerns.

And then her father, red-faced with wine, as he cut himself a chunk of cheese: "You've backed the wrong side, Will."

He was bright-eyed, genial, keen to pick a fight. His wife raised her eyebrows but said nothing. Jane turned away. Will, too, was reluctant to spoil the peace.

"A bad time for you Roundheads," persisted Richard Nowell. "Crushed in battles near Bath and in Wiltshire, our good Prince Rupert capturing Bristol. What a general he is!"

But Will would not be baited. After all, it was true. Things were going badly.

"And Newbury last week," goaded his father-in-law. "Another failure for you."

And now Will had to respond.

"I don't think so, sir. Your Royalists retreated. Our army returned safely to London."

"But not a defeat for us," came the counter. "A wise decision

232

to withdraw because of a lack of gunpowder, I'm told."

"Shall we call Newbury evens, then?" said a conciliatory Will, aware that Jane approved his avoidance of argument.

"If you wish." But said with the magnanimity of the victor, emptying another glass of Will's fine wine. "The tide is with us. Better think again, Will, before it is too late."

"But the tide turns."

12 DECEMBER 1643

Candles flickered from their iron brackets low down on the tall stone pillars, the high arched roof in shadow. A pale light from the transept window.

Will's ungloved hands were icy, but Westminster Abbey was crowded with members of the Commons and the Lords. Warm breath hung over them in the cold air like mist. The funeral service was over and the body of John Pym was being interred in the north ambulatory, by the chapel of Edward the Confessor.

A murmur of hushed voices, the pad of feet on stone, rustle of clothes. Will, wrapped in gloom, not wanting to converse. John Pym had died a painful death from cancer of the bowel.

It was a bad end to a bad year.

But many of both Commons and Lords, friend and foe, recognised Pym's qualities. Will believed Pym, almost single-handedly, had held Parliament together through titanic tussles on the most fundamental themes. He had been the driving force, a unifying force, and Will feared that things might now disintegrate.

Even Ingilby, no friend of Pym, had said, "A supreme lawyer, a master tactician."

"And brave," added Will. "He risked his life for his cause."

For many weeks afterwards, the most palpable aspect of the Commons for Will was the absence of John Pym, the space he left.

Will was in bed at home with a fever when Thomas Harrison flung open his bedroom door and, cloaked in a smell of leather, horse and sweat, rushed over to grab Will's hot hand.

"The Lord is with us, Will. Praise the Lord!"

"Keep your distance, Thomas. We need a fighting man like you to be fit, not fevered like me."

Harrison retreated to a chair. "It's fighting that keeps me fit, and the Lord's grace."

And so Harrison told the story of the great Parliamentary victory at Marston Moor, near York.

"You know the man John Lilburne?"

"Yes, I do. I watched him being whipped in the streets some years ago. A real champion of free speech and prepared to suffer for his principles."

"Well, he's a Lieutenant-Colonel of the Dragoons now. Yelling like a dervish, he led a running march and cleared a ditch of musketeers, and that gave Cromwell his opportunity. His Ironsides forced the Cavaliers back, including Prince Rupert's finest men. It was hand-to-hand sword point, vicious. By nine o'clock we'd cleared the field of Cavaliers, recovered our ordnance and carriages, captured their ordnance and ammunition, and chased them towards York." His voice rose in excitement.

"I feel better already," said Will. "And your part?"

Harrison grinned and threw his arms out. "Let's just say there was a three-mile trail of dead Cavalier bodies: 4,500 dead and 1,500 prisoners."

Will felt part ashamed and part relieved he had not been there. Was this a real turning point in the war?

"And now I'll leave you to your sweaty bed and shit-smelling room. But, Will, I tell you: that Cromwell is something of a man."

A week later Will and Ingilby met in a corridor outside the Commons. MPs were milling about.

"Is that the man you mean?" asked Ingilby, a look of distaste on his face.

"Aye. MP for Cambridge. Not much to look at, is he?"

"Well, that explains his provincial clothes."

Cromwell wore a plain cloth suit with a speck or two of blood on his collar. A bulbous nose and warts on his chin.

"He makes a powerful speech," said Will. "I remember his first speech in Parliament argued for the liberation of John Lilburne, who'd been imprisoned by the Star Chamber. Four days later, Lilburne was freed."

"And Lieutenant General in the Army now, I believe."

"Yes, leading the cavalry of the Eastern Association."

"The famous Ironsides, eh!" Ingilby scoffed.

Will's eyes blazed with sudden anger.

"Always the mocking observer, Francis. You never commit because you live by no values."

He turned away and entered the Chamber. Cromwell had begun to give his report on the battle of Marston Moor. Will listened; it was not a voice to inspire, thin and sharp and monotonous – but with a driving intensity.

Cromwell ended: "It had all the evidences of an absolute victory obtained by the Lord's blessing upon the godly party principally. Whenever we charged we routed the enemy. God made them as stubble to our swords."

Not God but man, thought Will, uplifted and emboldened. This man was a leader.

SEPTEMBER 1644

"Pat-a-cake, pat-a-cake, baker's man,
Bake me a cake as fast as you can,
Pat it and prick it and mark it with B
And put it in the oven for baby and me."

Will was in the garden, kneeling, Robert standing opposite him. They were patting hands and knees as Will recited the rhyme, Robert grinning. Three-year-old Robert knew the words but wouldn't sing them: a kind of defiance Will loved.

A set of small skittles lay scattered on the gravel. Robert, his fingers stained with blackberry juice, had been throwing a ball to knock them down.

It was a mild, still September day, Susannah gurgling in her cradle, Jane discussing herbs with the gardener. A couple of hours of peace before the irascible Commons.

Will ruffled Robert's hair, grabbed him and swung him round, Robert laughing, legs outstretched.

Then the door into the garden opened: Jane's father.

"Ah, Richard, good day to you," said Will, putting down Robert, who ran to his grandfather who bent and kissed him.

"Not at the talking shop, eh? Some sense at last."

He shooed a reluctant Robert off to his mother.

"Take care, Will, that you don't end up on the wrong side. There will be reprisals, and you have a lot to lose."

Robert was peeking over the cradle at his sister.

"More defeats for you," continued Richard. "From Cornwall to Scotland, I hear. Cavalier victories. The omens are not good." He smiled.

Will dreaded Richard's frequent visits. Will and Jane had learned to circumscribe themselves, their conversations meeting only at compatible points. Wrangling was avoided. All this careful work was threatened by Richard's bluff and triumphant goading. He drove a wedge between them.

So Will held his tongue. But also, partly, because he feared his father-in-law was right. Was he putting his family in serious danger?

That was why he must be in Parliament this afternoon.

"Sorry, Richard, I must go."

Richard disappointed, raring for an argument as usual.

The door of the Painted Chamber was not quite closed, voices raised in argument. Will pushed it open: a dozen or so men standing – MPs, Cromwell, others. Heads turned towards him.

"Join us, Mr Nailor," said Cromwell. "You were on the committee that drew up the Remonstrance, weren't you?"

"Er, yes, I was." Will rather daunted by being addressed so directly by the Lieutenant General MP.

"So your opinion will be valued."

Will recognised two Army generals.

"But I'm not a military man."

"No matter. It is not military tactics we are debating."

Indeed they were not. It was the Earl of Manchester, Commander of the Eastern Association, who now pointed his finger at Cromwell. "You, sir, want to live to see never a nobleman left in England." The man's jowls and chins were quivering with fury.

Cromwell shook his head.

Then Ludlow stepped forward. Was he the Wiltshire Commander?

"The plain fact is," fumed Ludlow, "you nobility have no further quarrel with the King. You would make terms with him."

Nods and ayes around the room. Aggressive.

"And when the King is re-established," continued Ludlow, "he will not lack the means to revenge himself upon those who adventured to resist him in his illegal and arbitrary proceedings. And that is most of us here." He spread his arms to encompass the room. "We who are defending the rights and liberties of the nation."

More grunts of approval.

Then came another voice, quieter, from the window.

"Posterity will say that to deliver us from the yoke of the King we have subjugated ourselves to the yoke of the people. Is this the liberty for which we shed our blood?"

It was the Earl of Essex, Captain General of all the Parliamentary forces.

Shouts and anger and blustering.

How would Pym have handled this? thought Will. But Cromwell was now the main man in the Commons, his reputation built on his victories with his Ironsides.

Will knew the size of the problem Cromwell faced. Parliament was united no more. There was the Peace Party which wanted to negotiate with the King, and there were those who wanted to fight on and defeat him utterly. But beyond the arguments and the men of principle there were petty personal feuds, bickering, men looking after their own interests or seizing opportunities to enrich themselves.

"And you, Mr Nailor," said Cromwell when the noise abated, "you are not yet a fighting man but where do you stand?"

It was not a difficult question, but the high-born generals and the expectant Puritans were equally intimidating. Presbyterian MPs were now opposing the Army rank-and-file, heavily influenced by the Levellers, who wanted freedom of religion and equal rights for all men. All eyes were on him. This was his moment. He took a deep breath

"In my opinion, it is clear we must defeat the King. Rule by Divine Right is a nonsense. Parliament must be supreme."

There was a moment's silence, the Earls sniffed, and then there were cheers and hands clapping Will on the back.

Cromwell now confronted Manchester and Essex.

"We have lost too many battles. The latest battle at Newbury in October was ours for the winning. You were there, gentlemen, in command. I believe you were unwilling to prosecute unto a full victory because you want accommodation" – he spat the word out – "and terms which do not bring the King too low."

The Earls stared down the accusation, heads raised, supercilious with this fenland farmer.

Cromwell continued, his voice strident and grating, "The Army must be put to another method. The war must be prosecuted more vigorously, because the people can bear it no longer."

There was a finality that brooked no argument.

Will was emboldened now. "I fear the Presbyterian faction fundamentally wants the Army disbanded or sent out of the way to Ireland to fight the Catholics. I think they are more against their own Parliamentary Army than their real foe, the King."

"You speak like a true man," said Cromwell, putting his arm around Will's shoulders.

The Earls of Manchester and Essex moved towards the door. At the threshold, Manchester said to Cromwell, "Your officers are not men of estate but such as are common men, poor and of mean parentage. When I look upon your regiment of horse, I see what a swarm there is there of those you call godly, precious men. Some of them profess they have seen visions and had revelations."

He said it with contempt. Cromwell surged towards him but Will and others restrained him. The Earls were gone.

APRIL 1645

By God, this man wrote the truth! Will closed the pamphlet, put it on his desk, drank some more wine and stared out of his office window. Grey clouds drifting, but in his head a tumult: ideas, excitement, a need to do something.

How much he wanted a wife who could discuss these things. Alice! She would have loved it, inspired along with him. John Lilburne, the whipped man. He read again the title of his pamphlet: *England's Birth-right Justified*, and the opening words: *I, with my one poor Talent, have used my best endeavours to shew the maladies and remedies of this sick, swooning, bleeding, and dying Nation.*

Monopolies was the theme! Lilburne's first thrust had been against men like him, guilds such as the Merchant Adventurers, *a company of private men who have ingrossed into their hands the sole trade of all woollen commodities that are to be sent into the Netherlands.* Power and profit restricted to a few. Did it have to be that way? That was what Lilburne asked.

Will went to the door and shouted for John Boon. He wanted to share this and wanted some confirmation, some like-mindedness.

"What do you think of this, John?" he asked as soon as John appeared. "You know our government has vowed to extirpate popery and prelacy but you also know it has just made an Ordinance to continue the strict payment of tithes."

John nodded.

"I voted against, of course," said Will hurriedly. "But listen to this: *Take tithes away and we will uproot the papists, for the Clergy are such greedy dogs that they can never have enough. Priests, who form not more than a thousandth part of the population, take a tenth, even a seventh, part of the products of a man's labour, for which they have laboured with their hands or with the sweat of their brows.*"

"Your man Lilburne," said John. "Of course he's right. Did you expect me to say otherwise?"

"No, John, I didn't. I wanted you to steady me. And now I'm raring for an argument. If my father-in-law disapproves, then I'll know Lilburne is right and that I'm on the right side."

Will strode out, leaving John smiling, bemused, and hurried the half mile to Richard Nowell's shipyard and knocked at his office door.

"Come in." Richard Nowell's gruff voice, an order.

He looked up as Will went in. "This is unusual. What can I do for you?"

"Disagree with me."

Richard laughed. "How do you mean?"

Will pulled a chair up to the desk, held out the pamphlet and stabbed at it with his finger.

"Listen. *Just, equitable and reasonable taxation lays the burthen upon the strong shoulders of the rich, who onely are able to beare it, but spareth and freeth the weake shoulders of the poore.*"

"Balderdash and hogwash!"

"But why?"

"The more tax I pay the less profit I make. The less profit I make the fewer wages I can pay and men I can employ. And as for the poor, most of them are idle or stupid and have no initiative."

"That's what I wanted to hear. Thank you. If that's what you think, Lilburne must be right."

He stood up.

From the chair behind his desk, Richard said, "What a man my daughter has married. You were alright until you became an MP. You've got in with a gang of troublemakers. God help Jane and my grandchildren."

But Will had closed the door and was out on the street. He was like a man possessed, seeking signs. Ingilby was next. Will pushed his way through the narrow, crowded streets. Then stepped aside into a doorway. He watched the rush of people: were they all backsliders? Their faces were worn, tired and desperate. All were struggling to survive, all persuaded their reward lay in heaven. Few if any could read Lilburne. Even fewer do anything about it. This is how life was; they had their place, nothing would change.

Yet the workers' sons in his school learned as fast as Robert. Given the chance they were not thick. They were shrewd, too.

Richard was wrong. Society was wrong. There were fairer ways.

He elbowed his way into the stream of people and made for Ingilby's offices.

"Will," he said, "this is a pleasant surprise, an excuse to have a break from my legal obligations."

He pushed aside a scroll of documents.

"Ale?"

"No thank you. I just need to hear an answer to a question."

Ingilby raised his eyebrows. "Ask away, my friend."

Out came the pamphlet again, the finger jabbing again. Do you agree with this? *Parliamentary Ordinance and the Stationers' Company suppresse everything which hath any true Declaration of the just Rights and Liberties of the free-born people of this Nation and under pretence of searching for scandalous books call smiths and constables to help them break open and even riffle houses, chests, trunks, and drawers, to rob and steal from law-abiding Citizens and carry them before Committees of Examination and even to prison."*

Will stared at Ingilby, challenging him.

Ingilby looked back and stroked his beard.

"A monopoly of printing," said Will, "censorship of any views that those in power feel threatened by."

"No need to spell it out to me, Will." He looked towards the window, the faint sound of yells on the street.

"We are living in perilous times, Will. I fear anarchy could be round the corner. It is easy to stir up the poor and ignorant with wild ideas and give them hopes that will be dashed. That disappointment, together with cheap ale, can lead to riots, riots to killing, and killing to a greater tyranny. Those in power have the power and incentive not to give it up. The losers will be the same losers: those people out there who have shoved and cursed you. Those people you and some of your colleagues wish to save, and who will in the end be betrayed by you."

It was not quite the answer Will had expected. "You truly think that?"

"I do. But then you know I have no belief in the goodness of man. We are all charlatans of one degree or another though we like to pretend otherwise. We are all selfish – even you, with your idealism and your philanthropy. They make you feel good. That's why you do it."

242

"So cynical."

"I plead guilty. We shall see."

So Will left.

It was late when he arrived home and he went straight to his study, lit candles, poured wine and read again the last lines of Lilburne's pamphlet.

Oh Englishmen, where is your Freedoms? And what is become of your Liberties and Priviledges that you have been fighting for all this while? Look about you betimes, before it is too late, and give not occasion to your Children yet unborne to curse you, for making them slaves by your covetousness and faint-heartednesse. Therefore up as one man and in a just and legall way call those to account, that endeavour to destroy you and betray your Liberties and Freedomes.

Will laid the pamphlet down on his table. Outside the window it was now dark. His room was in shadow except for where the candles burned and guttered in the draughts. His own two children, Robert and Susannah, were privileged, but if this unjust and unfair society continued far more than their privilege would be lost.

He closed his eyes and sat back in his chair. In his mind shone a bright light, as if a curtain had been drawn back and he could see clearly for the first time. This was common sense, not revelation, this was seeing it as it was. This was what he should be about – in the Commons, fighting the Presbyterian compromisers and in the Army, fighting the King and all he stood for.

Next day, Westminster Hall was packed. Beneath the buttressed oak hammer-beam roof adorned with angels, below the seventeen statues of kings of England, the stallholders were doing a brisk trade. Seamstresses and milliners called out their wares; customers selected gloves and ribbons; men turned pages at second-hand book stalls; publishers sold pamphlets, some from under the counter. Groups of lawyers left the courts, buttoning up the pockets of their breeches' pockets. MPs gossiped and conspired: high spirits and loud voices among the Parliamentarians.

A small knot of people was grouped around a man Will recognised. His hands were waving in the air, his arms gesticulating, head thrown back, voice loud even above the hubbub.

"Isn't that John Lilburne?" he asked, nodding his head in their direction.

"Freeborn John? Aye," said one. "A brave man."

"With his customary rabble rout, ragtag and bobtail," scoffed Ingilby, passing by.

"Excuse me, gentlemen, I need to speak to him," said Will.

Will pushed through the crowd and joined the listening group. The man's eyes were so direct, almost black. Shaven chin, moustache, long thin sloping nose, hair cropped short on top, curled about the ears, mouth animated as he spoke.

"I have read your *England's Birth-right*," interjected Will. "A strong statement and true."

"That's why I'm here," replied Lilburne. "Your Parliament is setting up a Presbyterian church. Well, do as you think fit provided you leave my conscience free. I printed my pamphlet so other people would know what was happening."

"Forced to print on an illegal press and without licence, I presume."

"How else can we do it? The Committee of Examination has sent stationer Nicholas Tew to Fleet Prison for it." He laughed. "A *scurrilous, seditious and libellous pamphlet* they called it. Are we not allowed to speak our minds these days, under this new Parliament which is supposed to be there for the people? The Star Chamber may have been abolished but its work goes on. So much for the freedom of the press."

He turned, doffed his hat and strode off with his band of disciples. Will watched them go. He realised that, like so many others, he had been hooked by Freeborn John. More than fascinated, he was awestruck by him.

He knew that the Presbyterian-dominated Parliament had taken up the very weapons it had once abolished. He'd been horrified at the return of the strict control of the press that followed. Searches were now made for printing presses engaged in 'scandalous' printing; those presses were destroyed, and the printers, vendors and writers imprisoned. A special licenser had been appointed. No book could be printed without licence and without being entered in the Register of the Stationers' Company.

What did fighting for Parliament mean anymore?

A fight against the King's divine authority, a fight against the sly return of Popery. A fight above all for liberty of conscience and liberty of speech. Fine principles, but Will knew he had not the strength of conviction to fight alone. As part of a group, yes, part of an army, with comrades in a joint endeavour, but not like this strange, bold man.

★

Three weeks later Will learned that Lilburne had been arrested on a trumped-up charge of defaming the Earl of Manchester. The Lords immediately took up the case on behalf of the Earl. Lilburne was arrested and arraigned before the House of Lords. But he refused to accept the authority of the Lords, refused to kneel, put his fingers in his ears to avoid hearing the charges.

"I have," he said, "learnt better religion and manners than to kneel to any human or mortal power, however great, whom I have not offended."

To Will's disgust and despair, the Lords pronounced him guilty of high contempt to the honour of their House, sentenced him to a fine of £2,000 and imprisonment in the Tower during the pleasure of the House. His pamphlets were to be publicly burned by the public hangman the following Monday at the Old Exchange in London and New Palace Westminster.

The unelected were defending their cronies. Why seek to get rid of the King and yet keep the Lords? It was illogical.

A petition with 10,000 signatures asked for the redress of grievances and for Lilburne's release. It was ignored.

Another Large Petition, as it was called, initiated by the Levellers, attacked Parliament just like Lilburne's *England's Birth-right*. Both these petitions were also burnt by the hangman at Westminster and the Exchange.

Lilburne remained in the Tower. Will, frustrated and angry, was powerless to do anything about it.

MAY 1645

One evening in May, after supper, Will and Jane sat either side of the low-burning fire. The last of the light filtered through the windows. A comforting smell of food, fresh scent of rosemary and thyme that Will had deliberately brushed against, a splash of red fashionable tulips in a copper vase. Children in bed.

They had talked about Susannah's first words, about Robert's ceaseless talking and his efforts at bowling along a hoop, his animated recitation of *Cock-a-doodle-do, My dame has lost her shoe*.

"He has a love of song," said Will.

Jane was embroidering, her fingers deft.

Will knew he would fracture this harmony.

Silence, except when Jane's dress rustled as she shifted her arms, or logs settled in the fire.

He had no choice, cleared his throat.

"I must speak with you on a serious matter," he said.

"I know." She did not look up.

"How do you know?" Sounding petulant.

"It's been obvious since I heard you talking with my father about the New Model Army. I wondered how long you would put it off." She threaded some green cotton into a needle.

"Ingilby has refused to fight for either side," said Will. "He says shedding poor men's blood is a vulgar way of solving political differences."

"He's right, isn't he?" A pause. "And you?"

"Jane, you know I am Cromwell's man, and I know it pains you and your parents."

"Does it pain you enough?" Firing these questions, her head bent, not looking at him.

"We will never agree on this. If I thought I could convince you, I would try."

"So, you have decided to join this unified New Army with its regular pay, promotion on merit not birth and its Puritan independents?"

Although annoyed by her apparent dismissiveness, Will kept his voice calm. "I want you to understand. Please. You have your principles, Jane. Do I prevent you from going to church? Do I refuse to see your parents because they are on the King's side? Well, I have my principles, too."

"So, you have decided?" she repeated.

Will stood up. "I have to fight for my principles, otherwise I could not live with myself."

And now Jane did look up at him, a cold challenge in her eyes.

"You need to live for your children and your wife."

She stood, placed her embroidery on a side table and left the room.

It was the inevitable conclusion. There was no appeasing her, and there was no avoiding his duty.

When he went upstairs to bed, he did as he always did: looked in on his sleeping children. He could hear their soft, regular breathing, Susannah with her arms still above her head, as when she was a baby. Was he making the right decision, and was it for the right reason? He tiptoed over and kissed each of them on their forehead. The soft innocence of their skin.

"I love you," he whispered.

Three days later, Will proudly joined Major Bethel's troop, part of Colonel Whalley's Regiment of Horse in the New Model Army.

Between Will and Jane, silence now seemed preferable, and with the silence grew a coldness.

JUNE 1645

A month later, Will was part of an army besieging Oxford, the King's headquarters. News came of a great victory at Naseby in Yorkshire. Manchester and Essex had been removed from their posts. The New Model Army, now under the command of Sir Thomas Fairfax and Oliver Cromwell, had routed the Royalist Army at Naseby in Yorkshire. A small group of Royalist cavalry escaped but all the infantry were killed or captured, artillery and the baggage train captured.

In the baggage train were the King's private papers. They contained damning evidence that he had sought help from Irish Catholics and the Catholic nations of Europe. Cromwell seized upon them with glee. How they would fortify the Parliamentary cause!

25.

WITCH-FINDERS

1645

At nine o'clock next morning, under a warm sun, chattering groups of people wound their way through the small town to the meeting house. Six men carried a long table and placed it in front of the entrance. On one side were placed eight chairs, on the other side, one. The crowd assembled including many who wanted to give testimony. James and Alice were among them. Alice was deeply afraid for Ellen: she had witnessed the power of superstition at home and in Holland. She knew how easily mobs could be inflamed. The dignitaries filed out and took their places, grim-faced and soberly dressed: Mr Ludlow, the magistrate of the General Court of Plymouth, the treasurer, two deacons, Samuel Wilton, the Reverend Hooker and two representatives of the colony of Connecticut.

Then the Constable brought Ellen, still in chains, her hair and dress spattered with straw, looking down at the ground, face pale and drawn. Alice gasped and a cry went up from the crowd, a primitive noise that made the hairs on her neck stand up. The Constable thrust Ellen roughly onto the solitary chair, where she faced her questioners. Alice looked along the line of severe men facing Ellen: not a trace of compassion in their faces. The two deacons who had been at the arrest looked upon her as if she were already guilty. Samuel Wilton was smirking.

Mr Ludlow read: "Ellen Clark, you have been brought forth on this day having been accused of having familiarity with Satan, and thus having conspired with him to complete his many works against this town including sorcery and murder."

Ellen gasped and gave a strangled cry.

Murder! Alice just stopped herself from leaping up and yelling, "Liars!"

"We will hear testimonies from those who make the accusations and you may be asked to answer further questions about the allegations. This inquiry will determine if your case should be presented before the General Court at Hartford for a formal charge of witchcraft. Do you understand?"

One by one townspeople came to the front and spoke of how Ellen had bewitched their horse or caused a fire to spread and, most importantly, brought about the deaths of children and family members. She sat with head bowed. Alice knew some of these were people who had been thankful for Ellen's cures. Now they spoke of her use of the savages' cures; of the dark angel the little girl had seen just before she died; of the Dark Lord two boys had seen her commune with in the woods.

"Her medicines were evil potions and toxins. We presumed her to be healing when she was murdering."

And here Ellen jerked her head up and shouted: "'Tis a lie! A lie! I am not a murderer. God knows I am innocent. I cured people not killed them."

The crowd hissed.

"Her medicine brought her hexes and spells upon us."

"Why did her family never ail while all around her neighbours died?"

Shouts of approval from the crowd.

"What say you," asked Mr Ludlow, "about these Indian remedies?"

"Yes, I did use them because I have seen them work. And there was so much illness and so many came to me for help that I ran out of English remedies and had to use Indian ones more."

Her voice had grown stronger as she spoke.

And then James moved to the front. Alice saw Ellen's eyes follow him.

"May I speak now, esteemed magistrates, select men and clergy?"

Wilton frowned and seemed about to object, but the panel of magistrates nodded and required the crowd to be silent.

James turned to the crowd.

"I think there is devilry here," he said, "but it is not in Ellen. It is here among us all, that is how Satan is working. Think back, citizens, to the times before this pestilence when many of us had ailments and aches and pains which Ellen cured. People went to her for help. They trusted her. They came to the market and my store and bought her medicines and teas and potions. I see many faces here who bought them from me, happily. Why? Because they had seen how they worked and cured their loved ones."

The crowd was silent, Alice proud of how brave he was to stand against them and the magistrates.

"How can she or any one person be responsible for this latest pestilence?" James continued. "It is not the work of the Devil nor our sinfulness nor even the work of God. Diseases come, like scurvy or the flux or even the plague; they are natural things, borne in the air or food or brought by animals. In helping to cure so many people, Ellen risked her own life. Her remedies did not always work but that is not because she does the Devil's work; it is because people were already too ill. She is become a scapegoat. It is horrible and does not become us. We live by the law, not superstition."

But there were hissing and catcalls.

Alice could not let that intimidate her. Controlling her nervousness, she stood and came to the front.

"I heard the rumours and the accusations," she said, "and then my son lay at death's door, the doctor having done his best but not able to help further. I too had my suspicions about Indian medicine. In my desperation I called for Ellen's help. She came and treated my son and now he is fit and well again. I know she cured him and no one else. She is an innocent woman. I beg you to cease all this and let us come to our senses."

There was a moment's silence after Alice spoke but then more bawling and shouting down.

Mr Ludlow stood up.

"I thank you all for your testimonies. We must now see if there is any physical evidence against Ellen Clark. Mr Samuel Wilton has a book from England, *The Witch-Finders' Manual*, which explains how we seek this. We must set up a committee of women which will search for any marks of the Devil on Ellen's body. We will convene here again in three days' time. Constable, take the accused back to her prison."

The Constable grabbed her roughly by the arm and dragged her off to throw her into gaol.

The committee of women was formed: the spouses of the men behind the table. One of the representatives of Connecticut suggested that Alice be one of the committee so that it would be fairer and look better, and she would be only one. The women did not like it but Mr Ludlow saw the advantage. Alice did not like it either, but being a witness for Ellen might prevent some cruelties or at least she would be able to report them. And she would be the only friendly face amongst the persecutors.

The magistrates, reading from the manual, had decreed that Ellen was to be kept awake all night. Supervised by the committee of women, the Constable brought in a wooden chair and tied her to it, forbidding her to close her eyes. She was to stay in this position for twenty-four hours to see if one of her familiars came in search of nourishment from a secret teat on Ellen. The committee worked in shifts to keep Ellen awake, hitting her, kicking her chair or screaming in her ear. They questioned her repeatedly. Alice was appalled but helpless.

Exhausted, her head slumped, Ellen could only croak: "God knows I am innocent. You are wrong to treat me so."

She begged for water and Alice insisted on giving her some, much to the disapproval of the others.

Just before dawn, Alice and the deacon's wife were on duty. The wife had zealously kept Ellen awake by slapping her cheeks, and yanking her head back by the hair saw what they were waiting for. Suddenly the wife stood stock-still and screamed. She pointed at a rat sneaking into the shed through a hole, heading for the bowl of stew Ellen had left untouched.

"Her familiar, the minion of Lucifer!" shouted the wife triumphantly.

"Don't be ridiculous," remonstrated Alice, terrified by how this would be interpreted.

When this was reported to the magistrates they decided the next step was for the women to examine Ellen's body. Ellen was kept awake all morning and Alice managed to give her some fresh bread and cider. The examination was to be in the house of Samuel Wilton so they could see better than in the shed.

Led by the Constable the small procession of women made their way to the big house, watched by scowling bystanders. In the large drawing room, furniture had been pushed to the side, covered in sheets, and a space left in the middle. Here a single truckle bed had been placed. Light streamed through the window onto it. It was like a sacrificial altar, thought Alice.

Ellen was hysterical when they told her they were looking for signs or marks where imps or familiars had suckled. Alice could not believe the venom she saw in the faces of these prosperous, respectable women. They had been turned into witches themselves.

"You deserve this, witch," they said and laughed.

They forced her to undress until she was entirely naked. She had never been naked with anyone except her husband since she'd been a young child. She tried to cover herself but they grabbed her arms and held her legs and laid her on the bed. They ignored the visible moles and wart on her arm because evidence had to come from those parts of the body which were not exposed or scarce talked about. So they examined under her arms, spread her legs and peered closely, seeking the skin tag or mole that would prove the case. It was as if the task had released some long pent-up sexual crudity. Disgust and lasciviousness warped their faces. But they found no moles, birthmarks or extra nipples. Ellen was shivering uncontrollably – with fear and humiliation as much as cold. Alice wrapped the bed's sheet around her and sat with her, ignoring the committee's orders to leave her alone, though she knew this could look bad if the bloodlust and the witch-hunt continued.

When it was reported to the magistrates that nothing incriminating had been found, they consulted Matthew Hopkins' manual and ordered that the women were to shave all the hair from Ellen's body. Alice's protest was dismissed. Once that was done they were to stick or cut her with sharp implements to see if a previously undiscovered teat would appear.

Alice held Ellen's head and stroked her forehead. Ellen no longer struggled, compliant and unmoving as they shaved her. She closed her eyes and Alice sensed her go deep inside herself, absenting herself. Alice watched the women run their fingers across Ellen's body. They turned her over and she did not resist, every inch being examined. They turned her on to her back again and Alice watched the fingers trail across Ellen's breasts, the stippled aureoles around her nipples. They did it in a concentrated silence, just a rustling of their sleeves and skirts. They were absorbed: it wasn't just the power they were exercising, it wasn't just that they were doing this in the name of the Lord. Something shameful had been licensed, something forbidden allowed. They were Ladies of Misrule.

They scrutinised every part of her body, pricking it with pins and a paring knife. Occasionally they broke the skin and blood trickled. But it was as if Ellen did not feel it, as if she was not there.

But still they found nothing. They worked meticulously on Ellen's vulva. Indeed, thought Alice, they were examining a quim for the first time in their lives, discovering their own bodies as well as Ellen's. Alice herself had never seen the intricate folds that frilled the hole through which, unbelievably, a baby's head could push and emerge. She looked away. This was rape. Then Ellen's body jumped and she gave a cry of pain. Alice looked down and saw a pin was being jabbed into the outer folds of Ellen's genitals. They did it again. Again Ellen cried out in pain.

"For God's sake," shouted Alice, "have you no pity?!" *No Christian charity,* but she didn't say it.

And then the Reverend Hooker's wife: "We have found it, the secret teat."

Such fevered, excited chatter among the committee women. Alice could almost taste the unctuous piety in their voices.

She could see nothing like a teat or a mole or a growth of any kind. But she knew the men would not refute the women's testimony. And if she, Alice, said anything, she would be the next to be charged. A mania had overcome the place, a madness. The Devil was only an excuse for the worst kind of human behaviour.

"Get dressed now," said one of the magistrate's wives.

"You can no longer pretend you are not what you really are," said another.

Alice helped Ellen put on her ragged, dirty clothes.

"And you," said Alice, unable to hold her tongue, "you are unable to hide the beasts you have become in this room."

Cold and condescending, the others left the room.

Ellen dressed but still shivered with fear and humiliation, Alice trying to comfort her. But Ellen was still in some far-off place.

Eventually Alice called in the men.

"Just as we expected," said one of the deacons.

"Aye," said Mr Ludlow. "Now she must sit in that dark shed for two more nights, with a night watchman to keep her awake. Perhaps she will learn to admit her undeniable guilt."

So she was returned to the shed and Alice forbidden to go near it.

For the next two days Ellen was taken to the house for more questioning by the magistrates and clerics. Alice, heart thumping with silent rage and frustration, and the committee listened to the same charges and stories repeated.

Quietly, hardly able to speak, her tongue swollen and her mouth dry, Ellen protested her innocence.

"No one has enquired after your well-being; the whole settlement has abandoned you," Wilton said brutally. "The only companions you have are the Devil and his consorts."

Alice protested but was threatened with removal if she did not close her mouth.

Late in the afternoon of the second day, Ellen slowly stood up, supporting herself on the back of her chair, and said she wished to make a statement. Permission was granted.

"I do not understand the cruelty you have shown against me. My fate has been decided," she said in a wavering voice. "Whatever I say, I will be found guilty."

"No, Ellen, no, please, no!" Alice blurted out. An admonishing frown from Ludlow.

"The Dark Lord who met me in the forest was Satan and not the old Indian woman's son. Perhaps the Indian remedies were at fault, perhaps I have unwittingly killed people and created misery. Perhaps I am full of sin, and not the community. And this is my punishment."

Alice cried out, "Why are you telling these lies?" Then caught Ludlow's eye.

Ellen looked exhausted, beaten, her eyes dull. She sobbed out her confession, "I now want only to leave this world where I have tried only to do good but instead have caused misery and mistrust."

Alice felt utterly helpless, beaten herself.

The following morning Ellen was brought back to the meeting house in chains and made to repeat her confession in front of a large group of citizens. She confessed her pact with the Devil. Alice and James were horrified.

"You cannot do this," pleaded James. "What you are doing" – and here he pointed at the magistrates – "is truly the Devil's work." But he was roughly bundled out of the building.

The magistrates were satisfied. They had all they needed to send Ellen to Hartford for trial and probable hanging. As they spoke, Ellen raised her head towards James and Alice at the back of the group. Her eyes beseeched them: *What else could I have done?*

Alice noticed Wilton had said little, but he hadn't needed to. All he had had to do was set the ball rolling. As she had feared, using these trials was his way of worming his way back into public acclaim and respectability.

Next morning, Alice and James watched as Ellen was taken to the river and led in chains to the shallop which would take her to Hartford. As the boat was pushed off from the bank, she took one last look back at the settlement where she had lived a bare eighteen months. Alice tried to catch her eye, but what encouragement could she give?

26.

KENTFORD HEATH AND PUTNEY

1647

Will started, half sat up, rested on an elbow. Damn! What had woken him? Some soldier's nightmare cry? That bloody tussock in the small of his back? He needed sleep. He lay back. Damp was seeping up from the ground; low voices, snores and grunts, cries, horses shifting. He craved sleep because it closed down his thoughts, thoughts which now opened up: the horrible polite indifference in which he and Jane now lived; being away from Robert's new skills with spinning tops and Fox & Geese. Will loved his son's competitiveness. And away from Susannah with her doll's house and the new rocking horse she loved to ride, and her chatter.

No! And he screwed his eyes shut. He fidgeted into a new position, wrapped his cloak around his head, tried to concentrate on tomorrow. But the tussock was still there and he was wide awake. He'd be better out of the tent, and he needed a piss.

So he stood up and stretched, circled his shoulders and found a bush to pee in.

Melancholy: almost pitch-dark, half a moon with clouds scudding over it, black tree shapes around the heath, a hint of light in the east, dew on the ground, a breeze shuffling the leaves. Horse shapes, their munching, smell of fresh horse shit, fires burned low with men lying huddled round them, tents, a sentry or two. Nearly dawn on June 4th 1645 on Kentford Heath.

Seven regiments of foot and six of horse were due here today, all from the New Model Army.

The demanded rendezvous: a culmination and a next step.

He was right to be here. When they were older, his children would understand why he had left them to fight. And Jane's indifference had only spurred on his commitment to the cause.

He had played his part, risked himself and fought in the Commons for these brave men who slept or dozed around him. He was proud to be here. Proud to be with them, accepted by them. Part of a fellowship.

He smiled to himself as he remembered that day in the Commons.

Parliament had received a *Representation of the Army* signed by 223 officers. He had stood and given impassioned support for their grievances.

"This Parliament has still not settled arrears of pay for the Army, the Army that has fought for the freedoms and rights of our people. Disbanded soldiers are already being harried in court for their seizure of horses, under orders from their superiors. They can be hanged for this. It is a disgrace. Is it wrong to want relief for widows, orphans and the maimed?"

Cries of "Hear him! Hear him!" from the benches behind, but he saw only disdain on the faces of the mostly Presbyterian MPs opposite. Ingilby appeared amused. The Presbyterians' intentions were clear: afraid of the growing power of the New Model Army they wanted to disband it or send it under new commanders out of the way to Ireland. Only after disbandment would they settle the arrears. No one believed them. And, of course, they also wanted to negotiate with the King.

"This is a dangerous petition," came the counter, "putting the Army into distemper and mutiny. Those who continue to promote this petition shall be proceeded against as enemies of the state and disturbers of the public peace."

"This is self-seeking treachery and ingratitude," fumed Will. "You will inflame the Army more."

In this struggle between Parliament and Army, Will now clearly knew where he stood. Which was why he was here on the Heath. At last he felt he was in step with John Boon, old Arthur Babthorpe and John Lilburne.

The New Model Army, incensed by Parliament, became even more politicised. Will watched as the common soldiers took the initiative. Eight regiments of horse elected adjutators to represent them. There were meetings of horse and foot regiments which chose committees from every troop, who then met the adjutators of horse. Each foot soldier contributed four pence, half a day's wages, towards the expenses of the meeting. Army adjutators and London radicals, including Levellers, communicated in coded letters, signed by numbers not names. Will was thrilled and impressed at the speed and efficiency of what had happened. There was now a mixed civilian and military network operating beyond the reach of Parliament.

Lilburne had played his part, too. From the Tower he published a letter to Cromwell:

> *If tyranny be resistable, then it is resistable in a Parliament as well as a King. King Charles his seventeen years misgovernment before this Parliament was but a flea-biting in comparison of what this everlasting Parliament already is... the Commons of England may bid adieu to their Lawes, Liberties and Freedoms unless they speedily take a course for the electing of a new Parliament."*

This further stoked the Army's opposition to Parliament, which was still attempting disbandment.

Now as dawn lifted the lid of darkness up from the Heath, soldiers rose from their sleep, horses were fed and other regiments arrived. Wagons full of ammunition and surgeons' chests creaked along the tracks, troops marched in, coarse greetings were shouted. Sir Thomas Fairfax had made his decision: the regiments would not be disbanded. He would defy Parliament for the unity of the Army. Will watched him go on his great skewbald horse from regiment to regiment, speaking a few words, greeted with cheering acclamation. Cromwell was somewhere there, too, having ridden from Westminster to join the rendezvous.

Before the sun was too high, representatives were called together. Will was one of them. Propositions were put and discussed; the debate was sober, intense and well-disciplined; much tobacco was consumed. After four hours they had agreed upon *The Solemne Engagement of the Armie*, and Will was more proud of it than anything else he had achieved. It was the product of unity between officers and rank-and-file and went way beyond a repetition of Army grievances. It was agreed that from now on there should be a Council of the Army consisting of two officers and two soldiers elected by each regiment, including adjutators. Decisions were to be by majority vote. This was revolutionary in itself.

The *Engagement* went on to propose a purge of *corrupt and delinquent MPs*, a fixed limit on the length of future parliaments, a re-drawing of constituency boundaries so they were more equal, the end of the King's power of arbitrary dissolution, the right to petition, and *provision for tender consciences* – which meant religious freedom.

It concluded that *they had taken up arms on behalf of people's rights and liberties, that as freeborn people of England they were entitled to resist the oppression, injury and abuse of Parliament, that the meanest subject should fully enjoy his right, liberty and properties in all things, that every yoke be removed from the people's necks.*

The Army was now directly challenging Parliament. Will was with the Army but was still an MP. There would be conflict to come, both on the field and in the House.

261

As the Army set off to march to London to put further pressure on Parliament, amazing news was brought.

It had not been a dignified royal story when it was pieced together. The King had fled from his headquarters in Oxford, his hair cut short, affixed a false beard and dressed as a servant. Will recalled a conversation in Westminster courtyard.

"Has the man no dignity?" drawled Ingilby.

With only his chaplain and a single manservant, the King had made his way to Newark to join the Scots Covenanters.

"His former enemies," scoffed Will. "Has he no principles?"

"The Covenanters support the principle of having a King, and that's his main principle," said Ingilby.

The Scots took him to Newcastle, but in January 1647 they handed him over to Parliament for £400,000.

"That's the Scots principle – money."

"Cheap at the price," Charles had quipped, and was placed under house arrest at Holmby House in Northamptonshire.

And now King Charles was in the hands of the Army, taken from Holmby House in Northamptonshire, and was being escorted to the new Army headquarters in Putney.

On 6th August a detachment of troops marched into Westminster, escorting the Independent MPs, each soldier wearing a laurel leaf in his hat.

Then the whole Army marched through the City. Will rode with them. It was like a march of triumph: crowds cheering, the tramp of boots, the red coats of the musketeers and pikemen, the buff leather coats of the cavalry in tight formation, light flashing on pikes, breastplates and helmets. Will imagined Lilburne, still in the Tower, with pen in hand, listening to the tramp of feet and clatter of horses' hooves. This was a disciplined force to be reckoned with by King, Presbyterians and citizens. But underlying that was a unity, a sense of right, an evangelical progress towards a new kind of society.

And this evening he would at last be with Robert and Susannah again. It was for their future he was riding with these men.

The cold stone of the pillar pressed into his shoulders, whetting his mind. From the shadowed west end of the chancel, Will watched. About twenty men stood in groups in the old church, their conversation steady but muted – as if by the age of the place, by its dampness and gloom, by the weight of the meeting to come. In the dim light, among the Puritan black hats and jackets and the soldiers' buff leather jackets, pale faces turned towards each other, nervous, expectant.

It was November 1st 1647. This meeting had been called by the new Council of War. There were the representatives of the army regiments: officers and elected adjutators. Will was an elected adjutator, from Colonel Whalley's regiment of horse. Here, today, where for centuries births and deaths had been solemnised, there would be a re-birth – a bold, possibly reckless, new beginning. That was Will's fervent hope. All depended on Cromwell's reaction. He looked down at his hand holding the newly printed *Agreement of the People.* His grip was tight, his knuckles white. He relaxed his fingers and took a deep breath.

Will watched as, in the shaft of light below one of the plain glass arched windows to his left, Fairfax stooped. A tall man, his bald head gleaming, he listened to the stockier Cromwell, whose lips were close to Fairfax's left ear. As Cromwell spoke, Will saw his yellowing teeth, the wart on his chin, his hard blue-grey eyes, his shoulder-length brown hair. Fairfax nodded, spoke briefly, straightened up.

They were two of the Grandees, as Lilburne had christened them: the powerfully-built Sir Thomas Fairfax, Commander-in-Chief of the New Model Army, Black Tom because of his dark eyes and swarthy complexion; the shorter, thick-necked, broad-shouldered Lieutenant General Oliver Cromwell. Easy to see that he had excelled at football, cudgelling and wrestling at Cambridge University: Old Ironsides, face rough-hewn, much more the Fenland farmer than the Inns of Court lawyer, shirt soiled as usual, his plain clothes cut by a country tailor not a fashionable London one.

He knew they were nervous of the level of dissent in the Army – and it was no longer just about conditions and pay. The Leveller-inspired adjutators were stirring up ideas about the voting franchise, about inequalities and rights, about what should be done about the King – radical ideas that excited Will, that would make the rich and powerful tremble, and not just Royalists. So the Grandees had summoned this meeting of the Council of the Army in this church of St Mary of the Virgin, on the banks of the Thames in Putney where the army was quartered. They were expecting to debate *The Case for the Army*. This was a document which argued against their own *Heads of the Proposals*, which was a compromise from Parliament requiring the King to formally share power with Parliament but on the same limited franchise as already existed. The King so far had stubbornly refused even this compromise, but many in Parliament were still hoping to make an accommodation with the King.

Will looked for Commissary General Henry Ireton, Cromwell's son-in-law, and found him standing silently beneath another of the windows. The Grandees needed to be here. They wouldn't have seen the document Will was holding, that would be presented to the meeting for discussion. This 28th day of October 1647 could be a day to go down in history.

In the centre of the chancel was a large plain oak table with benches round three sides of it. Two chairs were placed at the head. Faces glanced sideways, conversation stuttered as the men watched Cromwell and Fairfax move to stand behind the chairs, Cromwell's big hands resting on the back.

"Gentlemen," announced Cromwell. For such a burly man with such a presence of authority, his high-pitched voice was incongruous, almost amusing. "Let us begin."

He gestured towards the empty benches. He and Fairfax sat down, the others took their places. Henry Ireton sat in the middle of one side, Colonel Thomas Rainborowe opposite him. Will wondered if that was deliberate. A shuffling and a settling, wary eyes glanced quickly round, weighing up, a setting down of beakers and tumblers of ale. Will counted seven elected adjutators like himself, seven officers, two civilians and a chaplain. Cromwell leaned forward, thick forearms on the table, holding the pamphlet. He lifted it up.

"*The Case for the Army*," he said. "Who wishes to speak first?"

Edward Sexby, adjutator and trooper, raised his arm and brandished another pamphlet. Cromwell nodded.

"This is the paper we wish to discuss today," Sexby pronounced brusquely, "not the one you hold."

Will and the other adjutators slapped their copies of *The Agreement of the People* on the table, something defiant in the way the action was co-ordinated. Copies were slid in front of the Grandees. Fairfax ignored it, his face expressionless. Ireton turned the pages and scowled. All looked at Cromwell. Will held his breath. This was the moment. Cromwell adjusted his weight a little and leaned back. Finally he said: "I have not seen this paper."

"Nor I," said Fairfax abruptly.

"Nor I," added Ireton.

A tense silence. Cromwell looked levelly round the table, seeking each man's eyes. Fairfax bent towards him but Cromwell with a slight gesture of the hand stayed him.

"It is Army business?" asked Cromwell.

"Indeed it is," said Sexby. He was a wiry man, back bent almost like a hunchback, glittering blue eyes in his gaunt weather-beaten face, a trooper in Colonel Fleetwood's regiment, a tough soldier, one to have on your side.

"We will continue," said Cromwell.

Ireton glanced at him, disapproving. Fairfax stared up at the window. Will felt the tension round the table relax. He breathed more easily and felt a renewed respect for Cromwell.

"In all we say," continued Sexby, "we wish to prove ourselves before God as honest men. The cause of the army's misery is this: we have laboured to please a king and I think, unless we go about to cut all our own throats, we shall not ever please him. And we have fought to support a House which will prove rotten studs – I mean the Parliament, which consists of a company of rotten members."

Here Sexby glared fiercely at Cromwell. Too strong, thought Will. Don't antagonise at the outset; remember who you are addressing, acknowledge the ground he has ceded. But Cromwell's face was expressionless, though there might be a menace in his very stillness.

"Read the document," instructed Cromwell.

"First," said Sexby, "we do not want the King to share power with Parliament, as in your *Heads of the Proposals*. It is a woeful experience to depend for settlement of our peace and freedom upon him who intended our bondage and brought cruel war upon us. So this is the paper we wish to discuss today: *The Agreement of the People*. This paper is proposed by the adjutators of the five regiments of horse and has the general approbation of the army at Kentford Heath and the joint concurrence of the free commons of England."

The two civilians nodded firmly, Wildman and Petty. Will had met them briefly in London in March, introduced by Sexby.

"Read out the first article," said Cromwell.

Sexby read: "*That the people of England being at this day very unequally distributed by counties, cities and boroughs for the election of their deputies in Parliament ought to be more equally proportioned*" –

and here he paused before continuing – "*according to the number of inhabitants.*"

That was the crucial word, thought Will, *inhabitants.* Not men of property.

Ireton flung his copy onto the table, shaking his head. Cromwell read the words again to himself then calmly laid his paper on the table. Looking directly at Sexby, he said in a measured way:

"This is a very great alteration of the government of the kingdom since, I believe I may say, it was ever a nation."

A few nods around the table.

But it was Rainborowe who spoke: "Sir, if writings be true there have been many scufflings between the honest men of England and those who have tyrannised over them. The people of England are not born to any of the just and equitable laws we have; they are entrenchments on the once-enjoyed privileges of their rulers."

Henry Ireton jabbed his finger on the paragraph and thrust his head forward. Ireton was a Commissary General of the New Model Army and a Member of Parliament.

"Does this mean that every man that is an inhabitant is to be equally considered and to have an equal voice in the election of representatives?"

Incredulity was in his voice as he emphasised the words *equally* and *equal.* He looked around the table, challenging, upright in his chair, clean-shaven, firm mouth set in his austere face. It was Rainborowe who spoke again, so quietly that the men had to lean forward to hear.

"I think that the poorest he that is in England has a life to live, as the greatest he."

And Will was moved by the simplicity of the words, their essential rightness.

There were nods and noises of agreement round the table. But Will saw Fairfax was frowning. One or two of the officers seemed taken aback at hearing words they had signed up to spoken aloud – and directed at the two most powerful men in England. Cromwell put his elbows on the table, rested his chin on his hand and said nothing. Rainborowe continued, again quietly but his voice charged with certainty.

"Every man that is to live under a government ought first by his own consent to put himself under that government. It is his birth-right."

Ireton gave an exaggerated sigh, straightened the paper in front of him precisely. He began: "No, sir, no person has a right to choose those who shall determine what laws we are ruled by – unless that person has a permanent fixed interest in this kingdom."

He held up his hand to forestall an interruption.

"Birth-right? Yes, birth-right to air and place and ground and the freedom of the highways. That is due to a man by birth. Indeed, as Rainsborowe says" – and here he nodded towards him respectfully – "the meanest man in England ought to have a voice in the election of the government he lives under, but only if he has some local interest."

And now Ireton warmed to his argument: "Those that have the meanest local interest – a man that has freehold property bringing in rent of forty shillings a year – he has now as I speak" – and he prodded the table with his finger – "as great a voice in the election of a knight for the shire as he that has ten thousand a year. If we go Rainborowe and Sexby's way and take away the forty shillings a year qualification, we shall plainly go to take away all property and interest that any man has."

He took a drink of ale, as if this rounded off his argument, and wiped his mouth with the back of his hand.

Rainborowe continued: "I ask again: how does it come about that there is a voice for some freeborn Englishmen and not for others? I still desire to know how some men and not others have the right to elect."

And here he thumped the table. Will eased his collar, his neck moist with sweat.

Rainborowe was not for compromise. Cromwell was frowning, Fairfax staring at the ceiling, Ireton shaking his head.

For the first time civilian John Wildman spoke. He was a fat puddingy man with a round face, small eyes like raisins and plump cheeks – and a sense of indulgence that did not extend to the monarchy. He was a strong republican, Will knew.

"The question is whether any person can justly be bound by a law, who does not give his consent that such persons make laws for him."

Ireton smiled in that superior way he had, steepled his hands on the table and moved into lawyer style. "The original power of making laws does lie with the people, but by the people is meant those that are possessed of the permanent interest in the land."

Now Rainborowe spoke. His eyes blazed beneath his thick dark eyebrows as he growled: "Truly, I think we are still where we were. One part of the people make the other five to be hewers of wood and drawers of water, so the greatest part of the nation be enslaved. And I do not hear any argument given but only that it is the present law of the kingdom. We must agree that liberty and freedom is for all the people."

Will could find no fault in that argument. Clever, thought Will, but cleverness will not win the day. Nor did it soften his wooden chair. He shifted his weight and sat straighter.

Sexby, stern and measured, his passion controlled: "We have ventured our lives in order to recover our birth-rights and privileges as Englishmen. But by the arguments urged against us here, we have none. Except a man has a fixed estate in this kingdom he has no rights. I wonder how we were so much deceived. I do think the poor and meaner of this kingdom have been the means of preservation of this kingdom." He looked round, challenging them, fist raised and clenched. "And now we demand the birth-right for which we fought."

Rainborowe bellowed: "I would fain know what the soldier has fought for all this while. Has he fought to enslave himself, to give power to men of riches, men of estates, to make himself a perpetual slave?"

The representatives thumped the table in agreement, nodding their heads, saying *Aye, aye*. And Will was with them, inspired by Rainborowe's certainty, half out of his chair to hammer the table. Outside, in the grey Thames, he knew the tide would be turning, rising up the river to challenge and mingle with the seaward flow. And here, in this building of stone and glass, heavy and light, clotted with five hundred years of ritualised prayers and promises and pleadings – here now a current was rising and turning, refining. Will felt it stir in the hairs on the back of his neck, and he shivered.

Now Cromwell raised his hand. "Let us not spend more time in these debates but let us apply ourselves to such things as are conclusive: everybody here would be willing that the representation be mended, that it might be made better than it is."

Will nodded. He had to give him credit. Cromwell had listened attentively, chaired the meeting well, allowed people to have their say, been fair.

Sexby came in again, his voice taut with emotion. "I am sent by my regiment, and if I did not speak these things I should think I were a covenant-breaker. Many of us fought for those ends which we have now learned were not those that caused us to go through difficulties and straits and to venture all in the ship with you. It had been good in you" – and here he pointed his finger at the three Grandees – "to have advertised us of it," he ended sarcastically.

Ireton leaned back in his chair, even-toned, conciliatory: "We did fight for the liberty of Parliament. I agree that Parliaments should be successive, not perpetual, and the distribution of elections more equal. We need to appoint a committee of some few to consider this."

There was a silence, as if the argument had lost way, the gusts of words abating in this compromise.

Will, uncomfortably aware he had not yet spoken, took a deep breath and cleared his throat, and said, "All people have a liberty and power to alter and change their constitutions if they find them to be weak and infirm."

As soon as he said it, it seemed a statement of the obvious. The only response was Rainborowe, who nodded vigorously. Cromwell stared at him and leaned forwards, elbows on the table again. "Gentlemen, we are going round in circles like crazed sheep. We will vote on this by a show of hands. I will give you a moment to gather your thoughts."

Will was sure most had made up their minds some time ago. The adjutators would vote one way, Ireton another; the officers he wasn't sure of. Hands raised tumblers to lips, mouths were wiped, the dampness of the church felt on the skin.

Cromwell: "All those in favour of extending the voting rights for Parliament to all free Englishmen except – and listen carefully before you decide – apprentices, beggars and servants: raise your hands."

Only three voted against. Fairfax, this man of war twirling his shoulder-length locks, had said nothing but voted for the motion. Will and the adjutators were exultant. Will fancied that the faces of the officers who had voted for the motion glowed with virtue – they knew they'd done something morally right even if it might not suit their personal circumstances.

And now, while there was a comfortable feeling of achievement and near harmony, Sexby chose this moment to raise the next crucial point in the *Agreement's* inevitable logic.

"I cannot but think that both the power of the Lords and the King was ever a branch of tyranny. And if ever a people should free themselves from tyranny, certainly it is after seven years of war and fighting for their liberty."

Then Wildman: "I fear that we are going about to set up the power of kings again, some part of it."

Will knew they were winding up to the climax of the argument.

Rainborowe weighed in: "You remember how we had no Parliament for eleven years? The King ruled alone. If those that make the laws can only do so when the King deigns to summon them, and cannot act except by such a call, truly I think that the people of England have little freedom."

This was the issue. Tempers were rising again, after the brief moment of agreement.

Now Captain George Bishop thumped the table. "I will tell you what distracts us in this council." He paused, all patience gone, eyes glaring, straightened his back. "I say that the reason is a compliance to preserve that man of blood." He almost spat out the words.

Man of blood rang round the church like a musket shot. The King, Charles, a man of royal blood indeed – but a man now steeped in the blood of this war, Englishman against Englishman. At last the argument had arrived at its appointed destination.

There was a sharp intake of breath around the table, the tension ratcheted up.

Wildman looked directly at Cromwell and said, "But it is very questionable whether God intends there to be a way left for mercy upon that person."

This was the very nub.

"Take care, Mr Wildman," interrupted Cromwell. "We cannot appeal to the mind of God because we cannot so clearly know the mind of God." He stood up, straightened his back and stretched his shoulders. "Gentlemen, we have talked a long time. There is much still to dispute but our minds ache and our bellies need bread and cheese. So I will now adjourn this meeting to another time. There is much business to attend to outside of this Council and we will meet again as soon as is possible. I thank you."

But before anyone else could rise, Rainborowe said: "I move that the army might be called to a rendezvous again so that the troops can be consulted."

Fairfax and Cromwell looked at each other.

"Agreed," said Fairfax.

But Will felt it was a weary, tiresome consent. And maybe to be regretted. The Army gathered together would be a powerful force. And the Army was behind *The Agreement of the People* – angry at broken promises over pay, bitter at King and Lords and Presbyterian Parliament.

Rainborowe was raising the stakes. Will caught Rainborowe's eye: his half-smile, his nod, a raising of his beaker, an acknowledgement. The Council broke up, chairs scraping across the stone floor, small knots of men talking excitedly.

27.

TRIBULATION

1646-47

For two weeks Ellen had to stay in her cell in Hartford gaol, stone-walled and damp, waiting for the spring session of the Connecticut General Court to begin. James and Alice came and were permitted to give her a feather mattress, blankets and food. James paid the gaoler extra so she would be better fed and more softly treated.

"No matter what happens, Ellen," said Alice, "we know you are innocent. They have forced you to do this."

But Ellen made no reply.

"Already she is preparing to depart this place," Alice said to James on their way home.

On their last visit, when they knew the date of the Court session, Ellen told James he must not attend the trial. He had publicly defended her so strongly that she was frightened they would be suspected of being in league with her, such was the hysteria in the area. Ellen would permit no argument. If he cared for her at all, he would grant her this last wish so she could rest easy. He must know the possible danger.

"I would like to be there," said Alice. "So you have one friend."

Ellen nodded, managed a sad smile but said nothing. She seemed grateful she would not be entirely on her own.

They both hugged her as they left. Alice held her close and knew it was a farewell. The outcome was inevitable. The way Ellen held her and buried her head in her shoulder showed that Ellen knew it too. At the door of the cell, finally, James turned and looked at Ellen. For a moment, before she averted her eyes, Alice saw in that look not just sadness but love. So something had remained. And she loved him for that loyalty.

The authorities were determined to do it properly. This was to be the first case of witchcraft to be tried in all the English colonies of North America. The Deputy General of the Colony was to be prosecutor. The magistrates who formed the judges' panel included Mr Ludlow and Samuel Wilton who was still public notary. The jury consisted of twelve publicly esteemed men.

On 28th May 1643, sitting at the back of the court, Alice heard Ellen Clark's trial begin when Samuel Wilton, magistrate, stood and read the charge: "Ellen Clark, thou hast done works above the course of nature to the loss of the lives of several people including children in the town of Plymouth. The jury will hear all testimony. If you wish to bring forward your own witnesses, you may. The gentlemen of the jury will question you about evidence against you and require you to explain yourself. Is this clear, Ellen Clark?"

Ellen nodded. "Aye," she said loud and clear.

The same witnesses from Plymouth gave their testimonies, Dr Rossitter repeated his denunciation of Indian remedies, and the Reverend Hooker concluded his statement by saying: "It is with great sadness that I acknowledge Satan has infiltrated the life of this woman and thereby many lives in evil and horrific ways."

Ellen had listened in silence to the familiar stories. But at this point she looked around the court as she sought Alice's face, roused herself and retorted: "I have not made a pact with the Devil nor have I ever done harm to anyone. You know not what you are saying."

The Prosecutor ignored her and asked: "Ellen Clark, would you care to elaborate or comment on these incidents? The Court would like to hear."

It was all a charade, thought Alice, and everyone there knew it. Ellen stared at him coldly and said nothing.

"And how do you respond to the good reverend's comments?" continued the prosecutor.

Ellen looked at each of the jurors in turn, staring hard and cold into them. She said nothing.

"Very well, then. You have had your chance. I ask Samuel Wilton to make the final statement."

He stood up and spoke at length. "We must take action," he concluded, "as directed by the holy words of the Bible – *Thou shalt not suffer a witch to live.*" He glared at her: "Ellen Clark must hang for her injurious acts of witchcraft. I am grateful she was exposed before further wicked acts of evil could take place."

The fateful word had been said. It had been anticipated but the courtroom was still full of murmurs of shock. Alice gave a strangled cry and covered her face with her hands.

Wilton sat down.

Ellen looked along the lines of jurors. She was weary beyond measure. With difficulty she got to her feet, her chains rattling. The court grew silent.

Quietly, in an even voice, she said: "I am innocent, I am no murderer. God is my witness, I am no murderer."

Wilton sprang up: "You have already admitted your guilt at Plymouth. It is impossible to disavow your confession."

"You are a liar, Samuel Wilton. And you know you are. God knows I am innocent."

She sat down.

"The jury will withdraw," announced Mr Ludlow.

They were out for less than fifteen minutes, during which time there was chatter in the courtroom. Alice sat silent, bereft that she could not comfort Ellen. Ellen sat, head bowed, waiting for the inevitable.

The jury returned to their places and sat down. Samuel Wilton stood up and read: "Ellen Clark, thou hast given entertainment to Satan, the great enemy of God and mankind, and by his help hast treacherously committed murder and witchcraft for which, according to the laws of God and the established laws of this Commonwealth, thou deserveth to die."

He said it with such relish and, after a dramatic pause, continued, "You will be hanged at two o'clock tomorrow."

Ellen gave a low groan, slumped forward but almost immediately sat straight again. Alice wanted to console her, wanted to rage at the injustice and primitive superstition. But she could no nothing.

The magistrates decreed that after her death no one was allowed to mention Ellen's name. She was to disappear from the records. They would not allow such a black tarnish on their life to be known by future generations.

The gaoler took her back to her cell. As the court and crowd noisily dispersed, Alice remained seated, stunned.

Had Ellen found some peace in what she had said to the magistrates? God knew she was innocent. That was all that mattered. What men said and suspected and alleged meant nothing – they were men and therefore flawed, briefly self-important in this world. Perhaps it was better to put an end to this torture and humiliation by death. How could she have lived on if the verdict had been different? She would still have been deemed to consort with the Devil, she would have been ostracised – like the adulterous woman forever condemned to wear a scarlet letter A on her breast.

Next day, before daybreak and as agreed with Alice beforehand if this was the outcome, James slipped out of Windsor and rode his horse and cart through the forest to Hartford. The news about the hanging had arrived late last night. They could do nothing to save Ellen but if she saw them she might face her fate more calmly. Alice remembered the look of love James had given Ellen at her cell door. Ellen deserved to see that look again. It would give her strength. Alice would stand well apart from James so that Ellen could have him for herself.

So now, at the back of the square, they watched the bustle and commotion. Alice felt a disgusting excitement in the air; there was to be a spectacle, an entertainment, a change to the routine of their days.

Then the sound of a horse's slow clopping hooves on the cobbles; the crowd suddenly quietened and turned to look. The horse pulled a small cart; the cart lurched as its wheels slipped into ruts, the bailiff holding the reins. In the cart, a coffin, cheap and ill-fashioned, and on it sat Ellen in chains, still squinting at the bright light.

The crowd parted. Alice saw faces twisted with hate and fear, and a few – women – looking with pity. Someone spat on Ellen's face and she wiped it away.

"Whoah!" yelled the bailiff. Alice saw Ellen look up to the gibbet above her head, the rope dangling, and then at Reverend Hooker and Samuel Wilton, the Reverend stern, Wilton triumphant.

The bailiff turned to haul her up from the coffin but Ellen threw off his arms. Some of the crowd cheered, others laughed.

"Unchain her," said the marshal.

With ill grace he did so. Ellen threw off his hands and stood straight. She turned and looked out over the crowd, the yelling men, fists thrust into the air, bawling taunts and jeers – but some of the women were strangely silent, just watchful. Ellen's eyes ranged with an unnatural curiosity – as if, thought Alice, they were the spectacle not her.

Then Alice saw Ellen catch sight of James. Her eyes locked onto him. She placed a hand on her heart. Alice, quickly looking at James, saw he did the same. It was right and good.

The Reverend Hooker's deep voice came to her: "What say you, Ellen Clark?"

Calmly she looked directly at him. "You and others like you are responsible for this innocent death. God will bring his wrath upon you. Look for it."

The crowd cheered.

She turned to Samuel Wilton. "It is you who are the Devil's helpmate and one day the justice of the good Lord will find you out."

Again the crowd cheered.

She turned to look again at James. Again she placed her hand over her heart as he had done. She smiled, such a smile of loved and loving happiness. Tears welled up in Alice's eyes, sad but so happy that Ellen had this moment. This was a love that had persisted through everything.

The marshal placed the rough rope of the noose around her neck. She stared ahead, still smiling. Wilton nodded. The bailiff lashed the horse, which jerked forward, and the cart's wheels crunched round. Ellen's body dropped, her neck snapping so that all could hear it. But there was no cheer, just a groan. The crowd dispersed; the event had not been a celebration of good over evil.

Alice lost sight of James and watched the bailiff load Ellen's body onto the cart. She followed it at a distance as he took it to a shallow pit just beyond the edge of the burial ground. He threw her body into the coffin, nailed down the lid, levered it into the shallow grave and roughly shovelled a thin covering of soil over it. No witch deserved a proper burial.

Alice returned and found James sitting on his cart, morose and staring into space, the horse with its neck lowered, waiting. She stretched up and took his hand.

"She cannot stay where they have buried her," said Alice. "We will take her back."

She climbed up beside him, took the limp reins from his hands and flicked them. The horse moved slowly forward.

"Thank you," said James, his face still drawn after the harrowing hanging.

In the evening they came to the grave, scraped away the soil with a spade and lifted out the coffin. They placed it on the cart and rode homeward through the forest.

They took her to the farthest field of their farm, on the edge of the wood. Silent, intense, with a focused energy, James dug the grave. Together they laid the body down in it. Neither prayed, neither wept, just a silent grief.

Then they shovelled back the earth and replaced the sods of turf.

Alice put her arms round him.

"I would like a headstone for her," James whispered into her neck.

"Yes."

A girl from Walkden in Lancashire buried secretly by a wood in Connecticut.

A love that was not lost, just overlaid by another.

With James's head resting at her neck, Alice thought of Will. Was it the same for them?

28.

CORKBUSH FIELD

1647

Will licked raindrops from his lips, freshening his mouth still dry and sour from last night's ale, and wiped his brow with the back of his soaked leather glove. Cold raindrops infiltrated his collar and trickled down his neck. Flint's mane was plastered wet, his grey flanks greased.

They had ridden and marched to Corkbush Field in heavy rain. But it had almost stopped now, just a smear of drizzle in the air. Lined up were four horse regiments – horses whinnying, breath pluming the air, shaking their heads, metal bits clinking – and three foot regiments – men leaning on pikes, muskets shouldered, rubbing their hands to get the blood flowing, stamping boots into the squelchy grass. In their scowls and mutterings, shouted comments and gesturing arms, curses among the laughter, Will sensed discontent and insubordination. Anger was simmering in the drizzle.

Will watched Colonel Richard Eyres, returned from New England like hundreds of others. In front of each regiment he stood in his stirrups, raised his arm, his fist clutching a document.

"We stand by this, men!" he shouted. "*The Agreement of the People*, which we argued for at Putney and which was accepted by the Army Council. We must stand by this."

There were ragged cheers and the clashing of pikes. But some men were sullen, turning away and muttering to their comrades.

Major Thomas Scott was also exhorting the troops.

"We should do what they do in Naples in Italy. If any person there stands up for the monarchy, they are hanged at the door."

Guffaws and cheers, a few low hisses.

It seemed to Will this was desperate stuff, a last attempt to embolden the troops as they awaited the arrival of Cromwell and Fairfax. The high hopes of Putney in August had faded. The first betrayal: instead of one rendezvous of the whole army, which the Army had wanted and which had been agreed, the Grandees had decided to split the Army into three rendezvous. Corkbush Field was the first.

Divide and conquer. Cromwell the manipulator, backtracking.

What tactics would he use today? Attitudes had hardened on both sides. Only last week, the Commons had declared that *The Agreement of the People* was "destructive to the being of Parliament and to the fundamental government of the Kingdom." The Army Command had sent a Remonstrance to the House of Lords, condemning the Levellers for the anarchy they preached. In retaliation, army adjutators had warned the soldiers to defy their officers and had ridden to the soldiery in Southampton and to rouse the citizens of Bristol, Weymouth, Exeter and Gloucester. They had linked up with civilian Levellers in London, scattered copies of *The Agreement* in the streets, posting bills on churches and gates and docks inciting the people to "rise as one man and free themselves from the tyranny of their taskmasters at Westminster." Revolution was in the air.

Will shivered. His thighs were damp beneath his buckskin trousers and he shuffled restlessly, chilled, in his saddle. Below him, mist still hung over the River Lea down at King's Meads; behind him, cloud hung low over Barrow Green Common. Everywhere was grey.

Then out of the riverside trees came the sound of hooves, a small group of riders thundering up the field towards them, mud splattering, water spraying out. They wheeled to a halt, horses breathing heavily and pawing the ground. It was Cromwell, Fairfax and a small troop of guards.

Slowly, Cromwell turned his head to take in the whole assembly. He caught Will's eye, stared hard at him for a moment then turned away dismissively. Will had been about to acknowledge him with a nod. Was he being dismissed as a lowly soldier, an errant MP or a Leveller sympathiser? Whichever, it was a curt rejection.

Scott and Eyres continued to harangue the soldiers, trying to whip up their spirits while, seated on their horses, Cromwell and Fairfax watched, shoulders hunched, heads close together. A few nods then Cromwell's pointed arm. Four of the guards peeled away to seize Eyres. He shouted, "Traitors!" but did not resist. One of the guards grabbed Eyres' reins and led him back.

"You will be court-martialled, sir, for this sedition," barked Cromwell: "incensing the soldiers against their generals."

"Are you a general of your men or a traitor to your men?!" shouted Eyres.

Curses from the soldiers, threatening fists in the air, some taking a defiant step forward.

Scott was the next arrested.

Will watched the two led away. So the old order re-asserts itself, the Grandees: has nothing changed? More shouts from the soldiery, a clashing of pikes, spit gobbed onto the grass. But no concerted movement to surround Cromwell and Fairfax. No sense of a mutiny, just a sullenness. Taken off guard, shocked.

Then from behind the cavalry came another horseman. As he passed Will, he waved. A smiling determined face: Colonel Rainborowe. He now rode from division to division, exhorting them.

"Don't be cowed, men. We must stand firm on what was agreed at Putney by the Army Council. Stand firm on the principles we agreed."

Cheers and shouts of support.

Rainborowe turned his horse and approached Fairfax. The two men stared at each other.

"This is *The Agreement of the People*," Rainborowe said, and he offered Fairfax the rolled document. "We must all stay faithful to this if we are honest, God-fearing men. And here is a petition in support of it."

Fairfax stared at the proffered documents held in the stained calfskin gauntlet. Then he spurred his horse and rode straight past Rainborowe to the front of the assembled troops. Rainborowe was left stupidly with his arm stretched out. He turned to look at Will, and Will saw humiliation and fury in his face. Will shook his head in sympathy. Fairfax halted; his horse stamped and reared. He controlled it.

He waited while the troops grew silent. Then he took a sheet of paper from his pocket and began to read it out. Will and the troops listened to the short declaration.

"Adjutators amongst you have been guided by divers private persons who are not of the Army."

Civilian Levellers like Maximilian Petty and John Wildman, thought Will.

"They have spread falsehoods and scandals in print about the Army high command."

A low hostile muttering grew. Where was this leading?

Fairfax put the paper away in his pocket, looked up, his eyes scanning slowly across all the troops.

"This is not the time for a divided army. We must be united to keep what we have won through your bravery."

Fairfax paused, then ended, "If this dissent continues I will resign as General."

There was another gasp from the troops. Faces turned to each other in bewilderment. Will was astounded, immediately suspicious. A master stroke, a gamble, pre-planned. The troops worshipped Black Tom who had led them to so many victories. It smacked of Cromwell's manipulation. Soldiers' mouths were open with shock, brows furrowed.

"But if I stay," continued Fairfax, "I pledge your arrears will be paid. From now on you will be paid promptly and you will have indemnity for your actions during the war. There will be care for injured soldiers and soldiers' widows, and compensation for apprentices who left their crafts to serve in the Army with us."

Faces changed in an instant and cheers rang round the assembled troops.

Fairfax raised his arm to quieten them. "What you asked for at Putney will be agreed: a time limit set for this Parliament, freedom and equality to vote, redress of the common grievances of the people."

Clapping on shoulders, shouts of acclaim.

Fairfax stood in his stirrups.

"What say you?!" he shouted. "Do you pledge loyalty and allegiance?"

A great cheer went up.

"Then I will live and die with you."

A buzz of talk, shouting, laughter. A masterly performance. If he meant what he said and did what he said, all was fine. But Will was sceptical. Just words so far.

Then amid all the congratulations and good humour, relief, heads turned to the sound of another regiment of horse and one of foot marching down from the Common. As they neared, Will recognised Colonel Harrison with the horse and Colonel Robert Lilburne – brother of Freeborn John – with the foot. They had not been invited, Will knew, to this rendezvous.

Both regiments wore White papers in their hats. Peering closely, Will saw they were copies of the *Agreement*, with a motto on the outside in capital letters: *ENGLAND'S FREEDOM, SOLDIERS' RIGHTS.*

Fairfax immediately rode over to confront them. He spoke briefly and severely. He ordered them to remove the Whites. Harrison's regiment did so, and then pledged their loyalty.

But Will knew Lilburne's regiment was the most mutinous regiment in the Army. They stood, unmoving, surly.

"Take those papers from your hats," ordered Fairfax again.

"No," came the spontaneous response. "No."

Then Cromwell spurred his horse forward. Drawing his sword, he waved its gleaming blade as he charged furiously through Lilburne's regiment, scattering the men who dived for their lives.

"Remove the Whites!" he yelled in a fury.

Shocked and cowed by his rage, slowly the men complied. Papers scattered and crushed in the mud beneath their boots.

Rainborowe rode over to join Will.

"The greatest deceit," said Rainborowe.

"But clever," said Will.

"What we need is honesty and loyalty, not sharp wits."

"Remember him at Kentford Heath?" said Will. "He had the Army in his pocket, but now he is doing Parliament's work."

Then Cromwell bawled the order to arrest eleven ringleaders in the regiment.

"This is treachery," snarled Rainborowe. "I thought we were on the same side."

"He's setting an example for army discipline."

"Scapegoats more like," said Rainborowe.

But Cromwell wasn't finished. A field court-martial was convened and the eleven were tried, with three condemned to death. It took less than twenty minutes, the troops watching, paralysed with disbelief.

"The man must show mercy," said Rainborowe, his voice cracking with emotion.

Will had to restrain him. "It will do no good, Thomas. He will not back down, not in this public place. He knows the army respects him; now he wants them to fear him."

Cromwell ordered the three to throw the die. A colonel laid his scarf on the muddy grass. He and the three condemned mutineers stood at the four sides. The colonel handed the die to the tall, fair-haired soldier. He bent, coggled the die in his palm and threw it onto the scarf.

"Five," said the colonel, picked up the die and gave it to the second soldier, an older man, grey-haired and stooped a little. He bent and threw the die straight down with a kind of disgust.

"Four," said the colonel and handed the die to the last soldier, a young man, thick dark hair, broad-shouldered.

Less than an even chance, thought Will. Poor lad. Private Richard Arnold looked at the other three, turned to look Cromwell in the eye and smiled.

"I'm in God's hands," he said, tossed the die from one hand to the other, bent and threw it on the scarf. It tumbled over a couple of times.

The colonel bent down.

"One," he said and held the die up to show them all.

Private Arnold dropped to his knees on the scarf, looked up to the grey sky and crossed himself.

There was a low muttering among the assembly, cries of "Lord, Lord have mercy."

"There will be no mercy," said Will, disgust rising like vomit into his throat. "A godly man, certain that God is on his side, can be the most ruthless man."

"Ruthless and cruel and wrong," echoed Rainborowe. "This injustice will not be forgotten."

The colonel helped Private Arnold to his feet. He stood straight and looked straight at the assembled regiments while his hands were tied behind his back. He was blindfolded. The colonel marched him to the head of his regiment. The lucky soldiers who threw the five and the four were handed their muskets.

"Shoot him," said the colonel.

They looked at each other but they had no choice.

"Do they add murder to their sins?" said Rainborowe.

"Perhaps Cromwell will show mercy, away from this place. It would be a clever ploy."

"And so he plays with lives," said Rainborowe. "Like a god."

But Cromwell gestured impatiently towards the colonel. The colonel nodded. Private Arnold stood alone, head bent, lips moving in prayer. He raised his head to the sky, straightened and thrust out his chest.

"Shoot!" ordered the colonel.

With their backs to the regiments, the two soldiers raised their muskets.

"Fire!"

In the now total silence of the watching troops, two shots rang out, muffled in the grey dampness. The private's body crumpled to the muddy ground, his arms twitched and then were still.

A shudder went through the troops; a few, a very few, shouts of disgust from the back. Then a solitary soldier somewhere began to recite the Lord's Prayer and was immediately joined by everyone, voices intense and deep across the field, the final drawn-out amen first rising towards the low cloud and then sinking to the ground. A silence broken only by the horses whinnying.

As Cromwell turned away and rode back down to the river, even he must feel the hatred. Fairfax waited for him to follow the bend in the track into the trees, then ordered the Army to disperse.

They did so, slowly, orderly, subdued.

"And so we see that discipline wins wars," said Rainborowe.

"But makes enemies of friends," added Will.

"Remember, we don't fight for him, we fight for the people," said Rainborowe.

"God's commander can be the very devil," said Will.

Two troopers lugged the private's body onto a cart. A flick of the reins and the wheels began to creak downhill.

Will spat viciously into the mud.

29.

Aftermath

1647

A t home, for days James hardly spoke. He moved through his work routines on the farm and in the store silently and doggedly. At mealtimes he contributed only monosyllables to the conversation.

Was this more than the death of a friend, a youthful lover? wondered Alice. She recalled that soon after meetings with Ellen she'd often heard James whistling or singing. But he had abruptly stopped when she, Alice, appeared. If James had sought comfort with Ellen could she blame him? Since Nicholas's death she had kept an ice-cold bed.

Though this domestic tension held them apart, the settlement's reaction tethered them together. Because they had been so publicly outspoken against the witch-hanging, other people were wary of being seen with them for fear of being tarred with the same brush. On the streets, people averted their faces when they passed. The store lost customers. Only Alice's dissident women friends remained loyal to her.

But illness and death continued at a high rate. Some began to wonder why this was, now that the witch-perpetrator was dead. Had the elders and magistrates made a fatal mistake? The horror of the hanging – the first in the colony's twenty-five-year history – returned to people's minds: Ellen's last words and her dangling, twisting body.

Gradually, James and Alice were seen in a more sympathetic light. James was acknowledged by men as they passed him in the fields; trade in the store picked up. Samuel

Wilton unwittingly helped them, too. He bore himself about like a victorious tribune of the people: he had carried out their wishes and they should be thankful. His decisive, damning words at the trial had re-established his reputation as a leader with the Church and political authorities, but his triumphalism offended even them. As for the common folk, they detested his bragging, his presumption that he was their hero, his blustering loudness when in drink.

Over the weeks, as their isolation decreased, so did the awkwardness in the Parker household. Now Alice understood that James's feelings for Ellen had not invalidated his love for herself. She did not feel hurt. Slowly James came out of himself, and equally slowly Alice showed herself warmer to him: a hand on his shoulder, a soft word, a brief touch of fingers, a brushed kiss on the cheek. Eventually the night occurred when Alice turned to James in bed and kissed him. It was not a goodnight kiss but a long and tender one. James responded. The defences each had constructed were breached; the floodgates of affection opened and they made love with some of their old excitement and knowledge of each other's bodies. No words were said but both knew it was a new beginning. And they welcomed it.

Two evenings later they sat together in front of the fire with mugs of cider. There was an ease between them again. He had so readily come back to her; she had timed it right.

"I have been thinking about Samuel Wilton," said Alice.

"Is that good for you?" replied James.

"He thinks he's above the law," continued Alice, "parading about, putting on airs."

"He is above the law, the things he gets away with."

"I'm not sure. I'd like to put it to the test."

James glanced across at her, a frown, a quizzical smile.

"And I'd like us to do it together," continued Alice.

"A conspiracy!" James chuckled. "That sounds good. What's your notion?"

"It's more than a notion and not, I'm afraid, a conspiracy." She explained: "You know that second division of land he took over, next to our orchard and going down to the two rivers?"

"I remember him striding about down there, waving his arms and bawling instructions."

"I'm positive he's taken more than he should have," said Alice firmly. "If we could take him down a peg or two, that would give me great satisfaction."

"It's not revenge, is it?" He looked her in the eye.

"I hate him for what he did to Ellen. He's a loathsome man."

James looked away and nodded.

"But no, nothing to do with revenge. It's a question of what's right and wrong, whether there's been duplicity."

"So, what are we going to do?" asked James.

"Go to see Roger Ludlow."

"Ludlow? But he's a crony of Wilton's."

"You're right. But he's the deputy governor. We need his approval to investigate," said Alice.

"But why would he co-operate?" asked James.

"Because, although they may be cronies, they're all willing to use each other to their own benefit. At the trial Ludlow was happy to use Wilton to get the condemnation of the so-called witch. It gave him and the elders the justification to do what they had wished for a long time but feared because it would be unpopular – return to a more Puritan regime and strengthen the laws against tobacco and alcohol."

"*No use of tobacco in public, no lingering in the alehouse for more than thirty minutes*," he quoted. "The wives were pleased, but it didn't go down well with some of the men. The Puritans are in a minority now but still hold most of the public offices."

"The new laws are not only unpopular," said Alice, "they're difficult to enforce. I think Ludlow would quite relish the chance to make it appear that Wilton was the force behind them. That would prick his bombast and man-of-the-people act."

"Clever! If you're right," said James.

"We can only try. And it might even afford us a smile or two."

"Indeed it might." He smiled at her. "Not just a woman of principles, but prepared to stick her neck out for them. You're a brave woman, always have been. I'm with you."

"Of course, you must do the talking. Ludlow will take no notice of me. I'm only a woman."

"Only?"

Roger Ludlow's grey eyes, glaring out from their bony sockets, were famous: as unforgiving as honed steel to malefactors brought before him. His long thin face had that look of self-satisfied clerical virtue. His skin was that of a man who spent more time in offices than in fresh air. His grey beard and long, flowing grey locks signified experience and sobriety; his expensive black clothes, prosperity.

Such was the deputy governor of the colony who faced James and Alice across his broad, tidy, polished mahogany desk. Not a man to be trifled with. The man who had overseen the hanging of Ellen Clark only twelve months ago.

"You wish to raise a matter of land with me, Mr Parker?"

He was looking only at James.

"We do."

James looked towards Alice.

"Yes," she said, smiling at Ludlow, "my husband and I have a concern."

Ludlow's eyes flicked towards her as if he'd suddenly noticed something distasteful and out of place – a stain or a woodlouse.

"Speak on," he said, looking back at James.

"It concerns Samuel Wilton."

Ludlow nodded knowingly, a half-smile, steepled his long fingers with their prominent knuckles and rested them on his lips. "There is bad blood between you: the hanging of the witch. I will pay no heed to bad blood."

"You will see for yourself," said Alice, "if it is bad blood or a matter of fact."

"I will indeed make that judgement," he said, dismissing that tiresome woman well-known for her argumentative friends. "Now, proceed, Mr Parker." He leaned back in his chair and stretched out his long legs.

The power game: the petitioner and the office-bearer. His brother, the Archbishop and the King: writ small but the same.

James steadied himself. "At the original settlement, Samuel Wilton was rightly granted a prime division of land. Ten months ago, in view of his public service" – neither Alice's face nor Ludlow's flickered – "he was allotted a second division of land. This abuts my orchard near the foot of West Rock." A pause. "I believe he has taken more than his fair share. I ask that it be surveyed and compared with the original record of the grant. As the public notary, he will have recorded the transaction himself – and this, I think, merits some scrutiny… sir."

Alice looked sharply across at her husband. Not too much.

James had added the last word on the spur of the moment: a little subservience was worth it and he hoped Ludlow would not hear it as sarcasm or insolence.

Ludlow stood up and moved to stare out of the window at the street: hands behind his back, thin wrists, soft fingers that used a pen and not a plough, a tall man, spare of frame. Between his breeches buttoned at the knee and his buckled black shoes, his spindly legs were almost calf-less.

Alice wondered if Ludlow was thinking as she had predicted. She threw a questioning glance at James. To Ludlow's long back James said: "I ask only that a survey be done by one of your officers and the measurements compared with the documentation."

Ludlow turned and those eyes drilled into James.

"I understand what you ask. Is this request only on your behalf or on behalf of others?"

"To be true, it is only I who ask for it, but my neighbours have voiced the same concerns."

Ludlow returned to his seat. "Well then, Mr Parker, and Mrs Parker" – with an exaggerated grace – "in the interests of openness and fairness, I can see no objection to finding the facts. I must thank you for bringing the matter to my attention. I will call you back when I have some answers."

"Thank you, sir," replied both Alice and James. This time there could be no doubt about the sincerity of the 'sir'.

Ten days later James and Alice were back in the same room on the same chairs at Hartford. So was Ludlow. But there was an extra chair. On it, sat – or lorded – Samuel Wilton, preening himself in his bright blue, embroidered coat, casting supercilious glances at the Parkers, double chin thrust out pugnaciously.

On Ludlow's desk was a sheaf of papers and Ludlow was leafing through them. Alice saw how this was what Ludlow loved: stuff codified on paper in black and white. She watched Ludlow's lips twitch appreciatively, pursing. It was a habit, Alice assumed, as he perused a detailed sub-section of a regulation or recognised a relevant precedent. He was a man who approved order, punctuality, correctness, the routine liturgical demands of a Puritan Sunday. Alice understood that this was exactly the sort of man she and James needed at this point.

Wilton's patience was limited, his sense of hierarchy keen.

"I do not yet know why you have summoned me to sit here with these witch-lovers," he said.

"Pray be silent, sir; you will have the opportunity to have your say." Ludlow had not even looked up from the papers.

"I will have my say now!" Wilton stormed, his face red.

Ludlow, a touch of pink on both his cheeks, leaned back in his chair. He is enjoying this, thought Alice. He has all the information, knows exactly what the outcome will be: a lean cat playing with a plump mouse.

Wilton leaned forward and jabbed his finger at James and Alice.

"Whatever you have conjured up against me, it is the Devil working in you, the same Satan as worked in that witch Ellen Clark."

He turned to Ludlow. "They were in league with her. They spoke often together. They sold her Indian herbs and medicines in their store." Eyes blazing and pointing his finger. "Not a word they say can be believed. They are of the Devil's party; they should be banished from our community. I will recommend it to the court."

He had clenched his fists and thumped the arms of his chair, his feet tapping the floor, his cheeks trembling, breathing heavily. His waistcoat was flecked with phlegm.

Ludlow had watched with no change of expression, as if watching an unknown child have a tantrum. Now he sat up straight in his chair again, rested his forearms on the desk.

"Thank you, Samuel," he said calmly, nodding his head as if in approval. "I will bear your words in mind. But now to the matter in hand."

Alice and James had watched the short scene like spectators at a play, simultaneously caught up in it and at one remove, seeing the roles emerge. Wilton's threats were real but were they an attempt at a diversion? Ludlow was not easily diverted.

"It appears," said Ludlow slowly, running a finger down a set of figures, "that the amount of land granted to you ten months ago was twenty-four acres but, instead, you have taken fifty-two acres." He looked up, those eyes now piercing Wilton. "Can you explain?"

It was obvious that Wilton had been taken by surprise. It was as if his earlier outburst had exhausted him, as if, lunging forwards, he had been fatally wounded from the back. His voice was low and apologetic: "I fenced in my land without a surveyor. And if I took more than I should, it was a mistake for which I am sorry."

"It was more than an innocent mistake, it was a sinful miscarriage," Ludlow's voice hard as stone. He turned to James: "So your suspicions, Mr Parker, and those of your neighbours were correct." Back to Wilton: "You will be officially censured for this, Mr Wilton."

Wilton nodded and began to rise from his chair, his well-stuffed body seemingly as heavy as lead.

"But there is much more," said Ludlow. And James could swear he said it with relish.

Wilton sat down again, a sheen of sweat on his face.

"The records," continued Ludlow, again leafing through the papers and then looking up, "have been falsified. There have been crossings-out, additions, emendations. Is this your handwriting, Mr Wilton?"

He pushed a paper across the desk. Neither Alice nor James could entirely resist gloating at this unexpected turn of events.

Wilton picked up the paper, his hand trembling. "Yes, it is mine," his voice strangled, "but I can explain." His jowled face sagged, his body drooped. He shuffled uncomfortably on his seat. He cleared his throat.

"I am sure you can," said Ludlow. "But before you do and before you swear an oath on your honesty, as I'm sure you are about to do, I must inform you that here" – and he spread out the papers – "we appear to have three sets of accounts on this issue, all at variance, all favouring yourself and all written in your hand as public notary."

Elbows on his desk, again steepling his hands, his fingers lightly brushing his lips, he looked straight at Wilton.

Wilton swallowed, eyes lowered then flicking up at Ludlow in a mixture of confusion and pleading. Yet there was a pathetic defiance in him, not red with shame or guilt but with anger that he had been found out.

Now Ludlow put on his most formal lawyerly expression and tone of voice. "In these circumstances, swearing an oath of innocence or admitting to an inadvertent mistake, may I remind you, would be no other than a high breach of the third commandment."

Wilton slumped lower, his head on his chest. Alice may have felt a moment's pity for him, ashamed of her recent gloating, but James did not.

"On this evidence," continued Ludlow, "I am certain you will be voted out of office, your land reduced to what it should be, and you will be heavily fined. I shall also recommend that the Church excommunicate you."

Wilton slowly sat up straight. He narrowed his eyes at Alice and James with pure malevolence.

Ludlow ended: "Go, Mr Wilton, and consider yourself fortunate if you are not sent to gaol."

With a withering look at Ludlow, Wilton stood up, holding himself as straight as his ample paunch would allow in a final attempt at dignity, and left the room.

Later, James and Alice would agree they had seen two very different kinds of bully in a power play – both ruthless, both so certain of themselves, but one victorious and the other defeated.

James said: "We thank you and your colleagues for your work. We are very grateful."

Alice nodded and they began to rise from their chairs.

Ludlow motioned them to remain seated.

He said: "Wilton is not alone in his suspicions about both of you and the witch."

Alice saw James flinch.

"Indeed, to tell the truth, I have my own suspicions. Although I am sure Wilton will be punished as I said, there will be some among the elders and magistrates, some friends of his, some still beholden to him, who will not be happy at what they will see as your victory, the victory of the witch-lovers."

Alice and James frowned at each other.

"I fear it may be likely you could be brought to trial for the reasons Mr Wilton mentioned. We are a troubled community still. Deaths are still more frequent than they should be and people can be led to believe it is because you – particularly you, Mr Parker – are still living and prospering here. If there is a call for your banishment, or worse, I believe the fire of support for that action could easily be fanned."

Ludlow tidied the papers. "I would advise you to think on it. Wilton's case will be considered by the authorities next week. I think it would be wise if I had your thoughts before then. Thank you, that is all."

Alice and James could not hide from each other the sudden fear in their eyes. As they made their way home, all they could think was that they had plucked defeat from victory. Surely they had lost more than they had gained. And what now?

Next day, in the late afternoon, they walked together to the blackberry glade. It was a still June day, sun shining through the trees. It seemed the right place to go – where they had met over twenty years ago. They sat together on a fallen tree trunk. Decisions had to be made.

"They will do it, Alice," said James. "They will banish us."

"I have been trying to fathom why Ludlow warned us."

"Maybe he feels guilty. Maybe he wants no more weight of responsibility on his shoulders."

"Perhaps, but that hasn't bothered him before," mused Alice. "I think it's more about the power games they play."

"It's not like you to think like that."

"I'm learning. And my friends are opening my eyes. What do you think of my theory? Wilton's punishment, proposed by Ludlow, arises from our questions. Ludlow will be aware this might make him appear to be a witch-lovers' sympathiser. Now he has to redress the balance – by pushing for our punishment. Banishing us would make him the decisive player."

She glanced at him with her cheeky smile.

"Clever!" he said, with a grin. "But how did my straightforward Alice come to understand the mind of a conniving politician?"

He kissed her on the cheek.

"Just life?" she laughed. "Ludlow is giving us a chance to leave of our own accord before we're forced out. He wants to avoid another trial."

"He loves trials; they are meat and drink to him."

"But he does not like mob rule. It is dangerous, can get out of control. And above all, he believes this community needs to come back under control. Who knows what another witch-hunt may lead to – beyond the death of another innocent or two?"

Ellen's grave was only a field away. Alice wondered if James, too, was conscious of it.

"Would banishment be so bad?" she asked. "Others banished have set up on Rhode Island and it is a success. Why could we not do the same?"

"And give up everything we've worked so hard for? It's not right."

He got up and stood over her, with both hands gently tilted her face up to him.

"I think it is best if I go," he said softly.

"What do you mean, you go? You mean I stay?"

"I think Ludlow would accept that. He would have what he wanted and would make sure Wilton did not come after you, threaten him with prison."

James sat beside her again, took both her hands in his.

"I will go to England."

"England?"

"Yes. As you know, there is a war on, against the King and the bishops. I would dearly love to help get rid of them."

Alice tried to take it in.

"Your brother?" she asked.

"In part. I would be honouring him, giving him some kind of justice. Others are going, to fight for Parliament, hundreds of men from all over the colonies. I hear stories from Boston that my relative, Colonel Thomas Rainborowe, is foremost among the Army leaders. I would join his regiment."

"But, James, you are not a fighting man. You have said so yourself."

"But here is a cause I believe in. I can fight for that." A pause. "And I have something to prove to myself, and to my sons. And to redeem myself for Nicholas's death."

The name silenced them.

They heard the buzzing of flies, suddenly loud, a robin somewhere above, a scuffling in the bushes.

Alice put her arm round James's shoulder and said softly: "You have nothing to prove to anyone. That is foolish."

"I have fled before," he said. "But this time I flee to fight. And I am choosing to go."

Alice looked at him quizzically. "You know that is not wholly true."

"Perhaps I need to convince myself, then."

James shook himself, then spoke quickly.

"I will transfer the ownership of the farm and store to you. It will be done properly so you are secure. You and the boys will be fine. They are grown up now, strong and healthy and good farmers. And you know all there is to know about running the store."

Alice got up and wandered over to the edge of the clearing. She could not take it in.

"The blackberries are budding," she said. "Even a few flowers."

Sunshine on the thorns, on the green buds like beads, the purple stems, pink petals splitting the buds.

"I remember, all those years ago, my hands were stained with their juice." Without looking at him she said, "And that is the last I see of you?"

He came up behind her and she felt his lips on her neck, his hands round her.

"Of course not, you will not be so lucky."

"So what will happen?"

"If the war goes badly, I will return. If Ludlow is still in control, then we will have to sell up and move on – to Rhode Island, say. But if the war goes well, I will return here with guarantees in my pocket from Rainborowe and Cromwell and we will be safe to live out our days here. Peter and Giles have lived all their lives here, it is their home. I would imagine that that is what they would prefer. Then they would inherit all we have worked for."

Stepping away from him, Alice said, "And if you are killed?"

"I will not be killed. I know it. I am not a reckless man. I will take great care. I do not want to die."

"That is wishful thinking, James, as well you know."

She took his hand and they walked across the clearing to the trail. Subdued now, sad even, they paused to look around the place where they had met. Alice's eyes flickered towards where Ellen lay buried, then flicked away. She wondered if part of James's desire to get away was to escape his grief.

They turned for home. Each was subdued, anxious. After all the turmoil, they wanted to be together and safe. But that was now impossible. There was no choice: their paths must now diverge. And might never meet again, was Alice's unspoken fear.

Things moved quickly. That evening they told their sons, who said little. Perhaps, thought Alice, they looked forward to working on their own without their father, being in charge. The following day James returned to Hartford. Ludlow found James's proposal acceptable and seemed relieved not to have to shoulder more responsibility for suffering. Perhaps, beneath the layers, there was something decent in him. While in Hartford, James saw a lawyer and transferred ownership of all his property and estate to his wife. He signed the documents with a sense of relief. All was settled.

Five days later, with another twenty-five men similarly bound for England, James was climbing the gangplank of the *Anne* in Boston Harbour. Their sons had said their farewells at the farm. Only Alice was on the quayside to see him off. There were tears, of course, wishes and hopes – and fears. None spoken.

When the ship slipped out of the harbour, Alice turned the horse and cart to the warehouse of the merchant they used to stock the store. She watched men load up the packages, mostly linen and clothing James had ordered months ago. She thanked them and turned onto the road for home. The road rose out of the town along the top of a low cliff. Alice stopped and looked out to sea: James's ship under full sail was about to round the cape and begin the long crossing to London.

It was almost dusk before she reached their store. Giles was there to help unload the packages. As she arranged them more neatly she caught sight of a label. Her heart missed a beat. She felt a sudden hot flush around her neck.

The name of the London merchant that James had ordered from was Will Nailor.

This sudden reminder that he was living his life, in London. That they had both gone their separate ways, each unconscious of the other, creating full lives without each other. James and Ellen: would it be the same with her and

Will if he should come ashore here from a merchant vessel? A sharp pang of loss, a sense of possibilities forever unfulfilled, of a different kind of life never lived.

Now joined again, thousands of miles apart, by this frail coincidence, this order of sheets and blankets, breeches and skirts.

James was aboard ship, on the ocean. At home, at the back of a drawer, was a bent sixpence, forgotten for so long.

30.

BATTLE OF PRESTON

1648

It was August 1648, and Will was quartered in a farmhouse down a side lane behind the church of St Leonard's in the village of Walton-le-Dale on the River Ribble. It was, he supposed, only thirty miles or so from his own village of Worsley: a thirty-five-year journey he had not expected to fetch up here.

For the last three days his troop, under the immediate command of Colonel Rainborowe, had marched down the Ribble Valley from Skipton. Cromwell, they knew, was marching north having accepted the surrender of Pembroke Castle. Their pincer movement was aimed at the Scottish Engager Army, marching south from Lancashire. The imminent battle would be the result of another act of treachery by King Charles. From imprisonment in Carisbrooke Castle on the Isle of Wight, he had somehow signed a treaty, known as the *Engagement*, with the Scots Covenanters. The Scots would reinstate Charles as King in return for his officially establishing Presbyterianism in England. The battle would thus be a fight against Scots invaders, against the King and against Presbyterianism and the loss of religious freedom. A powerful motivation for his Puritan radicals.

Will supervised his troops in the yard at the back of the farm as they unsaddled horses, rubbed them down, fed and watered them and finally picketed them in the home paddock. Once that was done, Will made his way to The Unicorn Inn. Troop standards were slanting out of the window above the thatched porch, their red, blue and green colours stirring in the breeze. He made his way down steps and along an uneven passage into the taproom. A fire blazed in the hearth, logs spitting sparks, and light glinted on the demijohns and coloured bottles that lined the shelves. The place was packed with soldiers, the air thick with tobacco smoke, voices arguing and laughing but no fighting or drunkenness. Will shoved his way through to a small group of officers at a round table beneath a deep-set window.

Ale was brought. Will took a long drink and wiped his lips with the back of his hand.

"I needed that!"

He didn't know any of the four – three faces he could see in the flickering light of the fire. The fourth was framed by daylight in the window behind him, features hidden in shadow. All wore their New Model Army red sashes over their shoulders.

"Quarters up to scratch?"

"Aye, but the farmer's not keen," replied Will.

"How about his daughter?"

Laughter.

The face in the window leaned forward, daylight gleaming on his almost bald pate.

Will looked up at the face, now clear in the firelight. It was Rainborowe, not afraid to drink with his men.

"Good evening, Will, good to see you."

They shook hands.

"Did I ever tell you I sailed with a William Rainborowe, years ago, to Morocco?" asked Will.

"My elder brother, no less! To free the slaves?"

Tankards were raised and stories told of voyages and battles, of derring-do, escapes and wounds.

Another officer joined them and sat down.

"Will, I must introduce you to James Parker, a new member of your troop," said Rainborowe.

The man smiled, nodded, raised his tankard and took a swig of ale.

"James is over here from New England. Hundreds of them have come to fight for Parliament. There are exciting, new, democratic ideas over there – so my family in Massachusetts tell me. James will tell you all about it."

"Good to meet you," said Will.

Rainborowe continued his tales. He told of how he had watched smugglers and mutineers marched down to Execution Dock, dancing the hempen jig at low water, hanging there until three tides had overflowed them. "As a young man I watched the *Mayflower* sail out of Rotherhithe on the way to Plymouth and New England."

"My wife sailed out on the *Mayflower*," said James, glad to be part of the conversation. He hadn't shared his Indian war experience. "But we're both originally from Lancashire, not far from here."

"So am I," Will said. "From Worsley."

James laughed and thumped his tankard on the table. "Alice was from Worsley. But her father took the family away to Holland."

Alice! Will's stomach lurched, his heart thumped: a sudden image of her face and smile.

"And I'm from Walkden," said James. "Only a few miles away."

Will sat silent and stunned, taking refuge in drinking his ale.

"Perhaps you knew her," persisted James. "Ainsworth was her maiden name."

Another desperate long draught of ale, buying time.

"I was sent away to London," he stammered, "to be an apprentice."

"I didn't catch your surname, Will," said James.

"Nailor."

James sensed the blood drain from his face; he could hardly breathe. He took a drink, coughed and spluttered: the preacher's struggles in the river, his eyes bulging, bubbles rising from his mouth, then his body going limp. James's hands shook as he relived the murder.

He stood to bring more ale, to give himself some space.

More manly tales were told but James and Will were silent, each wrapped in his own thoughts.

It was very late when Will stumbled back to the farmhouse, too full of ale. He fell on to his bed and was immediately asleep. But in the early hours he awoke and tried to reproduce the conversation with James. He had wanted to ask if James's Alice had green eyes. Thank God he hadn't. There was no need: his Alice was James's wife. And now he would fight alongside James.

James, too, had woken in the dark. Will was the son of the man he'd murdered. Strange happenstance. How much did Will know about his father?

The following morning Will watched a fly crawl across his hand, across the veins and hairs, his hand on the saddle pommel. Casual. A slight tickle. It would be the salt of his sweat. His fingers were slicked with it. He shook his hand and the fly left. In its own time, just evading, no fear. To another hand or face.

The hum and buzz of a million flies among the lines of troops. Like the tension of a drawn bowstring, taut at his ear. A close, humid morning. He was sweltered: the padded buff coat under his breastplate and back armour was necessary, but the felt hat over his iron helmet was a mistake. A vanity. He licked the saltiness of the sweat on his moustache, swallowed. But his throat was parched, a dry obstruction in there. The damp air was thick and constricting, drawn tight. Sunshine shone pale through a haze; but in the west, over the town of Preston, a heave of black cloud swelled, loaded with thunder.

Will silently cursed his bowels. That urge in his arse again, the pressure to void. His heart thumping. Flint fidgeted and sidled, tossed his head, snorted – like the rest of the waiting troop of horses. Were the other men like him? They had talked quietly around the campfire last night, a little laughter among the words, the glow of flames, wood smoke. A calmness he had wondered at, James quiet and withdrawn. And later, he heard prayers muttered in the darkness.

Will looked across the mass of men and restless horses and saw him, his face seeming to look directly back at him. James raised an arm in instant acknowledgement, as if he had been waiting for Will to seek him out. Was James nervous, too? Had he fought before? Will thought of Alice, thousands of miles away, unaware her husband was going to risk his life this day.

Most men here were experienced soldiers, some of Cromwell's Ironsides who had fought at the great victory of Naseby, and other places too: battles, skirmishes. Hardened men. Survivors. Principled men, too, the famous godly men that Cromwell had gathered. On the long march Will had seen no drunkenness, no card or dice gambling. No food had been stolen from the villages, no women violated. This was a new kind of soldier. The New Model Army. Men who had accepted him though he didn't join in their prayers, men he could depend on today. Major Bethel's troop. Loyal to each other, disciplined. A team to fight with, to be protected by.

They would need each other today. Today was real, today would happen. And in the next hour. That rippling tremble in his arse again. Too late for that. He shifted in his saddle and looked down the gentle sloping Ribbleton Moor where the Parliamentary Army was drawn up. Down there in the valley was the River Darwen, narrow but deep, edged with marsh and reed beds. Across the stream the land rose, and there, on the ridge, seeming to tremble in the damp mistiness, were the Scots forces of the Duke of Hamilton. Their commander,

Major General John Lambert, had said that defeating them today would end the war. Their scouts had reported that many of the Scots guns had been abandoned, bogged down in mud. But two had been manoeuvred into position on the opposite slope.

Will's eyes followed the direction of their barrels down to the river, to the ford. And leading down to the ford, a little to the left of their position, was a sunken lane down which he and his comrades would charge – straight into the waiting guns. Unless their own artillery could destroy them. He had watched Scots Engager musketeers deployed into the hedges and drainage ditches along the lane.

Will checked, yet again, the two flintlock pistols in their saddle holsters. No carbines today, just pistols and sword. He half stood in his saddle to ease the cumbersome thigh-length riding boots of polished buff leather. Saw the eight-horse team led away from the thirty-pound culverin that he hoped would blast away the enemy's guns. Saw the light guns – drakes and sakers – on their grey gun carriages wheeled into position, powder and ball in place, crews ready. The ammunition wagon was already turning away, the draft horses straining into their collars as they moved back up the slope. The creak of the wagon, shouts of men. Jostling of horses. A mutter of thunder behind him. Air trembling. A poise, a balance, an expectancy.

For the love of God, before I shit myself or vomit, let's go!

Then the sudden shout of command from John Lambert, one human voice, so frail it seemed to Will, yet calling forth such power. Smoke from the culverin barrel and a deep boom that shattered the stillness, the sharper cracks of the drakes and sakers. The flash of replies from the Engagers opposite. Echoes across the moor, fading. A moment's silence ringing in his ears. Then another bombardment battered his eardrums and tore through the air. Two explosions opposite, where the enemy's guns were, and immediately trumpets sounded, barely heard, and great cheering from the troops of horse as Colonel Thomas Rainborowe's thousand yelling Roundhead musketeers, blue ribbons in their hats, charged down over the moor and marshes to clear the enemy infantry from the ditches.

Any moment now. The signal. With a great rasping sound of steel, Will's troop drew their short straight-bladed swords. Each side of him, men turned to each other, grinned and drew their lips tight. They were in formation, four abreast, all that the drove was wide enough for. He could not see James. Through the din, a trumpet sounded close by. Flint started, snorted. Then they were away, the front four horsemen with their standard, red with a white fringe, thrust high. And now his own comrades were yelling. They charged forward and down the slope and onto the lane, hooves thundering on the earth. It was a direct charge with sword points held out. Will was in the fourth rank. His blood was up, no thought of anything, just a rage. But the charge was disciplined, knee to knee to keep formation, the pace controlled. Now they were splashing through the ford, and onto the enemy slopes. Will was dimly aware of screaming men and horses, horses buckled on the ground, legs threshing, teeth bared. Swords clashing, musket fire, pikes jabbing and slashing. Yells, whirling horses, flurries of charges. He, too, was hacking with his sword, yanking Flint's head from side to side as he swung round to face a new threat. The shock of contact, resistance to his sword – armour, padded jacket, piercing of soft stuff. Blood on his blade.

Then in the melee he saw James, he and another man, unhorsed, back to back, blood streaming down their faces. Four Scots surrounded them, their sabres slashing down. Will saw James's arm savagely cut. He wheeled Flint and spurred him towards James, yelling and brandishing his sword. One Scot turned tail, a second Will pierced in the chest. But before

Will could turn and attack the remaining two, James had been felled, and the other man, now standing alone, had his throat slashed by an Engager sword and sank to the ground. Will could do nothing; the battle rushed on with him and then they were through the line.

A dim awareness that Colonel John Desborough's troop was following them as they found firmer ground on the higher slopes. The first lightning flashed as they charged the Engager cavalry. More reinforcements arrived with Lieutenant General Cromwell, and the Scots line broke, retreated and then fled. Cromwell halted the troops of horse on the ridge. Only now did Will return to sanity, his hands trembling, his breathing steadying, patting Flint on the neck, leaning forwards with words of thanks and comfort, the horse in a lather of sweat, men congratulating each other, wide-eyed, even a psalm being sung. But Will was crushed by his failure to save James. He had a raging thirst, but the day's work was not yet done. Black clouds were now overhead, thunder boomed and lightning flashed. Cromwell waited until the horse were reformed. Then the cloud burst in a torrent of rain. Will held his head up to it, opened his mouth, seeking redemption from the cool wetness.

Cromwell stood in his stirrups, raised his sword arm. "Ride them down!" he yelled.

So Will and the rest pursued and harried Hamilton's cavalry. Still disciplined, they cantered along the road towards Preston, its flames rising high despite the rain. They passed bodies and wounded men, horribly gashed, hiding in ditches and under hedges. Then they came into the burning town, set alight to delay them. Slowly they moved through and on the other side came upon the abandoned baggage and arms of the Scots Engager Army – overturned wagons, smashed boxes. Pickings for the infantry. There they halted, the rain sluicing down.

It was short-lived: the relief at surviving, the exultation of total victory, the possibility of the war being over. Will was overcome with sudden fatigue and tormented by James's death. He and Rainborowe plodded back through the battlefield. They looked down on bodies ripped by pike and sword and musket shot, distorted by a final agony in the churned mud. There were wounded, too, begging for death, some huddled like babies. Young faces, worn faces. A horse with two pikes buried in its belly. Flint had to pick a careful way through the mass of bodies at the ford. Most were Hamilton's men. So much bravery, so much grieving to come.

"Killed by the King," said Rainborowe.

"I'm looking for someone in particular," said Will. But he didn't give the name. It was Rainborowe who had introduced James to him but he needed to do this on his own. Rainborowe somehow understood, nodded and turned his horse away.

Will dismounted and led Flint slowly by the reins. Eventually he found James's body. Will knelt. Just another corpse, twisted, disfigured, ugly, meaningless now. Thank God he was not dying in agony. With his gloved hand, Will gently moved James's face so he could look at it – eyes staring, bloodstained, teeth bared. But a strong face. Will closed James's eyes.

This was the man Alice loved, whose sons she had borne, whose life she had shared, whom he had known for two days. It was for Alice's sake that Will had tried to save him. Will only realised that now. How could he get word to her? He wanted to write to her himself, as if that would comfort her more. But the shock of her husband's death would be bad enough. To see his signature at the end of the letter, out of the blue, could distress her more. He must get Rainborowe to do it; his own name must not be mentioned.

And Will felt a great hatred against the King rise up in him: all these lives wrecked so brutally at the behest of that arrogant

313

incompetent man who clung to his belief in the divine right of his ruling. Born to power and determined to keep it. But Will raged not just against the King but against the nature of men – to be violent, to hold sway, to coerce.

A victory in battle was never a victory; no less than a loss, it proved the failure and absurd cruel vanity of man. It was a vile necessary step towards an end.

Maybe, as Lambert said, this would be the last battle. And he could return to his children – having helped to bring them peace. Would that Jane could see it that way.

The rain turned to drizzle as he re-crossed the ford; the storm passed eastwards and the sky lightened.

31.

DISSIDENT WOMEN,

1648

"You really walked out of the service at the meeting house last Sunday?" Alice asked.

"I did."

"And you were on the front row as usual?"

"I was, with my husband."

Mrs Anne Eaton sat up straighter and smiled, eyes bright. Her husband was Theophilus Eaton, Governor of New Haven Colony.

They looked at each other, raised eyebrows and nodded approvingly. Alice was exultant. How angry and humiliated he must have been. There were five women sitting round the kitchen table: Anne Eaton, Widow Lucy Brewster, whose home this was, Widow Moore and her daughter Mrs Leach, and Alice.

Elizabeth, the servant girl, had brought them pastries and spiced cider.

Alice had a vivid memory of when she herself had walked out of a service all those years ago – thirty-three years and a lifetime ago. She wanted to tell her story, show solidarity and establish her credentials, but it would lead to other explanations she did not want to give.

"The sermon itself was almost too much for me but when they prepared to baptise an infant, that was when I left," continued Mrs Eaton.

"Are you an Anabaptist, then?" asked Mrs Leach timidly, as if the question itself were an affront. She was a tiny woman, thin-boned and sharp-faced: the very opposite of her mother who reminded Alice of Mary Cheever – broad-hipped, round-faced, burly as a wrestler, her hair untouched by grey.

"I believe someone should be baptised only when they ask to be and only when they can sensibly confess their faith in Christ."

Alice thought wryly that her father had led them away from Amsterdam to Leiden because many were beginning to think like Mrs Eaton. How bewildered and angry he would be to see his daughter a close friend of an Anabaptist. The twists of fate.

"And then you were summoned to a church meeting by the Reverend John Davenport himself?" Mrs Leach again, awestruck by the seriousness of this and its public nature.

"I was. To explain myself." She spoke with contempt, as if it were a supreme indignity. As Alice indeed thought it was.

"But you surely did that," said Widow Moore with the same relish she heard all stories of women refusing to comply meekly with men. "You are cleverer and more quick-witted than all the men there."

She ate another pastry and they all laughed.

"Do you know? I think I am," said Mrs Eaton, and they all laughed again.

Elizabeth brought in some chocolate drinks.

"That is the problem, of course," continued Mrs Eaton. "They disapprove more because I spoke about my changing beliefs only with a woman."

"Lady Deborah Moody?" asked Alice. They all knew that Lady Moody had been excommunicated from her church in Massachusetts for her beliefs.

"The men were angry. If I was reconsidering my beliefs I should have sought advice from my husband or any man of the Assembly."

"Or your pastor, John Davenport."

"Or him, indeed." Mrs Eaton wrinkled up her nose in scorn. "The Pastor, all severe-faced as if I was a child and he a schoolmaster, quoted me what Paul said in Corinthians: *If the women will learn anything, let them ask their husbands at home."*

"Only when we are widows are we free," said Widow Lucy Brewster.

"Something to look forward to, daughter," said Widow Moore. "And you, Alice."

"What have we come to, that we must look forward to our husbands' deaths!"

"So he lectured you?" asked Widow Brewster.

"He and two elders, in great detail. I decided neither to object nor yield but quietly held to my position."

"Here in this place," said Alice, "it is easier for a non-believer like me than for those, like you, who challenge some aspects of belief – and do it in public."

"The men do not like it at all," pronounced Mrs Eaton. "Women questioning them eats at their authority. They say it *undermines the stability of the family…"*

"*… which must always be ruled by men…"* interposed Alice, as if quoting from a well-known decree.

"*… and of the household, and therefore of the state,"* ended Mrs Eaton, tapping the table sharply at each phrase. "But in truth, it is their pride that is hurt. They feel threatened and humiliated. It is that which makes them take us to task."

"A fine thing for a humble man of the faith," said Widow Moore.

At that point, Elizabeth the servant pushed open the door and entered.

"Do you wish more pastries, mistress?" she asked.

Widow Brewster looked at her sharply. Elizabeth looked away, a slight blush on her cheeks.

"No, thank you, but the chocolate was delicious."

They all agreed. Elizabeth collected the cups onto a tray and left.

"And close the door behind you, please."

They watched as she did.

"*Thy desire shall be subject to thy husband and he shall rule over thee,*" whispered Alice mockingly.

"Even if he is not a godly man," added Widow Moore.

"But remember also," said Widow Brewster, "that God said to Abraham about his wife: *in all that Sarah hath said unto thee, hearken unto her voice.*"

"Good for God," said Alice. "But dare we repeat that? The pastor never quotes that to us. Would it not bring more wrath down on us?"

"They will have clever words for us. We can be sure of that."

★

"It just shows you: never trust a servant!" said Widow Moore.

It was two days later and the two women and Alice were leaning on the fence of the cow pen, keeping a watchful eye as their farmworkers in the byre milked the cows. Tails swishing as flies circled, the cows chewed the cud peaceably enough as their udders squirted milk. The sound of milk falling on milk, the rhythm of it – squeeze and pull, squeeze and pull – was homely and comforting.

"I agree with you," said Alice.

"But that Elizabeth," said Widow Moore, "I could see she was up to no good when we were at your house. And now for her to testify, on the gossip of Anne's own servants, that Anne would not lie with her husband after she was admonished by the elders, and caused her bed to be removed to another room, that is shocking."

"Denying conjugal fellowship," said Widow Brewster.

"A fine phrase," said Alice, laughing. "Well, she did right. Wouldn't we all like to do that sometimes?"

"Who's to say we don't? Or, in my case, didn't," laughed Widow Moore.

"Treat them mean, keep them keen. It worked for me with

my Nicholas," said Widow Brewster. "But he was a kind man, bless his soul!"

They turned to watch the maids carry the pails of milk into the shed. Who really knew what went on in people's homes and beds? thought Alice. What did they say of children? *Conceived in iniquity and born into guilt.* It hadn't seemed like iniquity with her and James. Fine fellowship, maybe, but not duty. How she missed him, and worried about him.

"But would we really want to be like poor Mary Drury?" put in Alice. "To have a husband who *never had fellowship with her nor was ever a bull,* as Mary herself put it, and *was incapacitated for the marriage estate*, as the elders put it."

"A mixed blessing," allowed Widow Moore.

"But an insufficiency sometimes to be wished for."

Alice brushed a fly from her face. "Judges can be so cruel. All men, of course, as if they understand everything."

A silence fell over the three of them: as if the faults and weaknesses of men – victims, oppressors, judges – had both united and dispirited them. They watched the cows amble back into the fields: blank-eyed, untroubled, udders swaying, bony haunches jutting. From across the fields they heard sawing and hammering – fence repairs, probably. Her two sons Peter and Giles would be doing the same around their new pasture, thought Alice. They were growing into strong young men already, Peter courting seriously.

The farms were prospering; people were busy as the seasons turned. The pastors gave their grave sermons. People were mostly cordial. But underneath, thought Alice, that was where the interest lay: God may or may not exist, but people certainly do. And people concealed things, perhaps the most vital things.

It was a pleasant sunny April day but now a sudden breeze came in with a chill. The women shivered and wrapped their shawls round their shoulders. New bright leaves on the bushes rustled.

"Let's go in," suggested Widow Brewster.

The others agreed and they turned to walk back up the track to their homes, stepping carefully to avoid the mud as much as they could.

"There are other rumours, too; we've all heard them, I suppose," said Widow Moore conspiratorially.

"About?" asked Alice.

"Dissension in Anne Eaton's household."

"And the elders are enquiring into that as well, I hear," added Widow Brewster.

"But those are private, family matters," said Widow Moore. "They need to keep their noses out. Interfering, prurient old men." She snorted in disapproval.

"Their argument," said Alice, "is that she will not be able to see the light of true belief while her private conduct is at fault."

"Ah! *Disarray in the family leads to disarray in religion.* What nonsense!" said Widow Moore. "As if shouting at my husband for walking into the kitchen with muddy boots – as I did almost every day, mind you, poor man – meant I was questioning the Lord's word."

"But that's what they believe," said Alice. "Domestic misbehaviour and religious error are inseparable. It serves their purpose to control us."

"But it's more serious in the case of Mistress Eaton. It does not look well with her husband as Governor. Won't people say, how can someone be able to order public matters for the common good if he cannot order his own private estate?"

"Look, a robin," said Alice, pausing and pointing to a fence post where the robin perched.

Did they all feel a moment of homesickness, as she did? Thirty-three years and still she could be caught by this sudden sadness. She imagined James seeing a robin over there in England, hearing it sing. Did he think of her?

"So, what is this misbehaviour?" she asked.

"Anne's mother-in-law Temperance lives with them—"

"Always trouble, especially with names like that," interrupted Widow Moore. "Mothers-in-law should be banished." And she laughed aloud so that the robin flew off.

"… and Anne is accused," continued Widow Brewster in a shocked tone, "of twice slapping her in the face at the dinner table."

"Oh, how I have been tempted!" laughed Widow Moore. "The grace of the Lord must have saved me."

"But the point," said Alice, "is that the elders say Anne has broken the fifth commandment – *Honour thy father and mother* – and the ninth – *Thou shalt not bear false witness.*"

"That is ridiculous," said Widow Moore in anger. "They are out to make her a scapegoat. To punish her as an example to all us women and keep us in our place."

"Poor woman," said Widow Brewster. "Maybe she is overwrought by all this about baptism."

"But she will not back down," said Alice. "She is a stubborn woman. We must support her. She is our friend. If they find against her, they find against us all."

Widow Moore halted and put her hand on the arms of Alice and Widow Brewster walking beside her. They all halted.

Widow Moore's eyes darted at each of them with nervous excitement. She bent her head forward. The others leaned in.

"My husband tells me," she paused, "they are bringing her to trial next week."

★

This time they were in Alice's house. She had invited Anne Eaton round and sent the servants out on various errands: provisions, wood-collecting. There were just the two of them, at the kitchen table, with two cups of chocolate. Alice cut them both slices of blackcurrant pie, the pastry glistening with sprinkled sugar.

"Help yourself to cream," said Alice.

"I will, thank you. I am in need of all the sweetness I can get." But she laughed as she spoke.

A low fire burned in the grate and there was a good smell from the cooking pot.

"It was terrible for you, Anne – and for me, too, to be among that congregation and hear their judgement."

"Yes, I cannot deny it."

"When you pleaded that no censure be passed upon you, I nearly wept."

"Nor did I accept that I had broken the fifth commandment. All I did was not acknowledge my husband's mother to be my mother." They laughed. "This pie is excellent," said Anne.

"So they excommunicated you."

"They did. I cannot attend church services, and if I want to listen to the sermon – as if I would – I must stand outside the door."

"You know, Anne, they are frightened. What if every wife refused to take religious instruction from her husband? What if every wife fought bitterly with her mother-in-law?"

"They would say society would collapse into chaos."

"By which they really mean they would have to share their power with women. And that is the crux."

The pie was finished and the cups were empty.

"But this is not over yet," said Anne. "My husband – the governor – says they are going to bring us all to trial, the five of us women."

"I have always expected that. To go on trial simply because we have been talking to each other."

"Ah, but about ideas which are none of our business."

"We shall see. I am looking forward to it. I think I would quite enjoy the disapproving looks of men: at last a sense of power."

"You are very fortunate, Alice, with your husband James. He did not discourage you? Bid you be quiet?"

"James is his own man. They do not know how to deal with him. He abides by the laws, helps people when they are in need, a good neighbour. But he does not attend church. He is, in a way, as much a threat to them as you are. He shows it is possible to be good but not godly. He has no time for them, the Church and civil leaders. A few, he thinks, are good men who want sincerely to help create a fair society. But most are in it for vanity, for being able to posture, and profit from their positions. James goes his own way and so supports me going mine."

"You must miss him sorely."

Alice sighed. "Of course."

"And is he an atheist, like you?"

"No, but nor am I. I have listened to him. He says it is a vanity to be an atheist, to be so certain. All we can know, he says, is not to know. And that is humility. Let each go his own way – provided they do not hurt each other. That is what we believe."

"Do as you would be done by."

"The same."

Anne left soon after. The talk of James had brought him back to the forefront of Alice's mind. She tried to prevent that because she was frightened for him. The war in England was going this way and that from all the reports they had. And she knew he was not a fighting man, yet needed to prove himself. That was a dangerous combination.

And Will: was he fighting, and on which side? And was it being disloyal to James to be concerned for Will?

It was partly to avoid these thoughts that she had become so involved with her friends, especially Anne Eaton. Like the Parliamentarians in England, her group of women had their vision and their battles. They, too, risked much; they, too, fought against entrenched authority, the divine rights of men.

She was looking forward to the upcoming trial: it was a chance to speak their minds to the community.

32.

EXECUTION

1649

Jane's soft fingers took his hand, gentle but insistent, the lace at her wrist brushing his skin, her face turned up to him, her grey eyes appealing. Will was startled. He could not remember the last time she had touched him.

"You will not murder the King, Will," she said quietly.

He was on the threshold, about to leave for Westminster. He had heard her come up behind him, her dress rustling, and knew immediately, with dread, that she would have a pronouncement. Something she needed to say to salve her conscience and torment his own.

"What will your children come to learn about you when they grow up, Will?"

He looked down into her eyes. That their father fought for what was right. But he said nothing. He could never convince her. A pause as they stood together, but so far apart. Then he leaned forward to kiss her forehead, and left.

His groom was waiting with his horse, Flint. Will stroked Flint's head.

"My boy, my boy!" he muttered, then mounted, shrugged the reins, a faint touch of his heels in Flint's flanks and they were on their way.

His wife's words had been neither entreaty nor advice, far less an instruction. Jane meant that a man as good as him would not be able to bring himself to kill the King and offend God.

But he could, and would. A death sentence after a trial was not murder.

As Flint made his way along Threadneedle Street, Will knew the King would already be in Sir Robert Cotton's house near Westminster Old Palace Yard, awaiting his summons from the Lord President of the Court. Over breakfast, a breathless messenger had reported to Will that when the King, at the Privy Stair, stepped into the boat which would take him along the Thames a crowd cried out and prayed for him. Worse, the watermen who had rowed the barge had defied orders and doffed their caps to him.

Will looked at the poor, working folk that Flint picked his way through on the crowded street. Did they not understand? Monarchy bred unthinking deference and subservience; divinely appointed monarchy sealed the social order – toilers or lords. For Will, having listened to the Putney debate, to Rainborowe and his Leveller friends, this wasn't just a trial of the King; this was a trial of fundamental injustice. And that was what the King didn't understand.

An hour or so later, in Westminster Hall, Will was impatient. He shifted his arse on the bench, tapped his foot, stroked his beard, rubbed his eyes and scratched at imagined itches on his leg. The High Court of Justice had been set up where Charles had hosted embassies and receptions in pomp and luxury, a just place for the just last act.

The Hall had been transformed as if for a theatrical performance. The tiered benches of the Judge Commissioners were newly covered in scarlet cloth. In front of them was the stage set: at the centre of the floor, behind a desk on which lay a cushion, was the raised chair for the Lord President John Bradshawe, the cushion and chair covered in crimson velvet. Next to it was the lectern for the Solicitor General; barely two yards away, the King's chair faced them. A wooden barrier separated this arena from the space which the public would soon fill. A dozen soldiers lounged there already, ready to keep order.

Will stilled his fidgeting. Dignity, calm. Gravitas. A Judge. For that's what he was: the preacher's son from Wigan in the far wild north-west now with the life of a king in his hands.

His fellow Commissioners around him on the benches were talking: tension and excitement in the greetings, and snatches of nervous, over-confident laughter. The headiness of power, the daring of the occasion. He looked down at his left hand, now resting on his thigh. He fancied he could still feel the unfamiliar touch of his wife's fingers there.

Since the start of the Civil War, his world and hers had drifted apart. She brought up their children, looked after the house and him. She prayed regularly in church and also, he knew, gave help to the city's hungry who suffered from the bad harvests and high prices, and to those dispossessed from their land and dwellings by the ravages of armies. A woman's world. He grew his business, fought in battles, discussed and argued: a world of action, ideas and principles, of pamphlets, petitions and remonstrances. A man's world. The worlds were equally real. But her domestic and charitable world was determined by his world: the nature of government and the laws it passed affected everyone's lives.

Which was why he was here, sitting in judgement. And why he would disappoint and horrify her, no matter the strength of his arguments. The distance between them would increase. And who could tell if they would ever be reconciled? This matter of the King split not just the country but families, setting brother against brother, son against father, wife against husband. Some believed they were going about God's business but Will did not have the comfort of that faith. He was working solely from his own sense of right and wrong. And he was conscious of the arrogance of that.

He watched the last Commissioners file out from the Painted Chamber onto the benches. Too many empty spaces. He reckoned only about half of the one hundred and thirty-five appointed Commissioners were present. He'd heard the reasons and excuses: illness, retirement, matters to attend to back at their homes in the country. More like faint heart, loss of nerve or an unwillingness to accept the legality of the Court. Or fear of ending up on the wrong side of history. He straightened his back, felt even more determined.

Kings had been removed, kings had been murdered but no king had ever been deposed by his own elected parliament. For those who believed kings were divinely appointed, what they were embarked upon was a crime against God himself, an assault on the divinely ordained world order. No wonder some quaked.

Even Cromwell was not immune. A short while ago Will had been in the Painted Chamber when, after prayers, news came that the King was arriving from Sir Robert Cotton's house. Cromwell had run to the window to watch him brought across the courtyard. He had turned to the others and said:

"My masters, he is come, he is come and now we are doing the great work that the whole nation will be full of."

But his face had been as white as chalk. Even their great leader was wrought up, almost overcome by the magnitude of what they were about to do, this defining moment without precedent.

Looking round, there were faces Will didn't know, and notable absentees: the Attorney General Anthony Steel who had suddenly claimed grave illness and an inability to discharge his duties. Chief Justice Henry Rolle and Chief Justice Oliver St John had refused to serve. And where was Sir Thomas Fairfax, the Lord General of the New Model Army? Surely he was not absconding? Tomorrow Will would suggest to the others on the Committee of Eight overseeing the management of the trial that the benches be reduced to make the court look more complete.

Now the door of the Painted Chamber opened and a wave of noise burst in: the shouts and clamour of the public waiting outside the north door. At the same time the MPs fell silent. In strode sixteen halberdiers, the bearer of the Sword of State and the Serjeant-at-Arms and Mace. Then came the Lord President John Bradshawe in a black satin gown held up by train-bearers and wearing a black velvet hat. Will could not prevent a smile: the black velvet concealed a bulletproof iron frame that Bradshawe insisted upon. He crossed to his raised chair, had his train arranged and sat down.

It was all a performance: scripted, dressed and choreographed like a court masque. When it suited, as now, the Commons could play the pomp and ceremony game, put on a play, although its Puritan members had shut down theatres.

Now the north gate was opened and the public crowded in to fill the allocated space. Shoving, laughing, some loud with drink, some eating hunks of bread: a motley band of what looked like apprentices, shopkeepers, housewives, come for a show, an entertainment. Silence was ordered and eventually, with the soldiers threatening to eject them, prevailed. But still they shuffled, restless.

"Bring in the King!" ordered the Lord President.

"At last!" said Thomas Harrison, who had come to sit next to Will. "It has taken too long and cost too many lives." Major General Harrison, MP for Wendover, had commanded the escort that finally brought the King to London. "We have him now."

"Indeed we do," replied Will. "But why so few of us?"

Harrison snorted. "Backsliders without backbone."

With a twenty-strong guard, musketeers and pikemen, the King entered. He strode forward, unhurried. The soldiers' boots clattered behind him. He wore his usual plain but rich dark clothes with the blue ribbon of the Garter on his breast and the Star embroidered on his cloak. Will guessed from his pallor and the shadows under his eyes that he had not slept much. But his grey hair and beard were neatly trimmed and he was hatted. His expression was serious, neither angry nor sad.

The soldiers peeled away to stand along the wooden barrier in front of the public who now pushed and craned their necks, a few ragged cheers muffled as the guards turned and scowled at them. The King stood and surveyed the scene, glancing from face to face along the crimson benches. He would recognise only a few among this group of goodly, well-affected men: the butchers and grocers and cobblers and cloth merchants like Will himself. They had been raised to authority in the New Model Army and risen to the challenge. Will felt a great sense of purpose, involuntarily stretching his shoulders and pushing out his chest. He knew pride was deemed a sin but he was proud to be among them, a group which was turning the world upside down. The King raised an eyebrow at the soldiers controlling the public crowd, standing at each side of the Commissioners and guarding every door to the Hall. He neither bowed nor raised his hat to the Lord President. Nor did the Commissioners raise their hats to the King. The King would not respect his accusers or the court. The Commissioners would not defer to the King: he was not a King, he was a prisoner at the bar.

The King sat, as Bradshawe had required, alone in a chair in the centre of the court, directly opposite the scores of his judges.

Harrison muttered: "Look at his impudent face, as if he has no guilt for the blood shed in these wars."

Will grunted. He interpreted the King's composure and self-control as the arrogance of one who had no shred of doubt that he was answerable only to God and certainly not to this court. Or perhaps his, too, was an act, and an impressive one, thought Will: king or no king, he was alone in front of threescore judges who would decide whether he lived or died. He must mask his fear, show no sign of weakness or nerves.

At last, proceedings began. The Act of Parliament for the trying of the King was read out and then, in the silence that followed, the Lord President opened with a summary of the charge. His words did not just fill the silence and space of the mighty Hall, Will knew they challenged and defied history. His eyes ranged over this Hall, built by Rufus, the son of William the Conqueror; it had seen kings and queens crowned for almost five hundred years, beginning with Richard the Lionheart. And now he, Will, was part of that defiance. He settled, concentrated.

John Bradshawe solemnly intoned:

"Charles Stuart, King of England, the Commons of England assembled in Parliament being deeply sensible of the calamities that have been brought upon this nation, which is fixed upon you as the principle author of it, have resolved to make inquisition for blood" – he raised his head from the paper and looked directly at the King before continuing – "have resolved to bring you to trial and judgement. And for that purpose have constituted this High Court of Justice, before which you are brought."

Bradshawe then looked to the Solicitor General, John Cooke, to proceed. The public quietened. In a measured way Cooke smoothed his papers on the lectern and leaned forward, his hands gripping each side. He turned his head to look round the whole assembly and finally looked directly at the King.

"My Lord," he said, "I am commanded to charge Charles Stuart, King of England, in the name of the Commons of England, with Treason and High Misdemeanours."

The King, wanting to interrupt, lifted his walking cane and touched Cooke gently on the shoulder. Will half rose from his seat. Immediately there was an indrawing of breath on the benches, tension tautened at this breach of protocol, a mutter from the crowd. But the silver head of the cane, resting briefly on the black gown of Cooke's shoulder, came off and fell to the floor with a clink. Will watched it, mesmerised, silver glinting, metal rasping on the stone floor as it rolled away into the shadow. Silence. A little nervous, stifled laughter on the benches. The public craned forward, mouths open. All eyes shifted to the King. He sat, for once uncertain. No one moved to pick it up for him. A pause, a stillness like a tableau, a poised moment. Without a change in expression, the King stood, stepped forward, stooped, retrieved it and placed it in his pocket.

Will breathed out, relaxed, somehow gratified. He noticed smiles, nudges and nods along the benches.

The Solicitor General flicked some imaginary dirt from his shoulder and proceeded:

"That the said Charles Stuart, being admitted King of England, and therein trusted with a limited power to govern by and according to the laws of the land, and by his trust, oath and office, being obliged to use the power committed to him for the good of the people, and for the preservation of their rights and liberties; yet, nevertheless, out of a wicked design to uphold in himself an unlimited and tyrannical power…" – he emphasised the word *tyrannical* at which the King half-smiled in ridicule and shook his head. Some in the crowd shouted, "No! No!"

Will understood why the King was incredulous, well aware that the Commons had imposed its own tyranny.

On 5th December last Will had been incensed as the Presbyterian-dominated Commons had voted 129–83 that they should again seek a settlement with the King. That same night a group of some of the defeated MPs, Will among them, and six army officers decided how to bypass the Presbyterian majority. Next day Colonel Thomas Pride, supported by Sir Hardress Waller and his regiment and Thomas Harrison, stood at the door of the Commons. Pride had a list of MPs who could not be trusted to implement the will of the New Model Army. One hundred and fifty MPs were refused entry to the Commons chamber and sent packing, to the jeers of the troops. Ingilby was one of them, shaking his head and raising an ironic eyebrow at Will as he passed him. Only seventy-five were allowed in.

Three weeks ago on New Year's Day at the start of the process towards the trial, Will had been in the Commons when this Rump Parliament – or arse Parliament as it was known on the streets – had declared it was treason for the King of England to declare war against Parliament and the Kingdom. But the following day the Lords had unanimously rejected this impeachment and adjourned for a week, hoping they could stall matters. When they returned to their chamber they found its doors padlocked. As Will had to admit to himself uneasily, the legality of the Commons itself had been undermined.

But it was for the greater good. That was Will's justification. Jane, had she heard this argument, would have given that superior smile, knowing that it was equivocating sophistry. Damn the woman! Will re-focused on the Solicitor General's words: "... to overthrow the rights and liberties of the people, yea, to take away all redress and remedy of misgovernment, which by the fundamental constitution of this kingdom were reserved on the people's behalf in the right and power of frequent and successive Parliaments."

Cooke paused and then more slowly said: "He, the said Charles Stuart, for accomplishment of such his designs and for the protecting of himself and his adherents in his and their wicked practices, to the same ends hath traitorously and maliciously levied war against the present Parliament and the people therein represented."

Cooke sat down. Mutters of satisfaction among the Judge Commissioners. The public seemed awed into silence. Harrison muttered, "That's told him straight."

Harrison never doubted, Will knew. He was known to break into a rapturous psalm of praise on the battlefield as the Royalists fell back. He was a leading Fifth Monarchist who believed that 1666 would see the second coming of Christ and the beginning of his 1,000-year empire that would end in the Day of Judgement. Will found Harrison's certainty shocking and ridiculous. But a man not to be taken lightly.

There was an awkward silence in the Hall; no one was certain what should happen next. Then the King stood. "First," he said, "I would fain know by what authority I am called hither, before I will give my answer. Remember I am your King, your lawful King."

"No!" was barked by voices on the benches. Will noticed that the King's customary stammer had disappeared completely.

Two or three uncertain voices cheered from the public and the guards turned towards them.

"Remember," continued the King, "what sins you bring upon your heads and the judgement of God upon this land. Think well upon it, I say, think well upon it before you go further from one sin to a greater. I have a trust committed to me by God and by old and lawful descent. I will not betray it to answer to a new unlawful authority."

This was the nub of it, thought Will. This is where we stand fast.

The King paused and spread out his hands. "Show me by what lawful authority I am brought here and I will answer the charge."

He sat down amid more cheers from the public and shouts of "God save the King!" at which Will saw the Colonel in charge of the guards urging them to cry "Justice! Justice!"

As had previously been agreed in the committee, Bradshawe replied: "It is done in the name of the Commons and Parliament assembled and all the good people of England."

The King laughed again, a brave laugh or a haughty dismissive one. Will could not be sure. The charge could hardly be in the name of Parliament which consisted of Commons and Lords and, indeed, King. It was brought by the Rump of Parliament.

But, to Will, legality was trumped by morality. It had to be if the status quo were to change. No matter what Jane thought.

And with the King's laugh Bradshawe declared the Court adjourned until Monday. The King was taken away, the public ushered none too gently out. The Commissioners agreed among themselves that tomorrow, Sunday, would be a fast day in order to seek the Lord's guidance more easily. To Will there was an arrogance in assuming one could interpret God's will accurately, especially when people who believed they could do so disagreed with each other. He bade farewell to Harrison. The man turned away, grim-faced.

As he rode home, Will's thoughts turned yet again to Colonel Thomas Rainborowe. How Rainborowe would have loved to be at the trial! Was it base or honourable to include revenge in his rationale? Less than three months ago, Royalist soldiers had murdered him.

Will still shuddered as he thought of it: his great friend and hero killed by subterfuge and slackness, dying not on a battlefield but in a street outside an inn in Doncaster. Will saw him as his mentor: the courageous commander on the battlefield, the radical thinker who at Putney had argued for one man one vote and putting the King on trial. He had convinced Will, guided him through his confusion to the views he now held so strongly.

But without the King's treacherous dealing with the Scots that had led to this second war, without the King's insufferable arrogance and refusal to compromise, Rainborowe would still be alive, sitting in the High Court, part of the imminent victory for his cause. The King, as leader, was responsible for his death.

This would be an honourable revenge.

Will did not hurry home. After the excitement of the Commons, he felt alone: his children would be in bed, Jane would civil but distant, the dinner she had supervised excellent. But, beneath that, censure and rejection. He felt Flint's warm body moving under him, the strong muscles, patted his neck. If only Jane and he were agreed on this. Instead of elation, he felt bereft.

When the Commissioners met in the Painted Chamber on the Monday morning – there were now sixty-two – they agreed that the King must not be allowed any further challenges to the jurisdiction of the High Court of Justice. Will argued strongly for this.

Once again in the Hall the public cheered when the King arrived. It drove Will mad. Solicitor General Cooke began by demanding, on behalf of the people of England, that the prisoner at the bar be directed to give his positive answer to the charge, either by way of confession or negation.

The King quietly but firmly defied him: "When I came here today, I did expect particular reasons to know by what authority you do proceed against me. Yet since I cannot persuade you to it, I shall tell you my own reasons why I cannot in conscience answer until I be satisfied with the legality of this court…"

Lord President Bradshawe lost patience: "Sir, you are not permitted to go on in these discourses. You are not to have the liberty to use this language." Bradshawe shook his finger at him, his red face thrust at the King. "How great a friend you have been to the laws and liberties of the people, let all England and the world judge." Nods and muttered approval from the benches. Bradshawe waved his arm imperiously, impatiently. "Take away the prisoner. The Court is adjourned until tomorrow at twelve o'clock."

As the King left, Colonel Hewson rose from the benches and cried out: "Justice! Justice on the traitor!" and spat in the King's face.

Will was disgusted. Proud of this Court of ordinary men, he was now ashamed of Hewson the shoemaker. That behaviour did their cause no good.

The King drew out his handkerchief, wiped the spittle from his cheek and said: "Well, sir, God has justice in store, both for you and me."

Will remembered Ingilby's words: *"Take care, Will, times can change – as you see – and then change again."*

The following day the stalemate in the Court continued and once again it was adjourned. Cromwell was livid. Pacing back and forth across the Painted Chamber, his energy pent up, he argued that there must be no further delay.

"The King has refused to answer and is therefore in contempt of court." His thin voice pitched even higher, rasping the eardrums like a caterwaul. "We must proceed to sentence now." And he glared at the silent Commissioners. Will nodded firmly in agreement.

But Ireton, a lawyer, argued that witnesses should be examined in order that their evidence might be published to justify the sentence – and that this should be done in private. Cromwell, shaking his head and grinding his teeth, was overruled. So Will spent the day going through the necessary charade, as he saw it. Twenty-nine witnesses, some from the Royalist Army, were led in and dutifully confirmed the King had led his troops and caused the death of many soldiers. The King's letters, captured at Naseby, were read, proving he was seeking the help of foreign troops while pretending to compromise with Parliament.

At the end of the testimonies the Commissioners debated. Adrian Scrope and other God-fearing judges looked for divine guidance. Scrope took out his Bible, held up his hand for silence and read out a passage from the Book of Numbers: *"That blood defileth the land, and the land cannot be cleansed of the blood that is shed therein but by the blood of him that shed it."* He repeated, *"But by the blood of him that shed it."* He looked around as if this was the defining argument. As it was: the King's life would need to be offered up in sacrifice. Cromwell was nodding vigorously.

Will strongly agreed but did not need the religious justification. He knew some Commissioners were uneasy: some, even at this late stage, hoped the King would be excused the charges or be punished in a way that did not end his life – abdication maybe. Others feared that if ever the monarchy returned, a future king would seek full vengeance against his enemies, primarily those here in the Court.

"It is a cruel necessity," concluded Cromwell.

Eventually the death sentence was justified because the King "was a tyrant, traitor, murderer and public enemy to the Commonwealth." For many, Will knew, they were doing what needed to be done rather than acting out of a hatred of the King himself. But for Will himself, not only had the King done wrong but the system of monarchy was also wrong.

Scrope declared: "I bear no more malice to the man's person than I do to my dear father. But I hate that cursed principle of tyranny that has so long lodged and harboured within him, which has turned our waters of law into blood."

Will disagreed: the King embodied this principle of tyranny, had argued to continue it, had refused to give it up. His guilt was personal.

On Saturday 27th January, a week after the trial began, the Commissioners in the Painted Chamber agreed the final wording of the sentence. It would be sent for publication at key points in the city. The King had been given every opportunity to defend himself against the charge, had chosen not to take them and, once condemned, must not be allowed to speak for he would be 'dead in law'.

Lord President John Bradshawe wore a new crimson satin gown as he, with the Commissioners, entered Westminster

Hall for the final act. It seemed to Will almost a funereal procession as they filed in and found their places. Frequently checking his bulletproof hat, Bradshawe gave a long speech which eventually the King interrupted. He asked for leave to present a proposal to the combined Lords and Commons which would reconcile all parties and bring back peace to the land. Will had heard rumours that he might abdicate in favour of his son Charles, Prince of Wales.

Bradshawe denied him. But one of the judges, John Downes, argued that the proposal should be heard. He forced a recess and the judges withdrew to the Inner Court of Wards. Will had never seen Cromwell so full of wrath at this further delay. Fingers bunched into fists, he snarled his contempt, foam flecking the corner of his mouth. He reduced Downes to tears. After half an hour Cromwell ended the muted discussion: "Waste no more time but return to your duty, lest you be accused for putting your hand to the plough and looking away." It was too late for any good to come of it and they would proceed. There would be no reprieve.

Back in the Hall where the King had waited, Will listened impatiently to Bradshawe's completion of his long-winded, self-important speech. Finally the clerk was asked to read the sentence. Cromwell sat, still as a stone, his face impassive. Will and the other Commissioners stared at the King as if holding their breath; the public, craning their necks to witness the King's reaction, shuffled their feet but there were no cries or exclamations. A tension in the room, as if before the first lightning of a storm.

In total silence, sweat glistening on his brow, the clerk cleared his throat and read: "For all his treasons and crimes this Court doth adjudge that he, the said Charles Stuart, as a tyrant, traitor, murderer and public enemy to the good of the people of this nation, shall be put to death by the severing of his head from his body."

There was a gasp from the crowd. As planned, all the Commissioners immediately stood up to express their unanimous support of the sentence. There was no cheering, just a sombre silence. The deed was finally done. All eyes were on the King. He had not moved a muscle, his left leg stretched forward languidly from his chair. He nodded slightly and stroked his beard, then asked if he might speak a word, quiet and polite but not beseeching. Bradshawe ruled that he could not be heard – and looked a tyrant himself as he said it, thought Will.

The King paled but recovered his composure and said: "If I am not suffered to speak, expect what justice other men shall have."

Guards bustled the King out of the Hall, some spitting on him and blowing pipe smoke in his face. Will overheard one guard, moved by the King's dignity, cry out, "God bless you, sir." For which the guards' commander belaboured him with his cane.

Back in the Painted Chamber, five regimental commanders were chosen, including Thomas Harrison, to decide on the organisation of the execution: on a scaffold in front of Whitehall on Tuesday 30th January.

When he returned home and opened the door, servants were strangely not in sight, children's voices eerily absent. On the long oak dining room table a sealed white note was lodged between a decanter of sherry and one glass. Will looked around to check he was indeed alone. He picked up the note, a faint trace of his wife's perfume, his name on the front in his wife's handwriting. He stared at it, knowing what it would say. A bleak emptiness inside him, matching his empty house. He sat at a window and read the note: Jane and their children had gone to stay for a few days with her parents. The message could not be clearer.

That evening Will ate alone in the house, eyed by his silent and – he was sure – disapproving servants. Without his children's noise and laughter, without his wife's familiar busying about, the place was cold and unloved.

He spent two days at his warehouse, irritable with colleagues and workers – sad, angry, worried for the future of his family. He respected his wife but would never agree with her on this. Would she come to understand him? Could they be reconciled?

On Monday 29th January, when Will returned to the Commons, the benches were almost empty of MPs. Many had gone back out of town to their homes. The Commissioners met in the Painted Chamber, only fifty-nine of them now, a subdued group. Spread out on the table was the death warrant. Cromwell asked for silence and said, "Those who sat in the High Court of Justice shall set their names to the death warrant. I will have their hands now." It was more of a demand than a request and was spoken in a tone that brooked no reservations. "God," he continued, "is about to bring His people into the Promised Land and his chariots are 20,000 strong."

Will presumed this referred to the Army.

Only a minute or two and he was at the front of the line. He stood by the chair, leaning his weight on his hands on the table. Slowly, deliberately, he read.

Whereas Charles Stuart, King of England, standeth convicted, attainted and condemned of high treason and other high crimes, and sentence was pronounced upon him by this Court, to be put to death by the severing of his head from his body, of which sentence execution yet remaineth to be done: These are therefore to will and require you to see the said sentence executed, on the open street before Whitehall, upon the morrow, being the thirtieth of this instant, month of January, between the hours of ten in the morning and five in the afternoon of the same day. And for so doing, this shall be your sufficient warrant. And these are to require all officers and soldiers, and other good people of this nation of England, to be assisting unto this service. Given under hands and seals.

Each word was separate and self-contained but linked in a chain he must follow: *severing of the head… before Whitehall on the morrow.* His heart was beating hard, his fingers trembled. Will sat down, took a deep breath and picked up the quill, rested the heel of his hand on the parchment to steady it. He heard the shuffling of feet behind him, mutterings; felt the pressure of the waiting Commissioners behind him insistent on his shoulders; but above him the weight of history and belief and majesty crowding in on him with looks of shock and voices of reproach and damnation.

He imagined Jane there, her pale grey eyes watching him, her face censorious.

He was about to sever a man's life; he was an executioner. But it was necessary, cruel but necessary. Right. It was right.

He focused his eyes.

Several signatures were already there: John Bradshawe, Lord Grey of Groby, Oliver Cromwell, Thomas Pride, Henry Marten, Thomas Harrison. His signature must be clear and unequivocal. He held the quill firmly, dipped it in the inkhorn and signed, smooth and steady, no decorative flourishes, black ink on cream parchment: Will Nailor. A statement as well as a signature. He used his signet ring as a seal, impressed into the red wax.

In Jane's eyes, he would now be a murderer. But in his own, he was a founder-father of a more just and decent world.

He replaced the quill; the nib would shortly need re-trimming.

He stood up, moved away for the next Commissioner, and re-joined his fellows.

Will did not want to observe the execution because when Jane returned – she had extended her stay at her parents' –

she would undoubtedly ask him if he had gone to see it. If he answered yes, she would be revolted by him. Had his signature yesterday also signed the death warrant for his marriage? How could they heal such a wound? But he had signed the warrant and this required him to see the sentence executed.

The officers in the Tower were ordered to deliver up the "bright axe for the executing of malefactors". When Will arrived, the scaffold was already erected outside the Banqueting House, the block and axe placed together in the centre. He was shocked to see the block was only six inches high, forcing the King not to kneel, as was customary, but to lie prone. Was this extra humiliation necessary? A new doorway, concealed with black cloth, had been knocked through the building's external wall to allow direct access. Four iron staples had been hammered into the scaffold floor with pulleys attached in case the King resisted and had to be forced into position for the execution.

It was bitterly cold; even the Thames had frozen over. Tower guards had reported the King wore two shirts beneath his doublet in case he shivered and this was interpreted as fear. The King emerged through the new doorway onto the scaffold and stepped to the breast-high rail. He did not falter when he saw the huge crowd which had come to watch, and the groups of soldiers, foot and horse with standards displayed, among them in case there was any last-minute rescue attempt or disruption. Even the rooftops were lined with people. Will felt some pity – even more, admiration. Was the King's heart, soon to be stilled, beating fast and hard? What emotions raged behind that set face? The crowd was eerily silent. The two executioners were dressed in long woollen smocks such as butchers wear, disguised with grizzled periwigs and false beards. Will knew the difficulties there had been in finding willing executioners. Then the King looked at the block. He asked if a higher one could be brought but this was politely declined.

The King spoke, from notes on small stubs of paper. The crowd was too far away to hear him but Will, close up, could. He spoke of his innocence and that he had not encroached upon Parliamentary privileges. So, his self-delusion must last until the end, and that reduced some of Will's pity for him. The King broke off when he saw one of the executioners touching the axe. "Hurt not the axe that may hurt me," he implored, surely mindful of the execution of his grandmother, Mary Queen of Scots, who had had to endure three strokes of the axe before her head was severed from her body. "Take heed of the axe," he repeated, "pray, take heed of the axe. Take care they do not put me to pain." In the end, he was a mere man, like the rest of us. But brave.

Then he resumed: "I have forgiven all the world, and even those in particular that have been the chief causes of my death. Who they are, God knows. I do not desire to know; God forgive them. But that is not all; my charity must go further. I wish that they may repent, for indeed they have committed a great sin in that particular. I pray God, with St Stephen, that this be not laid to their charge."

Not just a man, then, but with a nobility in his charity. Nobility to go with his foolishness and arrogance. He had brought this upon himself. And Will hardened his heart again.

William Juxon, Lord Bishop of London, had been with the King through his last hours and stood on the scaffold next to him. The King asked Juxon for his nightcap and pushed some of his hair up into it.

"Does my hair trouble you?" he asked the executioner. It did, so he and the Bishop tucked all of it up beneath the white satin so the King's neck was presented clear.

"I have good cause," said the King, "and a gracious God on my side."

"There is but one stage more," said Juxon gently. "This stage is turbulent and troublesome but it is a short one. It will

343

soon carry you a very great way. It will carry you from Earth to Heaven, and there you shall find a great deal of cordial joy and comfort."

"I go," said the King, "from a corruptible to an incorruptible crown, where no disturbance can be, no disturbance in the world."

"You are exchanged from a temporal to an eternal crown," the Bishop agreed; "a good exchange."

The King took off his doublet and draped a cloak around his shoulders. After raising his arms and eyes to the sky, the King lay down in prayer, his head on the low block. He stretched out his arms at the agreed signal and the axe fell in one powerful blow. Will flinched. The severed head tipped forward, fell, a faint thud on the wooden planking, shuddered, lay stone-still in a drool of blood. The second executioner bent, grabbed it, held it up by the hair, the mouth open in shock from that clean cleaving of the blade, the eyes closed. The crowd groaned and wailed. Not a cheer. And Will wanted to retch. He swallowed and swallowed again to control it. This was worse than anything he had seen on the battlefield. The ceremony, the cold-bloodedness, was barbaric. All through the trial he had not been able, not been willing, to picture this.

Jane was right, of course she was right, but in a way deeper than the doings of the world. But the doings of the world were what he was about, not the business of God. Now there was a new land – a promised land, if you must – to build, better, fairer. For his children and the common folk.

33.

1649

Alice held the letter in her hands. She knew what it would say.

A slice of bright May sunshine angled across the kitchen table at which she sat; a smell of fresh bread she had made that morning; the door open and hens clucking in the yard.

It was inevitable it would be like this when the news arrived: a double cruelty on such a spring day.

She unfolded the letter, took a deep breath and read it. Very brief, from a Colonel Thomas Rainborowe, sent onwards via a Rainborowe relative in Boston. *James had died fighting bravely in battle for a noble cause. Condolences. Signature of his commanding officer.*

It was anger Alice felt first: anger at James, anger at men who could so easily be persuaded to kill each other, anger at leaders – always men – who did the persuading. Anger at the stupidity and cruelty. And had he fought bravely? That was always the story. She hoped so but feared that, afraid and self-doubting, he had been easily cut down. And something insistent had always told her James would not survive the war.

Then came the grief – grief for a good man brave in so many other ways, grief for the end of a way of life, for the loss of her life companion, grief for what he had lost: the years of farming and living and loving, the satisfaction of old age he would never feel, not being able to watch his two sons continue his own life's work. Then came the selfish, for being left and abandoned alone. In the end, at the window that looked over the herb garden, she stopped the thinking and let her tears flow.

Then she went down the fields to tell Peter and Giles. They comforted each other. Alice knew her sons' sadness was genuine. They had loved their father. But she also sensed an almost immediate excitement in them: now they were truly men, with responsibility for the farm and their livelihoods. They were ready for the challenge.

The funeral was a simple one, well-attended in spite of everything, as if his fundamental goodness was recognised by the community. The service was in church but she insisted the burial was in the blackberrying glade where their life together had begun.

"All ground is equally blessed," she replied when the pastor said James should be buried in consecrated ground. But he wanted to avoid an unseemly argument and made no further objection.

Peter and Giles dug the grave, and only the three of them were there for the burial. No prayers were said, just a silence among the blackbird song.

As the days passed in her new life, and the daily tasks continued, she realised how glad she was that she had such strong women friends. She felt almost a recklessness about her in their disputes with the town's leading men.

She felt it as she and her friends went to trial. Alice knew the town saw them as a troublesome group of disputatious women, but also as a diversion and amusement. Many secretly enjoyed watching the authorities questioned and challenged. There was Anne Eaton, recently excommunicated from the Church (an act copied from the papists, commented Anne); herself and Mrs Leach, not members of any church; and Lucy Brewster and Mrs Moore, well-to-do widows and church members but always offering contrary opinions. They were indeed a pentad of dissenters and malcontents. *Pentad* was

James's word for them. He had had a secret fascination with old magic.

Alice enjoyed the scandal that surrounded them. She had witnessed it as the five strolled together down the lane to the meeting house on this warm early June day. Though they came under all the formality of an official summons, they had agreed they must look unconcerned. They chose to walk among the crowd which was gathering for the court assembly, acknowledging the good citizens and burgesses they knew with a nod and a smile, a greeting. When the women turned their primly-bonneted faces away in confusion and the men stared fixedly ahead, Alice laughed to herself. But she was also aware that there was a sullen churlishness about, one that could be turned to active malevolence. Others had been whipped and banished for less than she and her friends had done. They knew full well a sentence of a public whipping was more than a possible outcome. But they must show no fear of that.

She and her friends were charged with "severall miscarriadges of a publique nature". Inside the packed hall, full of whispering and none-too-discreet finger-pointing, the five women were ushered to their seats by three officious men. The women sat upright, hands on their laps, chatting unconcernedly, while they waited for the magistrates. Alice turned to look among the crowd for Mistress Malbon, wife of Mr Richard Malbon who was one of the magistrates. It was Mistress Malbon who was responsible for them being here.

Job Hall, a servant of Mrs Leach, had been on an errand at the Malbon home. She had asked him about the recent meeting of the five women at Mrs Leach's house, which had already aroused some public speculation. Job had felt obliged to report to her what he had heard.

There she was, Mistress Malbon, on the third row – with her narrow pursed mouth and supercilious heavily lidded eyes. Alice held her gaze for a moment then looked away.

Then Alice heard the whispering in the assembly suddenly cease. The three magistrates entered and took their seats at the table. These godly men had expressed no sympathy for her husband's death.

How tight a hold the Church had on this community, thought Alice as she watched them sit down, tidy their papers and look authoritatively around the room. Only male members of the Church could be free burgesses (which was why her husband James had not been one – and thereby he was free, he said, of *the petty insolence of office*), and only free burgesses could choose magistrates and judges. A close check was kept on behaviour but also, as this trial proved, on people's thoughts and opinions – women's, at least. It was people's very thoughts that made them people, believed Alice. And men, especially magistrates, would not allow themselves to be criticised. Here in the formality of the court, she realised, perhaps more than she had before, how much of a challenge the five of them posed. James would have relished this scene; she had a sense of him in her head. He had loved her argumentativeness. It had aroused him. There would have been play in bed tonight if she said what she wanted to say. A pang of loss, sharp, of loneliness.

Magistrate Malbon stood up. He was not a tall man, though he tried to disguise this with the steeple hat and heeled boots he always wore. Sometime I am going to investigate, Alice mused, about how many short men seek positions of authority. She thought it would be a surprisingly large proportion. James, she knew, had attributed it to the size, or lack of it, of the man's nutmegs and sugar stick. She must ask Widow Moore about it: she would be certain to have a raucous opinion.

"I bring this court to order," Malbon said, pushing out his chest like a pouter pigeon. He waited until there was absolute silence.

"The first charge against you, Mistress Alice Parker, is that you traduced and maligned magistrates in talking of the trial of Mark Meggs, Goody Fancy and William Fancy."

"Ah, yes!" said Alice. "We all recall that."

In mid-March Mark Meggs had been convicted of "sinful and lustful attempts" to rape Goody Fancy "in severall lewd passadges" in her cellar, in the corn and pumpkin fields, in the cow house and once while she was out gathering firewood.

The court had been agog as Goody Fancy described how Meggs "took hold of her, put down his own breeches, put his hand under her coates, and with strength and force laboured to satisfie his lust and to defile her."

The magistrates had ordered him to be severely whipped for his "filthynesse and villeny".

But what got people talking was the punishment meted out to Goody and her husband William. Goody had also been severely whipped for concealment of the rape attempts: she should have reported them to the authorities. She had not done so, she said, because her husband said her story would not be believed as she had previously been whipped three times for "theevery". And also because no rape had actually occurred. Her husband had persuaded her not to file charges.

So William Fancy was also severely whipped because, the magistrates declared, he had acted "as a pander to his wife when he should have been her protector".

"It has been testified that you, Mistress Parker, said that the criminals had been cruelly whipped and that your son had said he would rather fall into the hands of the infidel Turks or had rather be hanged than fall into the hands of the New Haven magistrates."

Again, a little gasp in the assembly. Alice smiled, remembering Peter's anger.

"I agreed with him, yes. Is it now a crime here for a mother to agree with her son?"

Malbon remained silent. The woman had not denied the charge. He was satisfied.

Alice smiled and nodded. "I do remember my final conclusion, which I shared with my good friends."

"And what, pray, was that?"

Alice waited for a moment, looked directly at Malbon and said, so softly that people had to strain to hear her: "I pray God keep me from those magistrates."

There was a gasp around the assembly. Alice imagined James's smile, the stirring in his breeches.

Malbon's mouth was twitching in anger. Then he found the answer. Smiling sardonic ally, he said: "Since you are here in front of us, it is clear that God did not see fit to answer your prayer."

This caused some laughter. A good response, thought Alice, amused and cross with herself at the same time.

"The second charge against you, Mrs Parker, is that you insulted and falsely slurred the godly witnesses who have testified against you."

Indeed she had. She had been summoned to a private hearing by this very Magistrate Malbon soon after his wife had reported the witnesses' accounts. She had been confronted by the accounts but refused to answer to them. Immediately afterwards she had hurried to Mrs Leach's house to confront her servants, Job Hall and Elizabeth Smith. She had not minced her words, berating them for telling half-truths and half-lies.

She had called Elizabeth "a brazen-faced whore" and said she would have "Job and his slutt, him and his harlot, to the whipping post."

"I cannot recall," said Alice. "I know I was angry – as you would have been – that my private remarks in a private house had been eavesdropped on by servants who then went running to tell tales. Is this how you want our community to live together?"

She must keep control, not become angry, stay calm. She continued to press: "Are you recommending all servants behave like this? Are you saying this is godly?"

Into the silence created by these rhetorical questions she added: "If so, it is a long way from the Mayflower Compact that began these colonies only twenty-six years ago. Do you think William Bradford would approve?"

William Bradford was still governor of the original settlement of Plymouth Plantation, a man greatly respected throughout New England.

Alice's rhetorical question was a shrewd one. She saw some of the congregation bend their heads; the magistrates took an undue interest in shuffling their papers; Malbon's mouth twitched repeatedly and he brushed back his hair from his face. He cleared his throat.

"This is New Haven, not Plymouth," he said primly. "We will stick to the matters in hand. And the next charge is that you all questioned in your discussion why Widow Potter" – and here he nodded in the direction of the woman, who was sitting at the back – "had not been allowed by the elders to be re-admitted to the Church."

"We did, indeed," said Alice. "Widow Potter had come to me and I asked her why this was the case. She told me it was because she would not separate from Edward Blackwell, even though the magistrates – including you, sir – had refused to allow them to marry."

"And what did you advise her?" asked Malbon.

"I advised them to appeal to the magistrates and, if they did not allow them again, then to take one another before witnesses and go to live together."

"And what authority do you have to give this advice?"

"As you well know, it is the English folk tradition."

And she had a fleeting image of Will by the river, making the same statement – and her rejecting him.

351

"Also," she said, forestalling a reply from Malbon, "I believe the magistrates were acting out of revenge."

The word brought a gasp from the assembly.

"Revenge against a woman who was excommunicated for previous disagreements, and against a man who had criticised you, Mr Malbon, for neglecting your duties."

Malbon's face flushed with anger. Governor Eaton came to his rescue.

"You did expressly cross the line," he said sternly, "to eat, drink and show such respect to an excommunicate."

"Widow Parker," said Malbon in his most oily voice, "more meekness and modesty would become you in this place. You are too full of speech and boldness. You have spoken uncomely for your sex and age. Your carriage has offended the whole court."

Alice raised her eyebrows in mock astonishment. "I thought it was the Christian way to forgive and to welcome sinners back into the fold. I plead guilty to that."

Governor Eaton wrote something on his paper.

It was then that Alice sensed a shift in the mood of the assembly. They could tolerate critical comments about magistrates – they would all have their own grievances against them – but her last, somewhat mockingly clever answer had implied a criticism of the ordinary citizens themselves: that they did not forgive as readily as they should. The guilt she had stirred made them resentful.

"Proceed, Magistrate Malbon," said the Governor.

"I turn now to Widow Brewster."

Alice sat down, turned and patted Mrs Brewster's hand, smiling with encouragement.

Lucy Brewster stood up. She was a tall woman whose clothes expressed her comparative prosperity. She folded her arms across her substantial bosom. She had a severe, down-turned mouth and pale grey eyes which glared directly at

352

the Magistrate. The assembly knew her as unafraid to speak her mind. Some of the women here, Alice was sure, secretly looked forward to this joust between Lucy Brewster and the magistrate. But the faces of most, she now saw, expressed a dislike of their self-confidence, of their uppishness. Many would like them pulled down a peg or two, back to their own level of compliance.

"It has been reported to us that you led your friends in a questioning of the Reverend Davenport's sermons and that—"

"She does not lead us," interrupted Alice. "She does not need to. We talk as equals."

The other four women nodded their agreement.

"Please keep silent. That is as may be. Nevertheless, it is alleged that you said that his sermons made your stomach sick and womble as when you bred a child, and that you instructed your son to make waste paper of your notes on the sermon."

Widow Brewster laughed. "Indeed I was sick, two or three times, from smelling an ill savour in that meeting house. Is a woman not allowed to be sick these days? I disagree with the Reverend Davenport when he says that only people coming in to his assembly will receive salvation."

"As do we all," interrupted Alice again.

"He takes too much upon himself," added Widow Brewster. "He is too full of self-importance."

And here she turned to direct her glare at Davenport who sat at one side. He appeared to shrink a little into himself, avoiding her gaze.

Magistrate Kimberley took over. "I now turn to you, Mistress Leach."

Widow Brewster took Mistress Leach's hand and helped her up and smiled at her. "Be of good heart, my dear."

Mistress Leach was quietly spoken, a delicate body and with hair greying before her time. Her husband was unlike James: he hated his wife's contentions at church and wanted only a quiet life, fearful that her opinions would reduce the income at his merchant's store. God and Mammon contended within him, thought Alice, though he would not be aware of it. But though her voice might be soft, Mistress Leach's mind was strong. Alice looked forward to the coming exchanges.

"You listened to a sermon by the Reverend Davenport on Ephesians 4, verse 11."

"Remind me, young man," interrupted Mistress Leach. "My memory is not as sound as it was."

She would remember every word, thought Alice.

"Could you, Reverend Davenport, please?"

Seemingly much displeased at this indignity, he rose and read: "*And he gave some, apostles; and some, prophets; and some, evangelists; and some, pastors and teachers.* That was the verse I took."

"Thank you. And what was your opinion that you shared with your friends?" asked Malbon.

"I said that these people have gone through the world and are now ascended into heaven."

"And is that all you said? Remember you are in church and have sworn on oath to tell the truth."

"I do not need you to remind me of that," she answered quietly. She spoke so softly that the assembly seemed to have to cease to breathe to hear her. "And I remember quite clearly what I said." She paused as if for a prompt. Heads twisted so that good ears pointed in her direction. "I said that now pastors and teachers are but the invention of men."

There was a gasp as people released their pent-up breath. It wasn't just what Mistress Leach had said, though that was heretical enough, but that she was brave enough to say it in public. But her bravery caused fear not admiration – fear of things falling apart. They turned to look at Reverend Davenport, who coloured red but thrust out his chin.

"And I also said," she continued, staring defiantly at the Reverend, "that this people are like the people at Sinai under bondage; a veil is before the eyes of ministers and people in this place, and until that be taken away they cannot be turned unto the Lord."

Again the assembly gasped. She turned to her friends and they all nodded in support.

Kimberley also nodded, satisfied he had the answer he wanted.

Her small chest rose as she breathed in. This time there was a slight quiver in her voice. It was still soft but there was an icy defiance in it: "I will go to none of you for any truth of my salvation. I am as clear as the sun in the firmament on that. If I am in error, it is to myself alone. You have no authority to examine me about it."

And now Kimberley controlled himself again: "Had you kept your error to yourself, yourself only would have been hurt, as you said. But it is not to be suffered that you should blaspheme and revile the holy ordinances of Christ and the Church and people of God, lying and spreading your errors to corrupt others and disturb the peace of the place."

What a patronising, sanctimonious fool, thought Alice, but the listening assembly voiced their approval. The old disciplines were reasserting themselves, confirming a comfort these uncomfortable women were disturbing.

Mistress Leach had not been cowed. The little woman, in her neat bonnet and gloves, looked back straight at him and said, "I wonder if you would ask the Reverend Davenport to read for me from Ephesians chapter 4, verses 14 and 32."

Kimberley nodded to Davenport, who took up his Bible with a little sigh of exasperation. He ran his finger down the page and cleared his throat.

"Speak every man truth with his neighbour for we are members one of another. Let all bitterness and wrath, and anger and clamour and evil speaking be put away from you, with all malice. And be ye kind to one another, tender-hearted, forgiving one another, even as God for Christ's sake hath forgiven you."

As he read, he looked increasingly uneasy.

"Thank you so much," said Mrs Leach and sat down.

Alice wanted to cheer. She put her arm around the little woman's shoulders and hugged her. Alice was not concerned with the arguments – to her it was all the same ridiculous question: how many angels can dance on the head of a pin? What she loved was the reverend being put down. She looked up at Davenport. From the colour of his face, from his scowl, from his restlessness and clenched fists – he was apoplectic. He deserved it. For a moment she remembered the groan as Will's father came under her hand, and the threat he had made. The same would happen here, she thought, she was sure of it. The breadth of an ocean did not alter men's behaviour.

The three magistrates conversed in hushed tones. After a few minutes Kimberley spoke into the shocked silence: "The evidence is full and particular and sufficient to convict you." He looked around the assembly

Now Alice and her friends were tense, the pain and humiliation of a public whipping very clear to them.

"You will be immediately fined, but we will confer further."

Alice breathed a soft sigh of relief. The crowd muttered to each other, their faces scowling. They were disappointed – they had begun to hope for a whipping and humiliation.

Alice was appalled at what she saw: the same cruelty as at Ellen's trial.

The court is concluded," said Malbon quickly, seeing the judges were in the ascendant. "The amount of fine will be announced later."

The magistrates gathered their books and papers and left. The assembly broke up into a cluster of conversations.

"You were all so strong," said Mrs Leach as the group walked home.

"They are enraged with us and bent on punishing us because we did not repent our statements or withdraw our criticisms of the Church," said Widow Brewster.

"They are not used to such obstreperous, vexatious women," said Alice, laughing.

"They are angry, I think," said Mistress Moore, "because no male Church member can effectively supervise us. Three of us are widows and beyond their control. We are not setting a good example."

"We have gone astray because we lack the religious guidance of pious men." Alice spoke this with mock formality.

They laughed.

"But the citizens grew hostile towards us," said Alice. "We did not win them over."

"They wanted us whipped," said Mistress Leach.

"And we may still be," said Widow Brewster. "They can find a way if they wish."

The five fell silent. How much now did they rely on the mercy of the magistrates they had traduced? That was the question in all their minds. And it was a chastening one.

They said their farewells as they turned towards their homes. They had had their say but their victory was muted. As she walked back, Alice thought that men could say what she and her friends had said, privately in their own homes, with impunity. Women couldn't because all their words and actions should be subject to supervision by their husbands or neighbours, the state and the Church. For women, such privacy did not exist.

More than that, she and her friends were women of some account and status. Some of them, Mistress Leach and Mistress Eaton in particular, offered an alternative interpretation to some of the Church's doctrines. They could become movers of dissent, and this could not be allowed. They had openly challenged men. Perhaps when the women in the gathering were back on their own, away from the emotions of the crowd, some would ponder their words. Maybe that was all she could hope for: that they had lit a spark. And that was dangerous.

She smiled to herself: that was a satisfactory outcome, after all.

She was indeed a vexatious woman – and James had loved her for it. As Will had done. Thirty years: she had grown up, remained true to herself.

They would not be whipped, she was sure. The magistrates would congratulate themselves on their magnanimity and issue them with firm warnings. And the sweet irony was that husbands – sole owners of property and chattels, except for widows like herself – would have to pay the fines.

In time the spark would kindle a fire, she was sure of it. Possibly not in her lifetime but she had played a part. And she should be content with this.

34.

DISILLUSION

1649

Will's right hand rested on his saddle pommel, loosely holding Flint's reins as he rode from his home to Westminster Hall. That hand, he thought, had helped turned the world upside down, his thumb and fingers forming his signature so clearly and deliberately.

But the streets had not changed at all: the same smells and rubbish, horses and carts, men's laden shoulders, women carrying buckets of water, calls of traders, curses. He must look to their eyes as he always did: a well-dressed merchant with his fine grey horse walking unhurriedly.

His head, though, was in turmoil. How could he feel exultant and fearful at the same time; stunned at the enormity of the royal execution but despondent at his empty home? Only the gentle swaying of Flint's rhythmic movement comforted him.

It was St Valentine's Day – how hollow that was to him this year – and Will was riding to the first meeting of the Council of State. As he approached the Exchange, he heard above the street's general bustle and noise the thud of hammers on stone. He reined in Flint behind a small crowd of onlookers. Over their heads he could see four men smashing the statue of King Charles in the centre of the square, each raising his hammer in turn. Already Charles' broken head and arms were on the cobbles, and now great ringing blows landed on the statue's chest. The crowd were not cheering; they watched in an eerie silence, faces sullen and frowning. Finally the statue fell from its plinth. The men vigorously attacked the legs and torso, splinters of stone flying.

Who had given the order? Or had the men taken the initiative themselves?

Will found the crudeness of it disturbing.

The other Councillors assembled, and at a half after eight Oliver Cromwell called them to order in the Painted Chamber. Within three hours they had set up one committee for the unification of the three kingdoms; another to deal with the famine in the north – after bad harvests, 30,000 had neither bread nor seed corn nor the means of securing either; others for the Army – which needed to collect money for soldiers' pay by loans from the city and the confiscation of royal estates – the Navy and Foreign affairs.

After lunch two simple resolutions were passed unanimously. First, the Monarchy was abolished – Kingship was "unnecessary, burdensome and dangerous to the liberty and safety and public interest of the nation"' Secondly, the House of Lords was abolished: "useless and dangerous". There was cheering and braying, fists thumped on tables, feet stamped on the floor. Harrison's eyes glittered like a fanatic.

Afterwards in the tavern, Will said, "Lilburne's gone very quiet. Is he ill?"

"Some say he's opening a shop, others that he's setting up as a coal merchant or a soap-boiler."

"He's disillusioned," said Will, "retired from the political scene. But I respect him."

"A mad man, no common sense," scoffed Harrison.

"A man of principle, I'd say. He feared that without King or Lords or a proper Commons, the Army might rule over us arbitrarily without declared laws. And it could if we let it."

"No fear," replied Harrison. "The Army fought for Parliament, not for itself."

They parted. Will thought Harrison's answer too easy, too dismissive.

But he rode home fully satisfied with the day's work. A new political order, a start made on tackling practical problems, a sense of progress. He paused at the square in front of the Exchange. Only the statue's plinth remained. He peered down at the newly carved words: *Exit tyrannus, regum ultimus – the tyrant is gone, the last of kings.*

A new free country. Why should he not feel pride that he had helped it into being? Why could he not just be happy?

★

The answer was at home. The rift in his marriage was now deep. Jane and the children were still at her parents'. So he threw himself into his business. He joined the Worshipful Company of Drapers and made plans to open shops in Bermondsey and back home in Wigan. He did deals in the coffee houses, where he preferred to drink the chocolate. He began to import cloth made from flaxen hemp from Russia, muslins and calicoes from the East Indies, and pioneered the export of 'medley', a cloth made from fine Spanish wool. He sought new markets in America, especially in Virginia and New Plymouth, but also in Sweden and Germany.

And Will also lost himself in the work of Parliament – driven by the fervour of creating a better society. There was indeed work to be done: the Council set to with the zeal of missionaries. Will had sight of a report by a French envoy:

> *"They live without ostentation, without pomp and without mutual rivalry. They are economical in their private affairs and prodigal in their devotion to public affairs, for which each man toils as if for his private interest. They handle large sums of money which they administer honestly, observing a strict discipline."*

361

It pleased him that men as disparate as himself and Harrison worked together.

It was a cold March day when Will left his unhappy house, head down and cloak wrapped close around him against a bitter east wind, and strode briskly down the cobbled streets. Rain was not far behind. He was headed for The Whalebone Inn on Bow Street. It was where Lilburne usually held court with fellow 'Whaleboners' as they were known, many of them Levellers.

Will pushed open the door and it closed fast behind him: a roaring fire in the great stone fireplace, groups of men sitting at tables, their faces lit by the firelight and the pale daylight filtering in through small, dirty greenish-glass windows. They were deep in conversation and few heads turned in his direction. He ordered ale, and a dented tankard was pushed towards him across the counter. Will took a drink and surveyed the smoke-blackened parlour with its massive beams – the smell of damp, stale beer and wet clothes in spite of the fire. And over there was Freeborn John, in a chair near the fire, his head tipped, listening, a rolled pamphlet in front of him on the table.

Will made his way over.

"Is there a space for another?" he asked.

"Ah, the MP again," said Lilburne. "Mr William Nailor."

The other men looked at Will, sour suspicion in their eyes, no respect.

Lilburne filled his goblet from a jug of wine, looked up, now a sparkle in his eyes, but his face was thin and tired. How many prison years and lashings had this man endured?

"You're on this Council of State, aren't you?" More a challenge than a statement.

"Yes, I am."

Lilburne launched straight in: "Our leaders take away the King and House of Lords and then overawe the Commons so that it is become the channel through which is conveyed all the decrees and determinations of your private Council of some few officers and peers. Of which you are one." He coughed.

The other men at the table grinned at Will, firelight bright on their teeth and eyes, enjoying Will's discomfort.

"No, it's not like that," answered Will.

Lilburne took a drink of wine, swilled it round his mouth and said, "And now they fight against Levellers instead of Cavaliers."

The landlord lumbered over and threw two more logs on the fire.

Lilburne was warming to his theme.

"What about the agreements made at Putney two years ago? You were present. The adjutators are now thrust out. They shot a soldier to death at Corkbush. They have weeded out good men. Meetings between officers and men are now forbidden, petitions allowed only if approved by officers."

All Will could say was, "I was there at Corkbush. I saw it myself. It was wrong and disgraceful."

"No marvel," said Lilburne, "if we are staggered in our belief of their integrity."

Angry mutters of agreement round the table.

"Our Army has been victorious. And for what have so many lost their lives? To be repressed with the same kind of repressions as the Kings and Bishops did before? And now, to prevent us laying open their treacheries and hypocrisies, they strictly stop the press. As you well know, it has happened to me."

"Now we see," continued Lilburne, "that they intended merely to establish themselves in power and greatness." He shook his head. "I have written it here." He held a pamphlet in Will's face and read from it, *"We were before ruled by King, Lords and Commons; and now by a General, a Court Martial and House of Commons; and we pray you, what is the difference?* And this afternoon I take it to the Commons, giving warning of the

363

most dangerous thraldom and misery that ever threatened this much-wasted nation."

Will was bewildered. It wasn't like that. It was as if all Will's work on the Council – the hours, discussions, decisions – had been for nothing.

The King had gone; he had to be replaced with strong leadership. Good men, like himself, were striving to create a better world out of chaos. It would take time. He gained no advantage financially or any other way from his position on the Council.

Lilburne's voice had risen. Other groups of men stopped their conversations to listen.

"Where is that liberty so much pretended and so deeply purchased?"

Tankards and mugs were knocked on the table. "You say it right, John. We are with you."

Their anger blazed at Will, their sense of betrayal. He had no place here. Lilburne's words were an indictment against him. He levered himself up from the tightly packed bench. All he could say was, "I think you speak some truth but not all." And he fled.

There was no comfort to be found at home; it was the place he found most lonely. And now Ingilby was keeping his distance. He'd been quite honest about it.

"I am shut out of Parliament by your democratic colleagues," he said, sardonically. "I earn my keep by being a lawyer and cannot discourage clients by taking sides. The King has gone but the future is uncertain. I must hedge my bets."

"Ever the pragmatist."

"Take care, Will, that the house of cards you are building doesn't come crumbling down and take you with it."

Troubled, guilty, doubting himself, Will sat in the Commons that afternoon. Were the views of the Whaleboners widespread? Was that how the people thought of the Council of State?

Accompanied by a crowd of supporters, Lilburne entered. He presented his *England's New Chaines Discovered*, his voice hoarse, a spare figure, his back bent over his papers. He spoke quietly, developing the arguments he had made in the inn. He thanked the MPs for their attention, summoned his supporters and left.

Four days later the Commons gave its response. Will could hardly believe his ears. First, it issued a Declaration and Order stating that the pamphlet "was false, scandalous and reproachfull, highly seditious and destructive to the present government and tends to division and mutiny in the Army." Second, the author or authors were guilty of High Treason and should be proceeded against as traitors. Third, that the specific offence was that "Lieutenant Colonel Lilburne did read the book outside Winchester House, where he resided, before a great multitude of people and perswaded subscriptions to it." Fourth, Oliver Cromwell authorised Edward Dendy, Serjeant-at-Arms, "to break open any locks and bolts whatsoever, to go to all dwellings and workhouses of those who print scandalous and seditious pamphlets, apprehend those printers and bring them before the Council, and to bring away the presses and all such pamphlets and papers." Furthermore, Serjeant Dendy was to provide himself with a drum, trumpet and guard and make Proclamation against the authors at Cheapside, the Exchange and the Spittle in Southwark. Fifth, that Proclamation was ordered to be made in all market towns in England. Sixth, all post was to be searched and all letters containing the pamphlet were to be stopped.

All this was a straight denial of all that Parliament and the Army had sought. Like Harrison and a few others, Will voted against all of this. They defied Cromwell, noted the disapproval on so many faces around them, but saw also some sheepishness in others not so brave.

"This was what we fought against," said Harrison.

"Freedom of speech is what we fought for," said Will. "Any criticisms of the Commons and Council must be answered, not outlawed. Lilburne is right, again."

The next steps were inevitable. In the early hours of the following morning an armed detachment of one hundred and fifty troops arrested Lilburne in his bed and marched him through the streets to the guardhouse in St Paul's. Three other Leveller leaders were arrested the same night.

Next day in Whitehall the four Levellers were examined by John Bradshawe and members of the Council of State. Will was among them. Overton and Lilburne refused to remove their hats, not accepting the legality of the Council. They just don't give an inch, thought Will, admiringly. They also refused to answer questions, to avoid incriminating themselves. Impatiently they were ushered to another room.

As soon as they were out, Cromwell thumped his fist on the Council table so hard it shook. "I tell you, sirs, you have no other ways to deal with these men but to break them in pieces."

He thumped the table again.

"Let me tell you that which is true: if you do not break them, they will break you. They will frustrate and make void all that work that with so many years' industry, toil and pains you have done. And so they will render you to all rational men in the world as the most contemptiblest generation of silly, low-spirited men in the earth. Sirs, I tell you again. You are necessitated to break them."

He thumped his right fist into the palm of his left hand. There were flecks of foam at the corners of his mouth when he finished, his face purple. Will had never seen him so enraged. Cromwell was a fearsome figure. He sat down but got up again immediately, wiped his mouth and continued. His quiet intensity now was even more disturbing.

"The country will never be settled so long as Lilburne is alive. I will stop his mouth or burst his gall rather than run the hazard of such discontents and mutinies as are daily contracted in the Army by means of his seditious scribbling."

The members were cowed. Will looked around. Would no one gainsay this bully? Could no one see the hypocrisy? But Lilburne had trodden on too many toes, told too many home truths. Will forced himself to stand.

All eyes turned to him. Cromwell glowered.

"I appeal for bail," said Will. His words were met with silence.

Rejected. Will shook his head in disgust. When had the movement lost its way?

The four Leveller leaders were committed to the Tower. It was the 28th of March, barely two months after the execution of the King. How had things so rapidly fallen apart?

However, the leaders were not abandoned by their followers. Only five days later a petition signed by 10,000 was presented on their behalf. But the Commons ordered the prosecution go ahead. Then came the *Humble Petition of divers well-affected women*, with nine hundred signatures, calling for the freeing of the four.

But the four Leveller leaders remained in the Tower.

Next day Cromwell's warnings came true. A regiment had been ordered out of London as part of a strategy to move troops to places where they would be less susceptible to Leveller propaganda. But a twenty-three-year-old trooper named Robert Lockyer, who had served in Cromwell's Ironsides, had fought at Naseby and been with Rainborowe at Corkbush Field, led a mutiny. The regiment was still owed arrears of pay. With thirty other troopers they seized the regimental colours and barricaded themselves in the Bull Inn in Bishopsgate Street. Officers brought some back pay but the mutineers refused to move. Finally, Cromwell and Fairfax arrived and the mutineers were forced to surrender by a company of Horse and Foot. Fourteen were taken into custody and punished. Lockyer was sentenced to death.

Lilburne and Overton petitioned Fairfax for mercy from their cells in the Tower. Cromwell was sympathetic, somewhat to Will's surprise, but Fairfax was adamant for execution. Army discipline overruled other deeper loyalties. Again, Will could not believe what he was hearing. He had to go and witness the betrayal.

Will watched as, accompanied by his sisters and cousins, Lockyer was taken to St Paul's Churchyard where he faced a firing squad. He refused to wear a blindfold.

He said farewells to friends and family and then addressed the firing squad: "My cause is just and I fear not the face of death. Fellow soldiers, I am brought here to suffer on behalf of the people of England and for your privileges and liberties. But I perceive you are appointed by your officers to murder me, and I did not think you had such heathenish and barbarous principles in you."

Colonel Okey, in charge of the detail, accused him of still trying to make the soldiers mutiny. To the watching crowd, Lockyer said, "I pray you, let not this death of mine be a discouragement, but rather an incouragement, for never man died more comfortably than I do."

Turning back to the firing squad, he said, "Shoot when I raise my hands."

They did so.

Another martyr, another betrayal, thought Will, to join Richard Arnold, shot at Corkbush.

Next day he attended the funeral. The Levellers knew what was required and organised it. A thousand soldiers paced before the hearse in files of six; the coffin was covered with a black cloth on which were sprigs of rosemary dipped in blood and, in the middle, the dead trooper's naked sword. Behind, came his horse, draped in black and led by footmen in mourning suit and cloak, while on either side marched three trumpeters. Two or three thousand citizens and soldiers followed in orderly file, ranks of women at the back. All the attendants, beside the black ribbons of mourning, wore the sea-green of the Levellers. At the churchyard thousands more waited, most wearing the sea-green emblem. No disturbance occurred. It was a ceremony of consecration and afterwards all returned quietly home.

What a magnificent affront to Parliament and Army, thought Will.

Will's life was now in turmoil: estranged from his wife, hurt by the absence of his children, appalled by the imprisonment of Lilburne and others in the Tower, moved by the petitioners and Lockyer's funeral. Everything he had come to believe was under attack, his great hopes were undermined, his friend and mentor Rainborowe dead, he was at odds with his hero Cromwell. Ingilby of course enjoyed the hypocrisy and broken promises of the politicians. Never had he felt more alone but at the same time hemmed in. Only his business was thriving but this gave little comfort.

He needed to escape the city, feel some different air, see the countryside.

★

"Move, God damn you!" Will shouted as he drove Flint through the barging crowds. "Out of the way!"

Faces scowled at him, curses were thrown, sticks raised.

To get away, to break loose beyond the Thames, beyond London. Some new air.

London Bridge – he loathed it now: the packed roadway always dark as dusk, loomed over by seven-storey houses, bawling, traders, short-tempered packed bodies, stink of offal and horse shit, taste of filth and rot on his lips. Flint, pressed in by bodies shoving into him, making his way.

They got through. Now in the open space, Flint was more relaxed, his ears up. Will let him amble, stroked his neck. "Easy, boy!"

369

He shook his head, breathed deeply, lifted his face to the breeze; patches of heath polished by the sunlight then damped by cloud shadows. To be free of it all: the crowds and stink of the city, the dealing and bargaining, pamphlets and arguments, petitions, aggression and suspicion, disappointments and petty rivalries, committees bogged down in details, disgruntled soldiers and mutinies; and the icy disapproval of his wife that was freezing his blood.

"To hell with it all! Come on, boy, let's ride!"

He spurred Flint into a canter and then a gallop, a gallop into peace not into a battlefield, into freedom and spirit.

Flint's pounding hooves, the strength of his body surging beneath him, grace and speed and rhythm, the rippling muscles of his shoulders, his snorting breath, the power and drive of his back legs.

Eventually they slowed to a canter, to a trot, to a walk. High on the heath, hearts slowing, breathing easing. Sweat on his face, hands loose on the reins. Flint's ears up, tossing his head, snickering.

Will leaned forward to pat Flint's neck. "Good boy!"

As the heath sloped slowly downwards, he could just see St Mary's Church at Putney, down by the Thames. The great Army Council debate had been there. Such high hopes, such passion. And now Rainborowe was dead, adjutators shot at Corkbush, Lockyer martyred, Army and Parliament at odds. The King had been executed but there were new conflicts; drab disagreements but the same problems.

They made their way down to the ferry at Putney and crossed the river. On they ambled past Fulham Palace, past market gardens and into the countryside.

At a crossroads he heard the sound of hooves, shouts and guffaws. A troop of horses rounded a bend, trotting, snorting, the riders with sea-green colours in their hats.

Will stepped towards them and a colonel reined in his horse.

"I like the sea-green," said Will.

The colonel's eyes suspicious, measuring him up.

"I fought with Colonel Rainborowe at Preston," said Will. "A great man."

Still suspicious.

"I heard him speak at the great debate in St Mary's Church, down there." Will pointed back towards the river.

A slight nod.

"I'm in Colonel Whalley's regiment. Captain Will Nailor."

"We're on our way to meet up with some of them," said the colonel. "There's a rendezvous arranged for Leveller regiments."

Regiments with grievances were assembling from Salisbury and Banbury and Aylesbury.

"Harrison's men?" asked Will.

"We're told so."

"Can I ride along with you?"

"The more the merrier. Richard Eyres." They shook hands.

"You were at Corkbush Field, weren't you?" said Will. "A New England man."

"That's me."

And Will wished James Parker was with them.

They rode up to Burford next day in the late evening in drizzle. The high street was packed with soldiers, rowdy with drink, virile with rebellion. Clumps of men, huddled together and laughing, arms round shoulders, telling their tales.

"About 1,200 of us here, quartered in barns and farms and suchlike. Mutineers!" said one and grinned, ale on his breath, gap-toothed, a scar on his right cheek.

"True believers!" he added, his reddened eyes raised to the sky.

He had *The Agreement of the People* folded into his hat band and a sea-green ribbon pinned to it.

At the Crowne Inn, Will and Colonel Eyres were given a small dark room to share for the night. Now, down in the parlour, already a fug of smoke, the sooty beams low, they shared a jug of wine. Knucklebones and cards at tables, clink of coins. Muskets stacked in a corner. Soldiers' and officers' voices loud with revolt, with shared grievance, with the expectation of confrontation.

"No Harrison," said Will.

"No, disappointing. But some of their men are here, and adjutators."

Among the bray of voices: "Ireland! We're not being sent to bloody Ireland!... Not before we get our back pay... Broken promises... Still no rights!"

The back of a hand wiped the ale foam from a moustache. "Ruled by the Council of State, as bad as the King... Worse! ... Adjutators banned from the Army Council."

The words of Lilburne.

A hairy fist, broken nails, waved *The Agreement of the People*. "None of this put into action." The fist slammed it onto the table. "Still only the same rich bastards allowed to vote... tithes not abolished... that liar Cromwell: he's a tyrant."

Voices louder, the stink rising off dirty sweaty bodies, calls for more ale.

"We must avenge the blood of Lockyer."

Fists raised in the air, great bawled cheers. Fellowship.

"Lockyer! Lockyer!"

"I heard a rumour – from the landlord," whispered Eyres to Will, "that an emissary from Cromwell, a Major White, is in some hidden room here negotiating with mutineer representatives, drawing up a document to take to Cromwell in the morning."

"This lot aren't in the mood to compromise."

Gradually the soldiers left for their billets and quarters, singing, reeling and swaying. Some stayed and slept, heads on arms on the tables. Quieter. Emptier. The stink still there. Spilled ale, crumbs of bread and cheese. Candlelight flickering in the draughts, and shadows, the fire burning low. Will and Eyres silent. Black night outside the windows. Midnight approaching.

And then a thunder outside in the street, hooves clattering by, great looming shapes of shrieking horses, flashing sabres in the light from the inn windows, musket shots, yells of anger then pain.

"Who the hell is that?!" cried Will.

"Not friend, so foe."

"It can't be Fairfax, he's over near Aylesbury."

"Cromwell, then," said Eyres. "Cromwell again."

The soldiers in the inn parlour stumbling for their weapons, Eyres shouting orders, a window smashed, Will stunned, pistol in hand. But who would he be shooting at? His own men? Then the door smashed open, a musket raised to the shoulder, flash of a shot; a soldier by the window cried out, spinning and falling to the floor. More new soldiers, no sea-green colours, crowded in through the door, metal clinking and glittering, shouting. Arms seized Will and Eyres, slammed them down into their seats. Will smelled horse and gunpowder. Eyres' soldiers were arrested, still only half sober, two with bleeding wounds, and led away.

Eyres questioned, cursing, arrested and led away.

Then, filling the doorway, Cromwell – his figure and stance unmistakeable – sword unsheathed. In his leather and metal and great spurred boots. He stared into the shadowy room.

"Is that you, Will Nailor?" he barked. He strode forward. "What in God's name are you doing here?"

Will stood up. These two minutes had decided him. "Not killing fellow soldiers... Lieutenant General. That's for certain."

He was ready to be punched for this insult, his body ready to spring, Cromwell or no Cromwell. The two were head to head. A poise and balance to be broken by a blow or a curse.

From behind the counter a man emerged. Cromwell turned to him. "Major White."

"Your negotiator" – the major emphasised the word – "Lieutenant General." His voice quiet, taut with controlled anger. "We were close to agreement before this... this..." – he looked around the room, saw the body of the dead soldier – "this betrayal, this murder."

Will saw Cromwell's fist tighten on his sword. Saw the battle in his face, the instinct to retaliate held and then suppressed.

"Let's sit," Cromwell said, gesturing to the empty chairs. "The rest of you, clear the room. Take that unfortunate dead man with you. Respectfully." Cromwell the politician now. "It is too late for more drinking." Even a smile.

Cromwell looked towards the landlord, still cowering behind the counter. "Some pie for us all. But wipe this table first. And bring candles."

The landlord hurried over, subservient, wiped away the food crumbs and ale pools, bustled away, shouting to his kitchen maid for candles. They sat down, the three of them, Cromwell on one side of the table, confident, Will and Major White opposite, angry and wary. A cat sidled under the table, mewing.

"We are not running a market stall," said Cromwell, his eyes intent, shining in the candlelight, switching from Will to White. "We are about God's business."

"That was God's business, was it?" said Major White, nodding towards the window where the soldier had been shot.

"Regrettable. But this is war and accidents happen in war."

"War?" put in Will. "Against your own men?"

"Again regrettable, but yes. I am protecting the Commonwealth."

White sniffed in disgust. Will shook his head, waiting for the platitudes, saw Cromwell pricked by their disrespect, anger flash in his eyes, saw the effort to control his temper.

"Let me ask you some questions. The Royalists are defeated." Elbow on the table, he raised his thumb. "Scotland is defeated." Now his first finger raised. "Both France and Spain want Charles Stuart to replace his executed father." Another finger. "Prince Rupert, the best Royalist general, is off the Irish coast with a squadron of eight ships." Another finger. "A Catholic army has been raised in Ireland." His little finger. "So, first question" – he spread his open hand – "where is any invasion of England most likely to come from?"

Cromwell leaned back out of the light, waited, almost lordly.

Will hated where Cromwell had led them: down a cul-de-sac to one obvious answer. He would not give Cromwell the satisfaction. White was silent, thin-lipped.

Cromwell smiled, teeth gleaming, the smile of a point won. "You won't say, but you cannot deny it. The invasion would come from Ireland."

He leaned forward again, elbows on the table, his profile outlined in the flickering candlelight. "Second question: can a divided army win a war?"

Rhetorical, patronising. This wasn't an explanation, it was a lesson: a schoolmaster and two awkward pupils who needed to be put in their place.

"Of course it can't," continued Cromwell, this time not waiting. "We must have a united army to prevent an invasion and keep the country safe. But these Levellers are trying to raise mutiny everywhere – in Wales, Bristol, Barnstaple, Portsmouth and the Isle of Wight, Lancaster." His voice rose as he listed the places. "So, my next question: if you were Lieutenant General of the Army, would you stand by and watch the army disintegrate and so open the door to Charles Stuart, or would you stop the rot?"

Cromwell's two clenched fists on the table. This time a genuine challenge.

But Will was up for it now.

"*The Agreement of the People* was approved by you and Fairfax and the Army Council at Putney. None of it has been implemented. None. And still there are arrears of pay." His turn to glare and thump the table. "That is why the army is in revolt; the Levellers have fertile ground on which to work."

Major White nodded in agreement.

"And who has not implemented it?" shot back Cromwell. "Parliament. You know, you're in it, an MP. You have not implemented it."

The cat jumped up onto the table, green-eyed and black. Will roughly shoved it off, opened his mouth to reply, but Cromwell held up his hand. "I am not accusing you, Will. I am more to blame than you. Holding the Army together is one thing, but politics is another."

He turned suddenly to the counter, shouted, "Where is that pie, landlord?" Turned back.

"We have put Parliament in charge. I know what you are going to say – that it isn't democratic enough, that it is still elected by the 'forty shillings a year' men. And you are right. But, and this is the point, we cannot work only with radicals; we will be able to govern this country well only with the agreement of moderate-thinking men. We have to broaden our government."

And this time, when he leaned back into the shadows, he seemed genuinely to want understanding. Seeking support.

"I didn't fight just to end the monarchy," said Will, "but to build something better and fairer in its place. To create something."

"It will be a slow process, Will, compromising here, bargaining there. It has taken more than a thousand years to end the rule of kings. It will take more than a few months to replace it."

Cromwell leaned forward, lowered his voice. "We must have peace now in our land. However much we may like their ideas, those revolters we call Levellers will bring more civil war and anarchy, more pain and death." He straightened up. The explanation was over.

The landlord brought a great steaming golden-crusted pie.

Cromwell wiped his dagger on his breeches, blade glinting as he plunged it into the crust, and cut a slice across the top.

"Will you join me, gentlemen?" he asked.

White and Will stood up. Cromwell looked up at them as they turned away. "There will be 300 of the mutineers locked up in the church by now." Voice harsh now, clipped, black eyes glossy in the candlelight, like beetles' backs. "The Levellers' War is crushed in the egg."

He slammed his thumb down onto the table. "Lilburne's seditious scribbling is behind this. Either he or I shall perish because of it."

But Will and White had gone. Cromwell stroked the cat that rubbed against his boot and started in on the pie.

Two days later, at nine o'clock in the morning, Will stood under the yew trees in Burford churchyard. Colonel White was nowhere to be seen. To the east, over trees and river, hung pale watery sunshine. Above him, lined along the roof leads of the church, mutineers slouched. Cromwell's orders, no doubt. Other mutineers stood around the churchyard, armed guards overseeing them. Blackbirds sang from the trees, leaves barely moved in the stillness. No human voices. A sullen silence. Will saw other faces, blurred behind the windows of the Lady Chapel.

Three men were led out from the church to the porch, blindfolded. The examples. Adjutators. Yesterday an Army Council court-martial had sentenced them to death. They had refused to put their names to a petition of penitence. Lined up against the west wall of the churchyard, the three men standing two yards apart from each other, hands bound behind their backs, unable to see the sun but faces upturned to it, warmed by it, Will hoped. Private Perkins, Corporal Church, Cornet Thompson. Three firing squads of four men each.

One of them spoke, voice strong, to the silent witnesses: "We die for what we acted for, the good and ease of the people who were under great oppression and slavery."

An order. Muskets raised to shoulders, taking aim. And the heads of all the watching soldiers turned down to stare at their boots, refusing to witness. "Fire!" Twelve shots rang out, three bodies twisted and fell to the grass, rag dolls stained red. Smoke in the air, a sharp smell of gunpowder.

A minute's stillness and then nearly three hundred men, on the roof, in the churchyard, in the chapel, raised their heads simultaneously and turned to stare at Cromwell seated on his horse in full battledress at the lychgate. Will, too. Still not a murmur of a protest. Silent loathing, silent contempt.

Cromwell stared back, his eyes roving over all of them. Then a twitch of the reins, the prick of a spur, his horse turning, leaving, hooves on the cobbles.

For Will, the end of a vision.

★

Escaping again, Will rode back into London, escaping perfidy, fleeing from his shattered dream. Lost in speed and movement, he spurred on Flint, riding late into the night, stopping at the Bell Inn in High Wycombe for food and a bed, too much ale and bad dreams.

Next morning on the road again, early. Instead of going to a comfortless empty home, he galloped straight to the yard at Westminster, threw the reins and a few pence to an ostler and, spattered in mud, climbed the steps into Westminster

Hall. A quick glance round: Harrison leaning against a pillar, laughing. Will marched over to him.

"And where the hell were you?" he demanded, thrusting his face forward, wanting to grab him by the throat.

"What?"

"Your men. You weren't with your men at Burford. Regiments were assembling – radicals, Levellers – a protest, maybe a mutiny. You should have been there."

Harrison snorted. "Games, Will, dangerous games. You should have been here, where the real work is."

Will's turn to scoff, turning away. But Harrison grabbed his elbow. Will swung round.

"Calm down," said Harrison. "Do you know what we actually did this morning?"

Will shook off Harrison's hand.

"We declared England a Commonwealth *governed by representatives of the people in Parliament without any King or House of Lords.* We did it, Will. England is a republic. A dream come true. We have abolished the kingly office. Worth celebrating? Let's share a jug of wine."

"It's you who's playing the game, Thomas. Swapping the fancy dress is all you've done. It means nothing if life doesn't improve for the ordinary soldier and the ordinary labourer. I'll celebrate when I see some evidence of that."

Will strode away. Within an hour his anger had been stoked higher. He learned that before Cromwell left for Burford he had sent 400 men from regiments hostile to Lilburne to guard the Tower because of rumours the Tower would be attacked to free Lilburne and his companions. Lilburne and his friends had been separated, deprived of pen, ink and paper and refused all visitors except wives.

His fellow MPs had passed the Treason Act which made it treasonable for civilians to stir up mutiny in the army.

"Treasonable to demand your rights!"

Harrison hadn't mentioned that.

Even an empty home was preferable to this place of scheming and compromise. By the time he strode through his front door, Will was sick to death with affairs of state, contemptuous of the poverty-stricken streets, raging at his wife's undutiful leaving, despondent about his absent children. He rapped out orders to servants for rich food – the only pleasure left. He had fires lit and his bed warmed. Alone at the head of the table, candles and firelight flickered in the gloom as he ate his supper: capon and pigeon pie, figs, apricots and red wine. He belched and farted unconstrained, wiped his lips with the back of his hand, ignoring the napkin. Crude freedom, but why not? Why mope? Jane had gone. Let go, Will, let go.

No, he must write that letter to her. But saying what?

He moved to the chair by the fire, staring into the flames, head warmed and muzzy with sack posset – eggs, wine and spices. To hell with it all. And fell asleep.

★

Two months later, on a hot August afternoon, Will was in his walled garden in a vine-shaded arbour. The gardeners had worked but the raised beds of herbs and plants were not as neat without Jane's supervision. The espaliered apples and pears along the south-facing wall were fruiting but Will knew nothing of pruning. Looking at the beds, he recognised only honeysuckle and parsley. How little he knew; how much he depended – the house, their home depended – on Jane. Over the weeks they had written occasional letters – Jane's about the children; Will's about the business, some servant matters, nothing about politics.

Two days ago he had finally written the letter. He had pleaded with her to return, said he missed her and the children, could not undo what he had done, could not pretend to regret what he had done about the King – and she would not want him to lie about it – but was sorely disappointed about what had happened afterwards, had misplaced his trust, wanted to talk to her about his future – if there was to be any – in Parliament. What was most important was the family being together.

Now, warmed by the sun, he awaited her response. Remembered his children's laughter in the garden bushes, games with them; remembered Jane's scent, sitting here together, the softness of her hand. It could not all be gone, could it? All gone and, in return, this Parliament – a compromised mess of broken promises and squalid bargaining.

Will took a drink of raspberry wine. His only solace was Freeborn John Lilburne: a man constant in his principles. From his doublet he took a piece of paper, a message brought from the Tower chaplain, from the still-imprisoned Lilburne. Will read it again with relish:

> *Tell your masters from me that if it were possible for me now to chuse, I had rather chuse to live seven years under old King Charles his government when it was at the worst before this Parliament, than live one year under their present Government that now rule. Nay, let me tell you, if they go on with that tyranny they are in, they will make Prince Charles have friends enow, not only to cry him up, but also really to fight for him, to bring him into his Father's throne.*

A thought too far, John. That could never happen.

Will picked up one of two pamphlets on the bench beside him. *An Impeachment of High Treason against Oliver Cromwell and his son-in-law Henry Ireton.* No sophistry there, then; straight to the heart of the matter. No author was named but everybody presumed it had been written by Lilburne. In despair at the

381

death by smallpox of his two sons last month, he had thrown himself again into his writing, rekindling his political fire.

Will opened the pamphlet and read it again.

O Cromwell! Oh Ireton! How hath a little time and successe changed the honest shape of so many officers! The final stage in the Civil War had done nothing else but set up the false Saint and most desperate Apostate murderer and traytor, Oliver Cromwell, to be King of England.

Yes! Yes! On the nail, my man. Will punched the soft summer air with his approval.

Another sip of raspberry wine. Was Lilburne deliberately putting his neck in the noose? Challenging the authorities to become himself a martyr, grieving for his sons, his life less meaningful?

The other pamphlet was even more inflammatory. He picked it up. *An outcry of the Youngmen and Apprentices of London.* Again no author but the tone and style were Lilburne's. It was a bare-faced incitement to mutiny. Addressed to the common soldier on behalf of the apprentices and fellow citizens of London, it asked:

Do you uphold The Agreement of the People so far as to use your swords in its defence? Do you allow of the late shedding of bloud of war at Burford in time of peace? You, the private souldiers of the Army, being the instrumentall authors of your own slavery and ours.

Will put the paper down.

Was it honeysuckle he could smell? Such peace in his garden retreat while outside a rage of passion and accusation. He was, he realised, not given instinctively to fits of passion about causes. But the Levellers, Lilburne and Rainborowe

382

had roused him to loyalties utterly unforeseen. Once, he had known which side he was on: Parliament against the King. But now? Maybe neither Parliament nor Army.

If Will was on any side, he was on Lilburne's. He looked around their silent, empty garden, just a robin hidden somewhere in the foliage. The King was dead, what's done was done. It was the future that counted, his children's future and the kind of land they would grow up in.

More raspberry wine. He swilled it round his mouth, the taste of a good, free England, swallowed it.

It wasn't a question of *if* Lilburne would be put on trial, but when and for what. A story was going the rounds that Lilburne's shoemaker had refused to make him a new pair of boots, saying that he would have but little time to wear them. But Lilburne commanded the boots be made to order: he would wear out his old boots and his new, too, as soon as Cromwell would wear his out. Typical Lilburne.

Will laughed to himself, closed his eyes, breathed deeply, felt the warm sun bless his face. If only this was all there was.

★

On September 18th Will received an answer from Jane. His fingers were trembling as he opened the letter. At first he dare not read it, just glanced quickly at the familiar handwriting. She would return home with the children at the end of October, when city summer fears of disease had eased with the coming of cooler weather. He read it again to make sure. No explanation, nothing about reconciliation or hope. But no recriminations either. He resolved that he and Jane would talk, but not about politics, unless she wanted to; there would be a new start, a renewal, a new softness between them. An acceptance of each other. But he was nervous, too.

At last, on September 19th, a warrant was issued for the trial of Lilburne. He was charged with high treason – for which the penalty was death.

Will feared for him, but at least Cromwell's rage and intimidation would play no part in it; he was in Ireland, massacring the Irish Catholics – in the name of God, no doubt.

On October 24th, a gusty day, rubbish swirling in the streets, Will queued outside the Guildhall. An MP he might be but he had no special privileges here. He heard angry curses, denunciations of Parliament, threats, defiance not deference as they shuffled towards the doors. Inside, in the public gallery, he was crammed in with the rest. The rowdy band of Lilburne's friends and supporters outnumbered the government's supporters by twenty to one. Opposite him were more spectators, equally packed, in a temporary stand built on scaffolding.

Lilburne stood silently at the bar. The emaciation that Will had seen before had gone but his struggles and disillusionment had left their mark in the set of his mouth and the challenge in his eyes. He looked respectable and Will could not prevent a smile: thick-set, dressed carefully in doublet buttoning down to the hips, with lace at the neck and cuffs, trousers slashed and decorated, good boots and spurs. Dressed for the occasion. Like a prosperous merchant. His hair was no longer curled back from his ears but hanging to his shoulders, somewhat grizzled with grey.

From the charge sheet the clerk intoned: *"You maliciously, advisedly and traitorously didst plot and contrive to stir up force against the government. And, though not being an officer or a souldier, as a false traytour, did maliciously indeavour to stir up a dangerous, distemper, Mutiny and Rebellion in the Army."*

Each word had been savoured as if it had been a sugared fig.

Lilburne stood silent and unmoving at the bar. At the still centre of the rowdy courtroom, restless with colour and gesticulations, shaking heads, catcalls, cheers and jeers, a rising stink of dirty jam-packed bodies – this man was on trial for his life.

The prosecution began by reading extracts from the pamphlets Lilburne had allegedly written. The Lilburne crowd cheered and stamped their approval. Lilburne motioned to them to be quiet.

A stream of witnesses was called claiming they had seen Lilburne holding proofs of the pamphlets, or giving them out at The Whalebone, or taking them for printing. More extracts were read out which got the crowd cheering again. Lilburne cross-examined all the witnesses on point after point, picking, probing, unsettling, through the morning and into the afternoon. Such stamina! At one point he demanded counsel. He was refused. He turned to appeal to the jury. All could see the lines on his weary face, his eyes deep in shadow.

But Judge Keble refused.

"You must clear yourself immediately of the charge of writing these pamphlets."

Almost complete silence in the court. Lilburne stood straight, raised his face to the ceiling and beyond, lifted and spread his arms in entreaty. "Then," he pronounced with his mighty orator's voice for the first time in the trial, "I appeale to the righteous God of heaven and earth against you!"

Instantly, as he uttered these words, there was a splintering crash and the scaffolding of the temporary stand came tumbling down, people falling to the ground screaming with shock and pain. Noise, dust, shouts, confusion enveloped the court. Guards rushed to help; the judges gestured to the court officials and hurried out. Lilburne, untouched in the centre of the court, himself looked thunderstruck. Then a faint smile crossed his face. Around Will in the permanent gallery, prayers were said, hands together in supplication.

It was the most convincing evidence for a long time that Will had seen for the existence of God.

Injured spectators were led away, protesting, the broken poles and debris removed. Silence and order were eventually restored, and Will saw that Lilburne had spent the time calmly studying his law books and papers.

The judges returned; the jury settled again. Judge Keble ordered Lilburne to begin his defence. But the tide was with him now. He wanted a delay, more time to compose himself and prepare.

"Sir," he addressed the judge, "if you will be so cruel as not to give me leave to withdraw to ease and refresh my body, I pray you let me do it in the court. Officer, I entreat you to helpe me to a chamber-pot."

Loud laughter from the public. Thumping and stamping of feet. It was a dangerous ploy, to make a fool of judges.

While it was being brought, Lilburne, unconcerned at the jocularity around him, studied his books, turning pages and reading them closely. The chamber-pot was brought in and placed on the floor in front of him. Lilburne looked around the court, saw grins on the faces of the watching public, severe frowns on the faces of the judges.

A shout from the gallery, just behind Will. "Come on, John, get it out. Show us what you've got!"

Ribald laughter.

Lilburne turned his back on the public – boos – and looked up at the judges, all eight of them. Made his decision. Facing them, he pissed into the pot, never taking his eyes off the judges. Cheers as the yellowish piss arced into the pot.

"Show them, John!"

The unfortunate officer took the steaming pot away.

Antics, laughter, jokes, but this man was now pleading for his life, accused of high treason. The play was over.

Lilburne began a long and detailed examination of the facts of his indictment.

Finally, weary and leaning against his chair, his voice barely a croak, he turned to the jury. "Gentlemen of the jury, my sole judges, the keepers of my life, I desire you to know your power and consider your duty both to God, to me, to your own selves and to your country. May the gracious assisting spirit, and presence of the Lord God omnipotent, go along with you, give counsel and direct you to do that which is just and for his glory."

All around Will voices cried "Amen! Amen!" and there was a great hum of talk.

The judges looked nervous and called for three more companies of soldiers.

It was five o'clock when the jury retired. The judges turned into their rooms. The extra soldiers stood uncertainly at the exit doors. Lilburne looked exhausted, his angular face grey and wan, eyes looking at the floor. The public were restless, some leaving the court and then returning. A bedlam of voices, calls to Lilburne to cheer him up. "We are with you, John!"

He sat there, awaiting a possible death sentence, oblivious of the support around him, lost within himself. Thirty-one years old but a veteran of causes and protests. Was this the end? The end of a principled life? In the centre of the arena, he was alone. Will could not guess what were his thoughts.

After an hour, the room getting hotter and sweatier, talk rising and falling, the clerk called the court to order. The judges filed in and sat at their places, looking grim. The jury was called in. They sat. A great silence fell.

"Are you agreed of your verdict?" asked the clerk.

"Yes."

"Who shall speak for you?"

"Our foreman."

He stood up.

The clerk said, "John Lilburne, stand and hold up your hand."

He stood but did not hold up his hand.

The clerk turned to the jury. "What say you? Look upon the prisoner. Is he guilty of the Treasons charged upon him, or any of them, or not guilty?"

The foreman cleared his throat. "Not guilty to all of them."

"Nor of all the Treason, nor any of them that are layed to his charge?"

"No," said the foreman loudly, "of all or any of them."

Then the whole multitude around him leapt to their feet, Will among them. Shouting, cheers. Applause. Never, surely, had such a noise been heard in the Guildhall. It lasted for half an hour, Lilburne being embraced a thousand times, smiling weakly, seeming on the point of collapse.

The faces of the judges were pale as, transfixed, they watched the celebrations. Lilburne freed himself from an embrace, turned to them, bowed just slightly. Sad and weary beyond all measure. But vindicated.

The judges retired. But Lilburne was to be returned to the Tower. He was too exhausted to protest. Escorted by soldiers, the accompanying crowd constantly cheered him, even the soldiers joining in.

That night from his bedroom window, Will watched the light of bonfires blazing in celebration in the streets of London.

It took two weeks for Lilburne and three other Levellers to be released from the Tower. Standing outside a coffee shop on November 8th Will and Jane watched the four of them, surrounded by cheering crowds, march down the streets to a great feast in the King's Head Tavern in Fish Street.

Ingilby was with them, lips curled derisively. But he always liked a spectacle.

To commemorate Lilburne's acquittal, a medal, made of silver and copper, was struck by the Levellers. On one side was the head of Lilburne, on the other the names of the jurymen. Round the head of Lilburne were inscribed the words: *John Lilburne saved by the power of the Lord and the integrity of his jury who are juge of law as wel as fact. Oct 26 1649.*

There was also a smaller medal, with a ring by which it could be suspended from a cord round the neck. Most of the cords, Will saw, were sea-green, including his own.

35.

RECONCILIATION AND PARTING

1654

Four days later, on October 30th, Will peered out of the front windows of his house: a cold day, blustery, rain in the air, light fading early. He turned away and paced again through the hallway and rooms. He was noticing things he'd never noticed before – the placement of a cushion or an ornament, the position of a chair – making adjustments, checking the table was laid correctly, adding a log to the fire, returning to the window. Jane and his children were due back before dusk. So tense: impatient, excited yet nervous and oddly self-conscious. He had ordered a thorough cleaning of the house, the garden tidied, last fruit picked and stored. For two days servants had been harried, checked on, admonished, thanked. He could do no more to welcome them home. He reviewed himself in the mirror: for the first time noticed grey in his hair, beard white in parts, the beginnings of pouches under his eyes. This was ridiculous – like a shy suitor, aged fifty-four and after ten years of marriage.

Was he expecting too much? Their marriage had voids within it, across which they had no contact: voids which denied vital parts of his nature. But there were also, somehow, long periods of contentment, of feeling settled and rooted. And his children, of course. Could something be restored at this fresh start? He had to hope for that.

A shout from the housekeeper. Will rushed to the window: hooves clattering near, the crunch of carriage wheels, two black horses reined in, the carriage coming to a halt.

He rushed to the door, opened it, saw the carriage door open. Down the steps jumped young Robert, ran to Will and clung to his legs, then Susannah, more dainty down the steps but running to him, too. He gathered them into him, clasped them and held them tight. Felt his face break, his mouth quiver, his eyes fill with tears. He kissed the tops of their heads, murmured their names.

Then he looked up. At the top of the carriage steps stood Jane, watching them. Gently, Will detached himself and went over to her. Their eyes met, direct, gauging each other. He held out his arm to help her down. Her hand in his, ungloved – she must have just taken it off for this moment – a surge of hope and confidence, her skin so warm, her dress rustling. Her pale blue dress, his favourite, her choice for today; another leap of his heart.

At the bottom of the steps he embraced her. But he felt her holding back, her arms not around him. He went to kiss her but she turned her face so he kissed only her cheek. A momentary pang of disappointment, but she smiled, held his hand, her grey eyes warm. A promise?

The children had rushed into the house.

"They're glad to be back," said Jane.

And you? he wanted to ask, needed to know.

He still uncertain, she so composed.

Three hours later Will and Jane sat at the table for supper, fire blazing in the hearth, candles on the table, lights glittering on wine glasses. The children had chattered ceaselessly with stories: Grandfather taking Robert fishing, Grandmother teaching Susannah some complicated embroidery, the riding they had done, trips to the coast. Will had romped with them, chasing and catching. Jane meantime had inspected the house; too dark for the garden. Now the children were in bed. Now it was just them, a new awkwardness.

"Thank you, Will."

"For?" He should be thanking her.

"The roast carp."

"Stuffed with almonds and herbs."

"I know. And my favourite pudding – apple pie and orange custard. And the plate of spiced dried apricots."

He smiled, not sure of the level she wanted.

She took the slices of lemon garnish off the carp. "The children needed their father. They missed you. It was not right of me to keep them from you."

He nodded, looked her in the eye. "*And you, Jane,*" he wanted to ask, "*did you miss me?*"

"But that's not only why we're back." She nibbled at an apricot. "Delicious!" Nibbled again.

Was this a game?

"And it wasn't because my mother insisted I should return out of wifely duty."

He dared a low chuckle.

"No, I'm back because I believe you are a man of principle."

Principle?

"In spite of what you did, or even because of what you did. I can never forget you signed King Charles' death warrant... but I have learned to forgive it. You were always a fair merchant, never a cheat or an exploiter. But your principles now are higher, I believe."

She wiped her mouth with her napkin. "They are very Christian." She smiled at him. Her lovely lips. "And you, a God-denying freethinker. That's progress."

She took a sip of wine.

"Say something, Will, you're not usually tongue-tied."

He looked at her, her slender fingers resting on the table, her fair hair gleaming in the candlelight, that slight ironical tilt of her mouth.

He wanted to say *I love you*. But even at this moment he knew it was too deceptively simple, a dissembling.

She was extracting some bones from the carp.

"It seems the revolution is abating," she said. "We may live in a Commonwealth and without a King but little appears to have changed. The gentry are relieved, more relaxed and are not worrying so much. The poorer folk are disappointed, disillusioned. Is that how you see it?"

She put a forkful of carp into her mouth.

Had her voluntary exile opened her eyes? Made her see that politics was important and affected everyone?

"Jane, I have seen innocent soldiers shot, shot only because they claimed their rights, shot on the orders of Cromwell. He is a traitor, as John Lilburne accused him. He has broken promises, ignored *The Agreement of the People*. I stand by that agreement." His voice had risen.

"I have read it, Will, but I had to buy it without my parents seeing. I felt like a naughty child again." She laughed. "And I loved the feeling."

"And did you approve of it?"

"I don't know as much as you, Will, about politics. But it seemed a Christian document to me."

Christian? Irrelevant, but now was not the time.

"A little more wine, Will, please."

She held the glass up, watched the firelight glossing the red of it. Cut into the apple pie, took a spoonful of custard.

"Will you stay an MP, in this so-called Council of State that some people say is more of a dictatorship than the King was?"

"I don't know, is the honest answer. It's what I want to talk through with you."

"But not now, Will, it's too late."

Not an outright rejection, then.

She stretched out her arm and took his hand.

"You are a good man, perhaps better than you used to be."

"And you are my wife again." He caressed her hand and her wrist under the lace edging. "I have been lost and miserable without you."

She sipped the wine, put the glass on the table and set aside the dish of apple pie.

"I am tired, Will."

He nodded.

She stood. "Sleep well," she said, and left the room.

Disappointment. He had hoped not to have another solitary night. Resentment flared for a moment. She needed more time.

★

1654

"Please go, Will."

As he sat beside her on the bed, Jane gripped his hands, her hand slicked with sweat, her arm trembling.

"There is nothing you can do."

Her face was drawn and blotched. He saw fear in her eyes as she waited for the next pain. He loved her so intensely at this moment, at the same time as he raged against a God who demanded this payment of agony as the price of a new life.

"I don't want you to see me like this."

Will's throat was choked; he could say nothing. The two midwives discreetly motioned him away. He leaned forward and kissed her on the brow.

"I love you," he said. He squeezed her hand and got up.

Her mother opened the bedroom door for him.

"Go to Westminster," she said. "We'll send a messenger when the child is born."

Will nodded.

He needed the exercise of walking. He needed his mind concentrated on something else. Yes, the Council meeting was an important one but his real motive in attending was to escape the pain in his wife's cries. He hurried through the crowded streets.

Before he entered Westminster Hall, he stood on the riverbank and watched the filthy Thames flow by. He closed his eyes. If only he believed in prayer. He would plead and beg on bended knee for Jane's safety. But he didn't believe. Instead he recalled a scene he would never forget: Jane cradling their first child, Robert, looking down as he sucked at her breast. On Jane's face a deeper happiness than he had ever seen, a sense of completeness and achievement. And he had a new level of respect for her. It was eleven years ago now and the scene had been repeated with Susannah two years later. Today the children were at their aunt Ann's house together with their grandfather.

He and Jane had been closer in the days after those births than they had ever been. All the differences between them about beliefs and politics had been subsumed in their new shared joy and responsibility: the miracle of the new life they had created. But then came the war, separation and, at last, reconciliation just four years ago. Since then, they had put their marriage together again. There was affection, respect, love of their children, an efficient household. It was not a bad marriage,

A sudden gust of cold wind from the river made Will shiver and open his eyes. He watched and heard the watermen: their harsh shouts and the thump of wood on wood as barrels were heaved and rolled. In the years since Susannah there had been two miscarriages and the despair that went with them.

Will had turned to the Bible, his wife's copy, for the first time since leaving home. Over and again he had read from Genesis: *And unto the woman God said, I will greatly multiply thy sorrow and thy conception; in sorrow thou shalt bring forth children, yet thy desire shall be to thy husband, and he shall rule over thee.*

And he railed against the God who had decreed this, and the deaths that accompanied it.

Jane had explained to him that this pain was a test. If she passed it, a new life would be born or she would enjoy salvation after death. Women were the suffering but anointed vessels of God's creative power. Will had not argued; there was no point. The whole of Jane's upbringing had led to this belief. They had not discussed it again, wanting to avoid discord.

Since the miscarriages they had seldom slept together. He had not trespassed on her body. Only once had they made love: he full of frustrated desire for her, his conscience weakened by wine; she compliant, desirous of some kind of intimacy. And God had taken his chance to set another test for Jane. That was cruel to her, and a wicked mockery of Will's self-imposed abstention.

When Jane had placed his hand on her belly and he had felt the child's quickening, he had felt the same wonder as before but now accompanied by guilt. They both knew what was ahead, and they both knew that Jane at forty-one years old was older than was safe.

Will heard the crash and rattle of an anchor chain from the Thames. What would be, would be. Jane had the best care he could buy. He turned away from the river, to the work of the Council and its meeting today about the remodelling of the Exchequer.

Through the afternoon and early evening Will and the committee were immersed in the design of ordinances to simplify the Protectorate's revenue system. The administration of the excise and assessment taxes and the confiscated estates of Royalists and Catholic recusants was to be centralised in a reconstituted Exchequer run by Treasury commissioners supported by a paid secretariat.

Pipe smoke was thick in the room when the door opened.

"Mr Will Nailor?"

Will looked up, alert.

"You are required at home."

He mumbled his apologies and left. Anxious now, a panic. Something was wrong, he was sure.

He ran home through the dusk, drizzle in the air, flung open his front door and rushed in. At the bottom of the stairs stood his mother-in-law, face haggard, red-eyed.

"What is it?!" yelled Will, pushing past her.

"Will, come in here."

She took his arm and led him gently into the living room. A midwife sitting by the fire got up.

"What's happened?" And he knew the worst. "Tell me, everything."

His mother-in-law nodded at the midwife.

"I'm truly sorry, Mr Nailor. We did the best we could."

"What? What?"

"Your son was born feet first and this meant he was strangled by his own navel string and was born... dead."

"But Jane, is she recovering?"

The midwife bent her head. Jane's mother spoke, her voice quavering.

"Jane died an hour ago, of bleeding and childbed fever."

"What?! Why did you not send for me earlier?"

She wiped the tears from her eyes. "She was in great pain, so low in spirit after the birth, and she wanted to make her peace with God."

"Did she not ask for me?" said Will, bewildered.

"She did not. It was difficult enough for her."

And Will sensed a certain pride in her daughter, a defiance of her son-in-law's non-belief. As if, at the end, right had been reasserted.

Will turned away, a shake of the head in anger and disbelief. Up the stairs and into the bedroom. The curtain was drawn, two candles burning by the bedside. A smell of herbs, the bedclothes neat and clean. Jane's head on the pillow, covers drawn up to her neck, arms by her sides, coins on her closed eyes. Her face placid. Will drew up a chair and took her cold dead hand in his. He stared at her face. The absolute absence of her, already. A helpless guilt. He wept. He kissed her forehead, as he had done only a few hours ago. His finger drew his tears across her brow. He watched them dry. A kind of baptism. He hoped she had found her peace with her God, her pitiless God.

He heard a door slam below, the deep voice of his father-in-law.

He had to face them.

Downstairs, her father's words were spat at him. "You couldn't leave her alone, could you? You're a murderer. And your children have no mother."

Will made no reply. It was what he thought himself. Jane's normally conciliatory mother ignored him.

Mother and father went upstairs. Will heard their quiet prayers. Then they left. Would they tell Robert and Susannah? Will shamefully hoped so; it was not a task he could face.

Will dismissed the servants for the night. He needed to be on his own. Jane's body was there, with the burning candles. But she was not.

So he sat in the living room, drinking wine, staring into the fire, watching the flames, hearing the logs and ashes settle. Jane's parents would want to take their grandchildren out of this godless house. They or Jane's sister, Ann, would bring them up. And what could he offer as an alternative, immersed as he was in the workings of the Protectorate and in his business? He was not skilled as a parent and the children needed a woman close at hand. And could he comfort them as they would need?

But he was afraid of losing them. Even if he visited regularly, they would grow up with values and experiences different from his. He refilled his glass. That would be difficult to witness. But the good of his children must come before his own satisfactions. And he was certain it would be what Jane would want.

Jane. He would sorely miss her: the home she had made, her small kindnesses to him. Her toleration of him, he supposed. Something more than affection had developed. It had been far from a marriage of just convenience. They had been happy for long periods of time. But he was not an expert in love. What did that word mean? It was sad but true that, in spite of all this, they had never been really at one. They early discovered that they could not talk about the subjects each felt passionate about: she about religion, he about politics. And this left a huge void between them. And in bed, too, there was a mismatch. But maybe there was between all men and women. Jane was dutifully compliant without ever being enthusiastic. Probably because he did not pleasure her enough. It was easier to blame himself. In spite of his success, he was a man of many failings and inadequacies.

He opened a new bottle.

And thought of Alice. Which he had not done for a long time. She'd been widowed seven years ago. Had she remarried? How life might have been different. And then he was ashamed again that, with his wife newly dead upstairs, he was remembering Alice. He emptied another glass.

When the servants came in the morning to clear and lay the fire, they found him asleep and snoring in the chair.

Five days later a small group of mourners exited the church of St Katharine Cree. Jane's parents had insisted on this church; Will had insisted the funeral be a small private affair. Only John Boon and Francis Ingilby accompanied Will. The bells that had rung in celebration of their wedding now tolled at her death. Now, with Robert and Susannah each side of him, Will walked behind her coffin as it was carried into the graveyard. Much against his in-laws' wishes he had given his children the choice of attending. They had wanted to, and not just to please their grandparents. Will was proud of them for not avoiding the misery and wretchedness.

They stood around the grave and the minister intoned, *"Man that is born of woman hath but a short time to live, and is full of misery. He cometh up and is cut down like a flower; he fleeth as it were a shadow, and never continueth in one stay."*

Robert and Susannah, holding each other, began to cry softly. Jane's mother stepped forward but Will put his arms around them and gathered them to him.

The coffin was lowered into the hole.

They threw handfuls of damp earth down onto it, small stones drumming on the wood.

"We commit her body to the ground, earth to earth, ashes to ashes, in sure and certain hope of the Resurrection."

His own sadness was subsumed in his love for his children. He felt the warmth of their bodies and let the words drift over him. The finality of Jane, the future of Robert and Susannah. The world was tipping.

"The grace of our Lord Jesus Christ, and the love of God, and the fellowship of the Holy Ghost, be with us all evermore."

"Amen" came the voices around him.

It was over.

John and Francis shook his hand and left. Will hugged his children. "I will see you tomorrow," he said. "I promise." And they left with Jane's family.

Alone now, Will turned and walked slowly away, stopped and turned. The gravediggers were already filling in the grave, big shovelfuls of earth thrown in, a joke made and a laugh. The bells were silent.

Back home to what? A house of silence, absence of movement, emptiness. Yet still so full of their lives. There would be no pattern or purpose there. He knew he must find it in his work at the Council of State. Amongst all the wrangling between the Parliamentary factions, he would try to stick to his principles and make this Protectorate work. Cromwell, he had to admit, was doing his best but the forces against him were growing. Self-interest and vested interests were ruling again. The King was gone but others with power used all means they could to retain it.

36.

QUAKERS

1657

Tiny, thin-boned, sharp-faced Mrs Leach tucked her change into her purse, leaned over the counter and whispered:

"Have you heard, Alice?"

"Heard what?"

Mrs Leach always preferred to create an air of conspiracy when she brought news.

"About the two Quaker women."

"Where?" asked Alice.

"In Boston."

"What happened?"

"The authorities somehow knew they were coming, from England," Mrs Leach continued, looking round to ensure no one had silently entered the store. "Before they even got off the boat they searched their luggage and all through their clothes, then riffled through all their books and tracts. They pronounced them heretical and blasphemous."

She mouthed the final words as if she were speaking to a deaf woman. Mrs Leach was not a churchgoer and relished this fellowship with another non-believer.

"What happened then?" asked Alice.

"They took all their books and pamphlets and the hangman burned them in the market square in front of the women. There was a crowd and they were spitting at the women."

"And they call themselves Christians – the godly elect."

Mrs Leach tut-tutted and left the store, her slight figure somehow augmented in authority, her low-heeled boots clipping purposefully across the wooden floor: a dissident woman still.

Such hatred of women, such arrogance of men. It was at times like this that Alice mourned most for the loss of her gentle, principled James. Not an ordinary man, his own man – and yet, in the end (she was convinced), killed trying to prove himself in manly ways.

It was two weeks later that her Indian store manager Nukpana brought more news.

After the book burning, the two Quaker women had been marched by soldiers for many days into the wild lands far from the white settlements. There they had been abandoned. Nukpana's own people had found them and cared for them in their tepees. But the women had insisted on being taken back to the nearest settlement, so the Indians had guided them. They would soon be in Hartford.

"They are like you and your friends, mistress," said Nukpana.

It was a compliment but rather out of date. Since the end of the trial, the antics of the "dissident women" had ceased. They had been significantly fined. All had admitted to each other their fears of public whippings and felt huge relief when the punishment was decided. Looking back, Alice had wondered at their recklessness, at the challenges they made and risks they took. They believed in what they did but Alice knew there must have been other issues: was it simply boredom or the freedom of prosperous widowhood, the lack of a man or the excitement of friendship, their age or the end of their courses? Whatever it was, they had, without any decision, settled for the quieter life, talking more guardedly among themselves but never publicly.

But Mrs Leach's report set Alice's fires burning again. She knew the reception the two women were likely to get in Hartford. The hounding and hanging of Ellen, though a decade ago, was still vivid in her mind. The same prejudices could easily be released again. She knew little about Quakers but their very name had produced a mixture of mockery and apprehension: trembling at the word of the Lord and shaking when moved by the Spirit. She knew they interrupted church services and showed no respect for ministers. She resolved to go to Hartford and help them if she could.

So the following Sunday Alice waited outside the Hartford meeting house. It was a sunny day but with a cold wind blowing. She had watched as people assembled and went in. Perhaps the two Quakers would be too fatigued after their experience in the forest, or ill. Or perhaps their faith had been tried too hard.

But then two women came round the corner of the courthouse and crossed the small square. They strode to the door of the meeting house, opened it and entered. Alice followed immediately.

The two women were already standing in front of the preacher in the pulpit: one was slight, short and red-haired, the other broad, taller and white-haired. Alice watched from the back. The preacher was shocked into silence by their sudden appearance, the congregation bewildered, all eyes on the two women.

It was the shorter woman who spoke, her voice ringing out in the silence: "Art thou a child of light? Hast thou walked in the light?"

She pointed up at the minister. "What thou speakest, is it inwardly from God?"

The minister's knuckles were white as he gripped the pulpit, his face red, his black brows scowling. "How dare you?" he thundered.

He stepped down and grabbed the short woman's arm.

"Hold thy hands off me!" she shouted.

The other woman wrestled the preacher's arms away. "Thou, man, blush and be ashamed of your actions."

The disrespectful, familiar *thous* offended his dignity. Alice had heard that Quakers used this form of address to show they counted preachers and ministers as not special.

"Get these silly, unruly women away," roared the minister. Four elders came towards them.

"Dost thou not see the eternal Son of God is in me, a woman?" challenged the white-haired woman.

"Dost thou, man, forbid me, a woman, to speak?" followed the red-haired one.

"Blasphemers!" roared the minister. "Take them to the gaol."

And now the red-haired woman began a piercing, buzzing chant, repeating the word *light* over and over again.

The elders now grabbed them and manhandled them towards the door.

"Baal's priest!" yelled the white-haired woman, her mouth flecked with spittle, as she passed within feet of Alice, before a hand stopped her mouth.

The congregation had been silent, heads turned and watching with open mouths the women's ejection. The minister was talking animatedly to some men at the front – Alice recognised Ludlow among them.

Then Alice left and followed as the women were taken to the same prison where Ellen had been kept. They were thrown in, the door slammed and bolted. The men looked fiercely at Alice. Maybe they recognised her from the trial. There was nothing she could do; she had to walk away. But she knew what James would want her to do. She was more nervous now, more aware but still determined.

The following morning Alice stood in the crowded meeting house.

At the front stood the two Quaker women, faces and clothes filthy but heads unbowed.

Governor Endicott stood up at the table at the front.

"You are Ann Austin?" he asked the red-haired one.

"I am."

"You are Mary Fisher?" he asked the other.

"I am."

But before he could speak further, the women protested that they had been stripped and searched that morning for signs of being witches.

"I have given birth to five children," said Mary, "and that search gave me more pain than any birth. It was savage."

"It was a man in woman's clothing who violated us," added Ann.

Alice remembered the pain and humiliation of Ellen that she had witnessed.

"No tokens were found on us," said Ann, "no moles or irregular marks but those of innocence."

Governor Endicott looked as if he would explode at the women's words.

"Be quiet, woman." His voice was all the more threatening because it was so quiet and cold. "You have brought here blasphemous scripts, and yesterday desecrated our service with profanities. Take heed: if you break our ecclesiastical laws you are sure to stretch by the halter."

It was his male authority as much as his religious belief that had been offended, thought Alice. Nothing changes.

"May we see these laws?" asked Mary.

"No, you may not."

Endicott thumped the table in front of him. His lips were thin, his eyes hard as stone as he glared at them. "You hold very dangerous, heretical and blasphemous opinions. You came here purposefully to propagate there heresies and errors."

He turned to the hangman and the gaoler. "Whip them," he said, "and then return them to prison until we can find a ship to take them back whence they came."

Most of the crowd bayed its approval.

The women were marched out to the market place, dragged to the pump, stripped to the waist and soused with water which was then jetted into their mouths and underneath their upturned skirts – to the guffaws of men. But Alice saw that some of the watching women were shocked.

Then the two Quakers were pinioned to the whipping post. The hangman was to lay on thirty lashes with willow rods, alternating his blows on the two backs. With each lash the crowd cheered. Blood flowed. The women flinched, but between each blow the women shouted: "Strike again; here is my back for you, strike on."

After twenty lashes the hangman paused. The crowd had gradually fallen silent as they watched the women's suffering and fortitude. In awe, thought Alice. Then two lashes later the two women began to sing, their voices quavering. Alice remembered it: the Magnificat, the song of praise by Mary, mother of Jesus. Each line fluttered out into the sunny silence and was followed by a blow of the willow.

My soul doth magnify the Lord
A blow.
And my spirit hath rejoiced in God my Saviour,
A blow.
For he hath regarded the lowliness of his handmaid.
A blow.
He hath scattered the proud in the conceit of their heart,
A blow.
He hath put down the mighty from their seats,
A blow.
And he has exalted the humble and meek.

And now, with each blow, the women in the crowd keened and groaned.

Endicott, sensing the change of mood, signalled to stop. The hangman threw the rods, now red with blood, onto the ground and untied the women. They slumped to the ground.

Endicott himself looked shaken and subdued. The crowd melted away, muttering.

Alice went to the pump, filled a pail with water and gently cleaned the women's bodies.

"To prison with them," said Endicott, recovering his severity now the crowd had gone.

The hangman and a soldier went to get the women up.

"Take thy hands off us," said Ann.

The men stood back. Was there sheepishness in their faces? Did they sense a special authority in the women?

It was Alice who helped the Quakers to their feet and to hobble to the prison. They staggered in and fell onto the filthy straw.

But the hangman would not allow Alice in.

"Governor's orders."

"I will come back!" Alice shouted, but got no reply.

When she returned early the following morning, the people she passed looked away from her. Alice felt there was a sense of shame now, as if, overnight, they had thought about the women's bravery and the cruelty unleashed upon them. Maybe they had even prayed.

So it was perhaps that the gaoler accepted the bribe she brought him, confident that the governor would turn a blind eye now the physical and public punishment had ended. The gaoler was disobeying the order that the women must not be allowed communication with anyone. The governor had also ordered that the women be given no food, just water, no reading or writing materials and that the gaol window be boarded up.

But Alice brought bread and mutton and clean shirts. She retched at the prison stench. The straw was a mire of pig shit and animal piss. The women cleared it away and Alice paid for fresh straw. The Quakers tended each other's wounded backs.

This was the first of regular visits Alice paid them over the following five weeks. Some of the townsfolk scowled at her, a few uttered comments, but mostly they ignored her. The authorities seemed content: their problem had been silenced and caged.

The women told her of the kindness of the pagan Indians: how they had provided them with dry clothes and food and helped them ford rivers on their way here. Slowly their backs healed and, in answer to Alice's questions, they explained their beliefs. They spoke of the Inward Light, a private inspiration that was in all people and which meant that each person could communicate with God without the need for ministers or preachers, sacraments, rituals or steeple houses or even the Bible. Women were equally worthy vessels and could be inspired to speak.

Alice laughed when they told her Quakers refused to take off their hats before magistrates. That would certainly have made Ludlow feel the world had been turned upside down. James would have approved.

No wonder, thought Alice, that the male Puritan leaders of Hartford felt that the Quaker women threatened the very foundations of their society. Her dissident women friends had, by comparison, only been playing games.

Alice could not fail to be moved by the Quakers' faith and honesty. They never tried to convert her and did not abuse her for her lack of belief. Perhaps it was because she was a woman or because she helped them. The Quakers, Alice decided, were just another sect, another group of Christians who believed they alone knew the real nature of God and what he wanted – like the Puritans, the Anabaptists, the Armenians, the Muggletonians, the Presbyterians and the Papists.

But what did move her most was their belief in the equal spiritual and social importance of women and how a new and fairer society could be created.

She remembered back about a decade ago to when the news came that the Parliamentarians had won the Civil War. She had been overjoyed.

Then the news had come that on 30th January 1649 King Charles had been beheaded outside Whitehall. Wilton and other Royalists had been appalled and also nervous that the new regime would somehow seek out Royalist sympathisers even here across the Atlantic. But most of the settlers were pleased, especially the Puritans. They had fled the King and his ways. For others it mattered little: there would always be somebody taxing them and laying down laws.

And then the news of her husband's death.

So much had happened since then.

Slowly, over the next weeks, as she remembered and listened to the women, she gathered her thoughts and came to a decision. James had died fighting for what was now called the Commonwealth in England. This Commonwealth was a revolutionary republic. James's death would be honoured and made more worthwhile if she somehow took part in the creation of this society.

The colony was changing: dissent was clamped down ever more firmly. Problems with the Indians had been increasing since the war with them: an Indian had been murdered and two white men hanged for it. It had been a brave and just decision but had inflamed many. The boundaries between Indian and white settler land became ever more blurred; settler livestock – cattle, pigs, horses, sheep and goats – were straying onto Indian land and eating their corn. Because settlers now no longer needed the help of Indians, they were more disrespectful of them. Indians were becoming poorer, and their land was needed by the increasingly overcrowded white settlements. A ship sailed out of Plymouth with 178 Indian slaves, following a law that declared that "no male Indian captive above the age of fourteen should reside in the colony".

There were reports of Indians gathering in large numbers, tribes making alliances, bent on revenge and the reclamation of their land.

The opportunity to help create the new Commonwealth and make it work, to have a positive new start, seemed an attractive alternative to living in this fractious and apprehensive land which had lost all its original pioneering Pilgrim values.

For the first time in many years Alice wondered what had happened to her brother Henry. And Will, of course. He too could be dead. She wondered what side he had fought for in the war. She could not believe he would have stayed out of it.

And then there was her son Peter and his soon-to-be-wife Martha. They would live on this farm, and though Alice liked Martha very much she knew from experience of the difficulties of two women living in the same house. It would be easier for the new couple if she left. So she made her decision. She went to lawyers and signed the legal documents that made her sons Peter and Giles official tenants of the farm until she returned. Without telling them she also made provision that they would become joint owners if she did not return from England. She retained sufficient money for herself.

After five weeks in prison, the Quaker women were put on a ship for England, the captain well paid by the colony to ensure they did not leave the ship until they reached the shores of England. Alice booked her passage on the same ship. Alice had been honest with them: she was not a Quaker, not even a believer. They were now firm friends, and the Quakers had friends in London whom Alice could stay with as long as she wanted.

There were tearful farewells with her sons. They wished her well but she could see they were eager to take full responsibility for the farm and store. And she loved them for it, for their confidence. They were grafters; they would be successful.

As the ship sailed out of the bay on a breezy, cloudy day, Alice remembered her first sight of these shores, and the man Wilton. What was then empty and dreary and wild was now a thriving settlement, a real society, but one so very different from that agreed in the Mayflower Compact. Why was it so difficult to live in harmony? It was certainly nothing to do with Eve and an apple.

She shivered and pulled her shawl around her.

She remembered watching James as he had sailed away from Boston, also with a mission. She remembered, too, the label on the goods she had taken back to the store: Will Nailor. What had the forty-odd years since she had seen him done with his life? Would she see him again? Did she want to?

PART FOUR

37.

RETURN

1658

December. A cold breeze chilling Alice's face; gloved hands, still cold, gripping the rail; a shiver running through her. The *Sapphire* pushing up the sludge-brown Thames, rubbish floating by. A stink off the river. Sails being furled, the yells of men, capstans clanking. Small boats everywhere, barges, cutters, weaving in between the big trade ships at anchor, cargoes being loaded and unloaded. The shore a clutter of buildings, and behind them a mass of dwellings under a shroud of smoke.

She remembered looking out at the shore of New England nearly forty years ago: bleak and empty, a silent challenge, but a beauty to its bareness. Today's grey, reluctant dawn crept over a cacophony and a frenzy, lay sullen over a brawl of orders and curses. So much anger and short temper in the air. She stamped her feet on the deck.

So this was the new Commonwealth. For seven weeks of storm and seasickness she had kept her spirits up, talking with Ann and Mary, but now – at the end of her journey, freed from the swell of the ocean – she sagged. She had made a huge mistake. Amsterdam and its energy she had loved but she had been young then. At sixty-two years old a big alien city was a different matter, she now realised.

The first blow had come at Plymouth, ten days ago, when news had come aboard of Cromwell's death. Already exhausted by the voyage, Alice had despaired. She had travelled here to help build Cromwell's Commonwealth, for which her

415

dear husband James had died. She had come too late. That bold, bright decision to leave her home and farm seemed now the stuff of stupid dreams. Cromwell's son Richard, they were told, was now Lord Protector. That seemed a betrayal, no different from a royal dynasty. A failure, a retreat. It was different for Mary and Ann, who were still below deck: they had their Quaker work to do.

A great splash as the anchor hit the water, the whirr of uncoiling ropes like demented snakes, orders bawled and sailors running from prow to stern.

"You women first off," snapped the mate.

They'd been just about tolerated during the voyage, mocked, sometimes insulted. The Republic hadn't changed the captain's attitudes, let alone his men's.

The three women were rowed ashore with their scanty luggage. It took the Quaker women some fierce wrangling before they managed to hire a small cart with a bony nag and a gap-toothed boy in ragged clothes. Welcome!

The narrow streets were already crowded. It seemed to Alice that everybody yelled and scowled; the streets stank of filth and rubbish. Thin-faced, barefoot children ran alongside, begging and then cursing. Alice hunched her shoulders, tried not to flinch. This was a wild and frightening place, dog eat dog, the Devil take the hindmost – and there seemed to be a multitude of the hindmost. She knew no one except for Ann and Mary. She felt alone and vulnerable, needing the blessing of a familiar face. Will! But perhaps his face would no longer be familiar, if he was still alive. And even if he was, he would have his life – married, children. She could not disturb that. And he would not allow her to.

In amongst the shops and rickety houses there were grand stone-built mansions. And amongst the rabble occasionally rode a well-dressed horseman with whip in hand, clearing the way. A new society? A revolution? She saw no sign.

The cart bumped and rattled over the cobbles, the young boy cursing. Alice closed her eyes and hung onto the cart side. She had a sudden overwhelming nostalgia for her farm, for being back with her sons, fighting no more battles, giving in, settling down quietly, looking forward to grandchildren.

But she was far, far away in this bedlam. How fanciful that she could make a difference, how ridiculous to have thought she could be a benefactor in the land of her birth.

"Here!" shouted Mary.

The boy savagely pulled on the reins; the horse's head jerked backwards.

They had halted outside a cabinet-maker's shop, a wooden building in a terrace. Alice looked up: three storeys high, each floor jutting out above the other so they seemed to be toppling over, casting everything into shadow.

Men and women hurried by, their backs loaded or with small handcarts, their faces grim.

Ann took her hand. "We have good friends here," she said.

Alice knew that somehow she had to draw strength from these indomitable women. She did not share their faith but maybe she could do some good. And so much good needed to be done.

★

Two days later Francis Igilby and Will Nailor stood at the windows of St Stephen's Chapel and watched the funeral cortege of Oliver Cromwell pass beneath them on the way to Westminster Abbey. Each had a goblet of red Spanish wine.

"Like the funeral of a king," said Ingilby. "Look!"

Will looked down. At the head of the procession the knight marshal rode, holding his black truncheon tipped at both ends with gold. Then came thirteen more mounted knights,

417

luxuriously robed, followed by the dignitaries of Westminster in mourning gowns and hoods, marching two by two.

"Gentlemen, ambassadors, knights, judges, aldermen, all in their mourning garb," intoned Ingilby sarcastically. "Inside, they will be celebrating his death. Don't you love the hypocrisy? For them, his death has been a long time coming."

Will looked at him. "You sound pleased."

"Indifferent, to be honest."

Will frowned. "It was a bold experiment, a noble attempt. But frittered away."

"Bold? Noble? Mad, maybe. When a visionary comes along, keep your head down and wait for him to pass." He nodded down at the procession.

Will took a sip of wine. "He was right, Old Ironsides. I still believe in the republic, Francis – no king, no divine right."

"No king? Look at the chariot."

Will looked at the chariot which was now passing, Cromwell's hearse on it, on a bed of black velvet, six banners bound in mourning veils on each side carried by generals. Behind came eight more army officers carrying pieces of Cromwell's personal armour.

"His body's lain in state in the Abbey for the past fortnight," continued Ingilby; "the man who hated idolatry became an idol for the people to gape at. His effigy with crown and sceptre, royal robes. His son anointed king after him."

"You know what's really sad about that? People still need a leader, pomp and ceremony. They don't believe in themselves."

"The people," scoffed Ingilby. "I presume you mean ordinary folk: labourers, craftsmen, tenant farmers, servants… women. They never got a look-in in your bold and noble experiment."

Will shook his head. "You're wrong. For a time they did – in the Army, in the House of Commons. Taking control and responsibility, winning battles. Debating ideas."

"Debating! I'll give you that. Hot air unlimited."

"I was there, Francis, at Putney, at the Army gatherings. Shoemakers, candlemakers, ploughmen. They had ideas, spoke them, put them into writing. Ideas that are surely right – about fairness and equality and rights."

"Endless arguments, you mean. Bickerings between Army and Parliament. And in the end these candlemakers were outmanoeuvred – in Parliament by the Puritans or the Presbyterians, by Cromwell himself. By the landowners, the merchants, the lawyers. Old men like us, Will."

Will leaned against the window frame. "And don't you find that sad and disappointing?"

"It's irrelevant what I feel. All I definitely know is that people will always require lawyers, whatever regime is in place. I'm still a Member of Parliament, Will, like you. But your votes-for-all republicans threw me out because they feared I wouldn't vote for them. Colonel Pride's Purge – remember? Ten years ago, and I haven't been allowed in the House of Commons since. That was your democracy. It seems like a lifetime ago: Parliament wanted to continue to negotiate with the King but the Army disagreed – your men of noble ideas – so they shut us out. The Army's ruled the roost ever since. Is that what you wanted? Rule by the unelected? That's like rule by the King – that king." And he pointed downwards through the window.

Will could not summon the energy to argue. What was the point? There was truth in what Francis said but it was too simple a judgement. Turning a whole country around, defying a thousand years of brainwashing by Church and state – perhaps too much for anyone.

"It was within our grasp," he said. "We got nearer to it than anyone else before. We could have done it."

"But now we have a new lineage. His son to replace him. But not for long, I feel."

"You dismiss it all, don't you?" said Will. "You think it ridiculous that we dared to dream dreams."

"Ah, Will, always the dreamer. But you are also a man of the world. How could you forget the shoddy ambitions of men, their shifting loyalties? Ideas are inspiring, as ideas. But it takes men to put them into practice – and men are mostly petty, vain and venal. Like me."

"Not all. Not John Pym or John Lilburne or Thomas Rainborowe. They were great men and suffered for their beliefs."

And Will remembered Lilburne's funeral just fifteen months ago. After his treason trial he had been banished and lived for two years in Amsterdam and Bruges. When he insisted on returning to England he was tried again. Although he was found not guilty of any crime worthy of the death penalty, Cromwell kept him in prison, afraid that Lilburne would whip up more opposition to what was already an unpopular government. He became a Quaker and was out on parole for his wife's lying-in when he died of consumption on the day before he was due back in prison. He was only forty-three years old.

His body was taken to the Mouth Inn in Aldersgate, a place where Lilburne had been part of many Leveller discussions and now a meeting place for Quakers. Will had watched as a mourner tried to throw a purple hearse-cloth over the coffin, but the Quakers insisted it was unadorned: "less pomp and more piety". Will was one of a thousand, he reckoned, who followed the coffin, carried on the shoulders of his friends, to its burial in the churchyard at Bethlem by Bishopsgate.

Free-born John Lilburne had been the strongest and most principled of them all. His treatment had been another betrayal by Cromwell.

"And what of Cromwell himself, Old Ironsides?" Francis's words brought Will back to the present. "You were a great supporter, then came to despise him, then worked for him in the Council of State for seven years. Was he a great man, too?"

Will took a deep breath. "In spite of everything, yes, I believe so. A great General who won the war, a bold man who did the unthinkable in executing a king. In the end, his job was impossible: to reconcile Army and Parliament with their different demands. I don't think anyone could have done it."

"But he abandoned his principles."

"I agree, some of them. He was afraid of anarchy and the breakdown of law and order. Too many had been killed in the war; the country needed peace above all."

Ingilby shrugged his shoulders. "He was a fenland farmer with an overweening ambition to be king. That surely is the irony and the verdict."

"Of the ignorant," Will snapped back. "He was invited by Parliament to be Lord Protector and only reluctantly accepted it. I would swear to that, for all his faults. And then he grew impatient, as I did, at the continual wrangling in Parliament and Army that prevented all reforms from happening, reforms his soldiers had died for. He had to take control himself, to push things through, get things done, to move the country nearer to what had been discussed at the Putney Debates."

"Have you read the epitaph on his tomb in Westminster?" asked Ingilby.

"Yes."

"Suitably ambivalent, don't you think? I'd like to know who authorised it. *Here lies Oliver Cromwell who, that he might be Protector himself, first brought the English monarchy to its knees.*"

"A travesty. That is so untrue and prejudiced."

"But he certainly stopped the people having fun: a fatal mistake in trying to win their hearts and minds. He appointed those major generals to run the country and they clamped down on anything that gave the people some amusement."

"Yes, that was the Puritan in him. I never agreed with it. You and I both like our fun. But he believed it was a godly approach."

Ingilby snorted. "Never trust a man who thinks he hears the word of God in his ears."

"You're right."

"And the result of it all?" continued Ingilby. "It's not just many MPs but the people too who talk of wanting a king back. And they don't mean Richard Cromwell. They hate military rule. Those major generals became tyrants and made themselves rich in the process despite their so-called Puritanism. And should we be surprised? Those who seek power, exploit power. Human nature will not change."

"A king will be worse."

"Without a doubt. And especially for men like you."

"Like me?"

"Regicides, Will, those who signed the old king's death warrant."

Will felt a jolt of fear. The great revolution had failed. He was angry and despairing. But that there might be imminent personal vengeance was a new thought, and a vengeance supported by the very population he had tried to help. That would be the supreme irony of fate.

He watched the chariot-hearse turn the corner of the Abbey and move out of sight. They had turned the world upside down, but if it now righted itself there would be another set of victims.

★

Less than half a mile away, Alice was also watching the funeral procession. In the two days she had been in London she had learned a lot about Oliver Cromwell, in particular about his persecution of the Quakers. Alice had been shocked. It was the threat they posed to the social order rather than their religious views that had provoked Cromwell's opposition.

What also surprised her was that most of the population did not mourn his death, although some did, she was told, and deeply. Looking round at the crowd, she saw no tears. She even felt there was a suppressed sense of celebration, that after the procession passed the alehouses would be loud with jokes and laughter. The austerity he imposed, the suppression of festivals and dancing and even of Christmas, was far more important than the primacy of Parliament he brought. Parliament was still an abstract, far away from the real lives of people, even in London. In fact, there was open talk of the desirability of a new king.

Richard Cromwell was unknown but already deemed inadequate. The Republic was in its death throes. All respect had been lost as Parliaments had been repeatedly dismissed by Cromwell, just as Charles had done. Rule had been by diktat and the Army.

That was the version Alice heard.

The whole purpose of her coming back to England had been destroyed within forty-eight hours.

Exhausted, hopeless, she watched the pomp and ceremony. There was a strange, sullen emptiness about it all. Horses passed, covered in black velvet and with plumes of black feathers, but the streets had been sanded and their hooves were muffled. The chariot on which Cromwell's body lay was also covered in black velvet. Its wheels passed without any clatter. The silence of the spectators was not one of respect or mourning but more of a sense of another impending change which would be imposed and of which they would be the victims.

Alice remembered the Mayflower Compact, signed by all men on board the *Mayflower* before they landed in New England. That compact, of community and mutual support in a new land, had lasted less than three years. Men worked better, it seemed, when they worked for themselves. It was the same here in England.

Was it human nature or was it the human nature of men? She thought of the Quaker women and Ellen, of Mary Cheever back on the boat in which they sailed to Holland all those years ago. Could, would women do things differently if they had the power?

By definition, the good were meek. But, as far as she could see, they did not inherit the earth. And if there was no heavenly reward, why be meek?

But that way lay despair.

Mammon and God. Was there no decent compromise?

Now, outside the west gate of the Abbey church, the procession halted. The coffin was lifted off by ten richly-robed men and carried into the church.

Whatever had awaited Cromwell, he had now met it: heaven, hell or oblivion.

The big question was, for her: what next?

Did she stay here in hope or did she return to New England in defeat?

It was obviously too early to make a decision. But she had already decided to travel up to Lancashire, to her old home in Worsley. Maybe her brother was there. Maybe he would be able to tell her about how her father had lived out his life. And she would try to find out something about James before he had left England.

And there was Will.

Was he still alive? Married and with children? Was he watching, she suddenly realised, this same procession? Had he been a Royalist or a Parliamentarian? Was he mourning Cromwell or wanting a king back?

Did he ever think of her?

Did he still have the bent sixpence?

And she fingered hers, that hung again like a pendant from her neck. She remembered how reluctantly she had accepted it from Will. How much that must have hurt him. Then, the dilemma had been to separate or not. Now it was to meet again or not.

38.

LANCASHIRE

1659

Nothing! Nothing left! Alice kicked at the dead frosted grass with her boot. Just a few pieces of rotting planks with rusted nails.

It didn't exist anymore, the hut on the bend of the river with the ash tree on the opposite bank.

Disconsolate now. She had walked out of the village along the frozen, rutted path by the river. Not a pilgrimage; that was a silly idea. Just eager to revisit her youthful self. And it was gone.

Yet perhaps it was fitting: if she had been able to step inside, it would have been a mockery. Or an accusation.

Even so, standing here with her warm breath smoking in the cold air, she could remember clearly: his red ribbons offered as a hand-fast, the beginnings of bright tears in his pleading eyes, his usually laughing mouth crooked and stiff with her rejection.

Her gloved fingers went instinctively to her throat where hung the bent sixpence, the other token of his love, his loyalty, his expectation. How could she have been so hard when so young? She hated that the last she had done to him was hurt him.

She shivered as she stood and watched the river flow. Along its edge, little isolated pools of water were iced over.

She had been right – but being right at that age, when she too was in love, was surely wrong. How could she have been so sensible? She had certainly loved him: his earnestness but with more than a touch of wildness, his integrity but with a dash of recklessness. She would have had a different life with him – more adventurous, more fraught?

She had loved James with a love deeper than anyone could have at the age of eighteen. They'd had a good marriage and a good life. James had encouraged her to grow in her own way, and at some cost. He had not been afraid that she was different and strong. She imagined Will would have been less predictable, more volatile. She wondered which parts of him life had enabled to grow and which had been suppressed.

Pointless nostalgia. Too late, irrelevant now.

She looked across at the ash tree, black against the cloudless blue sky. She had been right to walk here, after all. This day was perfect for these thoughts: the world poised in a frozen stillness; the tree wrapped in its bark like a tough shawl, stoic, waiting out the winter but full of potential life.

Safe in her warm clothes and good boots, this was – after all – a moment of calm beauty.

She began to stroll back.

After Cromwell's funeral she had deliberately not made any enquiries about Will Nailor. Instead, she had taken a coach on the fatiguing, uncomfortable journey to Lancashire. If she was to return to New England for good in the spring, all the promise of the Commonwealth now tarnished, she had wanted to take a last look at where her life had begun. Tie up some loose ends, try to leave with a sense of completeness.

She had three other places to visit today and the first was the furthest away but only a few miles: the village of Walkden, where James had lived.

The pony and cart dropped her in the centre of the village. In the village shop she asked for the whereabouts of the Fenton home. The shop girl took Alice into the back kitchen where the mother sat by the fire.

"The Fentons?" said the old lady. "A sad story."

No Fentons survived. The elder brother had been killed in a hunting accident by the King's men; the younger – James, he was called – had emigrated to America. There were suspicions he had fled to escape conviction for the murder of a nearby pastor. The parents had died soon after.

"Had nothing to live for."

Alice thanked her and asked for directions to the Fenton house. She wanted to see where James had lived.

The old lady told her. It was only a small village.

"Oh, and there was another sadness," she added as Alice was at the door. "That young James was betrothed and, many years after he left, she left, too, escaping a bad husband. She told me she would try to find him. In all of America. Impossible."

"Can you remember her name?" asked Alice. "The betrothed girl." She knew the answer but somehow wanted this old woman to say it.

"Ellen, I think," said the old lady after a long pause.

"Thank you," said Alice.

Outside, Alice drew a deep breath and walked slowly towards the Fenton house. What a life poor Ellen had endured, and with no happy ending. Her mind was back in New England.

Ellen had arrived at a difficult time in their own relationship, after the death of Nicholas. She had been cold to him, kept a loveless bed. Had he and Ellen made love, she wondered, snatching moments?

It had all happened nearly twenty years ago. If they had made love, she felt no betrayal or bitterness. James had been a good husband, a good father and a good man. Life was confusing and difficult.

How much Ellen must have retained her love for him, to cross an ocean in the faint hope they might meet again. Was that an unacknowledged part of why she herself had returned to England? To see Will? And did she love Will with the same intensity Ellen had loved James?

The Fenton house was empty and already crumbling, the door wrenched off its hinges. It added nothing to her knowledge of James; there was no sense of him. How could there be? It had been a fool's errand.

She turned to the inn and called for the carter. The day was still bright and there was time for her next visit, back in her home village of Worsley.

Outside the house she had grown up in, Alice stood and stared up at her bedroom window. There were different curtains. A brief unwanted image of what had happened to her in there. Far in the past, it had no effect now. The garden was laid out differently. She did not linger; she had no wish to speak to the current owners. Rather surprisingly, she felt little emotion for a place that had been her home for seventeen years. It seemed to belong several lifetimes away. Her mother's continual sadness was her dominant memory: sitting by the fire, her sewing box beside her, sometimes plying her needle skilfully but more often staring into the flames. She knew now it was the stillbirths and the miscarriages, and feared she had not been sympathetic enough.

She wondered how her father had fared with his new wife. Both would be dead now. And her brother? He had gone to sea in Amsterdam, fleeing their father's regime and expectations. How little she had known him. Had he prospered or had he died?

Now she turned along the lane to Will's house. Outside the gate she paused and looked up the garden path, the one she'd run down after walking out of Will's father's sermon. She smiled to herself: what a big thing it had been. She and Will laughing together, much more than a shared mischief. Will's loathing of his father and hypocrisy. She took a deep breath. The house was well-kept and she wondered who lived there now. Will had been an only child.

"Can I help you?"

Alice was startled.

"I'm sorry. I was just remembering. I used to live in the village. Used to know someone who lived in this house, but all a long time ago."

The woman's eyes twinkled. "Ah, a young love?"

Alice smiled but said nothing.

"It's a beautiful day but it's icy cold. Why don't you come in?"

Why not? thought Alice. She was curious, and there would be something painfully poignant about it. She realised she wanted to feel that.

As the maid prepared some bread and cheese and ale, introductions were made.

"Alice Ainsworth? And your family left here in 1613. I was only a little girl then but we still have links with your family."

The woman was Mrs Joan Whetstone. "I'm the younger sister of John Boon. I'm a Boon girl."

Immediately Alice remembered Will's story of his argument with his father about the starving boy, Andrew Boon, in the impoverished family.

"I can see you remember us."

Alice hoped her face had given nothing away that might offend.

"You wonder how we have come to live here in this grand house. And so you might."

Alice loved her honesty, felt at ease again.

"Yes, we were poor, my drunken father, my poor mother. But somehow I made a good marriage. My husband is the village smith. And my brother John has been a big help. We now run a store where your father once had his warehouse."

The place where she and Will managed to kiss a few times. How could she remember those kisses so well after nearly fifty years? Memory was strange.

"John lives with us at the moment. He should be back soon."

"I had a brother, Henry. Did he ever come back?" asked Alice.

"Henry? Indeed he did. He was your brother? What a story he had to tell!"

What had happened to her little brother?

"He was saved from slavery with the Barbary pirates by Will Nailor, who lived here."

What?! How could that be? Alice felt her face flush, her heart quicken.

What on earth was Will doing among the Barbary pirates? Or Henry?

"Will helped to set him up with a store at your father's old warehouse."

"But you said you now run that."

"Yes." Mrs Whetstone paused and cleared her throat. "Your brother had a terrible accident. He was gored by a bull in a field by the river."

To have survived the Barbary pirates and then to be killed in this parochial way. Her poor brother.

"And did he bring news of our father?"

"No, I'm afraid not. He knew nothing about him."

So she, Alice, was the only survivor, last of the line. What lives they had lived since leaving little Worsley.

She heard the outer door bang and Mrs Whetstone got up. Alice heard some whispering in the hallway and then a man entered, tall, bearded, sunburned.

"John Boon," he said.

Alice immediately recognised a family likeness: something in the set of his jaw and the blue of his eyes. She stood. "Alice Ainsworth, as was."

He smiled.

"I'm sorry, I don't remember you; I was only a boy when your family left, about ten, I think."

"We went to Holland but I've lived in New England for nearly forty years."

431

There was something in the way he looked at her, almost appraised her, which implied he knew far more than that about her.

He settled down at the table, buttering chunks of bread. "You knew Will, I'm told." Again that knowing glance, but friendly.

"Yes. We grew up together." Then added, "I was fond of him."

Joan looked across at Alice, a half-smile that asked if this was the young love.

"The best of men," said John. "He rescued me from my drunken father and poverty and took me down to London to work with him. He gave me a life."

He concentrated on his scones.

Alice wanted to know so much more about Will but had to contain her curiosity.

"Did he do well, then?"

"Exceedingly well. He became a very successful merchant."

"How on earth did he become involved with the Barbary pirates and save my brother – as your sister has told me?"

John did not answer directly. He seemed to be weighing up how much he should say.

Then he sat back in his chair, as if he had made the decision.

"Quite a history," he said. "Did you know Will liked to gamble?"

Alice thought. "I remember he used to play cards with the village lads – but that was largely to defy his father."

John nodded.

"Will made his money then gambled a lot of it away, unlucky business ventures, bets on cockfighting. He fled the country to avoid his debtors and possible prison. He sailed with the British navy to rescue Christians from the pirates. Then he decided to stay over there and set up as a merchant in Aleppo."

Aleppo, where's that?

"He made a second fortune and returned to England, paid off his debts and set up as a merchant again. I was his manager. He married and has two children."

Well, of course he did. Handsome, successful. He would have been a catch.

"And then he became an MP. Sadly his wife died giving birth to their third child."

So Will, like herself, had a death to grieve for. How long ago, and had he remarried?

But Alice chose the easier route: an MP? Will, an MP? That seemed preposterous. And the big question.

"May I ask if he supported the Parliamentarians or the Royalists?"

She held her breath and waited. This now seemed a vital question, as if the answer were a fulcrum and life could pivot on it. Had he fought against her husband James? John Boon paused again. Was she probing too much?

"He was a Cromwell man, a strong Parliamentarian, at least until Cromwell changed. Will Nailor is a member of the Council of State. Still is, but that counts for little now."

So his prosperity had not affected his sense of justice and his feelings for the poor. At least that's what she could hope. Doubtless it was more complicated.

"My husband came over from New England to fight for Parliament. He was killed in battle."

"I'm sorry to hear that. Is that why you're here?"

"Partly." She needed to know more. "So, did you stop working with him to come back here?"

She heard the bluntness of her question.

"Another story. I was a villain then but might soon be seen as a hero if a king returns."

Alice frowned. "Can you explain?"

He looked at her quizzically.

"I'm sorry, I'd rather not. Suffice to say that I was no longer safe in London. Will Nailor hid me, gave me money and sent me up here. He saved my life – for the second time."

He took a bite of cheese. "I've been here three months or so, but in two days I am returning to London," said John. "With all this talk of the return to a monarchy, Will could be in great danger. I must be there to help him if he needs me. He can still be a rash man, though he has sensible friends."

He stood up. "Are you staying in the village for long?"

"No, I was planning to return tomorrow."

"Why not return with me?"

Why not?

"Lodge with us for a couple of nights. We'll get your things from the inn."

It was so quickly decided.

After dinner that night Alice explained she had returned to England to work for the Commonwealth but had discovered that the Commonwealth was not what people wanted anymore. What had happened? Her husband had died in vain, fighting for the Parliamentarians. In response, John and Joan spoke of how promises had been broken: tithes were still collected; no more people were entitled to vote than when Charles was King; the same landowners still owned the land.

The country had then been put under military rule, with twelve Major-Generals splitting the country between them. The local one had been Major General Charles Worsley. He was a firm Puritan pushing for godly reformation. In doing this he had closed hundreds of alehouses to reduce drunkenness and blasphemy, banned horse races and cockfighting. John had supported most of it but it was men like the Major-General who had made the people want a return to a king. With no simple pleasures, they had only the drudgery of their lives.

It was a sad story, they all agreed. And now there was much uncertainty in the land.

Afterwards, Alice went to her bedroom.

She could not sleep. So much to take in. Crossing the Atlantic had been a mistake; she had arrived too late.

And Will a widower. What exactly did that mean to her?

But one thing was certain: John Boon must not tell Will that she was back in England. That was something she must do herself, unless she left for America without meeting him. She had left him once. Was it wiser to let sleeping dogs lie?

39.

LONDON AGAIN

1659

Will was more than glad to see John back again. He relied upon him to run his business and needed to discuss with him a possible expansion of trade into Virginia and new banking arrangements.

Four days later, John Boon knocked on the door of Will's office and opened it.

"Someone wants to see you urgently."

A quizzical look from Will, sitting at his desk. "What about?"

"Wouldn't say. Just that it was important." Will knew John sometimes enjoyed putting Will into unexpected situations; it was part of their friendship.

"Well, why not? Intriguing. Give me a couple of minutes."

John closed the door again. Will's right forefinger slid slowly down a column of figures in a large ledger. His lips moved as he calculated. He wrote a figure with a flourish and put his pen down.

He leaned back in his chair and looked out of his office window. It was a beautiful cold winter day, the sky a flawless blue, a half-moon still clearly visible west of the bright sun. Sunlight gleamed across the polished floor, a rich glow.

He could hear the rattle of shipping tackle and the yells of the wharf men.

He looked down at the ledger. He had meetings planned today with Ingilby, as lawyer not friend, and the banker Pinckney. Since Cromwell's death there was so much uncertainty and unrest. Even calls in Parliament – the Commonwealth Parliament, for God's sake! – for the return of the monarchy. Will had a clear image of his signature on Charles' death warrant. He would be a marked man.

There was a knock on the door and it opened.

A man stopped on the threshold, burly, a hefty belly, dark-haired, rough clothes, workmen's boots. He glanced briefly, aggressively, round the room and strode towards Will's desk.

Will stood up, nodded to John Boon in the doorway, who then turned and closed the door.

"You want to see me on a matter of some importance? Will Nailor."

He stretched out his arm for a handshake. The man looked at Will's hand and ignored it. His arms stayed at his sides, huge hands, a belligerent set to his round face, chin thrust out, small black eyes under a furrowed brow.

Will gestured for the man to sit.

No movement, that solid defiant look.

Will sat down.

"Well, could I have your name?"

The man was still staring intently at him, as if seeking something familiar in him. Then he looked slowly round the riches of the room, this tough man in his rough working clothes. The man's gaze returned to Will.

"Edmund Brentwood," he snapped out, shifting his weight from one foot to another.

Will nodded. "Do I know you?"

The man grunted, a crooked smile.

"You should."

Will frowned.

"You knew my mother very well." A slight scowl, almost a sneer, the voice challenging. "Thirty-eight years ago."

"Thirty-eight? That's very precise."

But suddenly Will understood: Edmund Brentwood.

His face must have betrayed his shock. The man nodded. "Your long-lost son." He took a half-stride forward and held out his hand over the desk towards Will.

Will did not shift, stayed in his chair.

"What do you want?" asked Will, his eyes measuring the man coldly, examining his face and body. He recognised nothing of himself in Edmund – or of his mother Lizzie for that matter.

Edmund stepped back, for the first time disconcerted by this rich man's icy look. It must be utterly alien to him, this luxury, thought Will. He would never have been in such a place before. It had taken guts to come here.

Then Edmund drew himself together again. "I'm thirty-eight. My mother died at the same age I am now, of some disgusting sickness that pitted her body with ulcers. She was in great pain."

Will stared at the man and did not change his expression. He held himself tight, refused to imagine the scene, would not be manipulated.

"There were five people at her funeral," continued Edmund, "only five to show respect to her. She never married, you know. Dedicated herself to me. She refused to give me your name, even on her deathbed. She was faithful to you."

His voice began to crack, his broad stolid face to break up, his jaw working hard to keep control.

"What do you want? Money?" Will's voice was as cold as the ice outside on the cobbles. He was shocked at how he had so immediately shut himself off, but felt no guilt.

Edmund shook his head, his shoulders slumped, his big hands in front of him twisting nervously as if he were washing them. Power become plaintive.

Then, again, Edmund gathered himself together.

"Money?" He looked around the room, gestured at the expensive furnishings and exotic objects. "It's all people like you think of. No, I don't want money. You insult me. You have given money, to my mother, to me for my apprenticeship." A pause. "And I thank you for that." Forcing the words out.

Will saw how much it had cost Edmund to say that. He was a straight man. Will had to admit he admired him for this struggle he was putting himself through. But for what? It still wasn't clear.

"I've found out a lot about you. You are an MP. My father an MP!" Edmund shook his head. "It took me two years," he continued, "to save money for my mother's headstone."

Still, Will said nothing, would acknowledge nothing, would not confirm Edmund's decency.

"I have two sons of my own," said Edmund, his voice strengthening again. "I could not walk away and abandon them."

Edmund did not have the words. Will realised that what Edmund wanted was recognition, to know that his existence mattered to his father.

Will glanced up at the window. The pale half-moon had faded and disappeared.

The truth was: Edmund did not matter to him, not a jot. Once the money had been arranged, and the banker's payments, life had rushed on.

Will stood up.

"I think you're a good man, Edmund," said Will. "I'm told you have worked hard, taken the opportunity at the bell foundry, become a master bell-moulder."

Should he add more? Give him something of what he had come for?

"I loved your mother, Lizzie, at the time. But I will say no more about it. I had my reasons. I paid my debts."

Will came round the desk and stood next to Edmund. Will was three inches taller but much the slighter man.

"But this is the end of it," said Will. "I do not want you here again. Our lives will continue totally separately. Do you understand?"

Edmund looked up at him. His eyes were hard as currants. He was plaintive no more. His truculence was back, together with a pride that he had come here and said what he wanted to say. And Will seemed to shrink, to diminish next to this ordinary working man who had dared to confront his father in surroundings that must have intimidated him. He had been wrong. The man deserved more of an explanation.

And then Edmund said, slowly, "And I have found out more: I know that you signed the King's death warrant."

Was that a threat of some sort, a promise of revenge? And suddenly Will was taller again, restored.

Will walked to the door and opened it. Edmund turned and followed him. At the threshold he paused and looked Will in the face, a slight puckering at the corners of his mouth, a smile beginning.

"The church of St Katharine Cree," said Edmund. "The bells that rang at your marriage there and tolled at your wife's death – I helped to cast them."

It was some kind of victory for him. Will knew that, as he left, Edmund felt himself the better man, a foundry worker compared with a wealthy merchant and member of the government. A better man than his father.

Will shut the door. So be it, he was happy with that.

But as he sat again at his desk, he thought back to Lizzie telling him she was with child and that he was the father: his fear and coldness, her anger and distress. He had little money then but his decision to pay her had been a simple one. Ingilby had been astonished at his decision: abandoned bastard children were all around, a fact of life. Will had told him the story of the starving Andrew Boon, and his father's words: that he would never forget. *"The Lord will visit the iniquities of the father on the children, to the third and fourth generation."* He could not be part of that.

He had paid his dues; he had made the right decision. But he could not deny that he had exploited Lizzie. He had not raped her but he had taken advantage of her. It was too late to make any more recompense. He had to live with that.

His father's words – *"to the third and fourth generation."* Edmund's sons were his grandsons. *"His iniquities."* Will groaned, closed his eyes and put his head in his hands. He had been too harsh; he had not given Edmund the recognition he craved. Why not? The meeting had come out of the blue; he had not been prepared. Edmund had dredged up a period of his life he had tried to forget.

Will knew he had not responded well.

Then it came to him: he would offer Edmund's sons places at his school. Yes, that would be a good thing to do. And would he want to meet his grandsons? Would Edmund want him to? Would Edmund accept the places? Would his pride allow him to accept this charity from his father?

That would be Edmund's problem. He, Will, would at least have made the offer.

40.

MEETING

1660

An early April day: sparrows chirping under the eaves, gulls raucous over the river, fitful sunshine at the windows, mullion shadows across the floor. Will was at his desk. A fire roared in the grate. A knock on the door.

"Come in."

It was John Boon. "A Mrs Parker to see you."

"Ah, you said, earlier."

Will was signing documents, head bent.

She entered, closed the door behind her. Stood just inside the room.

Will straightened the documents and stood up, behind his desk.

"Come in, please, have a seat."

He came round his desk and altered the position of the chair.

Alice by the door still. Almost a gasp, her hand at her throat.

So like his father: the way he stood, his straight back. His bulk. Greying hair, a silvered beard. Youth changed to mature man. Her stomach churned.

She wanted to flee. Such a mistake. This was not her Will. She couldn't move but her mind raced. What had she wanted to feel? Expected to feel? A return of old feelings? A dispassionate renewal of friendship? Nostalgia? Nothing? Certainly not this.

No recognition, no idea of who she was.

"What can I do for you?" asked Will.

How stupid of her to expect anything else: a strange woman suddenly appearing at his door. And he was frowning: he had other major worries, as she had learned from John Boon. His mind was certainly nowhere near forty-five years ago. Why should it be?

"Please," he said again. "Take a seat."

The fire. She already felt too hot.

He was expensively dressed but wore his clothes with ease, none of the puffed-up vanity of his father in his rich black clerical garb.

And there was no condescension in his voice. His accent had changed. A busy man with big problems, he had made time for her. John Boon had sworn he had told Will nothing about her. He had kept his word.

The first shock over, she regained her composure.

She walked forward and took the offered seat. Will returned to his side of the desk.

His blue eyes were paler now, wrinkled at the corners, the beginnings of bags beneath. His hands were on the arms of his chair: the same long slender fingers, but the backs of his hands now veined and spotted. He twisted a pen.

He was his own man, had a presence: mature, successful, the sum of his experience. Filled out, weightier. That ramrod Nailor back but without the arrogance, the conceit. Was the young man she had known still in there, behind the success, beneath the accumulated layers of his life?

"How can I help?"

And now she almost laughed at the absurdity of the situation. Her deceit. The unfairness of it. If she revealed herself, would he see it that way, too? The old Will would.

Then a stab of panic. Had she changed so much? Her face weathered now, not the pale complexion of her eighteen-year-

443

old self. Not quite so slender but she had not let her body go to seed.

And then a jab of anger. Why did he not see her? Could he be so blind or had he forgotten her entirely?

She was in control of herself again.

She had an answer prepared for his question.

"I am looking for a passage back to New England and I know you send ships there to trade."

She smiled at him.

And he saw the slight slant of it, saw the green eyes. And it began to dawn on him. Heart thumping, he began to search this woman's face, the shape of it, the cheekbones, those lips. But above all, the smile. And he saw the eighteen-year-old still there. Her boldness in coming, the straightforwardness of her request.

And she sensed his recognition, breathed deeply. More relaxed but excited now: a link between them.

"It's warm in here," she said. "Can I take off my bonnet?"

She did so without waiting for an answer.

He saw her dark hair, piled high and pinned. Streaked now with grey, stray curls – as ever – around her ears. Such a tenderness towards her.

And then a surge of warmth – as if he were on the tip of a wave rolling in from all those intervening years, returning.

He stood up.

"Alice," he said.

She smiled again, nodded, looked up towards him, her bonnet on her lap.

"Alice Ainsworth as was."

"The same, but different."

She felt a great burst of affection towards him.

He wanted to hold her shoulders gently, look into her face, rediscover.

She wanted to touch that small familiar scar above his right eye, a childhood injury.

She sitting, he standing. Awkward, shy. Knowing but not venturing.

"Some wine?" he asked.

"A little, please."

At a side table he poured two glasses.

"By the fire?" he asked.

"Not too close. I'm already warm."

He laughed and repositioned the chairs.

Each had registered the modified accent of the other – that seemed to signal the difference and distance between them now, and also between their younger and older selves.

They clinked glasses self-consciously, no toast.

Silence, staring at the flames.

Beating hearts, a tension, an unsureness about what the other felt.

A sense of possibilities: a wide view but not ready to step forward, off the edge. Impossible to know the consequences. Even if they knew themselves what they felt.

But those sudden surges of feeling, that recognition and affection. They were surely genuine, valid.

But where did they fit into all the complications – not just of their own lives now but of England itself, in turmoil and on the edge of more tragedy?

So they chose safe ground and talked of their families. This was a consolidation of their separate experiences, a pulling back from the brink, from connection.

Alice told him of going back to Worsley, of meeting John Boon there, of what he had told her of Will and of swearing him to secrecy.

Will laughed. "A man of his word, the best of men."

She spoke of her mother's death, the *Mayflower*, of her marriage and the death of her son Nicholas. Of her husband James coming to England to fight for the Commonwealth and being killed in battle.

"We met," said Will. "Before the Battle of Preston. He spoke of his wife, a woman called Alice who had sailed on the *Mayflower*. He spoke so lovingly of you. And the more he spoke the more I was convinced it was you. You were a rebel, he told me proudly. But I said nothing."

It discomforted her a little, that chance meeting. Being spoken of, both men with memories.

"We fought in the same regiment, under the great Thomas Rainborowe," continued Will.

"He was a distant relative of James, I think."

"Your husband was a brave man; he fought fiercely."

And Alice was glad of that, that James had found the sort of man in himself that he feared did not exist and that he so badly wanted to exist. Perhaps he had even felt at peace, at the end.

Alice spoke of her friends, the dissident women, of why she had come back to England, of her disillusion, the disillusion of the country. Of her wish to return to the New England farm.

Will filled in some of the gaps in what John had told her: of his wife Jane's death in childbirth, of his two children – Robert now seventeen and Susannah now fourteen – who lived with Jane's parents. He did not mention Edmund.

He spoke of his disillusion too, how Parliament and Army had not solved their differences, of his work in the Council of State trying to improve life for those at the bottom of the social ladder, of the change of national mood, of the danger he was sure he would be in if a new king was crowned, because he was a regicide. Of his plans to flee London and go into hiding.

They talked for hours and Will had food brought up.

Daylight faded and a rain came on, beating on the windows.

They were exhausted, emptied.

Will hired a small coach to take her back to the Quaker house where she was staying. He saw her to the door.

No arrangement was made to meet again. Neither dared to suggest it. There was too much to absorb. Neither slept much that night.

★

Next morning, Alice was due to meet a group of Quaker women who had been collecting names for a petition about tithes which was to be presented to Parliament. She had become particularly friendly with Sarah Marsden, a lively young woman from Manchester.

"We have collected 7,000 names from all areas of the country."

An outburst of applause and cheering. The document, fresh from the press, was held up.

Silence, and then parts were read out: "*We object to the forced payment of tithes, a papist tradition, for the steeple houses… How do you who are the heads of the nation expect we should pay your taxes when you suffer the priests to take away our goods, who do no work for us? … Stop the money-grubbing ministers extracting ten or twenty shillings for a sermon over the dead, for sprinkling babies… Stop the superstitious churching of women.*"

More cheers.

"We will take it to Parliament tomorrow. As many of us as possible must take it."

The group split up, Sarah and Alice agreeing to meet. Alice went off to her second commitment: working, as she had done regularly since returning from Lancashire, in the foundling hospital recently set up by the Quakers. The misery there kept her mind and body fully occupied. Only as she walked home did her thoughts return to Will. What next? She had resolved already to return to New England once summer weather came. There was nothing for her here; the Commonwealth was a broken dream. But what of Will? Did she want to be

447

with him, and what was she willing to give up for being with him?

Over the next few days Will and Alice walked in Hyde Park, opened to 'gentlefolk' by King James fifty years before. Will told her he had watched the trained bands exercise here at the start of the war. By one of the ponds, in the sunshine, Will shyly asked: "Do you still have the bent sixpence?"

For answer, she opened the top button of her blouse and pulled the sixpence out.

"It's travelled six thousand miles," she said.

And Will took out his sixpence. "To the Levant and back," he said, "in battles there and here. I wore it for luck. It worked!"

They pressed the sixpences together. And, at last, kissed. Tender, tentative, growing in confidence.

"The first time in forty-five years," he said softly.

They walked and talked on. Will's stories of his frustration in the Council of State during the Commonwealth, and his doubts about Oliver Cromwell, were matched by Alice's of her struggles against the ruling men of New England. The Pequot War and the Civil War. Building a farm and building a business.

Each felt a growing sense that the person they had loved at eighteen years old was still there now, had persisted through their very different experiences. It was a recognition they welcomed, something that bonded them together, the still centre at the heart of the storm of disillusion and uncertainty, disappointment and fear that swirled around them.

41.

AMBUSH

1660

A moonless night two weeks later, a brutal east wind whipping up the Thames and lashing into corners and alleys. Capes wrapped tight, bent into the wind, Will and John Boon hurried back from the warehouse towards Will's house. John carried a lantern, the candlelight meagre through the horn panes, bobbing.

In the narrow alleys the slam of a door, a raucous laugh, a dog bark, the trundle of wheels somewhere, their boots on the cobbles. Gleams of light from an unshuttered high window or beneath a door, a cat shape sneaking round a corner, a rat scurrying. Stench from the gutter.

But Will noticed none of this. His head was full of his meetings with Alice: the shock of recognition, the instant warmth of feelings, memories, the talking. But uncertainty – the meaning of it? Her smile but a certain reticence, even wariness. Their exchange of family information, pieces of each other's life stories. That long and lovely kiss! Could something reignite so quickly after such a long absence? Were his feelings real? How did she feel? He felt the sixpence on his skin, the sixpence he now wore again around his neck.

His life had been in turmoil even before Alice, and now the threat to him was mounting. Two days ago Charles, the putative king, had published the *Declaration of Breda*: that all would be pardoned, except the regicides who signed his father's death warrant. The king's health was being drunk in the streets and parlours. General Monck had returned from

449

Scotland at the head of an army and dissolved Parliament. MPs who had before the war wanted to settle with Charles were now reinstated; all Parliamentary proceedings since Pride's Purge had been erased. Will knew he was a marked man. Escape plans made with Francis Ingilby and John Boon had to swing into operation. And what now with Alice?!

"Shit!" cursed Will as his boot slipped in some soft noxious deposit.

He stumbled and regained his balance to see two shapes step out from the shadows at a corner. The sour smell of ale, the gleam of a dagger blade.

Will and John drew their swords.

"Will Nailor?" That voice.

"Who asks?" growled Will.

"The regicide?" came the same voice.

The bulk of the man, the sneering tone. Edmund!

"The very same!" came another voice, from behind. Will turned. Two more men, the sound of swords being drawn from scabbards.

"We arrest you in the name of Parliament!" Edmund's voice, intense, threatening.

"Parliament!" laughed Will bitterly. "This is not Parliament's doing. This is you, Edmund."

That name in his mouth. For the first time. And his mind clicked: no pistols. He wants me alive.

"Aye, Father, it is."

Will and John stood back to back in the narrow alley. Suddenly the first sword thrusts. Grunts. Lunges. A dagger thrust parried. Dodges and lurches. Clash of blades. The hilt of John's sword smashed into a face. A yell of pain. John's dagger slashed a neck, a gout of blood. One body on a doorstep.

A dagger stabbed at Will's arm. He leant away but was caught by it, a stinging flesh wound. But the man's thrust overbalanced him and Will's sword slammed into his stomach.

A scream of pain and Will kicked him away as he fell. The man crawled away and collapsed.

Two against two.

A dagger was rammed into John's breast. He staggered back.

"He has me, Will, I'm a dead man."

But his opponent was too drunk or confident, relaxed for a moment and John's dagger slashed his throat in return.

Will felt John's body slide down his back to the ground.

Now Will was enraged, beyond all reason. He fought as he fought at Preston. Edmund had never fought in battle for his life. Will was a better swordsman than his son; his passion for revenge was greater. Will was unbeatable. His dagger slashed Edmund's sword arm; his sword flipped away Edmund's dagger. Edmund turned but Will had him, flung him to the ground. Will grabbed Edmund's hair and ground his head into the cobbles. Ferocious. Will knelt next to him, his dagger at Edmund's throat. Pressure on the point, an indentation in the neck, a spot of blood.

To avenge the senseless death of good John Boon, to make sense of the lives lost in the now pointless civil war, to punish for the end of the dream of Commonwealth, to be a final desperate act before he fled for his own life.

The compulsion to push that dagger in, to kill this jumped-up man, his son.

Edmund's breath was foul with beer, an animal howling, black eyes pleading.

Himself gasping for breath, the pain in his slashed arm, teeth bared in anger. To finish it all before he fled to escape a torture that terrified him.

John Boon dead. And Alice, what of Alice?

Will laid his head on Edmund's chest, the point of his dagger still at Edmund's throat, a bubble of blood. He felt Edmund's heart pounding, and his own. Both of them thumping together, father and son.

And then he heard, clear as a bell, Alice speak: "What is the point of killing him? You are a better man than that. He has two sons himself. Do not, I beg you, continue the violence."

Will raised his head and stared at Edmund, now keening softly.

"You have murdered my great friend," spat Will.

"Not me."

"You would have me in the Tower and then be hanged, drawn and quartered."

Edmund tried to shake his head.

"And no doubt you would watch," continued Will.

His heartbeat was slowing now.

"But I cannot kill you. Not because you're my son, but because you have two sons of your own."

Will stood up and sheathed his dagger.

"Speak kindly of me to them."

Will turned, lugged John Boon's body to the side of the alley, laid it to rest on a doorstep and kissed his cheek. A life, a lifetime friend – murdered. In this sordid place. And for my sake.

"Farewell, John."

Clutching his wounded arm, Will walked quickly away. Not home now, but to Francis Ingilby's. He had to flee immediately.

And somehow he must get word to Alice.

It was suddenly obvious: if there was a future, he wanted her with him. If she would have him.

42.

DEPARTURES

1660

No, not to Ingilby's. Edmund might not have been acting on his own initiative. He might be part of a Royalist programme. There could be other Royalist agents looking for him, knowing his friendship with Ingilby.

To Alice, then, at the Quaker house.

He hurried through the alleys and streets, heart beating fast. He was a hunted man. At the end of the Quaker house street he backed into the shadows and watched. No one about. No alternative. He walked quickly up to the door and knocked. No response. He knocked again, louder, the noise seeming to echo down the empty street. It was about eleven o'clock, the last daylight long gone.

A bolt slid back, it opened a little; a slice of light and a woman's face.

"I need to speak to Alice Parker, urgently," he said.

"Who should I say it is?"

Who could he trust? Who might he endanger?

"Tell her it's Mr Worsley."

The door closed. He stood on the step, feeling exposed. A man came out of a house opposite, slammed the door and walked off in a hurry. A watcher? To inform someone?

Please.

The door opened.

"Come in, Will." It was Alice.

She closed the door behind him. They were in a dark narrow hallway, a pale lantern hanging, sounds of conversation from a nearby room.

"What's the matter?"

He told her of the ambush.

"They killed John Boon," he said, his voice breaking with emotion.

"John is dead?!"

Will still did not mention his son Edmund. Will pointed to the wound on his arm, the sleeve soaked in blood.

"Oh, Will." And she put her arm round him for a moment, then separated. "You cannot stay here. Too dangerous. Too many people here." She thought for a moment. "Wait."

And she went down the hallway and turned into a room. He was now dependent on her, in the very act of endangering her.

Alice came back, with another woman, younger.

"This is Sarah Marsden, a friend of mine."

Sarah smiled.

"She will take you to her house where she lives with her father, who is confined to his bed. It will be safe for you there."

Will thanked them both.

"Go now, quickly. The sooner you're off the street the better. I will come and see you tomorrow as early as I can."

It was only a short walk to Sarah's tenement house in Purple Lane. Not far from Gray's Inn, thought Will. In the kitchen, Sarah cleaned and bathed his wound. The fire had burned low.

"You must sleep in here. It is the only place."

She found him blankets, gave him a platter of bread and cheese.

"My father upstairs may disturb you. He has wild dreams. But take no notice. I sleep next to him."

And with that she went upstairs.

Will's arm was throbbing, his mind racing. Things had happened so fast. Somehow he had to talk with Ingilby. They had plans to put into operation. And business matters to sort, too. Eventually, as the last of the wood ashes settled in the grate and he thought sadly of John Boon, Will dozed off.

Next morning Sarah left early. Will expected Alice but she did not appear.

That morning, confined to the tiny hot kitchen and with nothing to do but stir the mutton stew that Sarah had made, Will cursed himself for being too complacent, for ignoring the warnings of Ingilby's legal mind. He had allowed this to happen to him. He had been preoccupied with Alice, had thoughts only for her. But it was not safe for Alice to be seen with him.

Ingilby had spoken with him about the *Declaration of Breda*, the Dutch headquarters of Charles Stuart. Charles' clever words of reassurance that might not mean all they appeared to say. Brandishing his copy of it, Ingilby had scoffed:

"And do I believe this? That *those who accumulated estates during the Civil War will keep possession of them*."

"How fortunate for you, Francis. That new estate you purchased in Lincolnshire at a knock-down price from a Royalist sympathiser who fled the country."

"Yes, Will. And he died abroad, I hear. So doubly fortunate."

"You played a canny game. Neither one side nor the other."

"I admit it, I am not a man of principle, like you, Will. And my conscience is easier for it. But there are dangerous words here for you, Will. Read this."

He handed Will the document.

Will read: "*We do grant a free and general pardon to all our subjects, of what degree or quality soever who, within forty days after the publishing hereof shall return to the loyalty and obedience of good subjects.* Can I stomach doing that?"

"If you wish to continue to prosper, and if you admit your dream is over. But it is not as simple as that. Read on."

And Ingilby pointed him to the next paragraph. "*Except only such persons as shall hereafter be excepted by Parliament.* What does that mean?"

"That means, dear Will, that a future Parliament might vote to punish the people who actually killed his father – the regicides, like you. And the new king would accept their advice."

"Lawyers!" spat Will.

"Lawyers indeed! But lawyers can help too, if they are on your side."

Impatient for Alice, unable to leave the house, Will recalled the amazing speed of it all.

A new Parliament had assembled. Called the Convention Parliament, summoned not by Charles, who was not yet king, but by "the will of the people". And this was a Parliament with a majority of Royalist sympathisers who had been booted out at Pride's Purge.

"It was all so predictable," said Francis. "I was there. I was one of those kicked out by Pride. I watched it all. First they agreed grants of money to the soon-to-be king: £50,000 to expedite his journey back to England. Then on May 1st they declared that *according to the ancient and fundamental laws of this kingdom, the government is and ought to be by King, Lords and Commons.*"

"May Day," said Will. "I remember it. Maypoles set up everywhere after being banned for so long. Bonfires, ringing of church bells. People on their knees in the street, drinking the king's health. It turned my stomach."

Only two days ago, Will had watched with disbelief the large bronze statue of Charles re-erected in the Guildhall. It had happened so fast: General Monck marching from Scotland with his Parliamentary Army, arriving in London in February then ordering the Rump Parliament to dissolve itself. Walking from home to warehouse, Will had seen rumps of beef roasted on every street corner; a great rump was turned on a spit on Ludgate Hill. Lads running about and laughing, shouting "Kiss my Parliament" instead of "Kiss my arse."

And the lesson of all this? wondered Will: the people are easily led, easily conned and fickle. The people he'd fought for, the people for whom thousands of men had died. And after all of that, still poor and hungry and exploited, they wanted a king.

He knew that the New Model Army's General John Lambert – hero of Parliamentary victories over the Royalists at Preston, Dunbar and Worcester – had been captured and was in the Tower. Colonel Thomas Harrison – with whom Will had fought at Preston and who he'd heard denounce Charles at Putney as "that man of blood" had also been arrested and sent to the Tower. The noose was tightening. The good, the brave and principled were now traitors.

In the late afternoon, Alice finally arrived and stayed only for an hour. She had spent the morning with Ingilby and she had proposals for Will to agree. Business that needed to be sorted immediately. Events were happening so quickly, laws and regulations made.

She and Ingilby had arranged John Boon's funeral – which Will must not attend, and nor would she. Will had bought from Alice what had been her father's land in Worsley and given it to the Boon family. Ingilby was at this very moment preparing documents that gave half of Will's personal estate to his children, and transferred the other half to Alice herself. At this, she paused, her look seeking confirmation. Will smiled and nodded. This was the confirmation he sought from her. Ingilby, she continued, was certain that Will's estate, if not disbursed, would be confiscated as soon as the new king was on the throne.

Alice would bring the papers for his signature tomorrow, early.

The plans that Will and Ingilby had already made for Will's escape, should that become necessary, were being finalised. All was well.

Then with a brief kiss she was gone and only her faint scent was left. Slowly his thoughts settled.

During their long conversations and walks their sense of companionship had grown, as well as the rekindling of their feelings. Alice's disillusion, Will's peril and the gathering momentum of events had made it clear that they would be together. Nothing had been said, no explicit commitment made, but now Alice was to be with him. The crisis had required decisions and they had worked and planned as a fresh partnership.

But she must not be imperilled and, once out of London, what then? Will knew the plan but now the practical details had to be sorted. And not by him. Alice and Ingilby were a formidable team. He trusted them. Anyway, he had no choice.

Sarah returned. Her father wasn't eating. Will had given him drinks of weak ale during the day, as instructed. He slept restlessly, groaned a lot.

"I think he will die tonight," said Sarah. "I hope so. It will be a mercy for him."

While Will ate some stew, Sarah went to sit with her father. She was a strong, stoical woman, Will already knew. She would mourn not the man in bed but the father she had known. Like Alice had told him about her own mother's death.

Sprawled in front of the fire, faintly hearing Sarah's soft, comforting voice upstairs and her father's weak moans, Will thought about the talks he and Alice had had after that first meeting. They had been a mix of the personal and political: how his and Jane's children were thriving at their grandparents, how he missed them. Will's meeting with Alice's husband James before the battle of Preston, their talk in the inn, how Will had half-guessed that the wife Alice James spoke of was his own Alice Ainsworth. But he had said nothing.

It was all he had left, thought Will. His only comfort. And the sixpence that was again hanging at his neck. At last he slept.

458

But he was woken in the early hours by a wail from upstairs, and then crying. Sarah's father's death. He would not disturb her. She would come and tell him in her own time.

Just before dawn, she came downstairs.

"It is for the best," she said, in response to his sympathy.

And then, like Alice, she was practical. Her father's body would be taken away this morning; Will must hide in the small storeroom. She would be here to make sure all was well.

And so it happened: Will crouched behind the door, among sacks and bags and tools, a mix of smells and damp; the clump of feet up and down the stairs, the drag of the body, words of respect, Sarah's thanks, the outside door closing, silence, the door opened by Sarah, dry-eyed and quiet.

"I must go to the Quakers' house," she said.

That afternoon, Alice arrived with a bag of documents. Will read through them quickly. It was all as expected. He signed them.

"Another part of my life over," he said, returning them to Alice. "You are amazing." And he held her hands.

Her smile, soft green eyes, the greying hair. "There is a future," she said.

"I hope so."

And then she was gone again.

It was on the fourth day in this prison sanctuary that Alice next arrived. This time she was in a fluster.

She took a piece of paper from her pocket. Will recognised Ingilby's writing.

"Francis gave me this. This morning the Commons passed this resolution."

She read: "*That all those Persons who sat in Judgement upon the late King's Majesty, when the Sentence was pronounced for his Condemnation, be forthwith secured.*"

"You must leave tonight," she said. "They will come searching for you."

"What about you?"

"I will come later, with Sarah. She wishes to come with us. Francis and I have last details to sort with your sea captain, Christopher Ward."

Will had selected him as the most trustworthy and loyal, with experience of sailing to New England.

"I'm glad Sarah's coming," said Will. The same disillusion, looking for a fresh start.

"Before dark, Francis will bring your horse to the place we spoke of. There will be time for you to leave the City through Aldgate before they close it."

He'd had no better horse than Flint all those years ago but his steel-grey Chert would carry him to safety. It would take him five days of steady riding to reach Ingilby's moated manor house at Somerby in Lincolnshire. There were coaching inns all the way up the Great North Road and it was a better gamble to stay in them, always busy with travellers arriving and leaving, than be a conspicuous stranger in small villages. Dangers both ways.

"We will join you as soon as we can," said Alice.

A kiss and an embrace and she was gone.

What a woman she had become! And no surprise. It had been unfamiliar for him, hidden away in this tenement, to have all these arrangements made for him. And stranger still that he, who had a lifetime of making his own decisions, had agreed so easily. It was to do with trust, with necessity. And, perhaps, a new-found peace with Alice at the centre of this swirling world.

That evening he thanked Ingilby.

"But you saved me, Will. Remember the molly houses?"

"Ah yes, the Puritan morality enforcers."

"Indeed. I escaped a fate worse than death, thanks to your warning. How they would have mutilated me. I was never so appreciative of your being on the Council of State and privy to such plans."

Will laughed. "I've never seen you move so fast, Francis. When I told you of the imminent raid on Miss Muff's you shot out of your office faster than an arrow from a longbow."

"I had to clear my chest there of all my... er... adornments and fripperies, and tell a few others. So here I am, still safe and well and whole, thanks to you."

"And, unlike me, safe under the new king. I'm told he will look more kindly than the Puritans on lewd practices."

Raised eyebrows. "Lewd, Will? So judgemental, not like you – a man on the run."

As dusk fell, Will walked Chert, loaded with saddlebags, through Aldgate. He paused and looked up at the spire of St Katharine Cree: marriage there, his children baptised and wife buried. Was the rest all delusion? All they had fought for, a sad, wild dream? This time, yes. But ideas had been set running that could not be suppressed. Others would follow and succeed.

He began to trot north. It was too dangerous even to say goodbye to his children; in any case, his father-in-law had for some time been very reluctant for Will to visit.

★

Christopher Ward's cargo and sailing plans, however, were not yet complete and could not be hurried. So, three days later, on 29th May, Alice and Francis were still in London. They stood together on the Strand to watch a very different procession from that six months earlier in December, the muted spectators of Cromwell's funeral.

The streets now were packed with jubilant crowds. Charles had arrived. Preceding the procession were troupes of morris dancers with tabors and pipes.

"A blessed return to the old customs," scoffed Ingilby.

Charles himself rode in a dark suit, raising his hat with its crimson plume many times. The streets were covered in

461

flowers, rich houses hung with ornate tapestries; bells and trumpets joined the cheers.

"Without a drop of blood, the kingship is restored," said Alice.

"And by the very army that chopped off his father's head."

The King passed under the gateway of the Banqueting House.

"Did you notice that?" asked Francis. "He glanced up to the site of his father's execution. It is not easy to forgive a father's murder."

Will, they knew, was safe in Lincolnshire with Ingilby's trusted household. But for how long?

"It's the new King's birthday today," said Alice. "He is thirty. He's not a handsome man – with that large nose and heavy jaw. I think he could be cruel as well as sad."

"His large nose will not put off the women," said Francis.

The fluttering pennants, squads of soldiers with shining armour, swords and shields, the clatter of hooves, horses' plumes, finery and rich robes.

"How they do love a pageant!" said Francis.

"And how I have had enough!" said Alice.

They turned away.

★

At dusk on an early June evening, Alice and Sarah arrived at Somerby.

The door was barely closed before Alice grabbed Will's arms.

"I am frightened, Will. We must away. We can wait no longer. Two of the judges who sat at Charles' trial have been arrested and sent to the Tower."

"There is no alternative to Captain Ward. We have to rely on him."

"But they are watching the ports now; Francis told me. Two other regicides, Carew and Corbett, have escaped by boat already."

Will held her close.

"They are closing in," she whispered, "just when we have found each other."

She had brought a scribbled note from Francis:

Parliament has issued a proclamation. Forty-four regicides are named, including you. These "who sat, gave judgement and assisted in that horrid and detestable Murder of His Majesty's Royal Father of blessed memory" are summoned "to appear and render themselves within fourteen days, under pain of being exempted from Pardon." Just like your Cromwell's Parliament sought seven deaths from among the upper levels of the King's supporters, now seven of the regicides must be held to account and the rest treated with comparative mercy.
But do not trust them.

Two days later Francis arrived at Somerby. He brought additional news that the public hangman had burned the books of John Milton at the Old Bailey, all Milton's savings had been sequestered and he had been imprisoned in the Tower.

"Though he is blind," said Francis.

★

It was there, in Francis Ingilby's moated manor house, that Will and Alice finally slept together.

"I am not the young girl you knew, Will," Alice had said. "My body is not the same."

"Nor mine," said Will. "And, if I remember right, we did not know each other's bodies. I was honourable." He laughed.

"And I virginal. Sensible above all."

And somehow, when they were naked between the sheets, there were no flaws. Their lives' experiences miraculously disappeared and it was just the two of them, now. A tenderness

463

as well as passion as they learned and ventured in their new, fresh pleasure.

"I have come home," said Will.

And Alice held him tight.

43.

PURSUIT

1660

W ill, standing back from the diamond-paned window, stared out at the rain and wind lashing the orchard. Last night, through the trees, he'd seen the glow of the bonfire in the village. The people celebrating God's preservation of the English throne. Bitter and angry, he'd watched sparks blown high in the air.

For eight days he'd hidden in this isolated Lincolnshire moated manor house at Somerby-by-Bigby, walking in the enclosed courtyard, occasionally enjoying the sun and fresh air in the walled garden, but usually confined to this small room. At first he'd been amused by the fact that his sanctuary room had once been a Catholic chapel, a card table now standing where the altar had been. In this room Mass had been said by priests constantly on the run from Protestant priest-hunters. The priests had been brave if foolish men, risking capture, the rack and then being hanged, drawn and quartered. Many had died in that gruesome way. Now he was hiding from Royalist regicide hunters, in terror of the same consequences. The irony had long worn off.

He'd waited, tediously playing patience and solitaire, reading, thinking of his children whom he would never see again, of John Boon's pointless death. His life was tumbling down and only Alice offered hope.

Francis had cannily purchased this manor when it had been sequestered from its Catholic Royalist owner. Still an MP in the Convention Parliament set up for the new King, Will's long-time friend had offered him this hiding place. Now he, Alice and Sarah Marsden were impatiently waiting for Captain Christopher Ward to communicate the final arrangements for taking them aboard for their escape to New England. The longer this took, the greater the risk of being discovered.

The new King had proved himself slippery, subtle and ruthless. No surprise there: weren't all men of power like that? Cromwell had been the same.

The King had taken Parliament's advice: the hunt for the remaining regicides was on. Revenge was in the air.

So here stood Will, as he did most daylight hours, staring at the door that led to the privy, the garderobe and its filthy escape route to the old priest hole. Constricted, fearful, helpless, he was going slowly mad, seething with impatience. The last message was that there would be a rendezvous with Captain Ward on the Humber Estuary coast very soon, but no date. Safety – or a chance of it – was imminent. That made the waiting even harder.

News came, too, of the arrests and committal to the Tower of the lawyers at the King's trial – Cook and Dendy, Broughton and Phelps. Thomas Harrison in the Tower was now bound in leg irons and chains, forbidden from receiving visitors or legal advice, with guards in his cell at all times to prevent suicide or escape.

And there was always the risk that one of Ingilby's servants might betray him for the bounty on offer. If capture and the rack were certain, would he have the courage – or was it cowardice? – to kill himself?

What he needed more than anything was space, to get out of this small cluttered claustrophobic room. To ride Chert down lanes, the wind and air rushing past his face; to be in the open, not having to hide; to be relaxed, not constantly wary.

There were shouts below, panic in the voices. Footsteps thundered up the stairs, the door thrust open.

Alice, eyes flashing, red-faced. "They're half a mile away, galloping hard. You must hide."

Will had to keep calm. They had rehearsed the routine. Down below he could hear the household rushing round, bolts slammed on doors that might delay for a minute. He opened the door into the privy room. Francis Ingilby rushed in.

"Never fear," he said. "The priests down there were never found."

"Your servants?" asked Will.

"Loyal to a man and woman."

Francis knelt down on the wooden floor. His fingers searched for the hidden mechanism that released the catch. A faint click and the covered wooden privy could be slid forward.

They peered down the shaft that led to the sewer. The wooden ladder nailed to the side disappeared into the darkness; a stench rose up the shaft.

"Down you go, fast but careful."

Will looked at him. "A candle?"

"No, impossible. We cannot take the chance the light will be seen. Now go. And don't fall. Not the place to lie in."

Will saw Francis was trying to make light of it, to be reassuring.

"No priests were ever found here," repeated Francis, putting a hand on Will's shoulder.

They heard hammering on the manor house door, oaths being yelled.

"The pursuivants. Now descend, and God go with you."

Will flashed a look. "I like your humour, Francis."

Will knelt at the side of the shaft, stretched his feet down into the darkness, found the rungs and stepped down gingerly. He lowered himself until his head was at floor level.

There was more bawling from below, a crashing of doors.

"For God's sake, go, Will," said Alice. She kissed her hand and placed it on his forehead.

Will transferred the fingers of his left hand from the floorboard to the top rung of the ladder, then his right hand. He stepped down. Above him the wooden privy was slid back into position, the lid closed with a dull thud. He heard Francis's footsteps across the floor. He was in total darkness. The shaft was narrow, his shoulders and back touching the sides. His feet found the lower rungs, his fingers gripped the upper rungs, a sickening slime on some of them. Will fought the urge to throw up. Tried to calculate to distract himself and keep control: the shaft descended the height of the ground floor room and then lower to the sewer tunnel. About twenty feet. So twenty rungs, then. Apart from the scraping of his clothes on the walls and the faint tap of his boots on the wooden rungs, there was total silence. No voices from above.

He descended, counting the steps, his fingers painful as they tried to grip the rungs, keeping his mouth closed, tightening his nostrils. At the bottom, he knew, was the tunnel, the house's sewer outfall discharging into the moat. He was waiting for his boots to splash into some foul liquid, to stand on solid stone. Eighteen, nineteen, a pause, his fingers burning with pain, twenty. He dangled his foot. Still space beneath. Twenty-one. And then his left foot splashed and rested on stone. His hands down the rung; his right foot also on stone. He was down. He stood there, sweating, trembling, hands still on the ladder. He looked up. Nothing, total darkness. Looked down: a faint small tremble of light on the disturbed liquid. How far away? And the stink! The shit and piss he was standing in. Again, the instinct to retch.

He heard boots stomping on the wooden floor above, several pairs. Harsh orders. Thumping – on walls, as they looked for hollow places. He had to get out of the shaft. He knew he had to turn to the right. He took his hands from the ladder, felt around him, needing something solid to keep him upright. If he tripped or fell into that... He felt stone, wet, rough, close to him on both sides, barely wider than his shoulders. He half-turned, stretched a hand behind him. More stone, slimy. He snatched his hand away, rubbed it on his jacket frantically. Turned back again. Stretched a hand forward, straightened the arm. Space. Nothing in front of him. This must be the tunnel. Gingerly he shuffled forward, small steps splashing in the water. Stopped. Put his right hand above him, felt the roof, barely a hand's width above his scalp. At least he was out of the shaft. He imagined the privy being slid forward, a sudden chute of light down the shaft, faces peering, hands over noses, seeing nothing now. To find him now, someone would have to climb down.

He breathed deeply, trying to ignore the nauseous stink. Retched, leaned against the wall. How long must he stay here? From here in the tunnel he could hear nothing from above. Total silence, total darkness, just stink, the taste of it on his tongue as soon as he opened his mouth, the wet rough stone. Then, ahead of him, at what must be the floor of the sewage tunnel, a narrow band of weak light, maybe a foot long. That must be the outfall to the moat, the slit.

He shifted his feet. There was a sudden splashing of water; something scurried over his boot. He felt the weight of it as it passed. A rat. Involuntarily he stamped, stamped repeatedly in a rage of horror. He took his hands from the walls. They could climb that rough stone, could leap to his shoulder, tail sliding across his face. He jerked one arm up to cover his eyes, but he lurched, almost lost his balance, had to find the walls. Stood upright. Trembling again. Sweating in this cold, damp, evil place.

The cold was seeping into his body. His legs began to ache and the bottom of his back. He tried to crouch a little to ease his back. He had to move. So he walked, ten steps along, turned, ten steps back. Sloshing in the dark, treading on God knows what. Getting used to the stink. He needed something

469

to drink, to refresh his mouth. His tongue was dry. Then he realised he wanted to piss. Well, this was the place. A wry smile. The slimy muck on his fingers from the walls. The wry smile became a grimace. Disgust.

So he held it in. And maybe it helped to save him, his sanity. His picture of himself: standing in a sewer, his boots in reeking piss, crossing his legs, his prick burning, unwilling to get it out. It concentrated his mind, took his thoughts away from discovery, the rack, the hanging, drawing and quartering.

But in the end he had no alternative. He wiped his hands obsessively on his jacket, with distaste took his prick out from his breeches and, oh the relief of it, pissed into the sewage, its sound loud in the confined space, scaring the rats, he hoped.

It was an event. The only event, apart from the rat over his boot. Time crawled by. He got colder, shivered, tried to beat some warmth into his arms, dared not stamp for fear of the noise. He just shuffled back and forth and leaned on the stone, back, left shoulder, right shoulder. The stone hemming him in. Images of disembowelling with red hot irons, a cheering crowd, fascinated and horrified, his own screams. No fine death for him. And what would happen to the good Francis Ingilby who had hidden him here? To Alice and Sarah? It was unthinkable. He imagined the Catholic priests who had stood here before him, upheld by their unshakeable faith. Faith had sustained them. Not him, not Will. He had only hope and luck.

So close, just days away from the good captain taking him and Alice and Sarah to freedom and a new start across the ocean in New England.

How many hours had he stood here? Now shivering uncontrollably, teeth chattering. On the edge of cramp in shoulders and calves. And then a noise, suddenly breaking the silence. A scrape of wood and light behind him in the shaft, blinding him momentarily. Terror. He cowered in the dark.

Still as a monument, but trembling not now with cold but with fear. Imagined a soldier's boots descending, the shine of his sword, his oaths in the filth. Discovery!

"Will!"

He stared along the tunnel.

"Will!"

He recognised Francis's voice.

Was he being coerced, a dagger at his throat? Alice threatened with rape?

"They've gone."

The voice came down the shaft.

Still, Will waited.

"It's safe."

What choice did he have? Either way – the pursuivants gone or not – he was known to be down here. Rescue or capture. If they were up there, waiting for him, the pursuivants would not allow him to stay here and starve to death. They would want a public ceremony, an execution, an example. They would drag him to it if necessary, out of this filth, up the shaft and eventually to the scaffold. If the words were genuine, he was safe. He almost collapsed at the thought of it.

No, he had no choice. He turned and, hands along the wall, retraced his steps to the bottom of the shaft, leaned forward out of the tunnel and peered up. Saw Francis's face framed in the privy frame.

"For God's sake, Will, climb up. This stink is unbearable."

So he climbed, still not sure if, just out of his line of sight, a group of soldiers stood, swords drawn, the Royalist agents triumphant.

It was harder going up than down, his fingers straining more on the narrow rungs of wood, hauling up his weight. He rested once, his back on the wall.

At last his hands reached the floorboards. His head and shoulders emerged from the shaft. He looked round the room:

Francis crouched, holding out a hand to help him, Alice at the back of the room, kerchief over her nose.

"You're safe," said Francis. "They've gone. No trickery."

His wrists were grasped; he stepped up the last rungs. He was hauled out and collapsed on the floor. He was as conscious of the filth and stench of himself as he was of deliverance. He wanted to mutter gratitude for his life but he couldn't, just lay there, his whole body juddering with cold and fear and relief.

"We'll get you cleaned up," said Alice.

Servants came and he was wrapped in cloths and carried out. Other servants were already sliding the privy back into place and cleaning the floor.

An hour later, scrubbed clean, in new clothes, he was eating a fine meal of venison, red wine in a glass in front of him.

"How long was I down there?"

"Six hours."

"It seemed like a whole day."

"They were thorough. It was hard not to show our fear. They were pounding the walls, measuring inside and out with long rods to see if there were discrepancies that would indicate a secret place. But Nicholas Owen who built that hiding place was a genius. They shifted tables, emptied trunks, examined beds, tore off wall panelling and part of the wainscot. Alice even gave them some breakfast, though at first they had locked her up. Afterwards they even searched under the roof tiles and climbed up the big chimneys."

"But, Will," said Francis, "we fear they may return tomorrow. They are still convinced you are here somewhere. They know we are friends. Tonight you must both leave, and carefully. They may have set sentries to watch."

Will nodded. Francis was right. They knew their next and final hiding place and the route to it: an abandoned boat shed in the marshes by the coast.

"I will be glad to leave," said Will; "the longer I am here, the greater the danger to you and your household. You have done enough for us."

Alice nodded.

Francis did not disagree.

"I will bring you information about the ship as soon as I get it," he said.

So their lives now depended on the good Captain Christopher Ward. He, too, would know of the bounty. There were now few men Will could trust.

*

Ten days later Will and Alice stood at the stern of Captain Ward's merchantman, *Poseidon*. The ship was bucking in the scudding wind, wave-tops white and blown. They were looking back at the rocks of Land's End, already fading into the evening darkness. Sarah Marsden was below deck, seasick.

"The last of old England," said Alice.

"Gone backwards," said Will, "to the bad old ways. People know their places again."

Sails were snapping in the wind which yowled in the rigging.

Arms linked, they watched the white wake of the ship.

"At last we're free, finally on our way," said Will.

Alice squeezed his arm.

"That's twice I've sailed out of the Humber Estuary, and twice I've left these rocks behind, both in September. Once, forty years ago, as Alice Ainsworth and now as Alice Parker."

"Soon to be Alice Newbury."

"This is becoming a habit: marrying men on the run, men who need aliases."

"What does that say about you?" Will laughed.

"That two very different women make the same choice."

"But you're the same woman, Alice. Underneath all the experiences, you're the same woman I knew when we were eighteen."

"You mean I haven't grown up?"

"Not in the fundamental way. The core of you. And that's the part I love most."

"We haven't lived together yet, Will. There's a lot for you to put up with."

Will's fingers brushed away the wind-blown hair from her face and he kissed her.

"I'm adaptable," he said.

He turned to look back but Land's End had disappeared. Robert and Susannah: he had hurt them, left them, not been able to explain anything to them. How could he live with that?

He stayed silent, felt Alice's hand squeeze his. Did she know what he was thinking?

44.

Epilogue

Edmund stood in the crowd at Charing Cross where Major General Thomas Harrison was unbound from the sledge that had pulled him from Newgate Prison to his place of execution – within sight of Whitehall where the King had been beheaded.

"Where is your good old cause now?" taunted a man.

With a smile, Harrison clapped his hands on his breast and said: "Here it is, and I go to seal it with my blood."

He stood on the gallows next to the rope that would hang him, and the instruments that would rip him apart.

He addressed the crowd: "The finger of God hath been amongst us of late years in the deliverance of his people from their oppressors. Be not discouraged by reason of the cloud that now is upon you, for the Sun will shine and God will give a testimony unto what he hath been doing in a short time."

A Fifth Monarchist, thought Edmund. To them, 1666 – only six years away – would bring the Day of Judgement.

Harrison ended: "I have served a good Lord and Creator; he has covered my head many times in the day of battle; by God I have leapt over a wall, by God I have run through a troop, and by God I will go through this death and He will make it easy for me. Now into thy hands, O Lord Jesus, I commit my spirit."

The hangman placed the noose over his head. It was only a short drop, and when the frantic thrashing of his body stopped he was cut down. As Harrison regained consciousness, his shirt was pulled away. The executioner sliced off Harrison's genitals, which were presented to him before being tossed into a bucket. He was then held down while a red-hot metal bored into his belly. The executioner ripped out his innards and burned them in front of him. At this, Harrison swung a punch that caught the executioner unawares. The crowd gasped in amazement. The angry and humiliated hangman plunged his dagger into Harrison's heart.

Harrison's head was severed, his heart cut out. Both were shown to the crowd – "Behold the heart of a traitor" – and met with shouts of joy. His body was then quartered.

Edmund was awed by the man's bravery and sickened by the brutality. Was this what he had wanted for his father? For this would have been his fate if he had captured him at the ambush. Could he have proudly told his sons of his part in his father's death? He was disgusted with himself.

His father could have killed him, had his sword point at his throat. But he had drawn back. The better part of him had prevailed. Edmund resolved now, in front of the bloody gallows with its bucket of entrails and the smell of scorched flesh, that the better part of his own self must prevail.

He turned away, horrified by the crowd of bestial men and women gorged with ale and butchery.

30 JANUARY 1661

This was the twelfth anniversary of the execution of Charles I. Francis Ingilby had been in Parliament when it was decreed that this day should become "the first solemn fast and day of humiliation to deplore the sins which so long had provoked God against this afflicted church and people; to be annually celebrated to expiate the guilt of execrable murder of the late King."

Now, at eight o'clock on a frosty morning, Ingilby stood before the gallows at Tyburn. Four horses dragged four sledges, on each of them a coffin: belonging to Oliver Cromwell, his son-in-law General Henry Ireton, Judge John Bradshaw, President of the High Court of Justice at the trial of Charles I, and John Pym.

The caskets were broken open and the bodies pulled from them. Cromwell's remains were wrapped in a green wax cloth, his torso clad in a copper gilt breastplate emblazoned with the arms of the Commonwealth.

The remains of the four men were hanged together, dancing on a gibbet, swivelling in various states of decay, in front of a crowd of thousands.

Ingilby was nauseated: the new King's need for revenge, the crowd's pleasure in witnessing it. He was amazed at his own bravery – rashness – in helping Will Nailor to escape. It was probably the only principled thing he'd done in his life. Not principled – that was the business of Will and the four corpses hanging in front of him – but out of friendship. Would Will really escape capture? Regicides were being tracked everywhere: in England and Europe, and, it was rumoured, agents to be sent to New England. Already successfully courting business among the returned Royalist elite, he would spread among them a story that Will Nailor had been assassinated by agents in Switzerland.

Even he, sceptic and cynic, had to admit that the Commonwealth had been founded on great principles. It was just that men could not make them work – which was no surprise.

Ingilby knew that at six that evening the remains of the four Parliamentarians would be beheaded, their bodies to be slung into a common pit, their heads to be stuck on spikes in Westminster, their eyes pointing towards the spot where Charles' scaffold had stood.

The stench of this raucous, insufferably ignorant crowd was unbearable. With his handkerchief at his nose, he left.

16 FEBRUARY 1661

Elizabeth Lilburne, widow of Free-bornJohn Lilburne, had consulted astrologer John Booker several times, but nothing in the stars apparently foretold the ending of her pension.

On her husband's death, three years ago, she had petitioned for the repeal of her husband's Act of Banishment, with its £7,000 fine, and for the continuation of his pension of forty shillings a week. She was in need of "some refreshment in the midst of distresse and sorrow, being att this time very ill and much declined of a consumption."

Oliver Cromwell had agreed and even oversaw the repayment of £15 arrears. Richard Cromwell had continued the payments.

But now, nine months after the crowning of Charles II, came the news that the pension was being stopped. She had two children to support.

Her friend Samuel Chidley had praised John Lilburne "as like a candle lighted, accommodating others and consuming himself".

And consuming his family, too, she thought.

21 JUNE 1662

King Charles, with his spaniels, was in a room at Hampton Court Palace, a room hung with tapestries, furnished with solid silver tables and Japanese lacquered cabinets containing vases of gold and silver. Music played and the guests played cards. £2,000 in gold coins lay wagered on the table. With a smile Charles noted three of his former mistresses were there. Now a French boy sang love songs while the fops and wits paid extravagant compliments to the ladies.

Even John Wilmot, Earl of Rochester, was there. Banished for a ribald poem he had written, and then forgiven because Charles was highly flattered by its opening lines:

Not are his high desires above his strength,
His sceptre and his prick are of a length.

Only that morning Charles and his entourage had attended the christening of the Countess of Castlemaine's six-day-old son, Charles Fitzroy, immediately entitled Lord Limerick by his father. Fitzroy was the countess's second child by Charles. He had insisted his young new wife, a Portuguese princess, attend. The countess was still tall and voluptuous, with blue-violet eyes, pale skin, full sulky lips and a mass of auburn hair. Queen Catherine was slight, coy and modest, and had crooked protruding teeth. Her humiliation had amused him.

A footman brought Charles another glass of wine, bowed and backed away. Charles sipped the wine. He liked the grandeur of Hampton Court, its gardens on the bank of the Thames. But he liked Whitehall better. It contained fond memories: of girls and actresses brought by river and then by private corridors to the King's rooms. His old friends and pimps, Baptist May and William Chiffinch, called them *supper companions* before dropping gold into their purses as the wherries took them away in darkness.

Charles beckoned Lord Ashley, one of the Treasury commissioners.

"Have my father's killers all been captured?" demanded the King.

"Nearly all," stammered Lord Ashley.

"I want every one of them."

Lord Ashley bowed.

"And who is that young woman?" Charles pointed across the room.

"That, I believe, is Frances Stuart. Just come with her mother from the French court."

"A beautiful woman. I must speak with her."

Sun warm on his face, blackbirds singing, wild flowers blooming, the river quiet and steady.

A slight rising of the bank now; steady pace necessary to avoid breathlessness. That wincing pain sometimes from right hip to knee: walk through it. But he was a fortunate man.

Seventy-two years old and white-haired, Will walked with a stick now, shoulders bent and back twisted a little. Alice walked with him, arms linked.

It was their favourite walk: along the Connecticut River in the small settlement of Springfield where they had lived for the last four years.

"Another winter survived," said Alice.

"And Judgement Day never came last year. John Boon and the Fifth Monarchists were wrong; 1666, the Devil's number," said Will.

Though neither spoke about it, other judgement days had also not arrived for them. Three years ago King Charles had sent commissioners to Boston. At the head of four hundred soldiers, they had arrived in four frigates with orders to first capture New Amsterdam from the Dutch, settle various land disputes in New England and round up any regicides still at large.

The story of William Goffe and Edward Whalley, both of whom had signed Charles I's death warrant, had been the talk of the colony. At first welcomed by staunch republicans, Charles' commands and threats had turned them into fugitives. They had feigned a journey to Manhattan, hidden in remote mills and caves, dived underwater under a bridge as the pursuing cavalry galloped overhead, even hid in a kitchen cupboard as soldiers searched the house. For six years they had eluded their captors and were now rumoured to have gone to Virginia.

But no one had come after Will, because he was believed dead. Francis Ingilby had used all the contacts he had to spread the story through court and Parliament of Will's death. With another regicide, he had been shot dead going to church in Lausanne in Switzerland: Royalist agents had hired a pair of thugs to kill him. Three pistol balls had torn him apart, his face smashed.

They had known none of this when they had sailed into Boston harbour six years ago. But fortune seemed to favour them: Alice was relieved that Wilton and Ludlow were dead. Then her sons Peter and Giles had bought out Alice's share of the farm, which meant that Alice and Will could move out to the edge of the colony of Massachusetts. This was the most independent of the colonies, already claiming it lay beyond the reach of Parliament's laws or the King's writ. They minted their own coins with *Massachusetts* and a tree on one face and *New England* on the other.

So here they strolled under the riverside trees, Mr and Mrs Newbury, respected members of the community, though neither of them attended church. They had retired from running a successful store, Alice still tending her garden, Will known to fast every Friday and always reading his favourite book *The History of the World* written by Sir Walter Raleigh while in the Tower, awaiting execution.

But even now there was the fear of a slip of the tongue or recognition by a new arrival from Old England. An unexpected knock at the door still made them tense; wary glances, a pause to let the heartbeats steady.

But mostly there was peace – though each had stories they wished to tell but had to conceal.

"I'll rest here," said Will as they came to a fallen ash tree on the riverbank. "You go on a bit."

Alice smiled. He liked time with his memories, alone.

"Half an hour," she said.

Will nodded. He settled down on the trunk to the usual thoughts.

No matter how happy he was, Will still had regrets which he could not dispel and – in a way – didn't want to. He thought of Jane. Had he loved her, really? Or had she just been the means to creating a family for him? And why had he wanted a family? Because it was what people did? And what was love, anyway? With Alice he had something that had endured for more than half a century – yes, broken and set aside for long periods, but so readily renewed: a core of connection and recognition that had remained unharmed. Fond though he had been of Jane, tender and caring, there had never been that deepness he now had with Alice.

His deepest regret was for the loss of his children. They would be adults now, Robert twenty-six and Susannah twenty-three, and they would not think well of him, the father who had left them. Not like Edmund, but a betrayal nevertheless. He could not escape the responsibility for fracturing their childhoods. What sort of people were they now? Had he damaged them? And all for a revolution that had collapsed and achieved nothing.

Once bitter and disappointed, he sensed himself more resigned, more able to live with doubts – one of the very few benefits of old age: an acceptance that accompanied the slowing of mind and blood. It had surprised him how old age brought more questions than answers, more doubts than certainties.

Walking on, Alice, too, did not avoid the past, but this was perhaps easier for her. Both Nicholas and James had been taken from her as a result of their own decisions. But still she felt guilt – that, had she been different, things would have turned out differently. Nicholas and James would always be part of her life here in New England. She would not put them aside, and Will accepted, even loved, that in her. She thought of Sarah Marsden, back in Boston, married well and now with one child. She would always be a force for good, wherever she was. But who knew what travails awaited her?

Will listened to the river idling past and watched Alice walk slowly back.

She sat next to him and waited, heard him sigh.

"I think we tried our best, didn't we?" said Will. "In our different ways."

Whenever he sat for a moment and contemplated, he drifted this way.

"Yes, I think we did," she replied. She knew he needed this occasional confirmation. "That's all anyone can do. You risked your life, Will. Never forget."

"You, too."

The flash of a fish in the river below.

"We've both had to flee," he continued. "But I believe we have helped set a movement rolling which will not be stopped. Ideas are difficult to suppress. Even if a king remains, Parliament will somehow prevail."

"I believe so, too. It's a kind of faith, I suppose."

He laughed.

She took his hand. "You know what I believe: that most people are good-hearted and will help each other if there is need – small kindnesses between people as they live together."

"And I say you're wrong about that. That is not sufficient. Small kindnesses between people allow unjust and unfair systems to persist – where the many are exploited by the few. The few know this. It is what they depend on."

Alice stood up. "It's a lovely day, Will. We can discuss these things inside, when it's raining."

"I enjoy those conversations. Now, please help me up."

She stood, stretched out her hands to grasp his, and Will levered himself up and straightened his back.

"But I am thankful for small things," he said. "Like the slice of your apple pie that I'm looking forward to."

"Small things," replied Alice, "like the bent sixpences you gave us and which we have kept all these years."

He nodded. Arm in arm they strolled back along the riverbank.

How strong she was, and sensible.

He laughed aloud, happy. She smiled and held him closer.

ACKNOWLEDGEMENTS

To Ian Plimmer who encouraged me to start on the challenge of writing a historical novel; to our manuscript group – Muriel, Joan, Neil, Chris – gave me invaluable feedback on my drafts; and to my partner Jan, a critical friend, first reader, continuity stickler, and huge support throughout.